*Hope you -
from "Daniel's life story".*

Terry Thompson
2022

DANIEL

PROPHET AT THE KING'S COMMAND

A NOVEL BY
TERRY THOMPSON

AMBASSADOR INTERNATIONAL
GREENVILLE, SOUTH CAROLINA & BELFAST, NORTHERN IRELAND

www.ambassador-international.com

ENDORSEMENTS

"The only problem you will have with this brilliant and inspiring novel by Terry Thompson will be laying it down. It is a spellbinding story with many great lessons of courageous leadership. Its contemporary resolution of the mysteries of the end-times will give you chills. Every few years, a particular Bible-based novel commands the attention of the Christian world. This is it for this decade."

MIKE HUCKABEE
Former Governor of Arkansas, National Television Personality,
and New York Times Best-selling Author

"This is one of the most thought-provoking Bible-based novels my wife, Ginny, and I have ever read. It is not only a gripping story of one of God's great prophets, but also a leadership case study and a survey of end-times prophecy. We were struck by how the challenges and dilemmas Daniel faced are similar to those we face today. Ginny and I do recommend this book to you! Enjoy reading as the story comes alive."

STEVE SAINT
Missions and Business Entrepreneur, Pilot,
and Award-winning Author of *End of the Spear*

"This is a stirring story applying ancient insights to contemporary challenges. Faithful to the biblical account of Daniel, with appropriate imaginative accents by the story teller, this novel both entertains and informs. It will help you be a better leader in adverse circumstances and understand global events as they are unfolding around us—while engaging you in a fresh way with the timeless story of a remarkable hero of faith."

DR. JEFF IORG
President of Gateway Seminary

"I can't stop telling my friends about this new book by my friend, Terry Thompson! Having been forcibly taken hostage myself, I truly sympathized with Daniel as he and his friends were taken captive from Jerusalem—"Where is Yahweh in all this?" I know about foot blisters from forced marching, starving, and bathing my stinky body in the river. What I didn't know is how much I would learn from this book, how entertained I would be, and how much I would be convicted and changed. Bible prophecy came alive as I read *Daniel*. The story is told so vividly that I cried when the Medes took over Babylon. I actually had to get up and get Kleenex! . . . and so will you!"

GRACIA BURNHAM
Missionary, Popular Speaker, and New York Times Bestselling
Author of *In the Presence of My Enemies*

"I have long believed that story is a powerful way to reach people with God's truth. Jesus thought so, too! The biblical account of Daniel is already one of the most riveting in the Scriptures. Terry Thompson wonderfully fills in the gaps with a captivating narrative that captures the tragedy God's people faced, Daniel's heroic and faithful life, and God's work through history from that time until now. Readers will savor the time they spend with Daniel."

DAVID GREGORY
New York Times Bestselling Author of *Dinner with a Perfect Stranger*

Daniel
Prophet at the King's Command, a Novel

ISBN: 978-1-64960-085-1
eISBN: 978-1-64960-095-0
Library of Congress Control Number: 2021930971

Digital Edition by Anna Riebe Raats
Edited by Katie Cruice Smith

AMBASSADOR INTERNATIONAL
Emerald House
411 University Ridge, Suite B14
Greenville, SC 29601, USA
www.ambassador-international.com

AMBASSADOR BOOKS
The Mount
2 Woodstock Link
Belfast, BT6 8DD, Northern Ireland, UK
www.ambassadormedia.co.uk

The colophon is a trademark of Ambassador, a Christian publishing company.

Dedicated to my wife, Linda.
Her inspiration and encouragement
made this project possible.

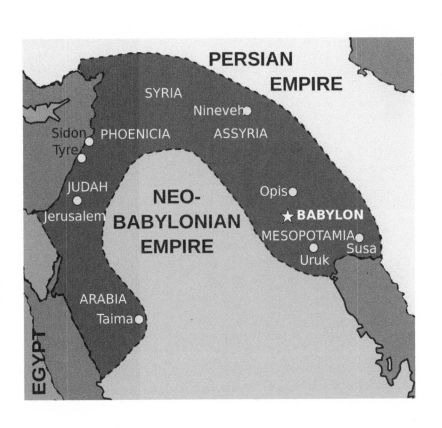

FOREWORD

THIS FICTIONAL STORY OF THE biblical prophet Daniel is a unique work that combines the integrity of the biblical account with extensive historical research of the main character's life and times. My many years of studying and teaching the Bible along with my experience in teaching and evaluating college graduate research projects were foundational to writing the book.

The story you are about to read is diligently aligned with the Bible. My speculation beyond the biblical account of Daniel's extraordinary life is in agreement with most respected theologians and Bible commentators. Certainly, imaginative liberty is taken where the Bible is silent, but nothing in the book contradicts the Holy Scriptures.

Dates, events, customs, and settings of the story are according to highly regarded scholarly sources. Where possible, names of people and places are from the annals of historical record. While captivated by the adventurous experiences of this biblical icon, you will be treated to an authentic journey through the cultures of the ancient Hebrews, Babylonians, Persians, Greeks, and Romans.

The book's content is also a case study in leadership. This godly, young Hebrew thrust into the highest echelons of a pagan monarchy created challenges beyond comprehension. As a high official of the world's greatest empire, he also had to maintain the confidence of his own enslaved people, which required the utmost in leadership ability and wisdom. You will be impressed and will benefit from the managerial principles that emanate from the pages of this book.

But this is much more than an entertaining and inspiring historical fiction book about a prominent Bible character. It is also an intriguing look into biblical prophecy focusing on the end times. More than any other prophet, Daniel received from God the most vivid dreams and visions of future events culminating in the return of Jesus Christ. At various intervals, these prophecies are explained in detail in setting changes to modern day, where a college student is being mentored in prophecy by a seminary professor. This unusual technique results in deep insight into God's plan for the end of civilization as we know it and the establishment of the Kingdom of Jesus Christ on Earth.

I also encourage you to read this book introspectively. At appropriate intervals in your reading, take time to consider how closely this story reflects your life experiences and the world around you. Concentrate on how it applies to you personally.

Finally, you will get the most out of this book by following the story in the Bible's Book of Daniel as you read it.

So, get ready to begin one of the most interesting novels you have ever read. Enjoy its biblical genuineness, its historical authenticity, its leadership principles, and its inspiring prophecy.

1

UNEXPECTED ENCOUNTER

DR. B. R. MCCARTY SAT across from Kyle Larson at the campus cafeteria table and struck up a conversation. Soon, both were talking about their holiday break and their respective interests. This unlikely affinity combination—the professor emeritus of biblical studies and the senior civil engineering student—made an unusual connection.

The conversation evolved into religion and the international news stories about the beheading of an American journalist by radical Islamists. Kyle had traveled internationally more than most of his peers and had been exposed to both elite and distraught social orders. But he found this jihad, void of any moral center or compassion, especially troubling. At home for the holidays, he had been bombarded with cable news and involuntarily subjected to the daily menu of world affairs, rather than his usual diet of ESPN and movies. He wished he had avoided the actual YouTube video of a beheading. The graphic scene now invaded his soul too often.

He had little Bible background and felt compelled to ask the professor whether he thought there was any biblical connection to what was going on in the Middle East.

"Oh, yes, definitely," Dr. McCarty said. "It all fits into the writings of the ancient prophets. From about 800 B.C. into the first century A.D.,

God revealed through His special spokesmen conditions and events of future centuries, including present day—even parts of our future."

"I've heard of Nostradamus, and I know there are prophets in the Bible, but I thought that was just stuff about ancient times."

The professor grinned. "These were well before Nostradamus—and legitimate, I might add. Everything prophesied by these biblical prophets has happened, except for that involving our future. And trust me, it will happen just as predicted."

The prospective engineer was fascinated by the professor's confidence. His first thought was that this old man was a religious wacko. But he was a Princeton seminary professor, for heaven's sake. "I'd really like to know more about that. Is there a book in the library I could check out?"

"I have hundreds of books on biblical prophecy in my office. That's what I've taught most of my life, and it's what I lecture on and write about in my emeritus position. Why don't you come by my office on the seminary campus soon, and I'll show you some information you'll find captivating?"

"Uh, I appreciate the offer, but I have a tough schedule this semester . . . probably not ready to add a Bible study."

"I understand. If you change your mind, just give me a call."

"Sure thing. Enjoyed meeting you," Kyle said, as he excused himself and departed.

*

The next afternoon, Kyle's Hydraulics class had just begun when his phone vibrated. It was his dad. Sensing it must be urgent, he walked quietly out into the hallway.

"Hey, Dad."

"Sorry to interrupt you, Son. I'll have to be quick. They're getting ready to escort us out of the building, but I wanted to contact you before you heard it on the news."

"What, Dad! What's going on?"

"Several people have been protesting across the street from the Stock Exchange for a few days. Well, today, looks like a bunch of outsiders have turned it into a riot. They're throwing Molotov cocktails, storming the gates, even some shooting. I heard at least one policeman has been killed. Cops are overwhelmed. I understand the National Guard is being called in. As you know, that's just three blocks from our offices. We now have a mob forming outside our building. We are vacating the place under police protection."

"Oh no, Dad! How can that happen so fast?"

"I hardly recognize our country anymore, Son. Seems we've been going downhill ever since the twin towers attack. It's surreal. I have to go. They're herding us out."

"I'll call you tonight, Dad. Be careful."

Kyle skipped his next class and spent the rest of the afternoon lying on his bed, mulling over the phone call and watching cable news. His mind was spinning with the holiday jihad beheadings, the professor's connection of prophecy with today's savage world, and, now, his dad threatened by anarchists.

And I'm here on a beautiful, laid-back campus with the only real challenge being my grade point average. I've got to get more into the real world and the cause of all the chaos. Maybe the professor does have at least some of the answers. But, man, I don't want to become a Bible-toting religious freak. I'm about to become an engineer.

That evening, Kyle and his dad had a long, deep discussion about the state of the world. He was surprised at his dad's anxiety about the future facing him and his brother. His dad was more transparent than he had ever been regarding his concern for his boys and potential grandchildren. Kyle knew this man he admired greatly was still raw from the day's experience. But he was rightly concerned about the culture that had lost its center in a single generation. A half-hour after the conversation, Kyle found the courage to make a call.

"Dr. McCarty? This is Kyle Larson."

*

A bit of uneasiness accompanied Kyle as he approached the office. He had never even been on the seminary campus before. The small, engraved sign next to the door frame read *B.R. McCarty, Ph.D., Professor Emeritus, Biblical Studies*. The door was open, revealing the professor at his desk poring over a book.

"Dr. McCarty," Kyle said with a tad of nervousness. He wasn't sure whether to just walk in or wait to be invited. "Kyle Larson again. I, uh, believe I have an appointment with you."

"Come in, come in, Mr. Larson."

Kyle was amused at the setting of the monstrous desk compared to that of the folding cafeteria table of their first meeting. The professor was a rather large man—not obese—just big and muscular for someone his age. But his physique now appeared smaller in the imposing office. He stroked his well-groomed, white goatee, then removed his wire-rimmed glasses.

With his gray cardigan, monogrammed with the Princeton logo, over a blue plaid, cotton shirt, he impressed Kyle as a neat, well-organized, but down-to-earth man. Two office walls contained bookshelves with volumes that he had obviously meticulously sorted and cataloged. A huge set of maps dominated another side of the room. On his desk were a few books, desk organizers, and a large, open Bible centered in front of him.

"Have a seat," he said, motioning to an over-stuffed chair near the front corner of his desk. "Tell me a little more about yourself. I remember you're from New York."

"Yes, sir," Kyle began. "I grew up in Staten Island. Graduated from Moore Catholic High. I played some basketball and was captain of our robotics team."

"Yes, I would have pegged you as a basketballer. What about family?"

"My dad is an executive with an investment firm. He works in Manhattan. Mom is on some charity boards and plays tennis. I have a younger brother graduating from Moore in May."

"What brought you to Princeton?"

"Dad graduated from here with an MBA. This is just where I—and everyone else—always assumed I would go if I could qualify. I plan to stay and get my M.S. in civil engineering here."

"Well, my story is a contrast to yours. I'm a California product. I grew up in a middle-class family. Got a football and academic scholarship to U.C. Berkeley. Majored in history. At that time, Berkeley was the epicenter of rebellion, anti-war demonstrations, drugs, and immoral lifestyles. It's sad how so many students were drawn into that campus culture; but for me, it seemed to push me away from it. It's like I could see it for what it was. The more I experienced, the more I wanted to be everything but that. Needed the scholarship, though."

Kyle was already finding this introduction absorbing, "Didn't you feel outcast, alienated?"

"Oh, it was a challenge. I just kept my head down and found consolation in a few like-minded buddies. We met for weekly Bible studies in our dorm rooms. I fell in love with a wonderful lady there. She shared my passion for the Lord, although she was rather liberal in those days. But I found that part of her charm. Jennifer and I married the day after graduation. In the fall, I enrolled in Golden Gate Seminary, now Gateway—something I never imagined I would do until weeks prior to graduation."

Noises outside the office announced the beginning of the evening class period. The professor got up and closed the door. He walked with a slight limp.

"Have you injured your leg?" Kyle asked before realizing the inappropriateness of the question.

"I think I got hit a few too many times on the grid iron," Dr. McCarty said, cracking a smile. "Most football injuries lie dormant until one gets about seventy."

"So, you enrolled in a seminary."

"Yes, graduated with a master's in theological studies. I surprised myself at how much I really got into biblical inquisition. It was like I had my life going in one direction—my direction—and God filled me with a passion for the complete opposite."

"Did you go straight into your doctorate program from there?"

"No. Like most seminary graduates, I pastored a small church immediately after graduation. Being young and overly ideological, I was determined to transform that church on several fronts. The problem was, they weren't ready, and . . . well, let's just say my pastoring career was short-lived."

The professor took a book off the eye-level shelf and handed it to Kyle, then repositioned himself in his seasoned leather chair.

"*The Late Great Planet Earth,*" Kyle verbalized the title of the book by Hal Lindsey. "I think I've seen this on one of my grandfather's shelves."

"It was a popular book for a couple of generations in the late twentieth century. I think the rise of the Soviet Union, the nuclear threat, and the instability of the Middle East had instilled an uneasiness in almost everyone. That, combined with the incomprehensible breakthroughs in technology—men on the moon and the computer revolution—had a lot of us wondering what the world was coming to."

Retrieving the book and holding it up as a prop, he continued, "Lindsey's timing was ingenious. The book became a best-seller as millions read about how all that was going on globally related to biblical prophecy. Although I had studied a ton about prophecy in the seminary, reading this was a catalyst for ratcheting up my interest in connecting the dots between the ancient writings and current, even future, events."

Laying the book aside, Dr. McCarty leaned a bit forward in his chair and looked into Kyle's eyes. "I suppose that is why I took a special interest in you at our impromptu dining hall meeting. You reminded me of myself about fifty years ago, utterly consumed by a determination to make sense of the times. That was a turning point in my life that began a journey immersed in the study of the prophets."

After a somewhat awkward moment of silence as both processed what was being discussed, Kyle responded, "Obviously, I'm not where you were then. Certainly not a Bible scholar. But I am very interested in the mystery of the prophecies, and I do think there has to be some meaning to what we are seeing, other than coincidence. So, what did you do after you stopped pastoring the church? Get a real job?" Kyle immediately realized his attempt at humor was actually disrespectful. "I'm sorry. I didn't mean to . . . "

"It's okay," the professor said, tilting his head slightly. "I suppose I have never had a real job—not what most people would define as a job. I wrote a review of Lindsey's book for a seminary publication, adding scholarly credibility to what many considered fiction. Surprisingly, the *Christian Science Monitor* republished my article."

He swiveled his chair 180 degrees to face an array of diplomas and awards filling the wall space behind his desk. Pointing to the upper left of the collection, he explained, "That is my Doctorate of Biblical Studies from this great institution. Princeton contacted me shortly after the article was published and asked if I would be interested in their seminary's doctoral program. It caught me completely off-guard, but I couldn't refuse the scholarship offered. Looking back, I can see this clearly as God's pathway for my life. He re-ordered my attention from worldly attractions to spiritually significant pursuits in seminary. Then He increased my passion for biblical prophecies and gave me an educational foundation second to none. Eventually, He set me on a platform of recognition as a subject matter expert in biblical prophecy. That is what I have dedicated my life to here at Princeton."

"I just want to say, sir, I really appreciate the time you are giving to help me make some sense of all that is going on in the world. I'm not sure where to start. I know very little about ancient history and probably nothing about prophecy. I doubt I'll ever comprehend it."

"Well, it would take several semesters to study it adequately, and even then, you wouldn't understand it all. I don't claim to understand it all. But if you will invest the time, I would like to show you some basics that are essential to a continuing exploration of the past, present, and future."

Kyle grinned, "Let's do it!"

Dr. McCarty turned in his chair to the large open Bible. "How about looking over my shoulder, so you can follow me in the Word."

With Kyle standing next to the chair back, the elder scholar began what would become several sessions of tutorial with his attentive protégé.

"The entire Old Testament—from Genesis to Malachi—covers the eons from creation to Jesus Christ coming to Earth. Every book points to Christ's arriving and establishing a spiritual kingdom on this planet. Although many of these first thirty-nine books of the Bible can be considered history or having other objectives, they all allude to a future time when God will no longer relate to His people through laws and rituals but through a more personal relationship of grace and forgiveness. But the books of prophecies—all seventeen of them—are written in more direct language concerning the future times, often in surprising detail. Although they sometimes contain poetic and rather cryptic prose, they reveal events, places, and people in advance—often far in advance—of the time of their writing."

Dr. McCarty leafed through his Bible as he spoke. "The prophets were typically warning of the evil ways of their audience, as well as God's consequential wrath if the people didn't repent. This Providential justice would often be predicted in terms of timing, location, and source. Almost always, though, woven throughout the prophecies were the counter messages of hope through God's ultimate compassion. This compassion is frequently presented as the Gospel, or good news, of the eventual appearance of the eternal King, Jesus Christ."

The professor asked Kyle to retake his seat. He turned his chair to face Kyle, crossed his legs, and folded his hands in his lap. He presented a half-hour synopsis of the entire Bible—Genesis to Revelation—from a big picture perspective. He slowed the pace at the intersection of the Old and New Testaments to highlight the keystone of the sixty-six books: the birth, death, and resurrection of Jesus Christ. Then he closed with a comparison of the Book of Revelation to the Old Testament prophecies.

"Are you hungry?" the doctor asked in an abrupt departure from his tutorial.

Kyle's raised eyebrows and rigid posture made his surprise obvious. "Um . . . sure. College students are always hungry."

Dr. McCarty pulled his phone from his sweater pocket. "How about a pizza? I'll buy. What do you like?"

After the pizzas were ordered, the professor refocused on the objective.

"To begin exploring prophecies, particularly as they apply to our future, we need to dig into the book of Daniel." The professor opened his Bible with one motion to the desired location of the relatively short, twelve-chapter book.

"Daniel lived in the sixth and seventh centuries B.C. He was born around 620 B.C. and lived to about 536 B.C. During those eighty-four or so years, the Hebrew people—the Jews--suffered one of the worst times in their history. Of course, the Jews have experienced physical and spiritual affliction from their origin in Abraham to the Egyptian slavery, to the exile in Daniel's day, to the last diaspora in A.D. 70, to the World War II holocaust, to the present threats from many powerful nations."

"I know something about most of that, except . . . what was that word, 'die . . . uh . . . sp . . . ?'"

"Diaspora. It means the fleeing and scattering of a population from their homeland. Shortly after King Solomon's tenth century B.C. reign, there was internal, civil strife, and the nation of Israel divided into two nations: Israel to the north and Judah to the south. It wasn't long until God became so displeased with their sin, He allowed Israel to be defeated by the Assyrians and taken into exile.

Later, Judah was also overrun by the Babylonians and exiled to Babylon. This was the first diaspora. Most of Israel never returned and were ultimately scattered throughout the Mediterranean lands. Judah's people, however, were allowed to return to their homeland and rebuild, although many chose to stay in Babylon. But that only lasted about six centuries. The Romans razed Jerusalem and most of Judah in A.D. 70, sending the Jews fleeing again throughout the surrounding nations. This was the last diaspora, and it left them without a homeland until 1948 when Israel was once again re-established as a nation."

Dr. McCarty walked to the large map on the side wall. "It's easier to see on the map. Come join me."

Choosing a particular map among several rolled up in an overhead encasement, he pulled it down like a window blind and locked it in place. Picking up an extension pointer, the professor began a mini lecture.

"You probably recognize the location of modern Israel," he said, pointing to the east end of the Mediterranean Sea. "This map is circa seventh century B.C. It shows the Assyria Empire from Israel and Judah to the Persian Gulf. If we overlaid a modern map, it would include the countries of Egypt, Israel, Lebanon, Syria, Jordan, eastern Turkey, Iraq, and Iran. In Daniel's day, it included Egypt, Israel, Judah, Assyria, Babylonia, and Medo-Persia. Assyria controlled most of the region in the eighth century B.C. and invaded the northern kingdom of Israel, taking almost all of their population to the Assyrian capital of Nineveh."

He traced the movement of the nations on the map. "Over a century later, the kingdom of Babylonia conquered Assyria and dominated the entire region. Babylonia's King Nabopolassar, with the help of the Medes, became ruler of the new empire. The Babylonians invaded the southern kingdom of Judah three times between 605 B.C. and 586 B.C. and took most of the country's Jews into exile in Babylon. Daniel, along with many other young men, was taken to Babylon in 605 B.C., almost twenty years before the ultimate defeat of Judah and the exile of the majority of the Judahites."

"So, Daniel was a part of the Jewish . . . diaspora," Kyle said to confirm he comprehended the tutorial. "If these were God's chosen people, why did He allow them to be conquered and taken out of their homeland?"

"That will become clear as we dig into Daniel. The same God Who loved His people passionately was also the God of perfect justice. Sin eventually brings justice in the form of consequences."

"Was Daniel one of the prophets warning the people?"

"No, not really. Daniel was a teenager when he was taken by force to Babylon. He was never the typical prophet of his day but became more of a seer, or a receiver of visions about the future. God gave most of the prophets supernatural knowledge of the future events, but none received more than Daniel. That's why he is a special source for understanding how events of the past and today relate to what is to come."

The professor tapped his pointer over Babylon and continued, "Babylon was also known as the center of the Chaldean Dynasty. It was from there that centuries earlier, around 1900 B.C., Abraham received the call from God to go from Ur of the Chaldeans to the land of Canaan. You might say that was the first movement of God toward creating a chosen people. Canaan, now Israel, was the land where the descendants of Abraham became God's special nation, according to His promise."

Dr. McCarty collapsed his pointer, tapped his index finger on Jerusalem, then stepped back from the map. "And what about Judah and its capital, Jerusalem? We could easily become caught up in the powerful empires and kingdoms, their risings and fallings, and lose sight of the fact that God's chosen people in His promised land were still His treasure. Judah remained the focal point of His creation. All the powerful empires warring against each other were doing so at the mercy of their unrecognized Creator. The defeat and exile of Israel was God's wrath applied as justice and corrective action for the egregious sins of His chosen ones. And it would become worse with Judah's lack of repentance and obedience."

Kyle realized that he had, in fact, lost the focus of the story, just as the professor cautioned against. The fascination with the warring empires had diminished his concentration on the most important people of that era. *What about Judah, indeed? What about Daniel?*

"From the time the unified kingdom of Israel split into the kingdoms of Israel and Judah in 930 B.C., Israel failed to produce one godly king. All of them led their people in ways of the world which God opposed. Despite the warnings of their prophets about the consequences, their immoral living resulted in the fulfillment of those prophecies. That is why Israel was conquered first, but Judah soon reaped the same consequences. She had a few godly kings, which apparently extended God's patience for a time.

"I'm going to stop here with the background study. We're now ready to look at the adventures of Daniel. It's time for a break, anyway; and if my timing is right, we should have some food appearing shortly."

Just then, there was a knock at the office door.

Kyle laughed. "You're a prophet in your own right, a seer of the pizza delivery."

As the student and the professor relaxed and enjoyed the nosh, they delved into the details of the life and times of the prophet Daniel.

2

INNOCENT BEGINNINGS

605 B.C.

The young man destined to have the greatest impact of many generations of God's chosen people was, for now, just an innocuous, Jerusalem kid. His highest teenage ambition was to beat his friends at Kugelach, or five stones.

He laid five small, smooth stones in the palm of his right hand. After three preparatory vertical movements of his hand, he thrust his hand upward, tossing the five stones in a cluster straight up to about an arm's length above his head. As the stones fell to the back of his hand, four of them planted solidly on his hand and fingers. The fifth stone glanced the side of his wrist and fell into the dirt.

"Oy!" exclaimed one of the boy's three friends and competitors. "You are too much for us—too much for any boy or man in Jerusalem!"

The fifteen-year-old neighborhood Kugelach champion paid no attention to their laments as he took long, deep, and rhythmic breaths, concentrating on his final feat. He had placed the dropped stone on the back of his hand with the others according to the rules. This toss, if successful, would win him the "fivesies" round. With slower preparatory lifts of his hand, he launched the five stones back into the air. Quickly turning his palm up, he snatched all five and slammed them to the ground in a gesture of sweet victory. Raising his hands, he spun around dancing in celebration. Very seldom did Daniel lose a Kugelach match as he and his three best friends met on the landing in front of his house just after noon almost every day, except on the Sabbath.

"Daniel, you all must head for the temple now," the soft, but authoritative voice of his mother, Nessa, called from just inside the doorway of the upscale, hewn stone house. "Be home before the sun sets."

"Yes, Mother," Daniel replied. The other three were supposed to play another "foursies" round to determine second place. But these four boys from prominent and noble families never challenged or even questioned instructions from their parents or other adults. Quickly, all four gathered their cloaks from inside Daniel's house. Daniel kissed his mother on both cheeks, assuring her of his return before sunset for the family meal.

The four walked abreast up the narrow stone street on the twenty-minute hike to the temple. All were about average in stature, with Daniel being the tallest by a small margin. All were uncharacteristically handsome by Jewish standards of attractiveness and physique. Their firm muscles gave evidence of their daily lifting and foot racing in friendly competition. This kind of athleticism was not the norm for most boys of Judah. But priests who tutored and mentored the youth of the elite families of Jerusalem made physical work and play mandatory as part of their religious and scholastic development.

The boys exited the prominent dwelling area, taking the everyday route by way of a marketplace street lined with merchants. They sniffed the various aromas coming from small booths owned by fabric sellers, meat and produce vendors, candle and fragrance makers, and bakers. The occasional set of steps that eased the rise in terrain through the long row of shops gave way to the long, uphill slope to the temple mount. All three were overhearing the public chatter about potential invasions by foreign powers but were giving it little attention.

The education of most Jewish boys was the responsibility of the parents with guidance from the temple priests. However, temple priests taught classes for children of the wealthy and privileged. The classes focused on Jewish law, languages, history, and mathematics. The sons of priests and nobles of royal ancestry attended these exclusive classes. Daniel's father, Karmiel, was chief of the national treasury. His father's long line of judges and rulers placed Daniel securely among the select young men of Judah—a small minority. They were appointed to a small group of peers whose headmaster was a temple priest who held classes in the outer courts of Solomon's Temple.

The four friends proceeded up the long ramp to the East Gate of the temple courts. The high wall around the outer court blocked the view of the temple until entering the gate. Temple gate guards recognized the boys as they approached and nodded as their clearance to enter. Walking past the east side of the temple toward the colonnade along the north wall of the outer court, Daniel gazed, as always, with awe at the indescribable magnificence of the structure. He was reminded it was King David's vision from God four centuries prior that was the genesis of the temple. But his son, King Solomon, had the blessing of directing its construction.

The boys walked toward their class table at about the halfway point along the colonnade. Several of the small classes of four to six students met in the mornings, and others met in the afternoons. Each priest taught both a morning class and an afternoon class. Daniel and his three companions were in their third year of formal studies.

The other classes were beginning just inside the long row of tall, white, granite columns that supported the roof extending inward from the wall surrounding the temple courtyard. Such open-air classrooms were the daily venue for these young men being groomed for leadership in the high offices of the land. Education on the temple grounds was mandatory for these selective heirs to greatness and special service to God. The prodigious temple dominating the mountain top provided an inspiring backdrop to their study area.

"Ah, welcome, my children," the priest greeted as he stood to meet his four students. He wore a white linen robe and a white turban with a gold rim at its base. "Daniel, I want you at my right hand today. Azariah, next to Daniel please. Mishael and Hananiah on the left."

Each day, the teacher seated his students in the order of his choosing, depending on whom he planned to give most attention to that day. Today, Daniel had the privilege—or burden, depending on how prepared he was—of sitting at that teacher's immediate right. The boys had no learning resources, other than the scroll lying on the table before them. It contained the writings of Moses, which had been revived for the people of Judah by King Josiah about seventeen years prior. The writings were in Hebrew, the predominant language of the people of Judah. Scribes had produced a few copies from the original document, one of which the teacher had access to. Almost all learning was by students' rote memory of these writings and the lectures from the teacher. The scroll was made of papyrus rolled at either end around wooden rods and inserted into a silver container. On this day, the teacher opened the writings to Moses' admonition to obey God's law.

"Let us begin, gentlemen," the teacher called out. "I will ask Daniel to read a portion of the writings of the fifth book of Moses. This is

Moses' record of what he said to the Israelites as directed by Yahweh just before they crossed the Jordan River into this promised land."

Daniel stood leaning over the scroll and began reading at the point where the teacher had placed his finger.

"See, I have taught you statutes and judgments just as the LORD my God commanded me, that you should do thus in the land where you are entering to possess it. So keep and do *them*, for that is your wisdom and your understanding in the sight of the peoples, who will hear all these statutes and say, 'Surely this great nation is a wise and understanding people.' For what great nation is there that has a god so near to it as is the LORD our God whenever we call on Him? Or what great nation is there that has statutes and judgments as righteous as this whole law which I am setting before you today? Only give heed to yourself and keep your soul diligently, so that you do not forget the things which your eyes have seen and they do not depart from your heart all the days of your life; but make them known to your sons and your grandsons."[1]

The teacher interrupted, "That's good, Daniel. Please take your seat. What is it that we, Yahweh's people, need to learn from this writing from eight centuries ago?"

Hananiah stood and answered, "That we are a special people with laws from Yahweh that will influence other nations as we live in the land He has given us."

"So, like good parents who guide their children in the way to live safely and prosper, Yahweh gives us guidance in the form of laws and

---

1 Deuteronomy 4:5-9

commands and assures us that we will be respected by other nations if we live by those laws and commands," the teacher responded. "And how faithful have we been to that?"

The students' silence portrayed their thoughts.

The teacher continued, "Yahweh led His people to victory under Moses' successor, Joshua, throughout the new land He had given them. But by the time Joshua died, His people were living heathen lifestyles of the natives of that land and worshiping their idols. Yahweh allowed the Philistines to conquer and gain control over His chosen as the consequence of their unfaithfulness. Eventually, they gained their independence back and decided to raise up a king of their own to lead them, although this was against Yahweh's will for His nation. King Saul was disobedient to the Lord and, because of this, was killed by the Philistines in battle. David was anointed king and ruled according to the ways of Yahweh, despite his personal failings. Later, David's son, Solomon, whose handiwork you see in the temple before you, led the people to respect the laws of Moses. But upon Solomon's death, our rebellious forefathers could not agree on a king and warred against each other, splitting the nation Israel into the two nations of Israel and our beloved Judah."

"Who will recite for me in sequence the kings of Israel?" the teacher quizzed his cohort.

All four boys stood.

"Azariah."

The fifteen-year old masterfully verbalized the twenty kings of the northern kingdom from 930 B.C. to 722 B.C., pronouncing each Hebrew name precisely from Jeroboam to Hoshea.

"And for a bonus prize, tell me which kings were recognized as faithful to Yahweh in their leading of His people?" the teacher asked.

"None of them, teacher."

"Correct. Your bonus prize is . . . You are permitted to sit."

The other three chuckled and gave a thumbs-down sign in Azariah's direction as a teasing gesture. The slight moment of levity was welcomed in the midst of the heavy discussion. But composure quickly replaced the brief light-heartedness.

"For two hundred years, the kingdom of our brothers to the north fell further away from Yahweh with each generation choosing to follow in the paths of their wicked neighbors. They crafted idols of foreign deities, practiced rituals of witchcraft, corrupted their Jewish bloodline by marrying women of other nations, and even sacrificed their own children to pagan gods. And every one of their kings, as well as most of their priests, encouraged such atrocities and often participated in them."

"Daniel, what have we learned about the ways of Yahweh during times of our transgressions like this?"

"He is patient, full of grace, and forgiving, but also a just Judge Who eventually punishes His children who willfully disobey Him."

"And how was His patience and grace demonstrated?"

"Through the prophets, He made Israel aware of their sin and disobedience, warned them of the consequences, appealed for them to repent and return to Him, and offered forgiveness."

"Who were the prophets that Yahweh called out to be His messengers to Israel?"

"Amos, Hosea, and Micah," the boys stated in unison.

"And did the northern tribes heed their messages?"

"No, teacher," Daniel replied anticipating the next question. "They suffered defeat by the Assyrians over a hundred years ago and were taken by their conquerors into exile as slaves."

"Mishael, what does this mean to us in our beautiful land of Judah?"

Mishael stood. "Like Israel, our southern kingdom of Judah has often been disobedient and worshipped other gods. Our prophets, too, have warned us and pleaded for us to turn back to the true Yahweh. Even though we have been attacked by Assyria and are now threatened by Babylonia, we have been spared conquest. We, too, have had kings who have led us away from the ways of Yahweh. But unlike Israel, we have also had kings like Jehoshaphat, Joash, Amaziah, Hezekiah, and Josiah, who were godly rulers who destroyed idols, punished evil, and led us to respect the laws of Moses."

"Azariah, we have been learning about the prophets Yahweh sent to us people of Judah. Can you name them in order?"

"Yes, teacher. Micah, Isaiah, Nahum, Zephaniah, and Jeremiah."

"You named five prophets of Judah and in the correct order. But remember Joel, even though he prophesied over two hundred years ago."

Azariah pursed his lips and nodded, frustrated that he had left out Joel, who admonished the people of Judah in their earlier years as a nation.

"We don't usually count yet another man among the line of prophets," the teacher offered. "But I think we should include Habakkuk among the prophets of Judah. He began prophesying only a few years ago but has become very worthy of our attention. Jeremiah is our modern-day prophet. We must listen to him carefully because he is delivering Yahweh's message to us, most of which is not popular with the public or even most of the religious leaders. He upsets many of my fellow priests quite often with his messages."

The priest transitioned the topic to the history of the people of Israel. His history lectures noted particularly that the northern kingdom had fallen to the Assyrians because none of their kings had followed God's command's closely. But when teaching about past kings of their own nation of Judah, he treaded rather softly on their misdeeds and the disobedience of the Judahites.

Few of the priests of the temple ever spoke against the monarchs, past or present. In fact, most would not admit there was any behavior among the people of Judah that would cause God to be displeased. After all, they were God's chosen and holy people. Unlike Israel, they were ruled by the line of David and surely found favor in the sight of the Almighty. In late seventh century Judah, religious leaders believed their kings were anointed by God and, therefore, could do no wrong. They considered the nation of Judah invulnerable as evidenced by its surviving the threats of their powerful neighboring nations.

Most of the priests and kings were heavily influenced by cultures of the pagan tribes native to their land. These tribes not only lived freely among the Jews but had been inter-marrying and integrating with the chosen ones for several generations. They had assimilated their idolatrous religious practices into those God had given Moses exclusively for His people. The temple priests had become reticent to maintain the purity of their rituals and had demanded their subordinate priests not make the letter of the law of Moses a major issue in their teaching.

The priest who had taught Daniel and his friends had not exactly honored the religious leaders in their attempt to control the teaching in the schools. Since his first class with the students, he had refused to overlook the sins of the past and present leaders in both the palace and the temple. Daniel and his friends had a unique and unabridged perspective of Jewish history that didn't mesh precisely with what was being espoused in the other classes.

"I have asked a student from the fifth-year class to read to you today from his assignment," the teacher announced as he motioned the handsome seventeen-year-old to approach their table. "You all know Ezekiel. He is studying to become a priest. He has been in the temple for the last three days transcribing some of the words of the prophet Jeremiah. The temple scribes will not copy Jeremiah's words, but, with my coaxing, they have allowed Baruch, Jeremiah's scribe, to bring some of the prophet's words into the temple to be transcribed by Ezekiel. I convinced the temple scribes to let Ezekiel use their ink and papyrus. As you would assume, they won't let him close to their precious parchment."

The papyrus used by temple scribes was from Egypt, where it was made from the Egyptian papyrus plant. The temple scribes were very protective of their limited amount of papyrus and ink. However, the priests' students—being future priests, scribes, and governing officials—were allowed a small ration for educational purposes.

Parchment as a writing surface had only recently become available. Made from a composite of animal skins, it was much more flexible for rolling into scrolls. It was also scarce and expensive.

Ezekiel expressed his excitement in being asked to transcribe some of Jeremiah's writings and read them to a lower class. His teacher would not allow the readings of the prophet in his own class. The whole issue of whether to acknowledge Jeremiah as a prophet was causing considerable conflict among the teaching priests. They had the same problem with Jeremiah's contemporary, Zephaniah.

Ezekiel positioned himself at the end of the table and unrolled a short scroll to reveal his handiwork. The words had been freshly stroked with a reed dipped in ink made of a solution of soot. The soot from the ashes of an acacia tree mixed with a tree sap for bonding produced the permanent, black Hebrew characters on the papyrus.

Daniel, Hananiah, Mishael, and Azariah stood without being cued as the scroll was unrolled. Although the words of the living prophet, Jeremiah, were not considered holy in the Hebrew culture, the boys had the greatest respect for them.

Ezekiel began with some introductory remarks. "Students, you know for many years our nation of Judah has drifted from Yahweh. Many of Yahweh's people now worship idols of the pagans who were in this land before He gave it to us. We know that even some of the children of Father Abraham sacrifice their own children to appease the Canaanite god, Molech. On our walk to and from these classes, we all observe images of idols made with Jewish hands sold in the marketplace. Are we any better than our northern tribes, whom Yahweh already gave up to the Assyrians and are now scattered among many oppressive lands?"

His voice increased in pitch and volume, "How long will Yahweh tolerate the people of Judah? You have heard your teacher tell of what Jeremiah is claiming Yahweh has revealed to him. Here are words I have copied from his writings being circulated among certain families in Jerusalem."

Ezekiel picked up the scroll and read aloud, "This is what Yahweh told Jeremiah:

"Behold, I am bringing a nation against you from afar, O house of Israel," declares the LORD. "It is an enduring nation, It is an ancient nation, A nation whose language you do not know, Nor can you understand what they say. Their quiver is like an open grave. All of them are mighty men. They will devour your harvest and your food; They will devour your sons and your daughters; They will devour your flocks and your herds. They will devour your vines and your fig trees; They will demolish with the sword your fortified cities in which you trust. Yet even in those days," declares the LORD, "I will not make you a complete destruction. It shall come about when they say, "Why has the Lord our God done all these things to us?" Then you shall say to them, "As you have forsaken Me and served foreign gods in your land, so you will serve strangers in a land that is not yours."[2]

"My friends," Ezekiel said, "I believe Yahweh is speaking to us through Jeremiah, and I believe our generation will see our nation conquered by a pagan nation. That nation will probably be Babylon, which has conquered Assyria and is already taunting us and is ravaging neighboring nations. Isaiah warned us over a century ago. How much warning do we need?"

The teacher interjected, "Ezekiel, if I didn't know you were preparing for the priesthood, I would think our Yahweh was preparing you to be a prophet in the likes of Jeremiah."

Ezekiel maintained a somber expression, thanked the teacher and the class of four, then rolled up his scroll and walked back to his class. The teacher didn't comment further on Ezekiel's readings.

The rest of the afternoon involved mathematical exercises using the basic decimal system with Hebrew alpha characters representing numerical values. As the setting sun approached the horizon, the teacher formally ended the class session with final comments.

"Enjoy the blessings of Yahweh on Yom Teruah," the teacher said, referring to the annual beginning of the High Holy Days. He reminded

2 Jeremiah 5:15-19

them that these ten days leading up to the Day of Atonement, or Yom Kippur, would begin at sundown in just a few hours. He then reminded them there would be no classes during the next ten days and to be preparing their minds and hearts for Yom Kippur. After this holy day, their class would begin testing in the Aramaic language, which they had been learning over the past year. The students were dismissed to complete their daily routine of physical strengthening exercises before returning to their homes.

All four young men took turns lifting different sizes of flat stones—first to knee level, then to the chest, then over their heads. This disciplined body building had produced larger-than-normal muscles over their limbs and torsos. Other than students of the temple ground school, few men in Jerusalem maintained such toned bodies that turned the heads of every young woman in the city. This physique, along with the outer garments and sandals of the best materials, made these young scholars immediately recognizable in the public venues as the elite of their generation. However, most of them—certainly Daniel and his three friends—dismissed the stereotypes they inherited and conducted themselves with humility and grace.

Through the descending, narrow walkways of rough stone en route to their residences, the boys were uncharacteristically quiet. All three were pondering the stark words of Jeremiah read by their superior classmate Ezekiel. Daniel's eyes were drawn more than usual to the miniature idols for sale on the tables at almost every storefront—little, gold-plated calves, miniature human-like silver figures with grotesque faces, phallic symbols, various images of Baal and Molech, and a number of bronze animal likenesses. He wondered how any descendant of the patriarchs could possibly purchase those images and take them into his home while still claiming belief in one God, the Creator, the omnipotent Yahweh, the "I AM."

Daniel was several steps away from the open door to his house, but he could already smell the pleasant scent of what his mother was cooking for the family's dinner. The smell of the baking Galilean fish was readily identifiable but not potent enough to cancel the sweet yeast scent of the wheat bread. Those combined aromas created an instant appetite in the teen.

He was hardly in the door until his younger brother and two younger sisters abruptly ended their play and ran to hug their brother. In order of their ages, their arms wrapped the first-born sibling's chest and hips, binding him with love and honor. It had only been a few hours since he had departed for school, but family was the center of life. A few hours apart left an emptiness in his soul that was always thrilling to refill.

Daniel moved quickly to the back room, where his mother turned from her meal task to welcome her firstborn home. Everything concluded early on Friday—school, cooking, work—so everyone could be unburdened and resting by sundown and the beginning of the Sabbath. Daniel was a mother's boy, like most Jewish boys having the proper respect balanced with a deep love. Kissing her face on both cheeks, he tried to hide the melancholy mood he was in.

"I am going to lie down just a moment," Daniel said to his mother as he headed into the adjoining room that served as the bedroom for him and his brother.

"All right, but your father will be home any time now, and we will be ready to eat immediately."

Nessa continued with the final touches of the dinner, the principal family meal. Other meals consisted of single servings of items, such as dates, grapes, pieces of bread, various nuts, etc. The evening dinner did not always include meat, but tonight, there would be fish. Four fish would be divided among the six family members. The fish, lying on a layer of olive oil in an iron pan, were presently baking in the conical stone oven with a flue rising through the roof of the house. Foods were also often cooked over an open fire outside in the back courtyard. The bread had just come out of the oven and was cooling in an open window. Earlier in the day, Nessa had boiled some beans over the outside fire. Everything had been seasoned with multiple herbs and spices. The meal would be topped off with pomegranates fresh from the market.

Daniel lay on his wool-stuffed mattress, staring at the wood rafters supporting the clay roof. Haunting thoughts of Yahweh's wrath bringing Judah the same destiny as that of Israel consumed his mind. It would be justice for those whose evil practices had beset the nation, but the vengeance would also include the faithful and righteous. Although he was young, innocent, and inexperienced, Daniel's mind had an unusually keen aptitude for understanding the ways of Yahweh. He reasoned that Yahweh's closest followers would pay the same price as those who rejected His laws when Providential justice was meted out on a nation. But those whose trust was in the Lord would ultimately be cared for. Yet he hoped with all his being that he would not see Jeremiah's prophecy fulfilled in his lifetime.

Mentally reviewing his dreams of becoming a government official of the Judahites, Daniel wondered whether those doors to the future would be abruptly closed by the conquering of his homeland. Would he even survive such an invasion? He aspired to be an officer in the royal court of the next king, who would hopefully reign in the manner of

Hezekiah and Josiah. His father had risen to a respectable position in the treasury of King Josiah and now served as King Jehoiakim's treasurer. He could probably sponsor his entry into that field of endeavor.

His parents often spoke of his becoming a scholarly scribe in the temple or maybe even a priest. However, the priesthood would require non-traditional ascension, since his family was not in the priestly bloodline, but the royal line. Furthermore, Daniel had seen too much hypocrisy and corruption among temple priests to want to pursue that realm. His innocent beginnings were giving way to stark reality.

As Daniel drifted into semi-sleep, the liberating moment was soon interrupted by the sound of his siblings celebrating their father's arrival. He rose to join them, embracing the father he loved and respected. In short order, the thirty-six-year-old patriarch of the family was sitting at the table with his children as his loving wife served the much-anticipated dinner meal on shiny, brass plates.

On each plate was a portion of fish, a piece of bread, and a serving of beans. Then, the mix of fresh fruit rounded out the meal. Beside each plate was a small glass of red wine and a pottery bowl filled with water for cleaning the fingers. The food was eaten by hand with no utensils. Regularly, throughout the meal, each person would dip his or her fingers in the water bowl to remove the olive oil and other food residue.

The family bowed as Karmiel began, "Blessed are You, our Yahweh, King of the universe, Who sanctifies us with his commandments and commands us to righteous living, and Who brings forth bread from the earth."

"Amen," the family responded in unison.

This mealtime seemed different to Daniel. It was quieter, except for the normal bantering among the three youngest children. His father didn't speak a word as they ate. As his mother rose from the table, she teasingly announced that she might find some fresh pomegranates as a special treat. As she placed halves of the fruit on each plate, the awkward silence continued.

"Is something wrong? Was my food not tasty?" Nessa asked.

"The meal was delicious as always, my dear," Karmiel replied. "I will offer the after-dinner blessing."

"Blessed are You, our Yahweh, Master of the universe, Who nourishes the whole world in goodness with grace, kindness, and compassion. He gives bread to all flesh, for His mercy endures forever. And through His great goodness we have never lacked, nor will we lack food forever, for the sake of His great name. For He is Yahweh, Who nourishes and sustains all and does good to all and prepares food for His creatures, which He created. Blessed are You, Yahweh, Who nourishes all."

All said, "Amen."

"Aviel," the father addressed his number-two son, "take your sisters outside and play some games until dark. I need to talk to your mother and brother."

This was unusual. Daniel sensed something very serious was about to be discussed.

3

TROUBLED CITY

THE MASTER OF THE HOUSE cleared his throat and spoke softly. "King Jehoiakim summoned us chiefs of the court and our highest military officials today. He announced that an envoy from one of our northern outposts had brought a message that the ruthless Babylonian army commander, Nebuchadnezzar, had overpowered Egyptian Pharaoh Necho's army at Carchemish in the north country. Necho appears to be retreating south with Nebuchadnezzar in close pursuit."

Daniel's eyes widened as he leaned closer to his father.

"Remember four years ago, our beloved King Josiah was killed in battle against Egypt in our effort to keep Necho's army from warring against Babylonia. We tried to stop Egypt's army from crossing our land and marching north to fight the Babylonians. We could not risk Babylonia turning against Judah. But what is our small nation against Egypt? They prevailed and have been battling Nebuchadnezzar's army ever since, while keeping outposts throughout Judah. They killed our king and have since controlled our nation. Try as we may to remain neutral, we seem to always be on the wrong side of the victors."

Karmiel paused and shook his head.

"Now, after ransoming our nation as a vassal state to Egypt for four years, we are finding ourselves threatened again by Babylonia, with whom we have been trying to avoid confrontation. If the Egyptian army is forced back to their country, Nebuchadnezzar's army will have every motive and opportunity to invade Judah and probably our neighbor Benjamin. Our forced alliance with Egypt since the death of Josiah has brought us a life of national poverty with oppressive taxes King Jehoiakim has insisted on paying to Necho. We are nothing more than a puppet of Necho's. Now, what has it gained us? Another enemy Egypt has stirred up, and we will likely be its next target!"

After a moment of stunned silence, Daniel spoke. "What is King Jehoiakim doing to prepare us for this, Father?"

"Tomorrow, a missive will be circulated throughout our troubled city and the surrounding provinces. It will order all able-bodied men from ages eighteen to thirty to prepare to supplement Judah's army. He will announce meetings and training beginning immediately to build up our fighting forces."

Daniel's heart raced as he flashed many thoughts of what an invasion by the Babylonian army would do to Judah, but most importantly what might happen to his family. His father could be executed, along with the king and his entire court. The words of Jeremiah read just hours earlier by Ezekiel surfaced in his head. He believed the words but had assumed they were describing years in the future.

Nessa embraced her husband and said softly, "Yahweh will protect us. He will show you how to keep our family safe."

"I know He has the power to protect us," Karmiel replied. "But He is also just. He was just with our kinsmen in Israel. Because of their rejection of His commands despite the pleading of His prophets, He removed His hand of protection and enacted justice, scattering His people to Nineveh and beyond. Are we incurring the same wrath from Yahweh? So many of the people of Judah are worshiping idols, turning their backs on the poor, lame, and widowed. Some are even sacrificing their children to a pagan god. And our king is depending on neighboring heathen nations to keep us secure."

Karmiel hung his head. "And I am no better."

"How can you say that?" his wife retorted. "You have devoted your life to serving this nation. You honored Yahweh in the court of King Josiah, the godliest of Judah's kings. If Heaven does allow the sinful land to be destroyed, you will be spared for your faithfulness, along with this family."

"My fear, beloved, is that I will not be found faithful," he responded. "I have led the collection of overburdening taxes from our people. Even though it was commanded by my lord Jehoiakim, it was I who increased the yoke of poverty among our people. It was I who facilitated the paying of redemption money to the enemy instead of depending on the redemption of Yahweh. And even if I were found faithful, when Yahweh's patience eventually gives way, His wrath falls on the just and the unjust without discrimination. Were there not some righteous people in Israel when Assyria's Shalmaneser laid siege on them and forced all people into exile?"

"What shall we do, Father?" Daniel's voice was cracking.

"We must trust Yahweh as your mother said but also prepare for what He may be bringing about. Whatever happens will be according to His purpose. We must pray more often, seeking His wisdom. We must follow His commands with discipline and determination. I also believe we should prepare by beginning to store up grain, dried fruit, and vegetables, oil, and wine. If Jerusalem comes under siege by Nebuchadnezzar, food will be in great shortage within the city walls. It is also essential that we not talk about this around the younger children."

Daniel lay in his bed that night unable to sleep. Well after midnight, he could hear the muffled voices of his father and mother. Unable to hear clearly what they were saying, he knew they were agonizing over the bleak prospects for the nation of Judah and for their family. Tomorrow, he would talk to his three friends about what was transpiring. Hopefully, Ezekiel would have a spiritual perspective on it. Maybe he would know Jeremiah's response to the news.

*

It had been a typical Shabbat—Saturday the Sabbath. The day had begun with Daniel's father reciting the requisite prayers and some passages from the Torah—all by memory—as the family was gathered around the table. No one had worked that day. In fact, no one was allowed to exert themselves in any way. It was truly a God-gifted day of rest. Nessa had prepared all food beforehand.

But now it was Sunday morning. Each family member had household responsibilities, except for their father, who had left early for work. Daniel knew his father would have many meetings with the other chiefs of the court, perhaps with the king himself regarding the ominous intelligence received on Friday. Daniel's first responsibility for the day was to go to the various food merchants and buy fresh fruits, vegetables, and oil for the family's next several meals.

Taking an often-used shortcut through a narrow alley, he stopped suddenly. About twenty steps ahead were several people descending a stone stairway from the upper floor of a residence. He was startled by the strange scene and sounds. A woman and some girls were trailing the rest while speaking softly to each other, obviously distressed. A man dressed in a brightly colored robe and a red turban was leading the group with a few boys following closely behind. Some other adults continued to flow out of the door. The alley was so dark that everyone was a silhouette. Except for the murmuring women, everyone was quiet.

As the entourage proceeded down the alley, Daniel resumed his trek. Maintaining a distance to avoid calling attention to himself, he observed the people in single file turn onto a seldom-used path behind the marketplace booths. Daniel paused, his curiosity mounting. This was a very mysterious occurrence. What harm would there be in returning home a little late with the food? As the odd mix of people disappeared over a hill, he lifted his tunic above his knees and trotted toward them.

After tailing the group for a while, Daniel realized they were almost to the valley of Gehenna. This was a huge, constantly burning garbage dump, where the residents and merchants of Jerusalem took all their refuse from food wastes to human excrement. Dead animals were also cast into the fires of the valley. The area emitted a rancid odor that permeated the whole city when the wind was strong from the south. The consuming fire burned constantly as it was fueled by a never-ending stream of organic waste. The odor burned Daniel's nostrils as he continued the slow descent into the valley, and the smoke hanging just above the ground evoked tears from his stinging eyes. Daniel remembered that a few of the prophets gave the name Gehenna to the eternal destiny of the unrighteous, which would also be characterized by never-ending fire.

The people he had been following had joined another assembly of what looked to be twenty to thirty men and women. They stood with hands raised forward, facing the rocky ledge just above the flames of the pit. Daniel had never been to this remote area of Gehenna before. He wanted to move closer to the assembly to quench his curiosity as to what was taking place. Carefully avoiding detection, he moved from one large rock to another, crouching as he ran to reduce his exposure. Finally, he was within about fifty steps of what had become a crowd of chanting people. His vantage was slightly up hill from the gathering.

Through the thick, dark smoke, Daniel could barely make out a statue of some sort in the pit just below the ledge. As the breeze redirected the smoke, a brass image of a human-like beast came into focus. It had an animal head, wings attached to its back, and arms stretched forward toward the ledge as if reaching for something. The roaring flames below the image leaped up to envelop the brass arms, giving them a red-hot glow.

Several men standing to the side of the crowd began beating loudly on drums. The man in the bright robe and turban began walking on a wooden ramp that extended from the ledge. In the man's arms was what appeared to be a young child. Daniel could see the child's legs kicking and could hear a faint cry over the sound of the drums. Most of the crowd began to chant to the rhythm of the drumbeat, "Hail, Molech!" "Praise to Molech!" "Molech, our god!" Arms were raised and waving wildly.

The man at the end of the ramp lifted the child above his head and cried out loudly, "May Molech show mercy on us and crush our enemies!"

As the frenzied crowd reached their loudest noise level, the man suddenly tossed the helpless child into the red-hot, bronze arms of the image. A piercing shriek replaced all other sounds. The small, limp body rolled down the arms of the image to the elbow bends and dropped out of sight into the raging fire.

The crying stopped. The drums ceased.

Daniel cupped his hands over his mouth to muffle his scream. His breath ceased; then he began short, rapid inhalations uncontrollably.

He felt totally numb as his knees gave way, and he slumped to the ground. Without warning, his stomach contracted, and vomit gushed from his mouth, filling his palms.

What have I witnessed? What horrid evil is this? I must gain strength to flee this dark place. Yahweh, save me from this Sheol and cleanse me!

Baring his legs to mid-thigh, he sprinted with all the energy he could muster back to the inner city. Reaching a tree next to a shop, he collapsed in its shade. The midday heat was miserable, but he was shivering from the chill in his soul. He felt dirty and in need of a bath.

After a while, his heartbeat and breathing rate reduced as he remembered his objective was to buy food for his mother. *She is probably worrying about me.* Hurriedly, he purchased the bread loaves, olive oil, and a selection of fresh fruit.

Daniel didn't acknowledge his siblings as he walked past them playing in the courtyard of their home. Laying the food items on a table, he disappeared quickly into his bedroom without speaking to his mother who was cooking at the hearth. He wanted more than anything else at this moment to avoid the rest of the world, including his family. His whole being seemed to be exploding with the vision of the ghoulish human sacrifice. He felt somehow a party to this dehumanizing act. Tears continued to fill his eyes. He craved a bath.

"Daniel, what is wrong?" the gentle voice of his mother inquired, only able to see the outline of his body beneath the wool blanket in the dim room.

"Nothing."

She left him alone, assuming another adolescent moment caused by a disagreement with a friend or the loss of a competitive game.

Daniel's father arrived just before sundown and was greeted just inside the door with a kiss. His loving wife knew his day had been stressful with the dealings of the national crisis. Within a few minutes, the meal was on the table, and the three youngest children joined their parents at their assigned places.

"Where's Daniel?" Karmiel asked.

"He's in his bedroom," Nessa replied. "He hasn't been out since before noon. I chose to leave him alone. He's out of character, but, sometimes, maybe a boy just needs his privacy."

"No. Sometimes a boy needs to respect his family and be at the table. He will be at the evening meal his mother has labored all day to prepare."

The stresses of the workday were surfacing as Karmiel rose from the table and entered the bedroom. "Son, come and eat with the rest of us. You're offending your family—especially your mother."

As he pulled back the blanket covering his son, he felt the wetness of it. He placed his hand on Daniel's back, which was soaked with perspiration, and heard him sobbing softly.

"Daniel, are you sick?"

"N . . . no, Father."

His father grasped his muscular arm and gently turned him over to reveal his flushed face with salty trails descending from his eyes.

Daniel wanted to confess what he had done and share the haunting experience, but he didn't think he could bear the pain.

"Son, I insist you tell me what is wrong." His father contorted to look into his son's eyes.

Daniel sat up enough to wrap his shaking arms around his father's neck and pressed his head against his chest. "Forgive me, Father. I followed a large group of people to the Gehenna valley. It was awful, Father. It was awful."

That was all Daniel's father needed to hear. He knew what had happened. He drew his son closer.

"Oh, my young, innocent child. I had so hoped you would not ever actually see this carnage. I wouldn't allow you to ever take any of our refuse to Gehenna, fearing you might see the Molech image or, worse, witness a human sacrifice. I'm sorry. I'm so sorry." Tears of both father and son were flowing.

"It was probably the son of our top military commander who was sacrificed. I heard yesterday at the palace that he had committed to King Jehoiakim to sacrifice his infant son. It was done as an appeasement to Molech that might bring victory over Nebuchadnezzar's army. I know that breaks the heart of Yahweh."

After a long pause, Daniel looked up at his father. "Some older boys at the school said they had seen the pagan rituals where parents would sacrifice their children to the fire god, but I hoped I never would. I assumed it could only be crazy people who would do such a thing. How can someone of rank and intelligence . . . ?"

Daniel's father's chest was pounding with what seemed to be a heavy mallet inside. "You shouldn't have followed that crowd, but I forgive you. You lost a lot of your childhood innocence today. Much of our nation is turning back to the evil that characterized us in the days of King Manasseh and the Ahaz reign before him."

Karmiel sat at Daniel's side on the bed.

"King Josiah, whom I served under for several years, honored Yahweh. He destroyed the idols throughout our God-given land and established the rightful worship of Yahweh and the legitimate sacrifices. He reinstituted the feasts. But within a few months after he was killed in battle, just four years ago, his son, Jehoiakim, began allowing our people to erect the images again and worship Molech, as well as Asherah and Baal. I am so ashamed the king I now daily serve to provide for my family is himself a worshipper of these pagan gods. Is there any wonder that Yahweh has removed His protective hand from us and is allowing Babylonia to threaten our existence?"

"Yahweh will not tolerate this rejection, will He, Father? Jerusalem will be destroyed and all Judah, just as Jeremiah has been saying and Isaiah before him. I'm scared, Father. We're all going to die."

"When you were younger, I would have comforted you with assurance that we will all be all right. But you are a young man, who has observed the wretched state of Yahweh's chosen people. I cannot be dishonest with you. I am afraid Yahweh's judgment is upon us. As I shared with you and your mother previously, we have been warned through the prophets. They have pleaded with our people to repent and honor Yahweh. It tears at my soul to have to tell my own flesh and blood that I do not see us avoiding His deserved wrath."

"But our family will continue to live for Yahweh. Right, Father?"

"Of course, Son. Even if we are the only family in Jerusalem who does."

Daniel's father wiped his son's tears with the sleeve of his tunic and, with his arm around the boy's shoulder, parted the curtain to re-enter the kitchen area. The mother and other siblings had finished their meal and left after clearing most of the table. Two bowls of inviting lentil and lamb stew and two small loaves of bread fresh from the hearth remained. Both ate silently, unaware of just how soon they would face the reality of their shared fears.

4

ATONEMENT SACRIFICE

TWO DAYS BEFORE THE DAY of Atonement, Daniel's father returned home late in the afternoon. He had been unexpectedly summoned by the king's messenger earlier that morning. Normally, there was no work performed during the High Holy Days. The palace's official activities would be ceased. The family knew something extremely important had occurred that required the recall of the royal staff. Karmiel asked the younger children to remain outside while he spoke with his wife and Daniel.

"King Jehoiakim announced this morning that messengers from our spies in the north country reported that Nebuchadnezzar's army had swept through Damascus and Dan. They are moving southward swiftly in pursuit of the Egyptian army, which is in retreat, having just passed to our west over the last two days. The spies also observed a ceremony at the foothills of the Nebo Mountains, followed by much reveling by his army. The strange event including music and dancing led the spies to conclude that Nebuchadnezzar had received a coronation in the field. His father, King Nabopolassar, was known to be failing in health. He must have died in Babylon. Nebuchadnezzar was seen leaving the camp the next day with a travel entourage. Babylonia probably has a new king."

"Does that mean their army will end their movement toward us, Father?" Daniel asked.

"Not likely. Their army is fierce and well-organized. They can operate without Nebuchadnezzar. What's more, Necho sent a team to inform Jehoiakim that Egypt was abandoning Judah, at least for now. Necho's men also presented a demand for food, supplies, and payment of our protection in silver and gold."

Daniel interrupted. "Why should we pay a defeated king further extortion?

"You should be king of Judah, my son. You are so wise for your young age. Certainly, King Jehoiakim would not agree to pay any more protection money to Necho. In addition to Necho's inability to enforce our payment now, we do not want Nebuchadnezzar to see us as a staunch ally of Egypt, remaining loyal even in their defeat. We would like nothing better than to be removed from the tyrannical control of Egypt. Unfortunately, we may just trade one oppressing king for another if Babylonia invades all of Judah. The combined armies of Judah could not withstand the thousands of Babylonian warriors."

"But, Father," Daniel interjected again, "Gideon prayed to Yahweh and defeated the entire Median army with only three hundred men. With Yahweh, we can overcome the Babylonian army."

"You are not only wise, Daniel, but your faith is greater than mine. Oh, that I had your faith. God surely has something great in store for you."

*

Daniel and his family entered the temple around nine o'clock on Thursday morning—what the Hebrews called the "third hour," being three hours after sunrise. It was just a short, quiet walk from their home. Even though worship and rituals in the temple had become infrequent and sparsely attended, this was Yom Kippur, the one day each year when almost every Jew turned out for the atonement sacrifice. This was the day that the high priest entered the Holy of Holies in the center of the temple to atone for sins of all Jews. It had been practiced by the Hebrew people since the days of Moses. Daniel always looked forward to this experience when he felt closest to Yahweh. The presence of His Spirit could be felt in a powerful way.

Daniel felt a particularly special need to receive atonement this year. He longed for relief of the guilt he harbored from observing the sacrifice to Molech. He felt unclean and in need of Yahweh's forgiveness. He knew his sin would be among those represented in the animal sacrifice as the priest would sprinkle the blood on the Ark of the Covenant inside the Holy of Holies.

Daniel's father entered the temple courtyard first wearing a traditional white mantle, a full-sleeved outer garment that flowed to the ankles with multiple folds and drapes. It was made of a light linen fabric imported from Babylon. On the bottom hem were a series of tassels, which the Torah commanded that Israelites wear as a reminder to keep the Lord's commandments. This mantle, called a meil, was only worn by men of rank in the Hebrew society. Underneath the mantle was an under-tunic made of wool that had short sleeves and was knee-length. There was no need for a cloak in the warm, early autumn temperatures on this tenth day of the month of Tishrei. Under both garments was a simple piece of cloth worn next to the body. Like a loin cloth, the front and back loosely stitched together between the legs. On his head was a light blue turban of fine wool cloth wrapped neatly and tightly. His footwear was recently purchased sandals with hard, thick, leather soles and leather thong straps tied just above the ankles. This attire was newer and of higher quality than that worn by the large majority of the attendees. His social position would always be identified by his higher grade of clothing.

Likewise, Nessa had selectively chosen her Yom Kippur clothing, the principal piece of which was a tunic. The women's tunic was two pieces of linen cloth joined in a seam along the top of the arms with a cut-out for the head. It had a seam running down both sides with holes for the arms. It had a bright red hem at the bottom touching the tops of her feet. This garment was gathered up in a bunch at the shoulders with a decorative metal clip and draped to fall gracefully over her body. Under her tunic were a loin cloth sewn together at the crotch and a long, narrow piece of cloth wrapped a few times snuggly around her upper body to cradle her breasts. Around her waist was a golden chain belt made by craftsmen that identified her as having above-average wealth. Her cloak of royal blue-dyed linen covered most of her tunic and included the requisite tassels around the bottom edge. Her long, black hair was wrapped in a piece of colorful patterned cloth that continued to encircle her neck framing her face. This combination scarf and neck wrap protected her from the sun but also sufficed as the head covering required of women in the temple. Expertly fabricated sandals adorned her feet. Accessories of fine jewelry were noticeable on her fingers and wrist as the status symbol of choice for Hebrew women.

Daniel was dressed much like his father, except for the turban. Most teenaged boys were bare-headed in public. His attire, including sandals, were the same as he wore to school, work, and play, except the newest and best were reserved for Yom Kippur.

The younger children wore only a tunic and the loin cloth under-garment, leaving the lower legs and feet bare. Boys and girls dressed in the same attire. However, the girls—regardless of age—wore a head cover in the temple usually consisting of a small, triangle-shaped scarf tied under the chin.

Daniel followed his father to the male seating section, while his mother, brother, and sisters took their place in the separate outer court-yard area. The women and children could observe the worship rituals and meditate but would not speak or take part in any of the processes. This was Daniel's third time to sit in the men's section of the temple, forward of the women, but behind the priests. That privilege was awarded after a boy's thirteenth birthday, the year he was considered accountable for the Torah's commandments.

Seriah, the son of the high priest, who was in line to become high priest, rose from his artfully crafted ceremonial chair and took his position before a large scroll lying on an octagonal table. He was dressed in a pure linen tunic, flowing in folds from his neck to his feet with long sleeves reaching to the wrists. A yellow cloak over-garment hung from his shoulders and was gathered at the waist by a white twined linen sash. His white turban was wound in a cone shape.

He began reading from the Torah the words of Moses, setting the stage for the imminent sacrifice by the high priest. The first reading was an instruction of the rituals of Yom Kippur. Then the young priest, turning both cylinders of the scroll to reveal subsequent writings, began reading what constituted sin and what sacrifices were required.

As the priest continued reading the word of Yahweh given through Moses, several of the men of the congregation were showing visible signs of remorse and contrition. For those who had prepared their hearts and minds by seeking the presence of Yahweh during the days leading up to Yom Kippur, this was an emotionally heavy moment.

Daniel could hear his father's soft sobbing and couldn't resist a quick glance, which revealed tears flowing through his father's fingers as they covered his eyes. Daniel's heart became heavy as his eyes also moistened from feeling his father's anguish. He sensed the guilt his father was carrying from the role he played in paying ransom to Egypt for Judah's security rather than depending on Yahweh's promised defense of His people. He had never felt closer to this man he admired so greatly. He shared the guilt of his father as he silently prayed that Yahweh would forgive them both. Although they had not rejected Yahweh, they had seldom spoken out against those who did. Both father and son were silently crying out to Yahweh to forgive them and to show them the right actions to pursue in the future to correct their mistakes. Both were well aware of the looming Babylonian army marching south and drawing closer. Both were praying that God would be merciful and provide protection of His people.

Daniel's mind switched to the scene of the human sacrifice he had witnessed. Suddenly, that evil act generated a personal conviction, and he swore before Yahweh to begin to fight against such a heinous affront to the Creator. He prayed for wisdom. This precious time in the presence of their Lord left these two men oblivious to the reading of the Torah and prayers offered by the priests in the ceremony of cleansing. Their hearts were being cleansed through their own appeals and personal repentance, as well as confession from the depths of their souls.

After the ceremonial readings and prayers, the worshipers, several hundred in number, moved to the perimeter of the courtyard.

The high priest, Azaryah IV, had been going through the ceremonial purification washings and changing of garments in private settings during the morning hours. Just prior to appearing in the courtyard of the temple, he had clothed himself in his special priestly garments for the sacrifices. Azaryah had participated in these yearly ceremonies as a young priest assisting his father, Hilkiah, in the years of King Josiah. This was only his third year to perform the sacrifices as chief priest assisted by his son, Seriah.

Azaryah entered the courtyard with the sounding of the temple trumpets and the beat of the ceremonial drums. His priestly robe was a sleeveless, white linen over-garment fringed at the lower hem with golden bells alternating with pomegranate-shaped tassels in colors of blue, purple, and scarlet. Over the robe was a richly embroidered, long, white linen vest called an ephod. It had two onyx gemstones on the shoulders engraved with the names of the twelve tribes of Israel. Fastened securely to the ephod was the priestly breastplate with twelve gemstones—four rows of three—each engraved with the name of one of the tribes. A white, linen turban adorned his head and displayed a golden plate inscribed with the words, "Holiness unto Yahweh."

At the high priest's command, the bull specially selected and inspected for the sacrifice was led in through the main temple gate. The bull had no blemish or impairment—the finest of all herds in Judah. It would be slaughtered to provide the blood as a sin offering for the high priest and his family before being placed on the coals of the altar. Just inside the gate, the bull's handlers, along with the priest's son, Seriah, immobilized the beast with ropes and dropped it to the stone floor with a thud and a flurry of dust. Saliva was spewing from its mouth as it bellowed in terror, pain, and anger.

Daniel and his father stood motionless on the periphery of the courtyard after they had maneuvered to a position with a clear view of the priest and the bull. Azaryah's loud and high-pitched confession over the condemned animal was the cue for everyone within earshot to fall prone on the floor. Fathers and sons lay with their foreheads and noses touching the warm stone courtyard overlays. The priest continued to cry out for Yahweh to remember their sins no more and to be glorified by the slaying of the bull lying at his feet.

As the prayer ended, Daniel rose and looked over the crowd. In a way, it was amusing to watch how people of all ages managed the act of rising from prone to standing. Suddenly, he gasped. His jaw dropped as he forcefully exhaled. Not more than ten steps away was the man he instantly recognized as the one who had presided at the sacrifice of the little boy to the fiery arms of Molech at Gehenna.

Daniel's knees buckled, and his breathing quickened. He was shocked at how such an evil man could join the presence of Yahweh's people on this holiest day of the year. Was he there to repent and confess? That would be too much to comprehend. Was he there because he was so out of touch with Yahweh, he saw nothing wrong with serving two masters? That was also unimaginable. Daniel became nauseous. He would not tell his father, desiring to not distract him from the ritual.

Seriah received a large knife from a temple servant and presented it ceremoniously to his father. With a precise sweeping motion, the high priest cut a deep gash into the neck of the bull, severing the vessels that immediately streamed blood into a bronze bowl placed instantly under the flow. The crowd yelled in jubilant mixed praises of "hallelujah," "praise Yahweh," and unintelligible shouts and screams, while jumping and lifting their hands heavenward. The sacrifice had been made!

The bull lay still and quiet, surrendering its life as a sacrifice for the sins of God's people.

Removing the blood-filled bowl, the high priest carried it carefully to the altar and poured most of it on the red-hot coals. Then he took a small shovel of embers from the altar and carried it under his arm while holding the bowl. Taking slow and deliberate steps, he walked past the laver wash basin and up the steps to the porch of the holy sanctuary. There, Seriah parted the curtains for his father to enter the sanctuary where the lampstand, the showbread table, and the altar of incense were located.

Losing sight of the priests, Daniel closed his eyes and visualized in his mind what he knew was taking place inside. The lampstand was lighted in the holy place day and night. The temple priests ensured the flames on all seven arms of the lamp were never extinguished and the incense was always burning. Daniel mentally traced the entire temple ritual.

Turning to Seriah, Azaryah handed him the bowl of blood and gathered several of the sticks and leaves of incense in another bowl. As Azaryah approached the thick, heavy curtain that guarded the Holy of Holies, Seriah stood behind his father. They were alone in the sanctuary. All was quiet in the room, partially because of the thick curtains around all sides muffling any sound, but there was also silence in the outer court as the people hushed in reverence to this sacred event. There was not a whisper, even from the children. This was the year's most sacred moment in the lives of the Jewish people. It was an eerie silence—a stark contrast to the raucous commotion surrounding the slaying of the bull just moments before.

Only the high priest could enter the Holy of Holies, the dwelling place of Yahweh, and only once each year during Yom Kippur. Seriah stood rigid in front of the burning incense that filled the room with a strong, but pleasant, aroma. Azaryah picked up a small oil lamp that had been placed next to the incense and draped its attached cord around his right forearm. Then he reached slowly for the tightly closed divide of the two huge curtains between the two inner columns of the entry to the Holy of Holies. Using all the strength of his left arm and shoulder while balancing the incense and the shovel of embers, he parted the curtains with a hearty exhaled groan. With barely enough room to slide his body sideways between them, he carefully held the bowl of incense in his right hand so as not to spill any of it. The curtains came together with a thud behind him as he suddenly stood overwhelmed with emotion and awe before the Ark of the Covenant. The flickering blaze in the small lamp barely provided enough light to see the silhouette of the ark.

As Azaryah's eyes grew more accustomed to the dark room, he began to make out more details of the ark. The solid gold, cube-shaped container housed the two stone tablets engraved by Yahweh with the Ten Commandments given to Moses. The sight was just as awesome as the first time this high priest had seen it in the first year of his anointing. The original contents included the budding staff of Aaron and a jar of manna, which were removed during the ark's brief possession by the Philistine enemies of Israel about four centuries prior. A few scrapes and dents were visible on the corners from months of abuse by the heathen tribes.

The ark was adorned at all edges with engravings by the artists commissioned by Moses. Fused to the top of the ark were the solid gold images of two angels facing each other in kneeling positions with large, feathered wings folded toward each other and touching in the center. Gold-clad, horizontal, wooden poles were held in place by gold rings on either side of the ark.

As the priest's eyes adjusted more to the darkness, he could not see much of the ark's former brilliance due to the centuries of annual staining from the sprinkling of blood first in the tabernacle tent, then in the temple.

After pausing to regain his composure and recovering from momentary hyperventilation, Azaryah forced himself to focus on placing the shovel of embers on the incense altar and pouring the incense over the embers. He closed his eyes and breathed in the sweet scent. It was understandable why Yahweh loved the aroma representing the prayers of His people.

Parting the curtains a little more easily this time, Azaryah reappeared before Seriah, took the bowl of blood, and reentered the Holy of Holies. Once again inside, he moved through the ritual of sprinkling the blood on the ark. He dipped his fingers into the bowl of blood eight times and, with repeated deliberate motions, flung the blood drops each time onto the ark's top and sides. He walked around the ark to sprinkle all four sides with the lifeblood of the sacrificial bull, most of which now lay charred and smoldering on the bronze altar. The bowl containing the remaining blood was placed on a stand at the exit from the room.

Still standing in the center of the holy sanctuary, Seriah saw the curtains part slightly at first, then just wide enough for his father to again move quickly through the heavy fabric, somewhat clumsily carrying the incense bowl, the shovel, and the lamp.

The father and son priests walked together from the sanctuary to the east side of the courtyard, where Azaryah laid his hands on a goat specially selected for sacrifice to Yahweh. As with the bull, he pronounced confession while the crowd again assumed the prostrate position on the stone floor of the courtyard. Taking the knife, he ceremoniously sliced through the blood vessels of the goat's throat, allowing its blood to flow freely into a bowl. Carrying the bowl of blood back into the Holy of Holies, Azaryah picked up the bowl of bull's blood, which had been left on the stand, and sprinkled it again with his fingers eight times on the Ark. Then, he took the other bowl and flung the blood of the goat eight times toward the Ark.

Following the precise instructions of the Torah, the high priest finally mixed the blood from the two bowls and smeared the bull and goat blood on the corners of the incense altar. Once again, he sprinkled the blood eight times on the Ark. The sacrifice was complete. The sins of the people of God were atoned for.

As he returned to the front of the Ark, suddenly the entire room filled with a smoke-like haze. There was no accompanying sound, no voice, no moving of the air, just instantaneous haze thick enough to block the view of the ark. Azaryah fell helpless to the floor on his knees. The presence of God was like a heavy weight pressing his body on all sides. He bent forward further to place his forehead on the floor. Although this was overwhelming to the point of near loss of consciousness, it was not unexpected. High priests through the ages had prepared their successors for this phenomenon. Although it was exhilarating, it was also dreaded because of its impact on the psyche of the only person who could receive it.

After a few minutes that seemed like hours, the haze cleared; the pressure of the room eased; and Azaryah lifted his head and faced upward. Tears streamed down his cheeks and neck. Raising both arms fully extended, he began whispering, "Yahweh, Yahweh!" His voice became louder until he screamed out over and over, "Yahweh, Yahweh!" Then, the chanting of the name turned to laughter. He laughed uncontrollably. This was the closest he would ever be to Almighty God until he was called to his eternal home.

Azaryah's face was ashen as the curtains slammed together behind him, never to be opened for another year. He walked unsteadily, handing both blood bowls to his son with shaking hands.

"Did it all go as well as you expected, Father?" Seriah inquired.

"Yes, Son. As Yahweh promises, He met with His people through His anointed. His presence was mighty."

"Even though you have described it to me before, I cannot comprehend it," Seriah responded.

"Nor can I, Son. But you will experience it someday. You will enter the Holy of Holies on behalf of your people. We must pray that the sins of our people don't become so terrible that Yahweh withdraws His presence from this temple."

Daniel smiled as the priests reappeared from the sanctuary. There was one more ritual required on this atonement day. Near the location of the animal slaughter, yet another goat was being held by one of the priests. Daniel watched with quiet anticipation as Azaryah and his son approached the "scape goat." Placing both hands on the goat's head, the high priest made confession for the sins of all the people of Israel asking Yahweh to forgive their transgressions. As this appeal was being voiced, all the people lay face-down for the third time in reverence and private confession.

Familiar with the process, the people rose to their feet just as the goat was released. They applauded and cheered loudly as several men chased the goat down the mountain, out of the city, and into the desert wilderness. The goat's destiny was to be pushed off the edge of a high cliff, symbolically taking with it the sins of the entire nation that had been transferred to it by the high priest during the confession. The men chased the goat to the precipice of the cliff and forced it over the edge to its tragic death.

5

WARNINGS IGNORED

ON THE WAY OUT OF the courtyard, Daniel caught another glimpse of the man who performed the baby sacrifice.

"Father!" he exclaimed. "That man walking next to a priest. It is him! The one who sacrificed the baby."

Anticipating his father's reaction, Daniel was surprised at the calmness and seeming disinterest with which his father responded. "Yes, as I thought, he is the top commander of our military. And, Son, what you don't realize is there are several men in this crowd who have sacrificed their children and other people's children at the burning shrine of Molech. Many more have done other heinous, idolatrous acts."

"Then why do they come here to the temple of Yahweh? Do they think such hypocritical and adulterous sins will be forgiven with the blood sacrifices and the scape goat?"

"I doubt that Yahweh, with all wisdom, judges them innocent. Only He can know their heart. If they are truly repentant, they can become innocent before Yahweh. But I imagine they are trying to please multiple gods, which violates the very first of the Ten Commandments. Their acts and their hearts are what is bringing the judgment and wrath of Yahweh on the whole nation of Judah. We are not better than Israel."

"I worry that we will see the wrath of Yahweh soon, Father."

"I worry, too, my son. Yet we must not enslave ourselves to fear. King David wrote, 'Though a host encamp against me, My heart will not fear; Though war arise against me, In *spite of* this I shall be confident.'[1] I am not afraid for myself, but I worry about you and your brother and sisters. I want you to marry, have children, and enjoy the life that your mother and I have enjoyed. I pray each day that Yahweh will have mercy on us and spare your life and those of your siblings if he unleashes His wrath on our land."

Daniel wanted to continue this conversation, but his friends had sought him out of the departing crowd and now gathered around him and his father. They were excited about all they had just experienced with their fathers. Yom Kippur was still new enough to these teenagers that it was definitely the most awesome time of the year.

The four young men and Daniel's father were reaching the bottom of the exterior steps of the temple when they were startled by a resounding voice from the top step. The distinct voice of this man was easily heard over the mixed, but muffled, sounds of the departing crowd.

"It's Jeremiah!" Daniel's father shouted.

There was an instant hush over the crowd as hundreds of Yom Kippur worshipers turned their attention upward to listen to the rather scruffy prophet on the landing. Daniel felt like he knew Jeremiah from all he had heard from his teacher, his father, and others. He thought of Ezekiel reading from Jeremiah's writing in a recent class. Some from Jerusalem followed him around the country, listening to his warnings. Most just listened out of curiosity when it was convenient.

"Hear the word of the LORD, all you of Judah, who enter by these gates to worship the LORD! Thus says the Lord of hosts, the God of

---

1 Psalm 27:3

Israel, 'Amend your ways and your deeds, and I will let you dwell in this place. Do not trust in deceptive words, saying, 'This is the temple of the LORD, the temple of the LORD, the temple of the LORD. For if you truly amend your ways and your deeds, if you truly practice justice between a man and his neighbor, *if* you do not oppress the alien, the orphan, or the widow, and do not shed innocent blood in this place, nor walk after other gods to your own ruin, then I will let you dwell in this place, in the land that I gave to your fathers forever and ever.'"[2]

Daniel tuned out Jeremiah's continuing message momentarily as he hung on to the words just spoken. *". . . if you do not shed innocent blood in this place."* According to his father, the atrocious murder of the baby by the man next to them in the courtyard was being repeated often by men claiming allegiance to Yahweh. Yes, Judah as a nation was shedding the blood of innocent babies.

The words of Jeremiah resonated in Daniel's mind: *"nor walk after other gods to your own ruin."* Many of Yahweh's supposed faithful were sacrificing to Molech, Baal, and other gods, as well as buying and selling idols from many stores throughout the city. Daniel had observed many other heirs of Yahweh's covenant with Abraham, who—although not outwardly following other gods—lived lives devoid of any connection to the one, true, Almighty Creator. He thought about how blessed he was to be the son of a faithful follower of Yahweh. His mind refocused on the further words of Yahweh coming from the mouth of His prophet.

"Will you steal, murder, and commit adultery and swear falsely, and offer sacrifices to Baal and walk after other gods that you have not known, then come and stand before Me in this house, which is

---

called by My name, and say, 'We are delivered!'—that you may do all these abominations?"[3]

Much of the crowd was dispersing, turning their backs on the prophet and mumbling among themselves. Several remained to shout profane insults. Only a few joined Daniel, his father, and his friends in listening intently to the ominous warnings.

"Therefore, I will do to the house which is called by My name, in which you trust, and to the place which I gave you and your fathers, as I did to Shiloh. I will cast you out of My sight, as I have cast out all your brothers, all the offspring of Ephraim."[4]

Jeremiah seemed to be just getting into his oratorical rhythm when, suddenly, two temple guards came running out of the temple gate toward the prophet. Shoving their arms under his and clinching him tightly, they lifted his body enough to drag him down the steps to the edge of the street. They pushed him into the street, where he stumbled and fell on the stone surface. Lying in the street, he received threats from the guards to imprison him if he ever again set foot on the temple grounds. Others encircled him, taunting him with jeers and threats.

Concerned for the safety of their sons, the fathers of Daniel's friends, Hananiah, Mishael, and Azariah rushed to their sides and urged that they all leave the temple area quickly. The four pairs strode past the spontaneous attackers of the prophet and headed down the street toward their common residential area. The four men knew each other well, having developed friendships through the close bonds of their boys.

---

3 Jeremiah 7:9
4 Jeremiah 7:14-15

Hananiah's father was the most vocal of the four. Keeping his voice to just above a whisper so as not to be heard by those along the sides of the street, he made his position clear. "I believe Jeremiah is a true prophet of Yahweh. With his warnings ignored, we are doomed by the wrath of the just Judge, Almighty Yahweh. According to the words that we just heard, Yahweh says He will cast us out of His sight just like He did with the people of Ephraim, which was Israel. We know where they are now—exiled slaves of the Assyrians or scattered who knows where."

"But what about us and our families?" asked Mishael's father. "We have been true to Yahweh. We have not murdered or sacrificed to Baal. We have raised our children to live righteously and honor Him. We have placed our children under the tutelage of the priests. Surely, Yahweh will spare us."

"We are all guilty. Each of us." Karmiel interrupted. "I am the worst. I have cowardly followed the instructions of King Jehoiakim for four years as his chief of the treasury without once even so much as questioning him. Is that not worse than sacrificing to Baal?" Karmiel wiped tears from his eyes. "I have been too ashamed to tell my family about some of these transgressions. I thought the Yom Kippur atonement would cleanse me, but Yahweh just told me through Jeremiah that I can't claim to be delivered from these sins and continue to act as I do."

Daniel winced at his father's confession.

Hananiah's father addressed Mishael's father. "You and I enjoy our blessings of wealth as store merchants. We do not sell images of idols as other merchants do, but have we spoken to fellow merchants about how their dealing in evil merchandise could bring judgment upon our land? I have not warned my customers about the risks they are taking by purchases that displease Yahweh. And why haven't each of us, as prominent men in this city, rebelled against the evil practices of our nation?"

"The Babylonian army is already somewhere in Judah," Daniel reminded everyone. "What if the judgment is upon us? Yahweh may have already made up His mind. What if Jerusalem is attacked soon? Will we run? Will we hide? Will we fight?"

The question unanswered, one by one, each of the boys and their respective fathers separated from the group to go to their homes. Myriads of thoughts surfaced in the four houses that evening, but few words were exchanged.

6

FORCED FAREWELL

DANIEL WOKE WITH A START and sat up reflexively in his bed. The blasts from the shofar pierced the quiet darkness as he gasped and held his breath. As he felt for his cloak and stumbled to the window shutter, he could hear his father in the next room also shuffling to open his window. They both came out of their rooms half-dressed and glared at each other as their eyes adjusted to what little light was emanating from the lamp carried by Karmiel.

"Is this it, Father?" Daniel asked in a high-pitched voice. "Are we being attacked?"

Panic! Blowing the shofars in unison with all their might, the watchman on the wall continued to trumpet the warning. The alarm sounded throughout the city as each house quickly became lighted and filled with cries of shock and dismay.

"I must get to the palace," Karmiel shouted to Nessa, who had now entered the room.

Daniel noticed his father was carrying a sword as he ran out the door. Immediately, he came back into the house and handed the sword to his son. "There are swords at the palace. You may need this. I'm sorry I never taught you to use it. I thought there was time." He kissed Daniel on both cheeks, embraced his wife, and ran back out of the house.

Daniel stared at the sword a moment, his hand shaking. He looked at his mother, who was now gathering her younger children around her, and said softly, "We need to pray."

*

By the time the sun was appearing, Karmiel and all other palace executives were in their emergency positions. Few were dressed and groomed appropriately. King Jehoiakim scanned the table, taking mental attendance of his staff. Everyone was talking feverishly among themselves.

"Quiet!" Jehoiakim yelled.

All heads turned to the king. "What's their status now?" he asked, leaning to his immediate right toward the emperor of the army.

"On the lower western slopes of the mountain. No movement. Looks to be about ten thousand, much less than a full field army, but that could be a deception."

"Is Nebuchadnezzar with them?" the king asked.

"We can't determine for sure. Our sources indicated he returned to Babylon for his coronation, but he could have returned swiftly afterward," the emperor replied.

"And the status of our army?"

"All are collecting their weapons and assuming their battle positions on the wall and at the gates. Warriors from outlying villages are arriving through the eastern gates. All twelve thousand soldiers should be in position by mid-morning."

The door to the conference room opened abruptly. The general entered and bowed toward the king.

"Request to speak to the emperor, Your Excellence."

At Jehoiakim's nod, the general strode to the emperor of the army, knelt at his side, and whispered his message.

"O king, we have our answer," the emperor relayed. "King Nebuchadnezzar is in command of his field army and has sent a messenger, now held at the Fish Gate. The king requests a meeting with you at the sixth hour halfway between your two locations. He said he has brought only half of his army in anticipation of us offering a bloodless surrender. The other half is assembled in reserve encampment a short distance to the west."

Jehoiakim looked upward and paused as if studying the ceramic tiles on the high ceiling. "Very strange. I expected an attempt to break through the gates by now. This may be a ruse—a plot to take me hostage—or worse."

He lowered his sight back to the staff. "What do you say?"

After a long moment of silence, Karmiel spoke up. "Perhaps the king and his army are battle-worn. They came from a long and bloody campaign with the Pharaoh at Carchemish, and Nebuchadnezzar has been traveling to Babylon and back. Maybe there is no more army waiting at the rear. They know we have been making large tribute payments to the Pharaoh. Maybe Nebuchadnezzar is ready to negotiate for those tribute payments to him."

"A very wise thought, Karmiel," Jehoiakim conceded, turning to the emperor. "If we can avoid bloodshed, I am willing to place myself at risk. How can we minimize the risk?"

"My staff and I will plan the rendezvous where it will be impossible for you to be killed or taken hostage," the emperor assured the king.

King Jehoiakim finished the short executive session with orders for each member of the royal staff to flesh out emergency plans quickly with their subordinates and reconvene the staff meeting just before the sixth hour.

At the sixth hour, the Babylonian army began to maneuver back down the mountain at a distance too far to be a legitimate threat to Jehoiakim. This was a condition penned by Jehoiakim on a small sheet of papyrus delivered to Nebuchadnezzar. Also, both kings would meet halfway between their two armies out of reach of either. The kings would be on chariots accompanied by only a driver and two bodyguards with short swords.

Karmiel watched from atop the western wall as King Jehoiakim stepped aboard his chariot wearing his full crimson regal robe and bronze helmet. The chariot was drawn by two stately steeds bred and trained specifically to transport the king. Their silver-embellished harnesses and braided manes and tails made them appear more ready for an official parade than a meeting with the most powerful man on earth.

"Hi-ya!" the driver yelled as he slapped the heavy reins on the backs of the two horses. They galloped down the long, sloping mountain as the royal staff stood next to the western wall to watch the dramatic event unfold.

Above them, on top of the wall, was almost half of the army of Judah standing shoulder to shoulder along the entire circumference of the city. Each man held a spear in one hand, and the other hand rested on the grip of his sheathed sword. All of them surveyed nervously the mighty Babylonian army in the distance. Their minds were haunted by visions of their families being slaughtered, their homes burned, as they engaged in close-order, chaotic sword fights with ruthless men of superior battle skills.

King Jehoiakim could barely see the opposing chariot raising a small dust cloud as the two monarchs sped toward each other. He rehearsed in his mind the exact words he would say, depending on the proposal his foe would bring to the rendezvous.

Their chariots passed each other and turned inward to halt within arm's reach, each facing their own respective armies as if preparing for a fast getaway. King Nebuchadnezzar was also lavishly attired in formal royal dress with a polished silver helmet. His chariot was appointed similar to that of his nemesis, being trimmed in etched gold with patterns of precious gems glimmering in the midday sun. Nebuchadnezzar began the dialogue without hesitation.

"I assume you speak Aramaic well enough for us to communicate in that language."

Jehoiakim nodded in acceptance. Although his preferred language was Hebrew, he, like most of the elite of Judah, spoke Aramaic adequately.

Nebuchadnezzar continued, "Greetings in the name of the kingdom of Babylonia! And, my heart-felt gratitude for the tour of your bountiful country and the use of its resources. As we pursued the humiliated Egyptian army through your mountains and plains, your cities showed great hospitality in surrendering their food and treasures in exchange for their lives. A few resisted but met our needs after we made half of their women widows and most of their children fatherless."

"If you have come to attack Jerusalem, you have miscalculated the strength and numbers of my army and their will to fight," Jehoiakim countered, knowing clearly that his army would actually be no match for the well-trained and equipped Chaldean field army. "Save the blood of your valiant men and continue on to Egypt to complete your conquering of their nation for the great kingdom of Babylonia."

Nebuchadnezzar laughed in a dramatic tone. "Surely, you must know Jerusalem is our immediate objective. We must control Judah to access the Mediterranean. Why would we delay? I have twenty thousand soldiers rested and eager to enrich themselves with the fortunes of your temple and then raze it to the ground. They hunger for your riches and for your women."

Jehoiakim studied his opponent's face and body language carefully. Even with Nebuchadnezzar's boisterous language, he sensed a tinge of hesitancy to do battle. "We are kings, but we are each with a conscience. We are sane, and no sane man wants to wage war if there is a better alternative."

"There is no alternative for me short of total surrender of the entire land of Judah. We came to conquer, but a bloodless surrender might be a consideration. Simply turn your kingdom over to me. I will install a Babylonian ruler on your throne, gain ownership of your resources, and collect taxes from your people."

"Is that your attempt at Babylonian theatrics? Are you the Chaldean king of jest? Would your plan be to assassinate me here and now and introduce yourself to my army as their new king?" Jehoiakim's jaw tightened, but he was also trolling for what his fate would be in such an agreement.

Nebuchadnezzar raised his voice and pounded his fist on the edge of his chariot. "You have no choice! I know the history of your people, their proud heritage of being an exclusive people of their God. I know of your sacred temple adorned in all its glory. You would be a fool to reduce all of that to smoldering ashes covering the bodies of most of your inhabitants and the rest being exiled as slaves. Do you want to have your place in the chronicles of your nation repeat that of Hoshea of Israel? Further, I would have no intention of requiring your head. You know your people. They are loyal to you. You would become a vassal of Babylonia."

Jehoiakim searched for words. He felt certain that Nebuchadnezzar was not going to leave empty-handed to fight another day. The only way Judah had survived the constant threats and skirmishes with Assyria for decades was through their extortion payments to Egypt for their protection. That security had now ceased. There was no other power to save them from Babylonia, he thought, unless it was Babylonia itself. He had been no more than a vassal of Egypt ever since the pharaoh had appointed him king of Judah. Would homage to Nebuchadnezzar be any worse? He would maintain his reign by paying tribute to the empire of Babylonia.

"You are thinking," Nebuchadnezzar said with a smirk. "You are a wise man, who recognizes reality."

Striving to appear strong-willed, Jehoiakim responded, "We will never surrender. But we have been paying tribute to Egypt for their protection. Perhaps we could come to a similar agreement."

The tense negotiations continued.

*

The executive staff was assembled around the conference table. The chief priest was present at the invitation of the king. Karmiel was seated between the chief priest and the emperor of the army. His mind was flooded with conflicting thoughts of his family's security, his responsibility to the kingdom, and his guilt for gouging the people with unreasonable taxes.

Jehoiakim entered from his chambers, still dressed in his formal robe worn during the fateful meeting with Nebuchadnezzar. He looked haggard and pale. The staff anxiously awaited his first words about the meeting of the kings.

His voice and body language divulged his stress level. "There will be no attack . . . no bloodshed."

The staff scanned the table for the reaction of their colleagues. No one spoke as all eyes returned to the king. Their initial relief was quickly replaced by confusion.

Jehoiakim paused, dreading to reveal the agreement concluded on the mountainside. "Judah's monarchy will continue without threat from Babylonia. I will remain king, albeit subservient to King Nebuchadnezzar."

Muffled groans emanated from around the table.

"The tribute we have been paying to Egypt, we will now pay to Babylon. We agreed on 150 talents of silver and a talent of gold each year."

"Your Excellence!" Karmiel spontaneously interrupted. "That is much more than we have been paying to Egypt—much more than the agonizing tax burden we have already been forcing on our people."

"Would the people rather be enslaved or, worse, die from the swords of Babylonia?" Jehoiakim snapped.

Karmiel exhaled forcefully in frustration.

The king looked into the eyes of his emperor of the army, inhaled deeply, and exhaled forcefully. "We will reduce our army by half, and Nebuchadnezzar will appoint one of his generals to replace you."

The stunned emperor's face instantly flushed. Everything inside him begged to erupt like a volcano. He was forming the words to curse the king. But he knew that any negative response would result in the loss of any status he had left within the kingdom, if not his execution.

"I understand, Your Excellence," muttered the emperor with his head bowed.

Perspiration was beading on Jehoiakim's face and hands as he spoke. "King Nebuchadnezzar will arrive at the Fish Gate tomorrow morning with a large contingent of his army. I will open the gate and invite him in. Our army will not interfere with anything they do. Some of his men will go into the temple and take whatever articles they desire. Others will help themselves to supplies from our city merchants needed for their journey back to Babylon."

Every member of the staff was in shock and disbelief. Azaryah, the chief priest, looked to the side, not wishing to make eye contact with the king. For any of them, to vocally object could be fatal. The king had struck the deal. It was not reversible, and any outward objection from his staff would be futile.

"That is all I have," the king concluded. "I will be in contact with each of you concerning the details. You are not to meet together without my presence."

As the staff was departing the room, the king called out, "Karmiel!"

Karmiel turned around.

"Karmiel, increase the tax levy immediately. Peace and stability are most preferable to losing those we love."

The king's treasurer paused, then replied, "Yes, Your Excellence."

"And, Karmiel."

"Yes, Excellency."

"You were the only one who challenged me. I'm choosing to overlook that once. Do not give me further cause to disgrace you and your family."

Karmiel bowed slightly, turned, and exited the room.

*

It was the second hour in the morning, the time when busy shopkeepers were normally opening their storefronts, early shoppers were appearing in the streets, and workers were heading to their worksites. But today, the streets were mostly empty. Karmiel was fighting off fear mixed with anger as he walked by the shops that were still closed. The few movements in the city were soldiers and those reporting to their palace responsibilities. Word had swiftly spread the previous evening that although imminent attack had been avoided, the enemy army would be entering the city early that morning.

Just inside the Fish Gate, a huge gathering of government and military officials awaited as ordered by King Jehoiakim. The entry street was lined with soldiers with bows, swords, and shields from one end of the city to the other. All weapons would stay stowed unless the unthinkable happened. This morning, the Hebrew army would be the protectors of Nebuchadnezzar and his men.

King Jehoiakim was positioned in his chariot at the front with his staff immediately behind him. He ordered the bronze-plated double doors unlocked and opened fully.

Shortly, several chariots with bowmen came into view from the left as their drivers reined their horses into a right turn and through the gate. Following closely behind was King Nebuchadnezzar in his royal chariot with foot soldiers at either side. Jehoiakim had his own chariot repositioned to the side of the street to allow unrestricted entry to the city. The two kings were meeting again in less than a day's time. They were both in formal robes and crowns.

"Greetings, King of Babylonia," Jehoiakim called out in Aramaic, his right hand lifted high. "Jerusalem is honored to be the first city in the Babylonian Empire to receive an official visit from the new king. Please accept our humble gratitude."

Karmiel whispered softly to chief of trade standing next to him. "This cannot be happening to our nation."

Jehoiakim ordered his chariot to be positioned to the left and abreast of Nebuchadnezzar.

Nebuchadnezzar's eyes scanned the city as the two kings moved forward. "You have a great city, and you are wise to ensure its survival. And your temple is truly a masterpiece of architecture almost as impressive as some of the structures of Babylon."

The Babylonian army paraded through a long stretch of the meandering street lined with Jewish soldiers and crowds of bewildered onlookers. Nebuchadnezzar lifted his arm to halt the march directly in front of the temple.

"I will now dispatch many of my men to enter the temple and obtain some of its most precious articles as part of Judah's tribute to my kingdom. My supply officers will also visit your merchants to receive their gifts of food and other needs necessary for our journey,"

"As agreed," responded Jehoiakim. He watched nervously as his people gasped, and some shouted curses at the pagans entering the temple. Anyone trying to intervene was quickly contained by the reluctant, but obedient, Hebrew soldiers.

Nebuchadnezzar continued, "I have prepared many papyrus sheets with my decree to all the people of Judah. The decree lists my laws and my demands, and it states the punishment my leaders will exact on them if they are not obedient. It explains how they will honor me and exalt the kingdom of Babylonia."

Jehoiakim was seething inside. *Is there no place for me in this kingdom?* he thought. *This is more than I agreed to.* "Do you not think that I am better able to communicate your wishes to my people according to our agreement?"

Nebuchadnezzar ignored him. "Quickly summon fifty of your young men who have been trained in the Aramaic language. These must be your wisest men, who are young enough to run throughout Judah and read my decree in your Hebrew language to those of Jerusalem and in all your cities and villages. These must be boys from your royal bloodline and the bloodlines of other nobles and high officials. They must have the education and natural skills and attributes to perform this task. Assemble them before my general in the temple courtyard."

"I will not allow you to remove the children from the city!" Jehoiakim shouted. "That was not in the deal."

"Soldiers, bind the king in chains. We will take him with us to Babylon."

*

Daniel had received a late morning message from his father delivered by a palace courier explaining all that had transpired that morning. His heart longed to be with his father and see everything that was taking place with King Nebuchadnezzar and his army in the city. But his mission now was to be obedient and stay in the house with his mother and siblings. He had been delegated by his father to be the family's defender in case this ominous, "peaceful" invasion by an enemy nation turned out to be a ruse. His conflicted feelings raged inside of him. He wished for a way of escape.

Suddenly, the door opened with no knock or announcement. Just inside the doorway stood a stranger, a soldier with a shield in his left hand and a sword hanging from his belt. His battle dress, equipment, and helmet were unlike anything Daniel had seen. The other man in the doorway, standing behind the stranger, was a Jewish soldier whom Daniel recognized. Nessa ran into the bedroom, where her other children were huddled. Her daughters were crying.

"Are you Daniel?" the Babylonian soldier asked gruffly in Aramaic, stepping forward toward him.

Daniel reached for the sword laying on the table beside him.

"No, Daniel!" the Jewish soldier cried out in Hebrew. "You will not be harmed nor will your family. Do not resist."

Daniel released his grip on the sword.

"His Majesty, Nebuchadnezzar, king of Babylonia, demands your services. You are to come with us peacefully," instructed the Babylonian soldier.

Daniel addressed the Jewish soldier. "My father is trusting me with my family's safety while our city is occupied by this army of snakes. I will not leave them."

"The city is peaceful," the Jewish soldier assured. "King Nebuchadnezzar simply wants some of our most capable young men to distribute and translate his decrees throughout Judah. We must take you to his general now."

Daniel's head spun with the dilemma. If he resisted, he might be killed, and his family would suffer. If he acquiesced, he might be forsaking his obligation to his father and his family.

"Go with them, Daniel," Nessa urged from the adjoining room. "You have no choice. We will be fine. Your father will understand."

Daniel needed advice from somewhere. His mother's words sufficed.

"Bundle up some extra clothes and essentials that you will need for your journey," the Babylonian soldier ordered.

"My journey?" Daniel asked with a sense of panic.

The Jewish soldier interjected, "You will be traveling for a few days around Judah reading the decree to our people. Prepare yourself for these travels. You will return soon to your family."

Moments later, Daniel left his family after quickly gathering a few belongings for the tour of Judah. He said farewell to his mother and siblings, hugging and kissing each one and assuring them of his love and his swift return. He walked up the familiar stone street between the two soldiers sad, confused, anxious, and angry. He just hoped he wasn't letting his father down.

Another thought plagued Daniel. *Where is Yahweh in all this? Is this the anticipated judgment?*

As they reached the pinnacle of Mount Zion, Daniel marveled at the throngs of soldiers, Babylonian and Jewish, in every direction. Some guided horse-drawn carts filled with various items of merchandise. Some wagons were loaded with fruits and vegetables as well as cured meat. There was a loud commotion among the people cordoned off by lines of soldiers.

The Babylonian escorting Daniel held a firm grip on his arm to avoid him darting into the crowd and disappearing. As they approached the temple, Daniel got a close-up look at Babylonian soldiers exiting with articles of gold and silver. They were depositing them in carts as if they were trash.

Just before reaching the temple steps to the courtyard, Daniel's eyes scanned the center of all the activity. He recognized King Jehoiakim in one of the chariots and assumed the man with a crown in the adjacent chariot was none other than King Nebuchadnezzar. Surely, his father wasn't far from the side of Jehoiakim. He decided it was worth the risk.

At the top of his voice, Daniel yelled, "Father! Father!"

His escort jerked his arm almost out of socket and slapped his face with an open hand. Both movements inflicted excruciating pain as evidenced by Daniel's shrill scream.

Somehow, through the maddening noise and chaos, Karmiel, who had been standing in silence beside the street, faintly heard the cry of his son. Looking in the direction of the temple, he soon focused on the shocking scene of Daniel and the soldiers.

Spontaneously, Karmiel bolted into the street with every intention of going to the aid of his son. After three strides, he received a sudden blow to his chest from a strong forearm. With his back to the ground in pain and shock, his eyes came back into focus on a long, glimmering sword, the tip of which was pressing into his abdomen.

"You not move!" the Babylonian guard yelled in broken Aramaic.

The commotion got Daniel's attention, and he watched the attack on his father now lying helplessly on the rough, stone street.

"Don't kill him!" Daniel screamed as he began to sob.

The two soldiers turned Daniel toward the temple steps and led him to the courtyard. There he saw numerous other young men—about thirty of them—lined up in an orderly formation. His eyes fixed immediately on two of his best friends, Hananiah and Mishael. As he scanned the assembly, he recognized all of them. Most were from his temple school. All were from affluent families in the city. Each had a bag lying next to them, apparently containing clothing and a few essentials like what the soldiers had instructed him to gather before leaving the house. He was placed in the back line as the hands that had gripped his arms so tightly were released. The relief of the pain was welcomed, but he was still overwhelmed with fear and bewilderment. He worried about his father.

As he looked around frantically, trying to assess the situation, someone was suddenly positioned immediately to his left.

"Azariah!" Daniel exclaimed.

The redness of Azariah's eyes revealed he had been crying. "What are they doing to us, Daniel?"

"Try to be brave," answered Daniel trying to subdue his own tears. "They said we were going to do some traveling to read some kind of decree throughout the land of Judah. Then we will return to our homes."

"But why us? Why not grown men?"

"I suppose because we are the learned elite, we are young and fit, and we are available," explained Daniel, although he was not sure his words were convincing, even to himself.

Daniel pointed out their two other friends in the group. "Let's see if we can move up beside them without being noticed. We need to be together, encouraging each other."

Eventually, Daniel counted fifty young men—healthy, handsome, and exceptionally educated. They stood in military-like formation, quiet and motionless, sweating profusely in the tortuous noon sun. They had been told that Nebuchadnezzar's general would be coming soon with instructions. Daniel and his three friends stood bravely shoulder to shoulder. Their exact destiny was still a mystery.

*

By late afternoon, the temple loot, food items taken from the marketplaces, and other valuables were organized in horse-drawn carts lined up on the main street leading out of the city. The marketplaces were virtually empty after having been ransacked by the enemy soldiers. Little of any significant value remained in the temple. The palace had also been relieved of many priceless treasures and its depository of gold bullion. Nebuchadnezzar's army had formed up in a long column in front of the Fish Gate. Daniel gasped as he saw King Jehoiakim bound in chains and tethered to the horse of a Babylonian soldier. He heard Nebuchadnezzar yell something to the soldier, who removed the chains.

Nebuchadnezzar laughed loudly as he glared at Jehoiakim. "You are free for now to remain here as my vassal. Your life will depend on your loyalty."

The victor of this bloodless confrontation, standing tall in his chariot, simply led the formidable army out of the gate without a word and headed north, joining the road through the northern mountain pass.

Midway in the convoy was the very conspicuous group of frightened and confused young men in traditional Hebrew attire surrounded by war-hardened uniformed men bearing shields and swords. Most of the soldiers were on horseback or wheeled conveyances, but the guards surrounding the Jewish boys were on foot for rapid mobility if needed.

Daniel was fighting anxiety as he looked back over his shoulder at the distant walls of his city. He was determined to be courageous but could feel the tears forming in his eyes and finding a path down each cheek.

Thankfully, this will be only a temporary absence from my family. Surely, no more than a few weeks of traveling throughout Judah. Will I have to travel alone? Can I travel with my three friends? When will we receive instruction? And why weren't we allowed proper farewells to our families? I miss mine already.

Daniel's thoughts were interrupted by Mishael at his immediate right. "The Babylonian soldier pulled me from my father's arms as one of our own soldiers put his sword against Father's neck."

"My father tried to rescue me while I was at the temple steps, and they shoved him to the ground. I didn't even get to say goodbye. I know they are horrified more than I of what might happen to me after our forced farewell."

The sun was approaching the top of the distant mountain range lining the west edge of the pass when the convoy stopped in an open grassy meadow. Chariots, wagons, and men on horseback circled the young men from Judah and their guards.

After a short period of mystery as to what was happening, a decorated chariot appeared, pulled by two white horses and carrying General Maoz in his bright red uniform. He had been introduced to them earlier in the temple courtyard. The general received everyone's attention as he ordered his driver to position the chariot in the center of the formation of the young Hebrew men.

He began speaking loudly in Aramaic. "Gentleman of Jerusalem, take your seats on the ground. We will bed down here for the night. We are now a considerable distance from your city. There are many layers of soldiers surrounding you to prevent any attempt of your people to rescue you, should they be that foolish. And if any of you would have a mental lapse and try to escape, you will be a casualty of the sword. Your dead body will be left for the birds and wild animals to feast on. You have a long journey ahead. In about six weeks, we will all arrive at Babylon."

7

TREACHEROUS JOURNEY

BABYLON? DANIEL'S BODY STIFFENED AS he gasped, then forcefully exhaled. He could not breathe in as if his lungs had collapsed. Immediately, he felt light-headed, like he was going to faint. He had felt this feeling of shock only once before when he watched the baby being sacrificed.

The young men began to murmur among themselves, no longer listening to the general's continuing statement. Their heads turned as each one looked for others' reactions, hoping to glean anything making sense of the alarming proclamation just heard.

"What is this?" Azariah shouted to Daniel. "We were told we would travel throughout Judah and return to our families!"

Daniel, still hyperventilating and feeling hazy, shook his head, trying to regain his composure. "Apparently, it was all a lie. We are captives being taken into exile." He couldn't believe his own words. Dozens of thoughts were racing through his mind. He visualized his family gathered in their home, wailing in agony over the likelihood they would never see their son and brother again.

"Close your mouths!" the general shouted. "Silence!"

The guards walked through the group that had just been designated as prisoners of the Babylonian army. With their knuckles, they struck the heads of those continuing to murmur until there was silence.

Calling another colorfully uniformed man to his side, the general finalized his remarks.

"I introduce to you Nebuzaradan, captain of the guard. He will be directly in charge of all you rats. He will determine whether you live or die. You will survive or perish on this journey, depending on how closely you follow his orders."

Nebuzaradan had three words for the young men. "You are mine!"

The general continued. "You will now lie down on the ground where you are and get some sleep. You will be walking from the rising of the sun until its setting tomorrow and every day until we reach the splendorous city. And one last warning, anyone who might attempt an escape to go back home will breathe his last breath right here in this camp."

Daniel lay awake for much of the night, agonizing over the complete upheaval in his life in a half-day. Somehow, even with the hardness of the ground and his travel bag for a pillow, he eventually drifted into sleep from total physical and emotional exhaustion. Little time had passed when he awoke suddenly, startled by the sound of loud voices and a shrill scream. It was unmistakably a scream of excruciating pain. Several other captives had also awakened. Daniel could see their silhouettes in the light of the half-moon as they sat up with heads turned in the direction of the commotion. Then, there was silence.

Getting back to sleep was more difficult this time as thoughts flooded Daniel's mind. *Who was screaming? Did one of the guards fall? Were some people fighting? Did an intruder get caught? Or . . . could it have been one of the captives?* But once again, he drifted into sleep.

The sun was still below the horizon when a guard walked among the slumbering young men. "Get up, you worthless Jews. On your feet!

You'll get a bowl of stew and a piece of bread before we journey a full day under the wretched sun."

Daniel could smell the aroma of the stew he saw cooking over an open fire. It was a familiar smell, since it was from the plunder taken from the street merchants in Jerusalem.

Thank You, Yahweh. He sent up a thought prayer. *At least the food on this journey will be according to the Talmud. It will all be from Jerusalem.*

After a sparse helping of stew and bread served with insults and threats from the guards, Nebuzaradan appeared on his chariot.

"Before we embark on today's journey, just a quick demonstration of how important it is for you Hebrew boys to heed our warnings. Unfortunately, last night, one of you decided we were not serious."

The captain looked to his left and raised his left arm. Shrieks and loud moans rippled across the ranks of captives as the horrid scene came into view. Two guards were at each end of a large tree limb with one of the young captives slumped over its middle. A sword protruding out of his back had been run through his torso from behind with the bloody, pointed end visible under his chest.

Daniel's knees buckled as his heart raced like it was about to launch from his body. Many of the young men cupped their hands over their faces. Next to Daniel, Mishael dropped to his knees. Spontaneous mumbling was heard throughout the assembly of captives.

"Don't attempt to break ranks like your foolish friend, or you will be the next example," Nebuzaradan scolded.

The cut limb with the young man's body still draped over it was positioned in the forks of two nearby trees. The owner of the sword, the obvious executioner, pulled the weapon from the body as calmly as if it were being used to butcher a sheep. He plucked a clump of grass and used it to wipe the blood from the sword.

The army with their prisoners at mid-section began the first steps of a long, horrendous march further north. Vultures were already circling overhead, ready to feast on a prominent Jerusalem couple's son who gambled on getting back home . . . and lost.

The road had been heavily used for centuries by travelers from as far north as the Black and Caspian Seas to as far south as Egypt. Running along and just west of the Jordan River, it was the passage of choice between the Arab desert and the Great Sea. Very few improvements had been made over the centuries. It was mostly a trail of beaten-out ruts formed by the wheels of wagons and chariots as well as thousands of horse and ox hooves. It was not a stable surface for walking.

"Do you think we will ever see our families again?" Hananiah asked Daniel as they trod under the scorching sun directly overhead.

"If we do, it will probably be later in Babylon," Daniel replied. "Remember how Jeremiah prophesied that our whole nation would be taken captive by another nation as a result of Yahweh's judgment on Judah's rebellious behavior? We are likely just the first fruits of that judgment. Nebuchadnezzar won't rest until he has conquered the entire nation. We can only hope that we see our families again as captives like ourselves."

Hananiah contemplated the unwanted answer to his question, then continued, "But why would Yahweh pour out His wrath on us first? As I look around, almost all of us were following His ways. We were studying His words and believing His prophets. Some among us were even preparing for the priesthood. We should have been protected from His judgment."

Daniel looked directly into Hananiah's eyes. "My father taught me that the closer we are to Yahweh, the more He reveals of Himself and the more He expects of us. My father did not follow other gods, and he made sure our family obeyed Yahweh's commands. Yet I saw him weep over his sin of carrying out King Jehoiakim's evil directions."

Pausing a moment to subdue his emotions, Daniel continued, "We children who claim to be pure in the sight of Yahweh are certainly not blameless. Besides, the purist of worshipers of Yahweh will not escape His wrath directed at their entire nation. I'm sure there were many in the northern kingdom of Israel who lived by the commandments and sacrificed only to Yahweh, yet they became slaves of Assyria, along with their rebellious neighbors."

Mishael had been listening to the conversation between Daniel and Hananiah. "I've been wondering why our captors chose us. Why did they choose me to be taken? Sure, we are all physically fit, educated, and from prominent families. But so were many other young men who were left with their families in Jerusalem. Ezekiel was older and wiser than many of us, yet he is not with us."

"No one can answer that," Daniel responded. "A better question is, why *not* us? If it is Yahweh's will for us to suffer captivity, He has purpose in it. We should not waste our time asking why but rather asking what He wants us to do in this unexpected upheaval in our lives."

As the second day of walking over rough terrain progressed, the minds of the Jewish lads shifted from fear and bewilderment to exhaustion and pain. Feet were swelling; knees and hips were aching; and the combination of sun and wind was burning their faces and hands. The only soldiers walking were the guards in the immediate vicinity, and those were cycling between walking to horseback riding. The young captives could not allow themselves to think about the length of the journey to Babylon.

Every day of the journey was the same. The sleeping army would arise just before dawn, eat a standard meal, and begin a long day's trek through the rocky terrain of what had been the nation of Israel. They would eat a light mid-day meal while on the move and stop just after sundown on the highest point available for defense advantage. After eating a hastily prepared evening meal, everyone, except rotating night guards, would lie down on the bare ground totally exhausted. Of course, King Nebuchadnezzar, his general, and the top staff had tents pitched which contained comfortable beds along with fine food and drink. These high command tents were protected by the army's most elite guards.

The convoy had forded the Jordan River just north of the Sea of Kinnereth on the fourth day. There was no delaying or breaking up of the formation to enjoy a respite in the water, except for a few soldiers who separated temporarily to refill the water containers. However, the waist-deep water did provide a welcomed instance of relief from the heat and the aching feet.

The route was the reverse of that, taken by the army just a few weeks prior as it pursued Pharaoh's army. This time, it had traversed past the eastern outskirts of Dan, which had been attacked and plundered by the same men who were now captors of the Jewish boys. No doubt, some Danite reconnaissance soldiers had discovered the Babylonians' movement far south of their position and had reported back to their superiors.

As Daniel gazed at the distant, damaged walls of the city, he could imagine them huddled in their houses in fear of the army making a second run on what little was left of their resources. Evidently, though, Nebuchadnezzar had no desire to be distracted from returning to his luxurious palace as swiftly as possible. This trip could not end soon enough for him, and there would be no delay or rest that wasn't absolutely necessary.

As Dan disappeared over the horizon, the entourage turned east along the foothill of Mount Hermon and onward toward the city of Damascus. Like Dan, Damascus had also been razed by this army recently and had been relieved of almost all its grain, wine, and precious treasures. Again, this new king of Babylon had no interest in the city now.

Turning back toward the north, the mountainous region began to transition into a vast plain. For the first time since the boys left Jerusalem, they could see no mountains directly ahead. The walking should get a little less painful. They overheard some of the soldiers discussing the route. Although their ultimate destination was to the southeast, they had to continue north to avoid the treacherous desert, which was not passable due to the heat and strong winds. Several more days would pass before they could change course to head along the Euphrates River directly toward Chaldea and, ultimately, Babylon.

As the sun set behind the mountain range, orders came to set up for the night on a plateau overlooking the gentler flatland. Freshly cooked food was distributed throughout the weary army and to the captives. Afterward, the guards directed now forty-nine young men to assume their prone positions on the ground for the night.

Daniel lay awake, unable to stop thinking about his family. He remembered his father quoting King David's words: "Though a host encamp against me, my heart will not fear; though war arise against me, in spite of this I shall be confident."[1] Suddenly, someone scrambled between him and Hananiah and lay still and quiet.

"Sh-h-h!" came the caution from the unknown intruder. "It's Segev."

Daniel and Hananiah recognized their older classmate.

"What are you doing here?" Daniel whispered. "You could get into big trouble with the guards."

Segev whispered back, "Some others and I were talking along the road today. Tonight will be our last chance to escape, since we will have no more rough mountains to hide in. We are spreading the word. Three of us will begin coughing later as a preparation sign. Then, one of us will fake a sneeze, which will be the signal for everyone of courage and faith in Yahweh to flee in separate directions into the mountains."

Daniel was shocked by Segev's words and immediately rejected the idea in his mind. "Have you so soon forgotten the blood-soaked body of our friend that we left behind the first night of our journey? Do you want us all to be killed and left here for the animals?"

"What we don't want is to die in Babylon as slaves of these heathens. It is worth the risks. Be brave and join us or live a hopeless life," Segev challenged, struggling to keep his voice from being heard by the guards. "You have only a little while to decide. Relay this to those around you and listen for the coughs and the sneeze."

"I can't believe this is happening," Daniel whispered to Hananiah as Segev slipped away.

"What should we do?" Hananiah asked. "If we stay, we may be treated more harshly; and if we run, we may be killed. Of course,

---

1 Psalm 27:3

Yahweh can protect us if He chooses, no matter which decision we make."

"It would be very unwise to try to escape," Daniel said, "but we must hear from Yahweh. Tell Mishael and Azariah what Segev and the others plan to do. Then, let's all pray for direction."

Daniel's heart raced as he buried his face in his hands and began whispering a prayer.

"Almighty, all-knowing Yahweh, You would probably prefer a priest or my father to be appealing to You for wisdom, but I am alone and without anyone to rely on. I am unprepared to approach Your throne. I call on You to make this camp Your tabernacle at this moment. Your captives, far outnumbered by Your enemies, must hear from you. If our captivity is Your will as a part of Your judgment against our sinful nation, I ask You to keep all of us together and alive as Your captive people. But if it is Your will that we flee in the night, I trust that You will protect us and gather us soon back in Jerusalem. What are we to do, almighty Yahweh? Use me as you desire."

Not sure what to expect from his short, whispered prayer, Daniel was instantly overwhelmed by a clear, although inaudible, Voice in his mind.

Get up! Get up! Speak! Speak loudly!

It was as if a Power outside of his own brought him to his feet. In the quiet darkness, standing near the center of the captives lying motionless on the ground, he began to shout with no forethought of what he needed to say. The words just gushed from his mouth.

"Friends and fellow captives!"

Immediately, four guards with torches for illumination started running from their perimeter position toward Daniel as he continued.

"In the name of Yahweh, do not do anything that will place your lives in jeopardy."

With that statement, voiced in Aramaic for the benefit of both the guards and the captives, the guards stopped just short of reaching Daniel's location. Their swords were drawn as they waited to see where he was going with his proclamation.

"Remain strong in the role that almighty Yahweh has ordained for us at this time. We are the first fruits of the righteous judgment that Yahweh has in store for the people of Judah. The prophets, including our own Jeremiah, have warned us and our brothers. It has begun. Our own obedience to His commands will not save us from being victims of the wrath. We are deserving by association. We cannot escape the judgment of Yahweh, and we cannot escape the destiny of Babylon. The will of Yahweh is for us to live for Him in the midst of our persecution, not to flee from what He has ordained for us. I plead with you, rest tonight. We have a long day tomorrow. Praise be to Yahweh!"

The guards kept their swords drawn, not knowing what might happen next as they stepped back to their perimeter positions. Daniel had fallen limp to the ground after his spontaneous oratory. He felt very strange, like something had overtaken his body and mind. He didn't feel the words had been his but that he was simply the mouthpiece. As he tried to assimilate all that had taken place since Segev's arrival at his side, he looked around the camp. There was an eerie stillness and silence. The area around the captives that had just been shaken by shouting and guard movement seemed strangely peaceful. It took Daniel a while to surrender to slumber. His last thought before sleep took over was in the form of a prayer. *Yahweh, I don't understand everything that just happened, but thank You.* The remainder of the night was uneventful.

The morning processes of feeding and preparing for the day's trek went as normal, except for most of the boys' avoidance of speaking or even making eye contact with Daniel. Many viewed his middle-of-the-night proclamation as shutting down their plan and making them feel foolish. Several of them, however, made a special effort to come to him and thank him for bravely speaking out. Daniel assumed from that point on, there would be division among the captives.

Walking in a clustered foursome, Hananiah, Mishael, and Azariah sought to comfort and encourage their friend.

"We've been together since we were babies, but I have never seen you so passionate and eloquent as last night," said Azariah.

"The passion was mine, but the words were not. I am certain that Yahweh was speaking through me. I have never experienced such a thing before."

"I agree with you fully. It is the will of Yahweh that we accept our present situation as His plan to deal with His people. I'm not sure where this will all lead, but I am His slave, not a slave of Babylon," added Mishael.

Suddenly, Daniel was startled by a firm grip of his arm.

"Come with me," ordered the Nebuzaradan. "General Maoz wishes to speak to you."

CRISIS LEADERSHIP

THE CAPTAIN LED DANIEL PAST rows of foot soldiers, mounted soldiers, and soldiers on chariots. No explanation was given, but Daniel assumed he was going to be chastised, or worse, for the previous night's episode.

After a walk at a swift pace that passed hundreds of men, the captain, still holding a firm grip on Daniel's arm, guided him to General Maoz's chariot in all its garish decor. "As you requested, Your Excellence." The guard crossed his chest with his forearm in a salute.

Without slowing the chariot, the general motioned for Daniel to board. The guard released his grip, and Daniel ran alongside the chariot until he could leap up to its floor. It was a very strange and uneasy feeling suddenly finding himself standing next to the general with the driver and bodyguard maneuvering for space on the small platform.

"What is your name, young man?" the general asked.

Daniel instinctively looked directly into the general's eyes out of respect and courage.

"Daniel of Judah."

"Ah, Daniel of Judah." The general smiled. "I heard a report that you created quite a stir last night."

"I did only what the one and only Yahweh caused me to do," replied Daniel, stretching to appear taller. He felt the urge to be somewhat defiant.

"Were some of your friends planning an escape?"

"I did only what the one and only Yahweh caused me to do."

"Your 'Yahweh' must be a wise god. If you had not denounced their plan, we would have far fewer mouths to feed today. But it would not be because of a successful mass escape; your friends would be lying dead among the hills and crevasses as fresh meat for the wild animals, as was your former friend."

"Yahweh will always protect us in His own way as long as we honor Him and follow His will."

"You showed unusually mature judgment, Daniel of Judah. Your courage saved the lives of your friends."

"Thank you, but I am only a servant of Yahweh."

The general paused the conversation momentarily, and Daniel kept quiet, looking straight ahead at the long convoy.

"I will announce to your friends and the guards that you will be my representative of the Hebrew boys—their leader—for the remainder of the journey."

Daniel was stunned.

"Sir, that is not my desire. I am no better than any of them."

"Of course not. If you wanted to be their leader, I would not have selected you. But you have earned this crisis leadership and my favor with your obvious wisdom and courage. You will be their connection to me. If there is a problem, I expect to hear from you. Of course, your requests to speak to me will go through Nebuzaradan. You are to keep your friends from rebelling and from any foolishness about escaping. Now, get back to them. I will make the announcement tomorrow."

Daniel was escorted back to his friends by the captain.

His three friends, as well as several others in his vicinity, maneuvered toward him after he was released.

"What did the general do to you?" Hananiah asked anxiously.

Daniel had thought through how he was going to handle the situation. Being evasive with his friends about what the general was going to do, then having them hear it abruptly from the general, would not be best. He wanted to tell them himself, so he could explain that it was not what he had wanted. Others clustered around Daniel.

"First, General Maoz was asking about last night. Of course, he thought I did the right thing. I told him it was not me but rather Yahweh using me to express His will. He then told me something I was unprepared to hear and did not desire. He will announce tomorrow that he is appointing me as his representative to lead the rest of the captives."

None of the others spoke immediately. They looked at each other for reactions. Finally, Mishael responded.

"I believe you that this was nothing you wanted. In fact, it will be a great burden on you. About half of our group are older than you, some over three years older. In our school, those older and at higher levels were considered leaders of the younger ones."

"Segev and some others probably feel that you spoiled their chances for freedom last night. They will not be happy that you are now their superior," Azariah added.

"I will not be their superior," Daniel objected. "I will only be the connection between all of us and the general. It could be a positive advantage for all of us."

By the evening meal, all forty-nine captives had heard the news of Daniel's new position. The communication didn't adequately convey

Daniel's humility and lack of desire for the position as it proceeded through several different voices. Nevertheless, most felt good about having one of their own as at least a semblance of a buffer between them and their captors. Some were skeptical of one of the younger among them having such authority. And a few saw Daniel as a traitor, who had finagled the favor of the general to get special treatment.

Awaiting the evening meal, Daniel was sitting in a circle with his three best friends when one who was becoming his nemesis joined their cluster.

"So, you sold out to the enemy and turned on your own people for the privilege of telling us what to do," Segev said. "I suppose we now have to be very careful what we do and say as you spy on us and run to the general if we get out of line. You have become just another Babylonian guard that we have to fear. Well, I don't fear you, Daniel. You foiled a perfectly good escape plan last night."

"I didn't ask for or desire this," Daniel retorted. "But after much thought, I believe Yahweh has bestowed it on me. I believe what I did last night was the will of Yahweh and that it saved many lives. It also led to this leadership responsibility, which is Yahweh's will to help us survive the rest of the journey."

"We don't need you in order to survive. I, for one, will not follow you," Segev snapped as he walked away.

During the evening meal, the general made his announcement as expected. For the second stressful night in a row, Daniel had difficulty sleeping.

After breakfast, as everyone was breaking camp, one of the guards rode into the group of boys busily gathering up their belongings. He stopped next to Segev.

"Come with me," the guard ordered sternly.

Confused and scared, Segev finished stowing his personal items in his bag and walked beside the mounted guard toward the front of the convoy.

As the young men began to murmur among themselves, Daniel was concerned about Segev. He was also worried that some of them would conclude that he had something to do with their friend's plight. Some were already eyeing him with accusing looks.

Now, as the newly appointed leader, I'm responsible for everything. Therefore, I'm to blame for everything. I'm sure the others think I betrayed Segev by telling the general that he was the instigator of an escape plan.

Daniel was convinced that God had given him leadership responsibility for the safety and welfare of the captives. Along with that appointment, though, came a heavy heart, caused by the rejection he was feeling from those for whom he was responsible. Few other than his three closest friends seemed to be accepting of him now.

Two days passed without seeing Segev. All the boys were speculating about what was happening to him.

"Some think they may have killed him," said Mishael as all three friends walked together abreast of Daniel to show their support.

"I don't think so," Daniel responded. "If they were going to kill him, they would have made a public spectacle of it."

"They could be beating him or starving him to force him to give names of others among us who may be potential troublemakers," Azariah suggested.

"Whatever they are doing with him, he must be rescued and brought back into our fold," said Daniel. "The general said I could speak to him about anything as the representative of all of us. Perhaps I need to accept that invitation now."

As the midday ration of food was being handed out, Daniel asked the guard to request of Nebuzaradan a short visit with the general that afternoon. With no response the rest of the afternoon, Daniel assumed the general was not going to be as accessible as he was made to believe. However, that evening, when the exhausted army once again stopped for food and rest, General Maoz rode up to Daniel's spot for the night. He motioned for Daniel to follow him as he rode out of hearing distance of the other boys.

"I understand you wanted a moment with me," the general said.

"Yes, sir." Daniel presented himself formally. "I want to appeal to you on behalf of the brotherhood of the Hebrews. I appeal for the return of Segev, whom your men led away two days ago. Is he alive and well?"

The general laughed heartily. "Of course, he is alive and well. We are keeping him in isolation, so he won't be tempted to organize another escape that would be demoralizing for my men and deadly for your men. It is also an example to all of you that rebellion will not be tolerated. Did your so-called brotherhood of the Hebrews think we would not notice which one of you was moving through your group that night, obviously planning something covertly? We will keep him under close observation until reaching Babylon. His isolation will be better for us both. You will not have to worry about him deserting or opposing you."

"If I may, sir, his release would increase my people's respect for your army and convince them that you value their lives. It would be evidence that there is no reason to consider escaping. Such a result of this meeting would raise their confidence in me as their leader and give me more credibility in assuring them of the benefits of their cooperation. I pledge to you that neither Segev nor any other among us will attempt any act of resistance under my leadership. His release would be best for us both."

The general's eyes panned the surrounding wilderness as he thought through Daniel's proposal.

"You are an impressive young man for a simple Hebrew, Daniel of Judah. You are testing me, and a man of authority does not like to be tested."

Daniel's heart sank. He feared that his boldness had jeopardized his privilege.

"Therefore, I will test you," General Maoz continued. "I will release your friend into your custody and see whether you can keep him under control. If he so much as looks suspicious during the rest of the journey, you will both find yourselves in isolated captivity."

"My deepest gratitude, sir," replied Daniel. "You will not regret this demonstration of mercy."

"Very well. Follow me to his cage."

"Cage?"

"Yes, we have cages for any wild animals we catch along the way that are edible. When the time is right, we kill and eat. Your friend assumed the role of a wild animal and was caged as one."

Daniel followed the general and his horse to a forward position in the convoy. He rode up next to a rolling cart covered with a sheet of fabric. The driver of the cart was ordered to halt.

"There is your troublemaker," the general jeered as he turned to ride away. "He is now your responsibility. I have important things to do."

Daniel stood in surprise and confusion. Was Segev under the sheet, which was draped over the cart? Was he supposed to take charge and rescue the prisoner, then escort him back to the others?

"Is there a person in your cart?" Daniel asked the driver.

"If you call a Hebrew a person," scoffed the driver.

Daniel's mind cycled between anger and caution.

"May I take him?"

"You heard the same words from the boss that I did."

Daniel approached the cart and nervously lifted the sheet.

"Daniel!" Segev exclaimed in a hushed voice, thinking he may have sneaked to the cart while it was stopped.

Daniel was shocked to see Segev crouched in a small, wooden cage barely large enough to accommodate his constricted body. His legs were drawn with his knees just under his chin. His head was bowed and touching the top of the cage. The stench of urine and feces stung Daniel's nostrils. Daniel noticed a chain was wrapped around some slats of the cage and covered the door. The end of the chain was anchored to the side of the cart out of reach of the cage's occupant.

Daniel quickly loosened and unwrapped the chain, then opened the door.

"Come on out. The general has released you into my custody," instructed Daniel.

Segev slowly inched his way out of the cage with some moaning from pain as he stretched his limbs for the first time in almost three days.

"So, the general decided to let me go?" Segev inquired.

"Only after I appealed to him and made promises I hope I can keep," answered Daniel.

Gawks and mumbling from the soldiers accompanied the two boys as they walked back to their fellow captives. Daniel's mind wandered as he tried to sort out the mixed signals from the general. On one hand, he seemed to be rather gracious in his treatment of his captives; but on the other hand, he could be ruthless and brutal, as in the murder of the escapee and the confinement of Segev. He whispered a prayer for wisdom and discernment.

"I can't believe you risked your leader status to rescue me," said Segev.

"We are in this together," Daniel responded. "We must never fail to defend each other, regardless of the cost."

"I will be forever grateful. I'm sorry." A tear flowed down Segev's dirty cheek, where tracks of previous tears were evident.

"It's all right. You have a lot of influence throughout our group. I need you to help me lead. We must be very wise in what we do and say as a group. The guards are very observant. It is evident that we will serve these Babylonians for a long time. We must make it as painless as possible. We must pray and listen for guidance from Yahweh. He is on our side."

As Daniel and Segev re-entered the formation of captives, they all cheered to see their companion back relatively unharmed. It was obvious to them that Daniel had leveraged his leadership at great risk to himself in order to rescue one of their own.

The next morning, Nebuzaradan began the day as usual with announcements to the guards and their captives.

"Shortly after mid-day today, we will move to the bank of the Euphrates River. This will be the first opportunity we have had to bathe and wash our garments. Most of you are very odorous by now, especially you Hebrews." The captain glanced at the captive formation. "We will wash ourselves and our belongings, then camp tonight at the river's edge while everything dries."

This was sweet news to everyone's ears. They had been on the treacherous journey for three weeks without any washing, other than a little water for their faces and hands every few days. Their clothing was badly soiled and repugnant. Just the thought of immersing themselves in the cool, refreshing river was exhilarating.

Trees became more plentiful, and many varieties of vegetation appeared as the army plodded over the gentle slope leading to the river. The constant dust kicked up by the feet of ten thousand men since leaving Judah subsided noticeably with the transition from barren trails to the grassy ground cover of the Euphrates valley.

A few horsemen had advanced ahead of the army to scout for a shallow location in the river that hundreds of people could wade into and wash themselves and their garments. The single trail divided into several alternative trails to various river crossings chosen by thousands of previous travelers. Everyone felt the air cool as they approached the river. Cheers went up from front to rear as the slowly flowing, sparkling river came into view. The convoy turned south to parallel the river's west bank so that everyone would eventually be next to the water.

"Everyone move to the water's edge with your bags," a guard ordered the captives. "Everything that is washable will be washed using the chunks of soap that will be distributed along the bank. Remove all your clothing and the contents of your bag. Scrub the wetted clothing with the soap and scour each item until it is clean. Then rinse it in the water. With another person, take either end of each item and twist it until you have wrung out as much water as possible. Watch the soldiers if any of this is unclear. They have done this many times. Lay all clothing on rocks and tree limbs to dry through the night. This will be the only time on the journey that you will be able to wash your belongings, so clean them well."

"Once you have everything washed, bathe yourselves with the soap. The guards will be watching you, so don't do anything foolish."

Daniel recalled that he had learned in school that the Babylonians were the first to make soap from animal fat and ashes almost two thousand years ago.

All the boys were anxious to get into the water, so there was no time wasted in stripping down, stepping into the cool, refreshing flow, and beginning the washing as instructed. Daniel looked around to make sure all the boys were complying with the directions. He purposely made eye contact with Segev. As far as he could see in either direction, thousands of men were in the river with a few standing guard at intervals along the bank. Four of the captive's guards had stayed clothed and at the ready with their swords drawn.

After the scrubbing and scouring, Daniel and Azariah paired up to wring out their clothing. They stepped out of the water together to place the clean items on some nearby rocks to dry.

"Have you noticed the Babylonians smirking and pointing at us," asked Azariah. "They can't resist humiliating us. They want us to feel ashamed and inferior, but all I feel is anger."

"Actually, I believe they are amused by us," Daniel replied. "They have likely never seen anyone circumcised before. This mark that Yahweh required of His chosen people is exclusive. Our captors are finding it quite interesting."

Azariah scanned the river full of Babylonian soldiers on either side of them.

"I find their uncircumcision interesting also—and rather disgusting," he said.

Both boys laughed loudly and ran back into the water. Daniel splashed Azariah in playful fashion. Then, he started splashing everyone within range. The water fight evolved into all the boys wrestling and dunking each other. It was the first time since their captivity that they had gotten to do anything close to recreation and play. Everyone in the captive cohort was laughing and yelling as they frolicked in the water like small children. The release of tension and pent-up stress was much needed and long awaited.

Daniel looked down the river at the nearby soldiers who had begun splashing and wrestling also. He wondered if his initiation of the water play had influenced his captors.

During the evening meal almost the entire army, as well as the captives, were still without clothes. The boys were joking about never having eaten while naked before. All freshly washed and dried clothing was retrieved from the bank of the river just before dark, and everyone settled in for a much-appreciated sleep in clean clothes and on soft grass.

"I feel strange in clean clothes," shouted one of the boys from the darkness.

"I feel strange with clothes on after our naked day!" announced another, followed by laughter rippling throughout the group.

"Quiet, you, or I'll throw you in the river clothed!" a guard yelled.

Daniel smiled to himself. *Even our enemies are light-hearted after a fun day,* he thought. He pondered further about the episode with the general and the experiences of this day. He sensed that his influence on his fellow captives and even on the Babylonians was somehow making a difference.

"I am only a youth, but You seem to be giving me influence over many people. Thank You, Yahweh," he whispered as he drifted into a deep sleep.

After the best night's sleep the entire army had enjoyed since Jerusalem, the caravan formed up to begin what would be another three weeks' journey. It would be less rugged now with frequent stops along the river as they paralleled its course. At the end of that course lay a world that Daniel and the other young Hebrew men could not have stretched their imaginations far enough to envision.

9

MAGNIFICENT CITY

AFTER ALMOST SIX WEEKS OF plodding through the mountains, across the plains, and along the banks of the Euphrates, the entire convoy was extremely travel-weary. Foot blisters had become painful wounds; second and third pairs of sandals were coming apart; clothing was worn and stained; and food was becoming scarce and stale. Wagons and chariots were causing problems, especially the wheels and axles. Most of the equipment had not had any significant maintenance since the army had deployed out of Babylon over four years prior. The horses and donkeys, most of which were taken from conquered lands to replace dead or crippled animals from Babylon, were moving slowly and painfully and in need of care. Journeys of this length always took a heavy toll in physical and psychological health of both man and beast.

The sun was high and hot as the trudging Hebrew boys lamented to each other about how debilitating the journey had been. Daniel felt compelled to offer an observation to several within hearing distance.

"It has been hard to bear, but have you noticed we all still have the same sandals and clothing we left Jerusalem with? And they are holding together. Our captors have gone through two or three sets of both. The Israelites experienced the same miracle with Moses in the wilderness. Yahweh has chosen to bless us this way because I'm sure we would have received no replacements."

"That is even more astounding when you consider that most of the captors got to be on horseback or in wheeled carriages at least some of the trip," one of the boys voiced. "But we have pounded the road in these sandals every day since we were taken from our homes."

"Have you so soon forgotten that I got to ride on a wagon for a while?" reminded Segev.

Everyone laughed. Segev had regained the respect of the others, including Daniel, since the caged imprisonment.

The past week had brought on a significant change of scenery. The land was beginning to look like the fertile green plains and valleys and forest-covered mountains of the Promised Land of Israel. That environment had disappeared many days before as the trek turned southeast from the Taurus mountain foothills near Haran. The present surroundings provided a pleasant sight and sweet aroma that were an enticement to progress forward. Even with the mystery of what their fate would be when they arrived at Babylon, the Hebrew boys were excited that the agonizing journey was about to end. They also assumed they would be supplied with more and better food, as well as new clothing and supplies.

Daniel was eating his meager evening meal of some stew concoction and stale bread when General Maoz approached on his chariot, called out to him, and motioned for him to come forward. Daniel set aside his bowl and walked toward the general as the other boys looked on.

"Yes, sir," Daniel greeted.

"Come with me to my tent. I'm celebrating the journey's near end with my other leaders before everything gets busy approaching Babylon. I have some fresh fruit and legumes there and wine that doesn't taste like soured grapes," the general said, smiling.

Like the others, Daniel had been constantly hungry, and he was becoming noticeably weaker physically over the last several days of insufficient nourishment. But he knew the rightful response to the invitation.

"Forgive me, sir, but I must not enjoy the benefits of your gracious invitation while my friends are receiving less food than they need."

The general smiled broadly and nodded. "I should have expected such a response from you, young man. I wish I could serve a banquet for you and your friends, but we are woefully low on food supplies."

"I understand."

"However, tomorrow we will arrive at the great city, if the gods agree. Then, you and your friends will eat well."

"Tomorrow, sir?"

"Yes. That is what I wanted to talk to you about. You and your friends will be registered with the king's court and provided rooms to live in, at least for a while. You will be billeted four to a room. King Nebuchadnezzar has sent word by advance courier for his court officials to receive you and your friends. They will account for all of you, resupply you according to your needs, and establish rules for your service in the king's court. Do you understand what I am saying?"

"Uh, mostly, sir," Daniel replied. "But if I may ask, what will be our duties, and who will oversee us? I will be relieved to relinquish my oversight of my fellow Hebrews to the court officials."

"You will all be serving at the pleasure of the king. Duties will be aligned with the talents and abilities of each of you. You will be enslaved servants, but you will be well taken care of if your performance is acceptable. Become slack in your duties, and you will join the ranks of regular slaves doing hard labor. As for oversight, you will all be under the ultimate authority of the chief of the king's court. His name is Ashpenaz."

"Will we all be directly under Ashpenaz, or will we be divided into work details under other supervisors?" Daniel wanted to get as many specifics as possible from the general to pass on to his counterparts.

"I'm afraid you won't be allowed to relinquish your responsibility that easily, Daniel. I have already sent a message to Ashpenaz with the advance courier telling him of your natural leadership abilities demonstrated on this journey. I recommended that he assign you as liaison between himself and your group. I suggest you speak to them tonight warning them to be on their best behavior, highly disciplined and courteous, and to make a very good first impression on the people of their new home."

Daniel's mind was processing the words of the general. This was the opposite of what he had wanted and anticipated. The stress of leading the other boys in the environment they had struggled through for the past six weeks was weighing heavily on his body, mind, and soul. He had been expected to exhibit the maturity of someone twice his age while maintaining the respect and loyalty of his friends as one of them. It had been a lot to ask of a fifteen-year-old. He had hoped and prayed to be relieved of these responsibilities upon arrival at Babylon. His disappointment was not hidden.

"You must be up to the task, young man. The assimilation of you Hebrews into the Babylonian culture and the palace environment will largely depend on you."

As everyone began preparing their sleeping pallets for the night, Daniel walked away from the group and knelt under a large sycamore tree. The tree towered above those around it as if to beckon the young man to find solace under its branches. The pressures of his unsought and unwanted responsibilities were weighing heavily on him. He craved clarification and guidance from outside his friends and his captors who had little to offer. He longed for wisdom beyond his own logic. Nothing about his situation was logical.

He humbly approached his only source of wisdom and guidance. "O, Yahweh of my fathers, Abraham, Isaac, and Jacob, hear my lament, my plea. I am unworthy and unprepared for the role You have given me to bear. Why am I here? Why is this happening to me? I am sick with desire to be home with my father, mother, brother, and sisters. My breath escapes me, and my heart pounds when I think of them. I am deeply distressed. I need to talk with my father. I feel so alone with nowhere to turn. I must turn to You and You only, Yahweh."

Tears flowed as he continued. "You know where I am and what You want me to do. I can do nothing without You. Reveal to me Your will and guidance. Fill me with Your wisdom. Tomorrow, as we arrive in Babylon, I will be but an ant among giants. What can I do, my one and only Yahweh? What can I say to Your chosen young men, some who are older and wiser than I? Do not desert me, Yahweh. Fill me with words of wisdom. Guide my steps. Show me what glorifies You."

Daniel was surprised—shaken—by his own words as he prayed. It was like the words were not his. They seemed to reflect the thoughts he was unable to express as they flowed from his lips. They were more eloquent than words in his father's prayers or even those of the priest. It was as if God Himself was choosing the words He wanted to hear. He ended the prayer with a final request.

"I am required to address Your young men now. Continue to provide Your words, not my words. Give me strength."

Some of the boys were already wrapped in their blankets for the night when Daniel stepped into their midst. He rubbed his eyes, still burning from the tears shed under the sycamore. He spoke in Aramaic with a loud voice that could be overheard by the guards nearby.

"Let me have your full attention. Tomorrow, we arrive at the city of Babylon. This wretched journey will be over. But the next phase of our lives may be just as challenging. You will see sights you have never imagined, hear things you don't understand, and do things you have never done. It will be essential that you be compliant, that you be disciplined, that you be patient, that you be courteous. We are captives of the Babylonians, yet we must be considerate guests. Place all your trust in Yahweh, the God of our fathers Who has been faithful even in our rebellion. Do nothing out of your own self-will, but only that which honors Him."

By that time, all the boys were out of their bedding, and most were standing in the dim, flickering light of the torches surrounding their camp. Oddly, Daniel was in direct line of some of the torches producing light unobstructed by object or person and giving him a brighter illumination than those around him. He continued.

"Our captors are heathens. They are enemies of Yahweh. Nevertheless, our Yahweh has used them according to His will to bring judgment upon our nation. This was prophesied for years by our prophets like Isaiah and Jeremiah as our destiny if we didn't repent and turn from our wicked ways. Our nation did not turn to Yahweh, and now our capture and exile are the first acts of that judgment. King Nebuchadnezzar has no regard for Yahweh, but he is being unconsciously used by Him to exact His judgment on His chosen people. Therefore, we are not to rebel against the kingdom of Babylon. We are to accept Yahweh's judgment and trust Him to lead us through it. So, tomorrow, be on your best behavior. Do not violate the teachings of the Torah but accommodate our captors within the boundaries of our godly principles."

Everyone was listening attentively without a word, including the guards who had drawn closer to hear the words of Daniel.

"General Maoz has informed me that we will be under the authority of the king's chief of the palace court. We will be servants in the king's palace. We will be well cared for as long as we perform acceptably. The general has recommended to the king's chief that he continue to use me as overseer of our group subordinated to his authority. I did not ask for this responsibility and did not desire it. In fact, I dread very much the burden of this responsibility. I am not worthy of it, nor am I capable of it. I will be depending totally on Yahweh for wisdom and courage in this role. I humbly ask you, my Hebrew brothers, to help me succeed in this role, so that we all may succeed. I need your prayers, your cooperation, and your loyalty. Let's get a good night's rest for strength and awareness tomorrow."

Daniel immediately wrapped himself in his blanket and lay down on the ground for the night.

"Thank you, Yahweh, for the words and the courage," he whispered as he closed his eyes. He hoped no one would come to him asking questions and offering suggestions because he had nothing else to say. No one did, and everyone was quiet.

*

The sun that provided welcomed warmth earlier that brisk morning now was uncomfortably hot. The journey-fatigued army and its captives were stepping a little more quickly in anticipation of their arrival at the largest and most magnificent city in the world now becoming visible on the horizon.

A tall, tower-like edifice appeared first, followed by other shorter structures. As the convoy drew closer, the cityscape's interruption of the flat plain expanded seemingly endlessly to the east and west. For the next hour of marching, the surreal view of the manmade skyline turned from an all-gray hue to distinct bold colors glimmering in the sun.

The river that had sporadically appeared to the east of the convoy's southbound course began to converge to within a stone's throw. Daniel could see the front elements of the army moving left toward a bridge across the river. The bridge appeared to be lined with people. He could see the tops of magnificent structures beyond the high walls of the city. Soon, the element of the convoy comprising the captives and their guards was also turning left in column formation toward the bridge.

The dusty road approaching the city became a hard surface of craftily hewn granite stone leading to the bridge. Many small sailboats carrying two or three men each leisurely floated up and down the river. Shouts of celebration could be heard from the throngs of people lining the walls of the bridge as they welcomed their new king and his mighty army back from their campaign. As the captives entered the bridge, a layer of crushed palm branches cushioned their feet. These branches—hundreds of them—had been placed on the bridge's surface in traditional homage to the king. Many of the greeters were also waving branches from the plentiful palm trees in the area.

As the captors walked in groups of ten abreast across the bridge, Daniel's eyes again caught the huge tower rising ominously behind the wall. It appeared to be in the early stages of construction with large bricks stacked to form the terraced shape. It was surrounded by ladders and scaffolding. Distracted by the activity on and along the banks of the great river, Daniel was surprised by the view of the arched gate through which he and his other captives were about to pass. The high stone walls lining the approach to the gate were adorned with images of lions, dozens of them, fabricated from red, white, and yellow tiles. Now just steps away, the gate was at least ten times the height of a man and was landscaped with endless shrubs and palm trees.

Daniel began to inhale the sweet scent of the flowers with every breath. In every direction, his eyes took in structures of magnificent architecture, trimmed and nurtured shrubs and flowers, and color-fully dressed people scurrying about in the streets. His breathing rate increased, and he could feel his heart pounding. He felt that he should have said something profound to his group as they entered the city, but he was too awe-stricken by the overwhelming scenes to form any words. It was difficult to comprehend they were entering their new home—a hostile and mysterious new home.

Once through the gate, tall walls again lined the broad street, this time displaying colorful bulls and dragons. *Such a contrast to the brown and gray simplicity of my beloved Jerusalem.*

The silence that had characterized the captives' approach to the city could no longer be maintained as they broke into simultaneous expressions of astonishment. The young men had discussed what their destination would look like, but none of them could have imagined the magnificence of the surroundings. Almost every building rivaled the size and beauty of Solomon's Temple back home. The designs and colors incorporated in every exterior were dazzling and far different from anything they had ever seen.

The tower Daniel had seen rising above the wall was now in full view. It looked like a huge, steep mountain, much larger than any man-made edifice he had ever seen or imagined. Even though it was obviously under construction, it dominated all other structures in the city. The contrasting brownish-gray unfinished stone gave it an imposing nature that raised chill bumps along Daniel's arms. The area around it was vacant and larger than the top of Mount Zion in Jerusalem that hosted the temple.

Element by element of the army systematically broke away from the convoy as it wound through the stone streets lined with unfamiliar, but beautiful, vegetation and tropical trees. The sweet aroma was mesmerizing. Finally, the hundreds of men, horses, chariots, and wagons in front and behind were paired down to the forty-nine exhausted young Hebrew men and their equally weary guards.

The now relatively small group of travelers walked out of the constant maze of tall buildings lining the streets into a striking open area that contained what looked like a huge palace. In close proximity on every side were other finely appointed buildings. Garish facades covered the front portico of the palace at the top of many ascending steps. The building looked to have four floors. Each floor had several exterior balconies accessible through large wooden doors framed by arches. The grounds surrounding the palace were covered with shrubs, trees, and flower gardens. Lavishly dressed guards with highly polished helmets and unsheathed swords stood watch in the courtyard. Similarly dressed entry guards at the giant doorway stood motionless at attention.

The captive's guards ushered them to the side of the palace under the shade of a columned pavilion.

After a moment of awkward standing in formation, the boys were greeted by a man who had walked from one of the palace exits accompanied by two other men on either side of him dressed similar to the other palace guards. The one on the left was carrying what looked to be a scroll canister and a small table. The man in the center was in a long robe with a red sash and a red turban on his head. He scanned the formation, stepping left and right as if counting everyone. He said something to the guard holding the canister, then began speaking in a loud and deep voice in Aramaic to his new guests.

"Greetings on behalf of His Excellence, King Nebuchadnezzar. I am Ashpenaz, the chief of the king's court officials, his most trusted servants. The king has determined that you are the elite of your Hebrew peers and may be worthy of serving him in his court. Whether you are worthy remains to be seen. I will decide that based on your performance over the weeks ahead. I have been given the duty of commanding all of you. That includes schooling you to the ways of the Chaldeans and our language, arts, and sciences. Your health and welfare will be my responsibility. Although you will be strictly disciplined for any failure to meet expectations, I have the power to make your lives more pleasant than common slaves. However, I have little tolerance for failure. Cross me or perform below my standards, and you will become a lowly servant like other prisoners of the kingdom."

Ashpenaz extended his arms from his side. "The royal palace in front of you will be your residence—your new home. You will be relegated to the servant's quarters, where you will sleep and eat. I will determine where and how you will serve. In a moment, my assistants will show you to your quarters and will outfit you with necessary clothing and supplies. But for now, I call out Daniel to come forward and stand beside me."

Daniel was shaken by the order. He had assumed his designation as leader of the group, which had been shared by the general the day prior, would be more subtle. He moved forward through the crowd feeling awkward and embarrassed, faced Ashpenaz, and bowed slightly. Ashpenaz placed his hands on Daniel's shoulders and turned him around to face the group.

"Daniel will be your peer leader," Ashpenaz announced. "You will respect and obey him. He will speak for me when I am not present."

Daniel was feeling very uncomfortable. Although he and the others knew this responsibility was coming, the abruptness of the declaration made him feel he was betraying his friends. He felt unqualified and unprepared for the assignment. Ashpenaz handed him the scroll canister, a reed quill, and a container of ink.

"Write the names and ages of each servant. When you're finished, my assistants will show you to your quarters. You will be divided four to a room. The younger ones will room with the older ones."

Ashpenaz departed as four assistants arrived and stood with the two guards. When Daniel finished the list of names and ages, the assistants and guards led the boys into the palace on the way to their rooms. One of the assistants asked Daniel to walk with them ahead of the formation, an obvious acknowledgement of his position for the observance of the others.

Inside the palace, after a short walk through an entry corridor, the building opened up to a huge rectangular great hall. The floors were marble with thick and colorful woven rugs. The main floor cascaded down two levels with three steps each to a sunken center floor adorned with blooming shrubs. Small plants and vines were appointed throughout the hall on all three levels. The upper floors were supported by marble columns a man could not reach around. All walls were covered with royal blue fabric. Statues of various Chaldean gods were prominent along the perimeter of the hall. Daniel recognized a larger image as Marduk, the principal god of Babylonia on a pedestal in the center.

He scanned the massive hall in amazement. It was more ornate than anything he had ever seen, even more so than the Jerusalem palace or even the temple. As the group filed into the mid-level floor, they stood around a small, round pool at floor-level that emptied into a trough. The water flowed into a small waterfall filling another pool in the lower floor. Assuming the role of a guide, one of the assistants gave the boys a short history of the palace.

"All visitors to the palace enter through this beautiful hall. It is also where we hold royal banquets and receive official guests. Notice the throne where the king meets with top staff. The original palace was constructed many years ago by the Assyrians for their governors over Babylon. However, what you see now is the handiwork of King Nabopolassar, who conquered the Assyrians in Chaldea twenty-one years ago. The plants and rugs were brought in by his son, and now king, Nebuchadnezzar. Our new king has a passion for plants. We will now proceed up the stairway to your quarters."

Daniel's eyes were drawn again to the statue of Marduk as they walked within arm's reach of it. The image with a tall, gold-plated crown, a long flowing beard, and a colorful robe with multiple folds stood about three times the height of a man. The sight sent chills over Daniel as he thought about the evil it represented. He wondered whether anyone in Babylon other than the captives would ever even acknowledge the one true God of the Hebrews.

The group walked up the staircase next to a side wall to the third floor. Daniel hadn't noticed that each floor had a walkway that encircled the great hall, providing access to long, perpendicular hallways lined with doors to rooms and offices. The assistant stopped at the third hallway and announced that this hallway led to the thirteen rooms which would be the accommodations for the servants until further notice.

"I will read the names of the four of you in each room based on your ages."

As names were called out, each set of four boys entered their rooms and deposited their bags with their total possessions on the cots next to the walls. A table with four chairs and a chest with four drawers sat in the center of the room. There were no windows. A small oil lamp flickered on the table.

Daniel now remained alone with the assistant. He had been thinking throughout the room assignment process that it wasn't going to work out evenly.

"You will have the last room to yourself. The leader gets a private room," the assistant said.

"I am honored to be given this position and to be offered a private room, but I would much prefer to have the same arrangement as my friends."

"I am only following the orders of my leader, Ashpenaz."

"Would you please relay to Ashpenaz that I am indeed grateful for the privilege, but my leadership effectiveness of these men will depend on my not appearing to be receiving special privilege. Our Hebrew culture would find my requested arrangement more appropriate."

"I'm sure Ashpenaz will insist on your having this distinction as the leader. That is our culture."

Daniel paused to think, then offered a compromise. "Then, may I request a different distinction? With all respect to your culture, allow me the distinction of choosing those who room with me. The others didn't have a choice. You would be showing favor to me by allowing me to choose. I humbly request that you reassign Hananiah, Mishael, and Azariah to my room. You would still occupy thirteen rooms; but ten of the rooms would have four occupants, and three of the rooms would have three occupants."

"As you wish. You know your people. I'm sure Ashpenaz has more important things to do than quibble over exiled servants' quarters."

Daniel was somewhat concerned that he might have begun his relationship with the assistant on a bad footing, but at least he had learned that future issues may be negotiable. And the modified room assignments would be an indication to the other young men, especially his three closest friends, of his loyalty to them. He would need this loyalty above all else for the challenges he would face even before this day was over.

10

DIET STANDOFF

EARLY IN THE EVENING, THE exiled servants were called to the first meal in six weeks not prepared by the Babylonian army field cooks. Daniel was eager to finally have tasty food in abundance. However, his heart was heavy regarding the meal. As he walked with the others along the third level walkway to the servants' dining room, he began feeling convicted about the Jewish dietary laws. Certainly, the boys had eaten whatever was served to them during their march to Babylon. They had not objected, rationalizing that it was not possible to honor every Hebrew restriction in their constantly mobile state. But they also realized that much of their food had been confiscated from the Jerusalem markets and was, therefore, according to law. Now the situation was different. They were apparently in their permanent environment. The palace surely had the capability to prepare food in ways different from local custom. He cringed at the thought of raising another issue with his superiors.

The young men were positioned three and four to a table according to their room assignments. Daniel and his three companions were seated on the front row. Ashpenaz entered the room and stood before the hungry group.

"You are about to enjoy a long-awaited meal after your many days of travel. Tonight's food will be typical of your daily evening menu.

It is the king's wish that all of us in the palace enjoy the same food he enjoys, even the servants. He insists every person in his court be healthy, strong, and able to serve him at their maximum capacity. The palace chief chef prepares the same items for everyone. You will gather here each morning and evening on schedule for a hearty cuisine. At mid-day, you will receive a light fare at your places of service."

Several servants appeared each carrying a large basin. They placed a basin at each table and poured water over each diner's hands as they were positioned over the basin.

The servants then began serving each table, beginning with Daniel's. He watched as a basket of thickly sliced bread, vegetables, and fruit was placed before him. So far, so good. Then came a stone platter stacked with what appeared to be beef steak and cubes of cheese covered with spices. Lastly, each preset brass cup was filled with wine from a large flask.

"We must not eat this food forbidden by the laws of Yahweh," Daniel whispered to his tablemates.

"But we have been eating unlawful food for six weeks," Mishael replied.

"But we never ate meat and dairy together. Most of what we ate came from Jerusalem," Daniel said. "And even though it was not prepared by Hebrews as required by our law, we had no choice. It was eat or die of starvation. Maybe we have a choice now."

Daniel looked around the room. None of the others appeared to have any hesitation of eating what had been place before them. They were gorging like starving animals. He didn't feel that he could ask everyone to refrain from eating what they had been served. They all knew the Hebrew laws, and each one was accountable before Yahweh.

"I believe we should fast for ten days as we pray for Yahweh's wisdom and favor in our threatening situation. Will you join me in eating only vegetables and fruits and drinking only water if I appeal to Ashpenaz?" Daniel asked the other three.

After a brief hesitation, they looked at each other and nodded. Daniel approached Ashpenaz privately.

"Sir, we are all extremely grateful to the king for his graciousness in serving us bountiful meals fit for royalty. However, we Hebrews have certain dietary laws commanded by our God that prevent us from eating much of what was served this evening and what will likely be served in the future."

"Surely, you don't reject this benevolent act by the king because of some religious preference from your past," Ashpenaz objected, openly agitated. "You are not in Judah anymore, Daniel; you are servants in Babylon and subject to the will of King Nebuchadnezzar. Besides, I am responsible for your health and physical development. If you become lean and frail from insufficient nourishment, I would lose my position in the king's court and likely my life. The king has no tolerance for such foolishness. You all will eat what is served and be thankful for it."

"Very well, sir. I appreciate your hearing my concern."

Daniel returned to his table, and Ashpenaz left the room.

"He was not willing to consider my appeal," Daniel reported to his three friends.

"I will eat only the fruit and vegetables and be satisfied before Yahweh," Daniel said further. "I encourage you to do the same, but that is a matter of your personal conscience and conviction before Yahweh."

All four boys ate the small helpings of fruits and vegetables, leaving the meat, cheese, bread, and wine untouched on the table.

Daniel asked one of the servers to invite the chief chef from the kitchen to his table, so he could thank him for the food on behalf of the entire group. Moments later, the server guided the chef to the table. All four boys stood.

"You haven't eaten," the chef exclaimed before Daniel could say a word. "Are you not feeling well, or is this a protest?"

"Neither," Daniel explained. "We are all grateful for the abundant delicacies. You have obviously served us a feast according to your commendable talents. It's just that the laws of Yahweh have restrictions as to what we should and should not eat and drink. We have enjoyed your fruits and vegetables, which are the only items on this evening's menu that were allowed for Hebrews."

The chef looked around the room. "Those at the other tables seem to be eating everything in front of them."

"That is their decision," Daniel replied. "Due to our circumstances, they have rationalized compromising our laws. But the four of us remain committed to obeying Yahweh in all things."

"Ashpenaz will not tolerate preparing different menus for you exiles," the chef retorted. "What will be next—someone wants goat's milk? I will not be part of a diet standoff. I am afraid of my lord the king, who has appointed your food and your drink; for why should he see your faces looking more haggard than the youths who are your own age? Then you would make me forfeit my head to the king."

"With all humility and respect, may I make one request that will, in time, resolve the issue?" Daniel asked.

With a nod from the chef, Daniel continued, "Please test your servants for ten days and let us be given some vegetables to eat and water to drink. Then let our appearance be observed in your presence and the appearance of the youths who are eating the king's choice food and deal with your servants according to what you see."

Hananiah spoke up. "If Ashpenaz is to be judged on how we are progressing physically, he should agree on the diet that meets that objective. He will praise you for your wisdom."

The chef was silent momentarily; then he knelt next to the boys. "I will accept the proposal; but if Ashpenaz finds out what we are doing, it will not be good for me. I will, of course, need you to explain what your dietary laws require."

Daniel breathed a sigh of relief. "You will not be disappointed. Thank you. You have been very gracious."

The chef listened attentively as all four boys discussed with him the requirements and restrictions of the Hebrew diet.

Before he departed, the chef had one last comment. "The food you were served tonight is the best possible for your physical development and health. Be prepared after ten days to join with the rest of your friends in enjoying the best diet the kingdom has to offer."

After the chef left his table, Daniel turned to the other three. "Yahweh has delivered us another victory for being faithful."

"What if we are not judged to be in better condition than the others after ten days," Azariah asked. "Even if we are better, they could judge differently."

"What Yahweh begins, He will finish," Daniel replied.

The next morning began with the assistants knocking on each door of the boys' hallway, waking them well before dawn. Each room slowly became active as the boys retrieved their clothing from their individual compartments in the shared chest. Their assigned attire consisted of tunics, cloaks, undergarments, and sandals. The clothing was designed much like they were familiar with, but the soft fabric and bright colors would take some getting used to.

While three assistants and a couple of guards waited, the boys assembled in the hallway. The last few to exit their rooms were chastised by an assistant. "You are too slow. Tomorrow, I expect everyone to be out of his room fully dressed and prepared for the morning meal in half the time of today's formation."

Once at their tables in the dining room, the morning meal was immediately served. Daniel noticed those serving were other young men with skin tones and facial features somewhat different from the typical Chaldean. He assumed they were fellow exiles from other conquered lands. The food placed on the table for Daniel and his three friends consisted of mixed greens, diced squash, beets, flat bread, and chalices of water. The other tables were being served slices of beef, strips of cheese, turnips, sweet bread covered with honey, and brass cups of wine.

"I trust your table's morning fare meets the standards of your God?" the server asked in a somewhat mocking tone.

"Yes, sir, it is perfect," Daniel responded. "We are humbly grateful. Please pass our compliments to the chef for this special accommodation."

The lead assistant approached the boys' table looking confused at their food. Before he could comment, Daniel stood and spoke.

"Sir, may I be allowed to reduce your time and effort of waking each room's occupants each morning? Would you be pleased to send a guard to knock on my door at the proper time and allow me to get everyone else up, dressed, and to the dining room? We would like to demonstrate our ability to meet your expectations with the least burden possible on you."

The assistant, clearly caught off-guard, paused momentarily, then answered, "Very well, I will consider this a test. You may conduct the morning preliminaries as you have suggested. But the first time your entire group is not at their tables at the assigned time, my men will resume that responsibility with harsher requirements."

"Thank you, sir. You will not be disappointed." Daniel was pleased that he had accomplished several objectives with the request. It diverted his attention from the odd food choices. It would elevate the group's confidence in his leadership; it would avoid possible conflict between the boys and the assistants during the wake-up procedures; and it would further convince the assistants that they could expect the utmost cooperation from their exiles.

After the meal was finished, Ashpenaz entered the room, spoke briefly to the assistants and guards, then announced, "I hope you had a restful night and a hearty meal because you have a full schedule of tasks today. This schedule will be typical of each day forward. In a few moments, you will form outside the palace for physical training. Then you will return to this room to hear the plans I have made for your three-year education and indoctrination program. At mid-day, in this room, you will receive a couple of pieces of food and a drink of water. Frequently in the afternoons, you will be escorted on visits to important sites around the city. During these tours, you will experience the Chaldean culture, our history, and our plans. You will go on your first excursion outside of the palace this afternoon."

Physical training that morning involved a very challenging race around the palace. The boys were divided into two-person teams. Each boy had to carry his partner on his back in a run that encircled the palace and returned to the starting point. Then the rider would become the runner and run the same lap with the original runner on his back. The two-person team that won by crossing the finish line first after the two laps would each receive a blue turban to wear until the next day's competition.

Each runner ran barefoot, dressed only in his knee-length tunic. To the surprise of most of the Hebrew boys, the first team across the finish line was Daniel and Hananiah. Daniel had chosen to be the runner for the second lap, thinking he could better catch up with any team ahead of them. The strategy worked. Coming in second were Mishael and Azariah. All four of them fell to the ground, completely exhausted and gasping for air at the end of the race. The four had pushed themselves extremely hard. They were immensely competitive, particularly among themselves. This race took Daniel's mind back to the temple school athletic games and even to their fierce competition in playing Kugelach. He tried to dispose of that memory flash, but it wouldn't go away.

After a brief time to recover from the race, the boys were formed up into loose rows and columns for exercises. The assistant called Daniel to the front.

"Daniel will lead the exercise. I will demonstrate each exercise element; then you will follow Daniel's movements and pace."

After each demonstration by the assistant, Daniel copied the movements but at double the speed of the demonstration. The exercises were strenuous with the movements stretching the muscles to extreme and requiring a great deal of strength. Daniel called for everyone to voice the cadence loudly by number. Soon, the participants began to moan and grunt heavily. When the assistant called to halt each exercise event, Daniel would lead at least two more repetitions before stopping.

Every boy was gasping for breath between each exercise. Grumbling ensued among the group. Finally, the assistant was satisfied with the effort and length of the exercise period and announced they had done enough for that morning. He made it clear though that he would expect improvement each day. While the assistant was talking, Daniel was jogging in place with his arms in exaggerated swings. One by one, the boys began to follow his last exercise that had not been demonstrated or directed. But almost all of them were not looking at Daniel as their heads were lowered out of exhaustion and frustration.

Back in the dining room around their respective tables, everyone's skin was aglow with perspiration. Large, wet circles under the arms of the tunics added contrast in colors. Sweat beads were still present on the scraggly beards of the older boys, which had not yet been trimmed from the exile journey growth. The younger boys, including Daniel, were still dealing with splotchy pubescent beards not thick enough to retain perspiration. The rank smell in the room was overwhelming but ignored.

11

CHALDEAN INDOCTRINATION

ASHPENAZ ENTERED THE ROOM WAVING his hand in front of his face mockingly showing his displeasure of the smell.

"I'm glad to see you enjoyed your exercise period," Ashpenaz began.

Eyes rolled and heads shook throughout the room.

"Your brains work better when your body is at its peak," he continued. "For the rest of the day, we will exercise our brains. For the next many months, you will be taught by my assistants and me how to be Chaldeans. You will become model citizens of Babylon, fitted for service to His Majesty, King Nebuchadnezzar. You will learn the finest standards of the Aramaic language. You will become speakers and writers according to communication standards expected of the royal court. You will learn the religions practiced by the land that has adopted you. The origins and histories of our gods will become very familiar to you. You will learn how to practice our religious rituals."

Daniel felt a tightness in his gut. *Another conflict we will have to deal with. How will we keep our loyalty and faithfulness to Yahweh while being confronted with the hedonism of this place every day? How can we be held accountable for learning the ways of other gods while not acknowledging them?* He prayed silently, *Oh, Yahweh, we are going to need Your wisdom beyond measure. I crave Your guidance. Keep us, Your children, devoted to You in unity.*

"You will become students knowledgeable of the sciences for which the Chaldeans are known throughout the nations. This will involve the realms of the celestial sciences of astrology and astronomy. Uses of oils and herbs for healing and nutrition will become part of your skills. We will give you much interface with our leading magicians and sorcerers, so you will learn of their arts and crafts. You will be experts in the history and geography of not only the Chaldeans, but also the Assyrians, the Medes and Persians, and the Egyptians. The fine arts of sculpture, painting, music, and drama will be easy conversation for you. You will be immersed in all of these subjects and more for the next many months of your Chaldean indoctrination."

Except for a short pause to nosh on the light mid-day meal and a quick time of rest, Ashpenaz continued the introduction lecture until time for the culture walk around the opulent city.

The forty-nine boys made their way down the busy streets with some semblance of formation while often giving way to the unappreciative pedestrians of the city. Ashpenaz was leading the group accompanied by his assistants and some palace guards. They were drawing many piercing stares and hearing occasional obscene insults from strangers as they progressed slowly toward the gigantic pyramid-shaped structure, which had appeared between and over tops of buildings several times along the walk. The exterior walls of most of the buildings were made of glazed brick, making them glimmer in the sun. Facades were in bright colors.

Ascending a steep hill, the boys stared in awe of the tall edifice now commanding their total attention. It was obviously in the beginning stages of construction. Daniel remembered not being able to take his eyes off of it when they entered the gate to the city the day prior.

Ashpenaz circled the group around him at the base of the mysterious cascading structure of brick with tar mortar. He began to explain the structure.

"This is the reconstruction of the tower of Babylon. It is the ziggurat called Etemenanki, which means 'house of the platform of heaven and earth.' It will reach higher than anything in the world made by man. Many Mesopotamian cities have ziggurats, but Babylon's will make dwarfs of them all. King Nabopolassar had hoped to see the project complete, but his son will now have the honor of celebrating the accomplishment."

"Ziggurats have been built where people have migrated from the historic tower of Babel. We believe the ruins that form the base of Etemenanki are from the original tower of Babel built here in Babylon long ago. This will be the resurrection of that ancient tower."

Daniel whispered to Hananiah, "This is amazing. They recognize the history of Babel from the first book of Moses. As we learned from the priest, the descendants of Noah built a tower in Babel, which displeased Yahweh, causing Him to separate the people into different lands and languages. Our captors and we get our knowledge from different sources, but the knowledge is the same."

The afternoon tour wound through other parts of the city, pausing occasionally for instruction on some of the many temples to pagan gods. Ashpenaz identified the Temple of Esagila as the shrine of Marduk, or Bel, meaning "the lord." He explained that even the rafters in this principle temple were clad with gold.

"Priceless articles from your Jerusalem temple have been stored in there and will soon adorn our temple to the pleasure of our gods," Ashpenaz remarked.

Muffled moans rippled over the group. As they approached the palace, Ashpenaz led them by the facilities housing the king's harem. He pointed out the queen's residence that was far more elegant than the others. Several of the young women were dancing together in the courtyard. Ashpenaz explained that they were practicing entertainment routines often performed for the king and his guests. He added that the practices also kept them in top physical shape.

That night, the small room that was now home for Daniel and his three friends had been quiet. The boys were readying themselves for a much-desired sleep. However, sleep any time soon seemed unlikely for any of them because of the flurry of thoughts and emotions welling in their heads. All of them were seated on their beds, contemplating the experiences of the day.

"My heart aches!" Mishael blurted out, his head bowed almost to his knees. "This place is awful. It's scary. I want to be home with my mother and father, my brothers and sisters." He began to sob.

"My heart longs not to be here, too, Mishael," Daniel responded. "But we are here by the will of Yahweh, and we must be strong. Yahweh is with us. He will protect us."

Azariah spoke up. "How can we stand another day like today? And another. And another. We are ordered around like slaves. How many more things will we have to confront like unlawful meals? How long can we hold up under the strenuous physical competitions and exercises? I wanted to place my hands over my ears during the lectures about heathen gods and their bloody history and over my eyes as we visited the pagan temples. They are trying to make us typical Chaldeans by packing our brains with evil things. I'm not sure I can make it through tomorrow."

"About the physical training, Daniel," Hananiah added, "I realize what you are trying to do in winning the races and leading the exercises. You are showing our captors that we can take what they demand and more, too. You are allowing them nothing to criticize us for. Am I right?"

"I'm just doing what I feel will assure Ashpenaz and the other of my leadership ability, so they will back off and let us rule ourselves as much as possible. The more they trust us, the less we will have to be subjected to their culture and the more we can honor our Hebrew faith and culture. I also want to convince our fellow captives I can lead in a way that avoids as much persecution as possible."

"You may overestimate our own people, Daniel," Hananiah advised. "From the grumbling and murmuring I heard today, I think they believe you are seeking favor from the enemy at their expense. They are wondering whether your leader assignment has gone to your head. I worry that they may revolt, which would be devastating for us all."

"And what do you each think my motive is?" Daniel asked, making eye contact with each of them.

After a pause, Azariah said, "Right now, I think the motive of all of us should be to get some sleep. We can evaluate our situation better tomorrow, having rested."

Daniel blew out the lone oil lamp and assumed a fetal position under his blanket. But sleep was not to be enjoyed immediately as worrisome thoughts haunted his mind.

Why does there have to be such conflict? Ashpenaz insists on converting us to the pagan culture of his world. His assistants watch our every move, ready to punish any infraction of their rules or disobeying of their commands. I must protect my people while pleasing our captors. Now my own people are questioning my leadership. I'm not even sure my three best friends are on my side. How can I lead these people in such a place as this? I am only a child. We are all only children. What will tomorrow bring?

Daniel finally fell asleep, silently crying out to God for help.

The young exiles' second day in Babylon was about the same as the first. Physical training after the morning meal was the worst part of the day. Daniel and his three friends gutted out the piggy-back run again to win first and second place. However, in the final lap, Daniel slowed purposely to allow Mishael, carrying Azariah, to take first place at the finish line. The blue turbans worn by Daniel and Hananiah during the morning had drawn jeers from most of their peers. They were more than happy to hand the turbans off to Mishael and Azariah.

During the exercise period, Daniel again showed no mercy in leading the effort beyond the requirements of the assistants. He led them at a faster rhythm and with more repetitions than necessary.

Following the classroom teaching and mid-day meal, the afternoon tour included a visit to the water source for the city. An under-water gate beneath the surface of the Euphrates River controlled water traveling through a large underground aqueduct below the city wall and into various access points in the city. This system provided ample irrigation for the myriad gardens, shrubs, and trees growing prolifically throughout the city. It also provided drinking water for every dweller in the city by a complex method of distillation. An important by-product of the underground system was the security advantage of not having their source of water easily destroyed by an enemy.

That evening, Daniel and his friends bedded down for the night extremely exhausted and without much discussion about the day. Emotions were still somewhat tense among the foursome. Before any of them had time to get to sleep, there was a loud knock at the door. Mishael, being closest to the door, answered. It was Segev.

"Come out in the hallway, now!" He ordered in a loud voice. "All of you!

Daniel's pulse raced. *What now?*

Moving into the hallway dressed only in their undergarments, Daniel and his friends could see the silhouettes of all the young Hebrews standing along the wall. Segev motioned for Daniel to follow him to a point halfway down the hall. They were in easy hearing distance of the rest of the group.

"We have had a meeting," Segev began. "We have some grievances—no, some demands—to raise with you."

Daniel's breathing rate quickened. He instantly moved from nervousness to anger. He thought he had gained Segev's absolute loyalty after rescuing him from the cage. Now, it appeared his repented nemesis was betraying him.

"During our journey, we all reluctantly sacrificed our freedom to become subject to your leadership. We didn't agree with everything you did, but it was ultimately to our advantage to allow you to lead us and represent us before our captors. Since we arrived in Babylon, you are attempting at every turn to make us look inferior to you, to elevate yourself in the eyes of our captors, to gain their approval for your selfish gain."

Most of the others were nodding and verbalizing their affirmation of Segev's words. The atmosphere was so heavy, Daniel felt like it was literally pressing on his shoulders.

Segev continued. "You gained the enemy's favor by unnecessarily relieving them of the morning formation burden, but you make us rise earlier and get to the meal sooner. You think you are holier than us with your special Hebrew diet. You have put at risk the endless portions we enjoy of the king's best food. You run faster than you have to, so you can win the races and wear that ridiculous blue turban. You lead the exercises like you are trying to kill us in order to impress Ashpenaz and his assistants."

Even in the low light, Daniel could see the redness in Segev's face. The blood vessels in his temples were swelling. He wondered when the diatribe would end.

"I have been asked to speak for my Hebrew brothers," Segev said, lowering his voice somewhat. "You must choose. Either stop leading us altogether and let the responsibility of our captors take its course or lead as one of us in opposition to our captors."

I doubt you have been asked to speak, Segev, Daniel remained silent. *I thought I could depend on you, but I see now you are still bent on being in control of this group. I do not sense that you are acting under Yahweh's hand. Yahweh, please give me strength and wisdom here. Give me words that will change the hearts and minds of my brothers.*

Daniel positioned himself in sight of all the others. He said nothing before making eye contact with each individual, except Segev, making a one-to-one connection.

"Brothers, please hear me out," Daniel began. "I would love to do exactly as you wish, but that is not Yahweh's will. We are all in the same predicament. As mere children, we have been ripped from our families, from loving parents and siblings, from the city and nation we loved, from our security, and from our anticipated destiny as elite countrymen. Now, we are the subjects of a harsh, pagan people in a strange, hostile land. We have nothing to hang on to but each other .

. . . and our Yahweh. We did not leave Yahweh in Judah. He came with us. Even though it was His will that we were the first to be exiled under His judgment on our homeland, He still loves us and wants to protect us if we stay faithful and true to Him. His punishment, as repeatedly warned about by our prophets, does not mean His rejection. He has always been a merciful God of second chances. What is most critical now is that we honor Him in our actions and stay unified in our relationships."

Daniel paused and again paced slowly, looking directly into forty-seven sets of other eyes, one person at a time.

"We know our captors see their sole purpose as preparing us to be servants of the king's court. What they do not understand is that they are part of Yahweh's plan for His judgment of His people. We should not see them as our enemy but as participants along with us in the Divine orchestration of events by the hand of Yahweh. Therefore, we must not resist them, except when their directions violate the commands of Yahweh, in which case we will not compromise our beliefs. Our objective must be to overly accommodate our captors in order to gain their trust and confidence. That will please Yahweh and will ultimately benefit us. That is why we must be very attentive in class, demonstrate extra exertion in physical training, show interest in their culture, be respectful. We can survive here in maliciousness against our captors, or we can thrive here by subjecting ourselves to them."

He paused again to allow his audience to process what he was saying. "There is another thing we must consider. We have learned it is common practice for Babylon to make eunuchs of enslaved exiles from conquered nations. They are castrated to keep them docile and passive, as well as to alleviate the risk of their violating the women they serve."

Grimaces and moans ensued at Daniel's graphic reminder.

"I have heard no implication that we will face such emasculation. I believe this is another confirmation of Yahweh's hand of protection on us. But we must not give our captors any reason to view us as a threat and lower us to eunuch slaves."

Daniel asked the young men to sit on the floor. They obliged, except for one. Daniel made his final point, standing toe-to-toe with Segev. They could feel each other's breath.

"Segev, you told me I must choose to either step down voluntarily or lead our opposition toward our captors. I will do neither. But I ask each of you to choose. Either choose a posture of antagonism from a few Hebrew boys against the kingdom of Babylonia or choose to accept the plan of Yahweh for our exiled co-existence with our captors. I will lead us in the latter direction. The choice is yours."

Daniel abruptly turned and walked away toward his room. His three friends followed. He didn't know what the others did afterward and didn't bother to find out. Nothing was said in the room until all four were back in bed. Finally, Hananiah broke the silence.

"Oy veh, Daniel. Awesome, but risky.

"Divine oration?" Mishael asked. "Where do you get those words?"

Daniel couldn't hold back a muffled chuckle. "I had no idea what I was going to say when I first opened my mouth. I continue to be amazed and humbled by Yahweh's provision when words beyond my capacity are needed."

"What do you think will happen?" Azariah asked

"We will all know tomorrow," Daniel answered.

The next day, Daniel continued with his leadership duties as if the confrontation of the evening prior hadn't happened. He seated the group in the dining room ahead of schedule with no involvement of the assistants. He again crossed the finish line first with Hananiah on his back, then led the exercises with no let-up from previous days. All the day's events followed the routine of days one and two.

In the evening, when Daniel knew everyone was making final preparations for bed, he asked his roommates for assistance. "I need your help. We have one more event tonight. Let us go knock on the doors of every room and tell them I am calling for a short meeting in the hallway."

Soon, everyone was accounted for and standing in the hallway in various stages of dress, looking confused. Daniel faced the wall and extended his arms parallel to the hallway.

"Everyone, please line up along this wall facing me."

"This will be a short meeting. You have had time to think about and, I hope, pray about what I said last night. What you saw in my leadership today was a continuation of how I intend to lead as long as I have your confidence and loyalty. I remain convinced that the behavior and demeanor that we are demonstrating is the right response to the demands of our captors and the response that will ultimately be to our advantage. My actions are in our best interests."

He stepped backward to the opposite wall.

"All who are willing to affirm me as your leader, step forward to this wall."

Daniel's three friends immediately stepped forward, followed by several others. Then, a few more moved after some side glances. Finally, there was only Segev standing alone. His head lowered as he slowly shuffled to join the others. Daniel stepped to a position facing them.

"The agreement we have just reached is the crossing of a threshold. From this point forward, whether we are captives for a year or we die here as old men, we will be unified. We will trust each other. We will help each other. We will hold each other accountable. If necessary, we will sacrifice our lives for each other."

Daniel paused to emphasize his statement, then continued. "There will be times when each of us needs encouragement. Sometimes, this may be in the heat of conflict when our captors' demands are too extreme or not permissible under our laws. I want us to adopt a code word that will generate strength and hope in times of dire need. You remember from our studies, my brothers, that the hope of all Hebrews is in the Messiah to come. The King will come from the line of David, from our own tribe of Judah, and will reign forever. He will save His people, Israel. That is us! That is our strength, our encouragement, our hope!"

"His name shall be Immanuel. Immanuel!" Daniel shouted. "Which means 'Yahweh with us'! The prophet, Isaiah, wrote that a virgin will give birth to a son and will call him Immanuel. Remember that word. It is our code word. Our captors will not understand it. We will shout 'Immanuel!' in public when any of us is in need of encouragement, prayer, and of a reminder of who we are. We are the children of Yahweh, Who will deliver us through King Immanuel!"

"Now, let us return to our rooms in peace and oneness. Sleep well, for tomorrow is another challenging day."

Without a word from anyone, the hallway quickly cleared.

*

After ten days in Babylon, the Hebrew captives were settling into the burdensome, but predictable, routine of intense learning, demanding physical training, and rigid schedules of other activities. There had been occasional bullying by the assistants and guards, as well as private grumbling and complaining among the boys. However, no significant conflicts had ensued as Daniel's principles for surviving and thriving as exiles were seemingly taking hold and his leadership honored.

Ashpenaz entered the dining room just as the morning meal was being served. He had been present every day either teaching in a class or leading a city tour or sometimes both. However, this was his first appearance at the morning meal since the first day after their arrival. He lifted both hands, signaling quietness and attention.

"As I told you on your arrival, the king instructed me to feed you the same diet he and his royal court were fed. He wanted to develop your bodies with plenty of meat, bread, and wine. However, on the first day, your leader, Daniel, petitioned the chief chef, saying that your Hebrew laws did not permit such a diet. He requested a different fare for him and his roommates. At great risk of offending His Majesty the king, I allowed the chef to prepare four meals for each seating in accordance with your laws as an experiment for ten days. I assumed at the end of ten days, the four at Daniel's table would be thinner and weaker than the rest."

Ashpenaz ordered Daniel and his three friends to stand at their table.

"As I compare these four with the rest of you, I judge them as stouter and more muscular than most of the others. I am also told that these four have been first or second to cross the finish line in the race around the palace every time. This fact has caused quite a stir among the king's court as we have discussed it. It also frustrated the king when I reported it to him. I regret allowing the experiment, but we cannot deny its results. Therefore, from this point forward, all of you will be served food that satisfies the laws of your Hebrew nation.

I will expect you to develop your bodies more aggressively and to see more balance in who wins the races. I will see you in class shortly."

Daniel's eyes scanned the room to see the immediate reaction of the group. To his pleasant surprise, there was no reaction. They all continued eating their last meal from the king's menu. He was pleased with yet another indication of the unity that had developed among them and their acceptance of his leadership. But he sensed there were bigger tests looming.

12

HISTORICAL REVELATION

Dr. McCarty's office smelled of the pepperoni and tomato sauce stuck to the empty box crumpled in the trash can. He and his inquisitive protégé had been discussing Daniel for four hours, breaking only for bladder relief and the delivered food. Kyle had never been so focused on learning anything and couldn't believe the time had passed so quickly.

"I've kept you much too long," the professor said, glancing at the Roman numeral clock above his door. "But you have been the most attentive student I have had in years. I couldn't give you enough of my favorite prophet. Let me close this session with some additional perspective."

Kyle repositioned in the chair and readied himself for beginning page eleven in his notebook.

The professor flipped the pages of his Bible to the left. "God loves His own as a parent loves his or her child but with a far greater love than we can imagine. He gives us every opportunity and reminder to live godly lives. But He is just. In His holiness, He cannot overlook sin.

"The Jews of both Israel and Judah had been instructed thoroughly regarding God's parameters. He warned throughout their history of what His wrath would entail if they were unrepentant and rebellious. Historically, as far back as 1400 B.C.—eight hundred years before the generation of Daniel—God was specific on the consequences of disobedience. Moses wrote the first words of warning in Deuteronomy, the fifth and last book of the Pentateuch. After God had given His people the Ten Commandments and assured them of their prosperity and security while they honored Him, He spelled out the punishment for rejecting Him. Listen to some excerpts from what is now chapter twenty-eight."

"But it shall come about, if you do not obey the LORD your God, to observe to do all His commandments and His statutes with which I charge you today, that all these curses will come upon you and overtake you . . . The LORD shall cause you to be defeated before your enemies . . . Your sons and your daughters shall be given to another people, while your eyes look on and yearn for them continually, but there will be nothing you can do. . . . The LORD will bring you and your king, whom you set over you, to a nation which neither you nor your fathers have known, and there you shall serve other gods, wood and stone. . . . You shall have sons and daughters but they will not be yours, for they will go into captivity. . . It shall come about that as the LORD delighted over you to prosper you, and multiply you, so the LORD will delight over you to make you perish and destroy you; and you will be torn from the land where you are entering to possess it. Moreover, the LORD will scatter you among all peoples, from one end of the earth to the other end of the earth; and there you shall serve other gods, wood and stone, which you or your fathers have not known."[1]

"Moses probably didn't realize the exact judgment God described through him would be meted out to his generation's descendants eight centuries later," Dr. McCarty added.

---

1 Deuteronomy 28:15, 25, 32, 36, 41, 63-64

"It's amazing that God warned them so clearly, and they paid no attention," Kyle said. "But I have to say, it seems that if He loved His own people so much, He wouldn't have done such a horrible thing."

"We must understand, the people who committed the sins caused the judgment. God only pronounced the judgment. Think of it this way. Let's say a thief broke into your parents' house and shot your mother and father in cold blood. The murderer came before the judge for arraignment, and the judge said, 'I see this is your first murder, and you have only a few thefts on your record. You seem like a good man, so I'm going to dismiss this charge. You're free to go.' How would you feel about that?"

"Of course, I would be outraged."

"Justice would not have been served, right? If we mortals require justice for wrongdoing, how much more would God, Who cannot be unjust, require it? Love requires justice."

Kyle nodded slowly.

"Almost a century prior to Babylon's invasion, Isaiah prophesied with specifics what would happen to Judah. He even wrote about the young men being the first to be taken captive. This is from Isaiah 39, recording his conversation with King Hezekiah."

The professor quickly located the scripture passage. "Behold, the days are coming when all that is in your house and all that your fathers have laid up in store to this day will be carried to Babylon; nothing will be left,' says the Lord. 'And *some* of your sons who will issue from you, whom you will beget, will be taken away, and they will become officials in the palace of the king of Babylon.'"[2]

---

2 Isaiah 39:6-7

"Whoa!" Kyle said. "Even after the fifty kids were taken by Nebuchadnezzar, no one made the connection to Isaiah's prophecy written a century earlier?"

"Oh, I'm sure Jeremiah and a few others did. But the vast ma[...] of the people apparently had no interest in the writings and [...] read them. The priests didn't want to believe God would jud[...] own. It was an inconvenient truth. They would only speak w[...] people wanted to hear."

"God was pleading with them right up to the time of the[...] but they wouldn't listen," Kyle said.

"Just before Nebuchadnezzar took the boys and treasures in[...] invasion, Jeremiah railed against Jerusalem for their being [...] to his years of warning. Listen to this from Jeremiah 25:

From the thirteenth year of Josiah the son of Amon, k[...] Judah, even to this day, these twenty-three years the w[...] the LORD has come to me, and I have spoken to you[...] and again, but you have not listened. And the LORD has sent to you all His servants the prophets again and again, but you have not listened nor inclined your ear to hear ... Therefore, thus says the LORD of hosts, *Because you have not obeyed My words, behold, I will send and take all the families of the north, declares the LORD, and I will send to Nebuchadnezzar king of Babylon, My servant, and will bring them against this land and against its inhabitants and against all these nations round about; and I will utterly destroy them and make them a horror and a hissing, and an everlasting desolation.'*[3]

---

3 Jeremiah 25:3-4, 8-9

"Note that Jeremiah eluded to not only his twenty-three years of prophesying, but also to many other prophets they had also ignored," Dr. McCarty added. "Just in the Bible alone are the works of seventeen prophets, all pointing to the ultimate judgment of Israel and Judah. There were many others whose writings were not canonized or have been lost."

"With all the warnings, I still wonder how they could not have recognized their plight and changed to avoid the consequences," Kyle said.

"I would like to answer that question with a couple of questions. Why are people today rejecting God? Why are they rebelling against His instructions presented clearly in the Bible? In the last half-century, He has been taken out of many areas of our lives. We have declined exponentially in morals and traditional values. The Church is being increasingly considered unnecessary. People have become more dependent on materialism, government, and technology than on the truths of God."

"So, why aren't there modern-day prophets warning us like those we've been discussing?"

"Well, we don't see prophets today like those in Daniel's time who received visions and audible messages from God. God tells us through the writer of the New Testament book of Hebrews that what He once spoke through the prophets, He now speaks through His Son, Jesus. We have the entire New Testament providing truths for living and warnings of sin's consequences. In addition, we now have the Holy Spirit to help us understand it."

"So, He doesn't speak through His people anymore?"

"Oh, yes, more than He ever did through the prophets. We have an abundance of pastors, Bible teachers, evangelists, Christian authors, and worship leaders who project God's messages to us constantly through our churches and various media. Plus, more recently, God has given us the technology of internet websites, email, social media, and eBooks. These provide instant access anywhere, anytime, to endless knowledge of His messages. God is far from silent today. He is calling out to this generation more loudly and more frequently than He ever did with the ancient Hebrews. We have absolutely no excuse for not understanding God's truths, His justice, and the rewards and consequences for our decisions."

After a still and quiet moment, Kyle replied, "Man, I've never thought about these things in my life. Judah back then was so much like America today. I want to know more, Dr. McCarty."

"We have just scratched the surface. There is so much richness in prophecy that God wants me to share with you. Just wait until you see what happens next in Daniel's life. But it's getting late, so let's wrap it up for tonight. How about we meet next time at my house for dinner? I would love for you to meet my wife."

"I don't want to impose. I sure wasn't expecting . . ."

"Not at all. Jennifer makes the best chicken cacciatore this side of the Mississippi. I say that out of respect for my mom, who lives on the other side of the Mississippi. She's ninety-two, still lives alone, and cooks her own . . . you know . . . chicken cacciatore."

Kyle chuckled. "Just text me with the day and time. I'll be there. Thanks."

13

After three grueling years of cultural indoctrination, Daniel, now eighteen years old, and thirty-nine other exiles were declared qualified for service in the king's court. Nine of the young men were determined inferior and assigned to lower-level servant positions outside the palace. The young men had received extensive education and indoctrination every day of the year. Their bodies were trim and muscular—fit for high endurance after the rigorous physical training. They had made hundreds of visits near and far to experience processes of the government, operations of trade and craft, programs of agriculture, practices of religion, and works of art. Stresses of frequent oral, manual, and physical tests were exceeded only by their comprehensive final examinations, which took a week to complete.

After a brief ceremony in the palace great hall with compliments from Ashpenaz, King Nebuchadnezzar made a grand entrance with royal trumpets blaring. His regal purple robe and garish red turban trimmed in jewels seemed to brighten the room. This was the first time the exiles had seen the king since getting a glimpse of him during his entry into Jerusalem. Remembering his appearance as a field army king made this royal palace regalia seem even more elegant. His former scruffy beard was now tightly waved, obviously by a hot iron. The king made a few remarks, then announced individual assignments.

"Based on my consideration of the recommendations of my chief of officials, Ashpenaz, I decree the following assignments," the king read from his script.

One-by-one, he went through the list of names, attaching a palace assignment to each name. Some were to become recorders of the king's actions and proclamations; some would be chefs; others were to serve as palace facility coordinators; and a few of the brightest would receive further training in the healing arts to ultimately attend to the sick and injured in the king's court.

Daniel's anxiety rose with every announcement, waiting to hear his name. Finally, there were only four names left.

"I have a special assignment for Daniel, Mishael, Azariah, and Hananiah," the king said. "You four will remain here with me for a moment after the others are released to Ashpenaz."

"But before you are dismissed, I have one more announcement. You are now all Chaldeans, citizens of Babylonia. You must release your ties to your Hebrew roots. Therefore, you will assume Chaldean names. You will use these names both publicly and privately from this day forward. Embrace these identities with pride."

The king called out the new names of each individual. "Liron is now Ramman; Zamir is now Nergal-Edir; Yadid is now Ishum."

He continued through thirty-six name changes without mentioning Daniel and his three friends. Daniel was uneasy and confused about the strange situation facing the four. He was confident they had performed with excellence over the past three years. Many times, they had discussed privately how, although applying their fullest effort, their superior successes had seemed supernatural. They believed God had shown special favor toward them.

Soon, the entire palace hall was vacated, except for the four young men and King Nebuchadnezzar. They stood motionless and noticeably nervous before him.

"I'm sure you are wondering why I singled out you four," the king said.

"Yes, Your Highness," Daniel replied softly, his head bowed.

"I have been receiving reports on the individual progress of all forty-nine of you since you accompanied me back from Jerusalem. You four have consistently been evaluated as the top performers in every aspect of your preparation for service in my kingdom. In fact, your final testing placed your intelligence and physical condition superior to any of my palace servants and advisors. I had not anticipated this level of qualification from any of you young Hebrews. Daniel, I was also made aware of your exceptional ability as the leader of your group."

The king paused and paced in front of them, eyeing each one individually.

"Therefore, I have decided to create four new positions in my court. You will be groomed for special service as my personal advisors. I must have the wisest counsel available to anyone on the earth. You will integrate with my palace magicians, sorcerers, and astrologers. They are in touch with our gods. I welcome your counsel from your Hebrew God. You will learn from my advisors, and they will learn from you. As you share your wisdom with the other advisors and they teach you the ways of their craft, I will expect far better counsel than I now have."

The four looked at each other in dismay. Daniel knew the other three were as shocked as he was. He was deeply honored and humbled by the appointment but at a loss as to how he and his friends could reconcile their Hebraic absolute beliefs with the closed fraternity of pagans.

"One last thing," the king continued. "I have saved bestowing your new names for this private setting. Daniel, your name shall be Belteshazzar. The name means, 'Bel, protect his life.' Hananiah, you will be called Shadrach, meaning 'under the command of Aku.' Mishael, you will become Meshach, which means, 'who is like Aku.' And Azariah will be known as Abednego. Your scholastic performance has earned you this name, which means, 'servant of Nego.' Learn the significance of those names, and you will bear them proudly as Chaldeans. Now, go to Ashpenaz, who will show you to your new quarters with the other advisors."

The new monikers were an embarrassment to Daniel and the other three. They knew from their religious indoctrination that the names reflected those of Babylon's pagan gods. Bel was another name for Marduk, the chief Babylonian god. Aku was the moon god, and Nego was the god of learning and writing.

As they walked out unescorted, Daniel glanced up at the huge statue of Marduk. *I have just been issued the official name of Bel, or Marduk, protect his life. My new name is "Marduk will protect me." What blasphemy against Yahweh!*

He prayed silently, *Yahweh, forgive me. I abhor this name. Show me and my friends what we should do to avoid alienating ourselves from You and our Hebrew roots.*

Again, the four would share a room. But this time, it was larger with four private cubicles partitioned with white linen fabric stretched over a wooden frame. Daniel placed his bag of belongings on his bed, which looked considerably more comfortable than what he had endured for the past three years. He viewed his semi-private area, glad to see the table, chair, and wardrobe just for his use. He was impressed with the chandelier of oil lamps already lighted. Opening the shutters of the large window, Daniel was refreshed by the sunlight filling the room and the pleasant view of the meticulously manicured palace gardens.

The roommates gathered around the wood-fueled furnace in the center of the common area of the room. Cool days were the norm for that time of the year, and nights would have been intolerably cold without the woolen blankets. The furnace was full of wood and warming the room on their arrival. Ashpenaz had explained they would no longer be keeping their furnace burning. Lower palace servants would be doing that chore.

"Brothers, we are in a very awkward situation, and I'm not sure how to react," Daniel said. "Yahweh has placed us in a position of great potential for influencing a dark culture. Perhaps He has orchestrated this miraculous assignment to show Himself as the one true God. The problem will be maintaining our positions while being true to the laws of Yahweh."

"Nebuchadnezzar expects us to just assimilate into his counsel of sorcerers and astrologers, who summon pagan gods and search the stars for answers," Azariah said.

"He thinks we will bring our Hebrew Yahweh into the mix, while accepting their gods as equal to ours," Mishael added. "We would be fools to be so unfaithful to Yahweh."

"Speaking of unfaithfulness, what do we do with our names?" Hananiah asked. "We were all named by our parents according to the attributes of Yahweh. How can I now accept being called Aku? And

Mishael, will Yahweh not bring further judgment on you for assuming the name that glorifies the moon god? Azariah, will you honor Yahweh by being named after the god of learning and writing? How do you feel, Daniel, about exchanging your Hebrew name, which means 'God is my Judge,' for one which means you are relying on the main god of the Babylonians for protection?"

"I have not been so afraid since the day we learned we were captives on our way to this place," Azariah confessed. "What is going to happen when the king learns we will not meet his expectations?"

"You each speak with a heavy heart like mine," Daniel said. "This is the most difficult test we have faced since leaving our families. We must give Yahweh time to speak to us. We must constantly pray for wisdom from Him."

As the sun set on their first day as members of the king's council of advisors, the four were shown to their new dinner table, where they first saw the other advisors. Daniel could think of nothing they had experienced over the past three years that made him feel as misplaced as this setting. He counted forty-four others, all appearing older than he, wearing white robes with brown hooded capes over their shoulders and hanging to their waist. Six of them were women. All eyes were on him and his three friends.

One of the older advisors approached the newcomers' table and placed his hand sequentially on each of their heads as a greeting. "Welcome to our clan," he said. "I am Bulludhu, the chief of the magicians. We are honored the king has added you to this family. I will be in charge of your accommodations and duties."

Bulludhu then turned to face the group. "Brothers and sisters, allow me to present to you the new members we have been anticipating.

We welcome Belteshazzar, Abednego, Meshach, and Shadrach. As you know, they are Hebrews from the land of Judah, and we will want to learn much about their God and their special knowledge and gifts. Now, let us enjoy our meals."

Daniel was surprised that the food served to their table was according to Hebrew law. That preference had obviously followed them through the palace kitchen channels. He wondered whether the other exiles were getting the same treatment at their assigned locations. He looked around the room, studying the group hoping for clues as to their personalities and how he and his friends could relate to them. There was focused discussion at each table, occasionally interrupted by laughter.

When the four returned to their room, each one had a white robe and brown hooded cape lying on his bed. A new pair of sandals was at the foot of each bed.

"I suppose this is the last official acknowledgement of our positions," Daniel said. "We now have our personal advisor uniform." He forced a chuckle. "I recommend we pray ourselves to sleep pleading for Yahweh to show us the way we need to react to all that has happened today."

The next day, Bulludhu escorted the four new additions on a tour of the advisors' section of the palace. Their new advisor attire felt awkward but also comforted them in allowing them to be less conspicuous. Bulludhu introduced them to each one of their colleagues individually. Some were in their work rooms reading; some were in corners of the rooms drawing or calculating with charcoal and slate; others were in the common area seated on the floor in small groups. Daniel was impressed at the intensity with which they all were conducting their duties.

A few were working on specific assignments from the king. Several were working on long-range projects to validate theories and policies for the kingdom. Some were simply studying stars and planets, comparing historical records of celestial positions with major historical events. These astrologers explained how relationships between heavenly bodies and past events could predict future events.

At their second evening meal, Bulludhu joined them at their table. "What are your thoughts after today?"

Daniel's three friends always deferred to him to speak first. "I was rather overwhelmed. I'm not sure what we can contribute to the wisdom and experience of the others."

"Oh, but you will," Bulludhu replied. "You were chosen from the brightest Jerusalem had to offer. Besides that, we are familiar with your God's miraculous feats performed among your people. But our gods would be very angry if we tried to use the powers of your God for our good. We need you to be the channel through which your God will conduct His mighty deeds for our favor."

That expectation made Daniel nauseous. *Yahweh must be laughing at you right now.* "We hope to not disappoint you," he replied.

"The four of you will bring a welcomed freshness to our work. I plan to separate you, allowing each one to contribute to one of the various functional cohorts. Each of the four cohorts will now consist of twelve advisors. Belteshazzar, you will be in the cohort led by Arua. They are studying the art of dream interpretation. Meshach, I am assigning you to the astrologers under our chief astrologer, Nin-girsu. Abednego will study the spells and incantations from the ancient Sumerians with the cohort of Khu-hea. And, Shadrach, you will learn the magician craft with our chief of magicians, Amilanu." Bulludhu then walked each of the four to his assigned group and gave initial instruction regarding their assimilation.

After spending the next day learning the purposes, processes, and procedures of the groups, Daniel and his friends returned to their quarters. Daniel had not been able to eat much of anything from the dinner table due to his nervousness and pressures from the day of spiritual darkness. He felt the need to say something to his roommates that would bring some sense and clarity to the outlandish experience. However, his own conflicted soul left him with no ability to reconcile their dilemma.

Hananiah broke the silence. "I cannot do this! I am supposed to learn to perform miracles through magic by calling on the gods of Babylon. Amilanu said that every day, we would read about and discuss the crafts of Sumerian magicians of old and practice them, striving for perfection. We will be in demand by the king when the supernatural is needed. We in this room know for certain the only legitimate miracles are those of Yahweh. He is our Master. How can we serve many masters?"

"We can't serve many masters," Mishael said. "And being faithful to Yahweh in our present situation will get us reassigned to low-level servitude or death. I think I would prefer either to what I am facing now. Watching the stars to predict the future is not my calling. It is an offense to Yahweh."

"I slept very little last night as I appealed to Yahweh to reveal His will and purpose for us in this pagan land," said Daniel. "I didn't receive an answer. Throughout this day, I felt I was abandoned by Him. But I am just now sensing clarity as to what Yahweh desires of us. Keep in mind, we did not choose to be here. It was chosen for us. We may be the victims of the sins of our people and the first action of Yahweh's judgment, but we did not reject Him. Therefore, if we remain faithful to Him, He will remain faithful to us."

"But for us to remain faithful to Him means opposing the Babylonians and their gods," said Azariah. "That would mean slavery or the grave."

"Not necessarily, although we must be ready to accept those consequences if that is our destiny," Daniel continued. "But I believe Yahweh has us here for a purpose—perhaps to shine His light on this dark culture. A few with the power of Yahweh can make a difference in the many with manmade gods. He will show us how to survive, maybe even thrive, taking our place among these heathens while being unshakable in our commitment to Him."

"But we would be disagreeing with everything the other advisors profess," Mishael said.

"So be it," Daniel replied. "As long as we show respect, we would only be carrying out our instructions from Butludhu to add our Hebrew God to their sources of wisdom. When they speak of their gods in the stars, tell them we believe our God made the stars. When they try to craft miracles from magic, let them know that we believe only Yahweh can perform miracles. As my colleagues study dream interpretations, I will pray that Yahweh shows me how to interpret dreams better than they can."

This discussion continued into the early hours of the morning, ending with a unanimous conclusion that they would trust God to keep them in their assigned positions while they maintained their faith and loyalty to Him.

*

After three months of intense study and experimentation in the realm of dream interpretation, Daniel's cohort had made little progress. Numerous times, members had described their personal dreams for the others to interpret. As they would call on their various gods for insight, Daniel would pray to Yahweh for the meaning. Receiving nothing from Yahweh, he would not contribute anything to the effort. The few successes of the others were deemed invalid as being nothing more than random chance.

One morning when Daniel's cohort gathered for their day of study, they were surprised to find Bulludhu sitting on a cushion in their meeting area.

"Pardon my intrusion, gentlemen, but I wanted to meet with you first thing this morning," he said. "I want to tell you about a strange dream I had last night before it departs from my memory."

Daniel could see from the body language of the others that they were as perplexed as he about this unexpected request. He assumed their chief wanted to examine their progress with his own personal dream to be interpreted. They all arranged cushions for seating, encircling Bulludhu, who began revealing his dream.

"Deep into the night, I saw four brown cows in a field, and one of them was far more beautiful than the others. The beautiful cow stood amid tall, luscious, green grass, but the other cows were eating from shorter grass of a lighter green. Then there appeared out of the wilderness a young, white calf, which joined the beautiful brown cow in the tall, green grass. The calf immediately began to grow, and its coat became shiny like the snow on the mountain tops. In just moments, it became much larger than the beautiful brown cow, and all the brown cows turned to face the white cow as if to honor it. At that time, I awoke and wondered what this dream could mean."

Daniel and the others realized immediately what Bulludhu was expecting.

"You have given us a challenging test," Arua responded to Bulludhu. "Allow us to delve deeply into your dream today and tonight. We will have you an interpretation tomorrow morning."

"Very well. I will be here anxiously awaiting your revelation," Bulludhu responded as he walked away.

For the rest of the day, the cohort worked feverishly to determine the interpretation of the dream. Daniel was amused by the bizarre initial methods of the others. "Please excuse me. I believe some time alone with my God would be my most valuable contribution to this matter. I will return shortly."

A nearby stairway led to a section of the palace's flat roof. Daniel soaked in the warm afternoon sun and the light breeze at this highest accessible level of the building. From there, he could see most of the city, which stretched almost to the horizon. The view of Babylon from that vantage point caused unexpected emotions to well up in his soul. For the first time in a long while, he felt the heaviness of being an exile in a strange land. Three years and many distractions had subdued thoughts of his family and homeland. Suddenly, the overwhelming magnitude of the city made him feel so misplaced and lonely.

Pacing slowly around the perimeter of the roof while scanning the cityscape, Daniel was reminded of another young man who had been taken from his family and thrust into a foreign land. Joseph, before his exile, had a dream about one of his sheaves of grain rising up over his eleven brothers' sheaves. Then his brothers' sheaves bowed down to his sheaf. In a later dream, the sun, moon, and eleven stars bowed down to him.

I memorized this story from the writings of Moses, and I recall that Joseph eventually ruled over all of Egypt as the Pharaoh's highest official. Thus, he ruled over his brothers, who migrated to Egypt.

Daniel ceased his walking and contemplated the story of Joseph further. He began to see similarities between Joseph's dreams and Bulludhu's dream. Daniel's mind was clearly focused. He dropped to his knees and gazed upward.

"Thank you, Yahweh, for revealing Bulludhu's dream to me."

Just before dark, he joined his other colleagues. They welcomed him back, anxious to hear what he had learned from his God. But first, they wanted to tell him what they had determined.

"We were finally able to find a very interesting revelation," Arua said. "The beautiful brown cow was Bulludhu. The white calf was the brown cow's spiritual alter ego that will elevate his status and influence with the king. Bulludhu will become one with the spirit and increase greatly in wisdom and reputation in the king's court."

Daniel turned his head momentarily, afraid that his laughing inside would expose itself externally. Composing himself, he told them of his revelation, entrusting to God the expected hostile response.

"I was placed with you in order to add the wisdom of my God to the sources we call on for our counsel. I took the description of Bulludhu's dream to Yahweh and prayed for a clear interpretation. I was surprised by His revelation, which is beyond my imagination. The large brown cow *is* Bulludhu. The other cows are all the wisemen who have long been subject to Bulludhu's oversight. Bulludhu enjoys fame and honor in the court of the king made possible by the wise counsel of his subjects. Then, the wisemen were joined by one from a distant land and a different culture. That one will surpass the others in wisdom and influence and will rise above even Bulludhu in the king's court."

Daniel could see the tension building on the faces of everyone else.

"Shall I assume this one who will supposedly have authority over us is you, young Belteshazzar?" Arua snapped, wagging his head and raising his eyebrows. "Surely you don't believe we will accept such an outlandish interpretation from your God. Bulludhu would be furious if he heard such a prediction. For your sake, he will hear only our interpretation. Otherwise, he would ask the king to banish you to the domestic servants' quarters as unfit for any advisory cohort."

Every element of Daniel's soul screamed for strong rebuttal of their response. But he felt an overriding call for restraint. "Very well," he said. "You have my interpretation representing Yahweh. Present what you wish."

The next morning, the cohort gathered early at Arua's direction to ensure that they didn't find Bulludhu waiting for them again. Before they could fully rehearse how they would present the interpretation, Bulludhu appeared in the doorway.

"Welcome, Chief Bulludhu," Arua said, motioning toward a fluffed cushion. "Please take a seat. We are pleased to have the interpretation of your dream. The stars, the gods, and the incense have all revealed the precise meaning of this complex vision from your sleep."

After Arua explained their interpretation, Bulludhu rose from his cushion with excitement. "That makes perfect sense!" Bulludhu exclaimed. "The gods will show favor on me and increase my standing with the king as his trusted advisor. All advisors will also benefit from such confidence from the king in our craft. I will anticipate the spirits of the gods as they inhabit my soul. We are experiencing a miracle, Arua. You are all miracle workers."

Since little was being accomplished in study or discussions due to celebration of the dream interpretation, Daniel departed early to have some time alone in his room. He needed to reset his mind and heart regarding his role and purpose. *If I understood God's interpretation of Bulludhu's dream correctly, I am destined to rise above all the other advisors. How can that possibly be?* He had difficulty focusing on his future because his mind kept drifting to the past. His soul ached for the familiar environs of home, his family, and the simple pleasures of Jerusalem. Oh, how he needed the embrace of his mother.

When his three friends joined him in their room that evening, Daniel told them of his experience. They were awestruck by what God had revealed to him on the rooftop.

"Surely, Yahweh has an incredible plan for your future in Babylon," Hananiah said.

"We were not torn from our families and homeland just to serve a pagan king in a godless land," Mishael added. "We are victims of the sins of Judah, but Yahweh is preparing us for something beyond our imagination."

The thee friends gathered around Daniel, cupped his head in their hands, and prayed long prayers of intercession and blessing on him.

14

For over a year since the interpretation of Bulludhu's dream, Daniel had been shunned by the men of his cohort. He spent every day with them studying the Sumerian historical writings about dreams, tolerating their prayers and rituals to their various gods, and watching their observations of incense smoke and oil shapes on water.

As opportunities increased for interpreting dreams of officials of the king's court, Daniel was in attendance but was never asked to participate. Remembering his prediction to excel to the position of their chief, they were unified in their efforts to not give that prediction any opportunity for fruition. Arua and the leaders of the other cohorts ostracized him and prohibited his access to any of the higher officials. The only communication they had with him involved routine schedules and duties. Through it all, Daniel remained disciplined in his responsibilities and never retaliated or demanded recognition.

One day, at midmorning, Bulludhu interrupted Arua's cohort. "Gentlemen, we have a request for a dream interpretation from none other than King Nebuchadnezzar himself. He is troubled by a strange, recurring dream that has kept him awake for several nights. He is well aware of the reputation your cohort has attained in interpreting dreams of many of his court officials. Quickly, bring with you any writings and equipment you may need and walk with me to the king's chambers."

Arua, surprised but excited, immediately gave directions. "Collect any Sumerian scrolls you may need, the incense and oil pots, and fire boxes."

Arua and his eleven other dream interpreters entered the king's outer chamber after two guards opened the tall, bronze entrance doors. After they had walked into the hall in ceremonial columns and stood at attention, Ashpenaz positioned himself before them and announced the king loudly.

"Behold the king of the great empire of Babylon, King Nebuchadnezzar!"

Bulludhu's wisemen, following his lead, bowed at the waist; then everyone took their seats on the floor. The king sat in a large, decorative chair of highly polished wood. The cushioned chair's arms and back were artistically carved in ornate designs. The king's beard was unkempt without the tight waves he normally displayed. He appeared to be somewhat disturbed as he fidgeted with his robe. After a lengthy pause that made his audience a little nervous, the king spoke.

"I had a dream, and my spirit is anxious to understand the dream."

After another moment of uncomfortable silence, Bulludhu replied, "O king, live forever! Tell the dream to your servants, and we will declare the interpretation."

"That is why I have you wisemen," Nebuchadnezzar raised his voice. "The command from me is firm. If you do not make known to me the dream and its interpretation, you will be torn limb from limb, and your houses will be made a rubbish heap."

Arua gasped, along with his men. Some began to whisper to others. Daniel was stunned, but silent.

"Quiet!" the king shouted. "But . . . if you declare the dream and its interpretation, you will receive from me gifts and a reward and great honor. Therefore, declare to me the dream and its interpretation."

Arua stood. "O king, live forever! You have the best interpreters of dreams of all Chaldea ready to serve you. Let the king tell the dream to his servants, and we will declare the interpretation."

The king rose from his seat, folded his arms, and spoke sternly. "If you are truly in touch with the gods and have perfected the crafts of the Sumerian astrologers and seers, you are able to see the dream I dreamed and interpret it. If not, what use would I have for deceitful advisors? I know for certain that you are bargaining for time, inasmuch as you have seen that the command from me is firm. If you do not make the dream known to me, there is only one decree for you. For you have agreed together to speak lying and corrupt words before me until the situation is changed. Therefore, tell me the dream that I may know you can declare to me its interpretation."

Bulludhu took a step forward and knelt on his knees. "O king, there is not a man on earth who could declare what the king has requested. No great king or ruler has ever asked anything like this of any magician, conjurer, or Chaldean. Moreover, the thing which the king demands is difficult, and there is no one else who could declare it to the king except gods, whose dwelling place is not with mortal flesh."

The king was enraged. With clenched fist above his head and his face red, saliva sprayed from his mouth as he yelled to his guards, "Destroy every wiseman of Babylon, these who have failed me today and all of the others. Kill their families and burn their houses. I will not have such imposters enjoying royal privileges and eating the king's food."

Daniel's heart pounded. His body shook. He wanted to flee, but there was no place to run. Chaotic movement and mumbling ensued among the condemned advisors. The guards began to encircle the group with swords drawn.

As they started to exit, the king called out, "My order includes the four Hebrews taking up space in my palace!"

Daniel overheard the guards talking about temporarily holding them in a prison room until their execution that afternoon. He recalled hearing frightful stories of King Nebuchadnezzar's temperament. He had supposedly had his brother and family killed during his coronation to ensure the brother would not take his throne while he rejoined his army in Judah.

The guards gathered up all advisors and marched them to the holding prison. Stuffed in the middle of the forty-nine prisoners inside the cramped room, Daniel began to inch his way to the front entrance, while praying silently for God's protection for him and all the others. The women were wailing, and many of the men were sobbing loudly. He could hear Bulludhu trying to reduce the panic with words of encouragement. Breathing was difficult, and the odor of perspiration combined with the dank room was sickening.

Eventually, he forced his way to the metal entrance door and found himself pressed up to the body of a guard. He had hoped to speak to a guard but hadn't expected to greet him this way. The guard pushed him back roughly and cursed.

"I have something very important to tell the captain of the guard. It pertains to the king," Daniel said.

"The captain will not listen to a dead man," the guard replied.

"I have a secret the king must hear before I die. I must tell the captain in private. If you refuse my request, the king's blood will be on your hands."

The guard stared at him grimly for quite some time, then turned to open the door. He clutched the nape of Daniel's neck tightly and led him to the captain.

"Forgive me, Captain Arioch," the guard addressed the captain. "This Hebrew is from the condemned wisemen and insists that he has an important message for the king."

Arioch growled and spat on the floor. "Make your statement quickly."

"Sir, for what reason is the decree from the king so urgent?" Daniel chose his words carefully. "We can surely interpret his elusive dream if granted a few hours to research it and receive Divine guidance."

"You must understand, the king depends on his seers, astrologers, magicians, and sorcerers to give him counsel beyond human capability," Arioch said. "He hears from the gods through them. After this morning, he is convinced that you and the rest are fake and that you have been playing him for a fool all along."

"We can redeem ourselves," Daniel said, hearing the wailing of his fellow advisors behind him. "By morning, we will have the interpretation the king needs. If not possible from collective efforts, I will have the interpretation from Yahweh, the Creator."

"The king will not show favor on you, Hebrew! He even made sure I understood that I was to kill you and your Hebrew friends, as well as the Chaldean wisemen."

"Please take me to him," Daniel pleaded. "Yahweh is a God of miracles. He will cause the king to hear me out. Letting me speak to him could save all of those condemned to die and please His Highness with an interpretation of his dream."

Waiting for a response that didn't come, Daniel made his last point.

"Sir, if the king is capable of such a rampage as witnessed this morning, who can say that he won't execute his court officials next—and perhaps his palace guards. We must appease him now. You have little to lose and much to gain."

As they approached the decorative steel doors to the king's chambers, Arioch warned Daniel, "I will go in and make your case while you wait here. If you try to escape, I will be a dead man and so will you before the sun sets."

"My feet will not move," Daniel promised.

Even through the thick wall and door, Daniel could hear the king's loud and agitated voice. He had no doubt that his request for a one-on-one audience with the now-enraged ruler of the empire would not be well-received. He hoped the king's paranoia would override his ire, leaving him curious enough to give Daniel a hearing. The door opened, and Arioch motioned for Daniel to come inside.

"With great reluctance, His Highness will hear you briefly. This had better be good."

Daniel stood nervously in front of the king and bowed at the waist. The king just glared at him, saying nothing.

"O king, live forever, I have come to assure you that your dream can be both described and interpreted by your humble servant. When you chose us four Hebrews to join your counsel of wisemen and women, I was overjoyed to hear you say you welcomed our counsel from our Yahweh. You also said you expected to receive even better results from all your advisors with the inclusion of our Yahweh. Yet my Yahweh, the God above all gods, has not been consulted in this matter. He will surely reveal your dream to me. However, I will need time to consult Yahweh regarding your dream. I beg you, Your Highness, grant me until morning to describe your dream and interpret its meaning. If my revelation is acceptable to you, I further plead that you spare the lives of all the wisemen and women, so they can learn more from Yahweh."

King Nebuchadnezzar stood. Daniel feared the king was about to lash out at him. Instead, he paced back and forth in front of his chair for an inordinate amount of time.

"Because of my goodness and against my better judgment, I will grant you until tomorrow's sunrise to consult your God. You and your cohort will, along with Bulludhu, stand before me on this floor and describe my dream. If you fail to describe it precisely and explain its meaning, I will consider all the wisemen and women of Babylon powerless and of no value to me. I will order the execution furnace to be fired up. You and all the other advisors and their families will be burned to death. I have spoken. Now, leave."

Arioch swiftly pushed Daniel out the door and escorted him back toward the prison room.

"Sir, I cannot adequately pray to Yahweh in the crowded and noisy prison room. Also, it pleases Yahweh when others are praying. Please excuse my Hebrew friends and me from the prison, so we can pray together at our residence, seeking the answer to the king's dream. Post a guard with us if you must, but we need a quiet and serene place to pray."

Grumbling exceedingly about the concessions he was being asked to make, Arioch eventually agreed to Daniel's request.

It was past midnight before Daniel and his three friends were alone in their room. A guard was posted outside their door. Daniel meticulously reviewed the past events of the day with the others. His faith would now be challenged more than any other time in his life.

"I have just promised the king of Babylon that I would describe and interpret a dream of which I have no knowledge whatsoever," he confessed. "Unless Yahweh chooses to reveal his dream tonight, we will not see another sunset."

"Nebuchadnezzar is determined to destroy all of his counselors, so he has given us an assignment impossible to accomplish," Mishael blurted, his voice breaking with emotion.

"The only hope for all of us is to cry out to Yahweh for mercy," Daniel said. "Let us lie down with our faces to the floor and pray in unison throughout these early morning hours for a miraculous revelation."

From that moment until just before daybreak, the four young men lay in a circle on the floor, head to head, pleading audibly and simultaneously for their God to show the king's dream clearly.

As the darkness began to dissipate into dim light, suddenly Daniel felt the eerie presence of someone else in the room. He looked up, and standing near the door was a figure in the form of a man. Although he had a human shape, Daniel could see the man was not human, because his face, hands, legs, and feet were glowing with a brightness that illuminated the entire room. Daniel squinted. No number of candles and lamps had ever produced such brilliance in the room. The man was dressed in pure white linen with a belt of gleaming gold around his waist. His piercing eyes were like white-hot coals.

Standing next to the man was a large, strange-looking, human-like statue. Although not emitting the brightness of the man, it, too, was glimmering from various metals that formed its structure.

Then, the man began to speak in the Hebrew language. His deep voice resonated loudly throughout the room, echoing off the walls and causing Daniel to cover his ears loosely with his hands.

"Stand, Daniel!" the man commanded. "I have been given a message for you."

Stunned and shaking, Daniel rose to his feet. He was still able to listen intently to the explicit description and explanation delivered by the man concerning the statue. Suddenly, the two figures disappeared as rapidly as they had appeared. The room was dark again, except for the faint light from a window foretelling the imminent rising of the sun.

Daniel's three friends were still lying face-down, engaged in their prayers.

"Did you see that?" Daniel exclaimed. "Did you hear it?"

"Hear what?" two of them asked in unison. All three stood slowly, exhausted from their intense prayers.

"Th . . . the man, the statue!"

"You're scaring me, Daniel," Azariah said.

"A man, maybe an angel, was just here in this room! You didn't see him?"

The three looked at each other, shrugging their shoulders. "Obviously, we missed something very strange," Hananiah said, not sure Daniel wasn't hallucinating.

"Maybe it was a vision just meant for me or a dream, but it was real—very real," Daniel said. "The man explained King Nebuchadnezzar's dream."

Daniel knelt with his friends as he thanked and praised God for His revelation. Just as he finished, three bangs on the door startled all four of them.

15

Daniel recognized the voice as Arioch's. *The day of supposed doom for all the wisemen and women of Babylon has begun. The day I was to die, along with my friends in the fire pit.* But he was certain he now knew King Nebuchadnezzar's dream and just hoped his interpretation would satisfy the king and spare many lives.

Having donned their wisemen outfits, the four headed for the door. Daniel noticed the sun's first rays through their window had cast a bright light on the floor in front of the door where the angel had stood. "Thank You, Yahweh," he whispered.

"Did your God tell you the king's dream, Belteshazzar?" Arioch asked as he and another guard escorted them toward the king's chambers.

"Yes, He did," Daniel replied with a voice of confidence. "Do not destroy the wisemen of Babylon! Take me into the king's presence, and I will declare the interpretation to the king."

"This should be interesting," Arioch said. "The fires are burning intensely in the furnace. May you disappoint the executioners."

"I have two requests," Daniel said to Arioch. "My three friends helped in obtaining the interpretation, so I would like them to be present in the king's chamber. I also ask that the dream interpretation cohort be in attendance, along with Bulludhu."

"You are trying my patience, young man."

"The cohort and I are in this together. We are a team of advisors. My interpretation will be on their behalf. Bulludhu oversees all of us and will be responsible for what I reveal."

Arioch sighed and ordered the other guard to release those requested and bring them to the king's chambers.

Soon, the dream interpreter cohort, along with Bulludhu, joined Daniel and his three friends just outside the door to the chambers.

"Ah, Belteshazzar, the savior of the wisemen and women of Babylon," Bulludhu acknowledged Daniel. "Arioch told us that you claim to have a revelation of the king's dream."

"Yes, sir," Daniel replied. "In a vision, Yahweh showed me the dream and its meaning. I am here to humbly present the vision to the king on behalf of you and our cohort."

"I see. I suppose we should thank you for delaying the death of us all until today. Your delay tactic has allowed us prisoners to see one more sunrise."

"I believe Yahweh will grant us many more sunrises after we redeem ourselves this morning."

"I also understand from Arua that your interpretation of my dream portended that you would rise in the kingdom to rule over all of us. The only one to rule over us, Belteshazzar, is the king, and his rule over us will end today as we all are marched into the fiery pit, victims of his insane ruthlessness."

The door opened, and Arioch led his prisoners into the chambers.

As they all stood before the king's empty chair, the crimson satin curtain parted, and Ashpenaz entered and proclaimed the king's entry.

Daniel struggled to maintain confidence in the opulent room graced with the king's presence in his regal robe and turban. He felt so overwhelmed, fearing his knees would buckle. *Who am I to be instructing the king? Yahweh, give me strength.*

King Nebuchadnezzar sat and leaned forward in his chair, "So, Belteshazzar, are you able to make known to me the dream I have seen and its interpretation?"

"O king, live forever. As for the mystery about which the king has inquired, neither wisemen, conjurers, magicians, nor diviners are able to declare it to the king. However, there is a God in Heaven Who reveals mysteries, and He has made known to King Nebuchadnezzar what will take place in the latter days. This was your dream and the visions in your mind while on your bed."

Daniel swallowed with difficulty from his dry mouth and breathed deeply. "As for you, O king, while on your bed, your thoughts turned to what would take place in the future; and He Who reveals mysteries has made known to you what will take place. But as for me, this mystery had not been revealed to me for any wisdom residing in me more than in any other living man but for the purpose of making the interpretation known to the king and that you may understand the thoughts of your mind."

Daniel began to feel a relieving peace. He sensed a renewing of strength like the second wind he got racing his fellow exiles during physical training.

"You, O king, were looking, and behold, there was a single great statue; that statue which was large and of extraordinary splendor, was standing in front of you, and its appearance was awesome. The head of the statue *was made* of fine gold, its breast and its arms of silver, its belly and its thighs of bronze, its legs of iron, its feet partly of iron and partly of clay. You continued looking until a stone was cut out without hands, and it struck the statue on its feet of iron and clay and crushed them.

"Then, the iron, the clay, the bronze, the silver and the gold were crushed all at the same time and became like chaff from the summer threshing floors; and the wind carried them away so that not a trace of them was found. But the stone that struck the statue became a great mountain and filled the whole earth."

King Nebuchadnezzar stood abruptly; his eyes widened, and his mouth gaped. He raised his hands. "I have told no one! No one in all Babylon could describe this dream to me, except it be revealed by a god."

Daniel knew by the king's confirmation he was speaking with the authority and influence of God. He continued. "This *was* the dream; now, we will tell its interpretation before the king. You, O king, are the king of kings, to whom the God of heaven has given the kingdom, the power, the strength and the glory. And whenever the sons of men dwell, *or* the beasts of the field, or the birds of the sky, He has given *them* into your hand and has caused you to rule over them all. You are the head of gold.

"After you, there will arise another kingdom inferior to you, then another third kingdom of bronze, which will rule over all the earth. Then there will be a fourth kingdom as strong as iron; inasmuch as iron crushes and shatters all things, so, like iron that breaks in pieces, it will crush and break all these in pieces. In that you saw the feet and toes, partly of potter's clay and partly of iron, it will be a divided

---

1 Daniel 2: 31-35

kingdom; but it will have in it the toughness of iron, inasmuch as you saw the iron mixed with common clay. *As the toes of the feet were* partly of iron and partly of pottery, *so* some of the kingdom will be strong and part of it will be brittle. And in that you saw the iron mixed with common clay, they will combine with one another in the seed of men; but they will not adhere to one another, even as iron does not combine with pottery.

"In the days of those kings the God of heaven will set up a kingdom which will never be destroyed, and *that* kingdom will not be left for another people; it will crush and put an end to all these kingdoms, but it will itself endure forever. Inasmuch as you saw that a stone was cut out of the mountain without hands and that it crushed the iron, the bronze, the clay, the silver and the gold, the great God has made known to the king what will take place in the future; so the dream is true and its interpretation is trustworthy."

Instantly, King Nebuchadnezzar dropped to his knees in front of his chair and bent forward with his face to the floor. Daniel could hear the gasps and murmurs from his cohort behind him. Both Ashpenaz and Arioch stepped toward the king to render assistance but stopped just a few steps from him, seeming to be conflicted as to how to react to this display of behavior never seen before.

Daniel was initially as shocked as everyone else but quickly realized that he was watching a man who was overwhelmed by the Spirit of God. Daniel knew the feeling. He had experienced the same just a few hours earlier in his room. The king lifted his head, while remaining on his knees. He ordered Ashpenaz to bring him gold coins, jewelry, and fragrant incense to present to Belteshazzar.

---

2 Daniel 2:36-45

"Surely your God is a God of gods and a Lord of kings and a revealer of mysteries, since you have been able to reveal this mystery,"[3] Nebuchadnezzar confessed. "Your God has spoken to me through you, Belteshazzar, and interpreted my dream that no one else could even describe—certainly not any of my other dream-seers." The king stood as his eyes moved past Daniel to the dream cohort focusing specifically on Arua, then Bulludhu. They both lowered their heads.

"Arioch, release the wisemen and women from the prison and bring them all here under guard," the king ordered, then left through the curtained entrance to his chamber. Ashpenaz followed.

The atmosphere in the outer chamber room where Daniel remained with his cohort and Bulludhu was filled with stress and animosity. The others were talking among themselves, but no one spoke to Daniel. He avoided eye contact, not knowing how to respond to the situation. Daniel had never felt so lonely and wondered if this awkward time was ever going to end.

The clang of the door lock announced the arrival of the rest of the advisors from the prison. Formed behind the dream cohort, they stood quietly. King Nebuchadnezzar entered the room again after yet another announcement by Ashpenaz. He stood before them, this time conducting himself more formally.

"Wisemen and women of my kingdom, as you now know, your friend Belteshazzar has described and interpreted my dream, which the other dream interpreters failed to do. For that, I am indeed grateful and impressed. I now know that the rest of you, although having provided me wise counsel and predictions in the past, are either losing your powers or have reached your peak of knowledge and wisdom. Or

---

3 Daniel 2:47

188 DANIEL: PROPHET AT THE KING'S COMMAND

perhaps your gods have abandoned you. After yesterday's disappointment, I lost all confidence in the whole lot of you. I wanted you all destroyed and your families."

Daniel didn't look behind himself but visualized all heads bowed. He was looking the king in the eye. The king paced in a circle as he spoke.

"However, Belteshazzar gives me hope. His Hebrew God is certainly present in his soul. He is wiser than any of you, and his God can do miracles through him for my kingdom. He possesses what I want all of you to possess. Therefore, I am going to withhold your execution. You will learn the wisdom of Belteshazzar. You will learn about his God. I am promoting him to oversee all of you. Beginning immediately, Belteshazzar is chief over all the wisemen and women of Babylon."

Daniel was breathless. Nebuchadnezzar nodded to Ashpenaz, who stepped forward with a heavy, dark blue robe draped over his forearm and carrying a decoratively carved, wooden box. The king took the robe, walked behind Daniel, and placed it around his shoulders. The white fur trim and gold embroidery appointing the robe rivaled the king's red ensemble in its majesty.

Ashpenaz opened the box and tilted it toward Daniel. He could see coins filling half of the box and pieces of jewelry lying on the coins.

"As a gift from me and a tribute to your God, I present you with 120 shekels of gold, a silver bracelet, a jar of the finest incense, and a gold emerald stone ring."

Ashpenaz whispered, "Put on the jewelry." Daniel complied with some difficulty, due to his hands and fingers shaking and feeling almost numb with shock. He wondered whether the dream interpretation and the subsequent events were not his own dream.

"Furthermore," Nebuchadnezzar continued, "I am naming Belteshazzar ruler over the whole province of Babylon."

Daniel gasped in unison with everyone behind him. He had learned all about the regional divisions of the Babylonian kingdom. He understood that he had just been placed in charge of the region from the mouth of the Persian Gulf in the south to several days journey north. The province lay from the foothills of the Median Empire in the east to the desert wilderness to the west. This was a vast area rich for farming, fed by the Tigris and Euphrates Rivers and anchored by the juggernaut city of Babylon.

Daniel searched for appropriate words that would both honor the king and pacify his colleagues but was so overwhelmed that only a simple response came to him. "O king, live forever; I am not worthy of such honor. I humbly and thankfully assure you of my faithful and fervent service to you."

"Come with me," the king said, smiling. "Ashpenaz, release the wisemen and women back to their homes."

Daniel followed the king through the fabric curtain, down a short hallway, and through a curtain of hanging beads into the king's private living quarters. Daniel had only imagined the opulence of the room he was about to enter, but what he beheld was far beyond his expectations. The stone hallway floor gave way to a thick, plush carpet artfully woven with floral designs. Large tapestries covering almost all of four walls hung from the edges of the wooden ceiling sculptured with figures of wild animals, mostly lions. The tapestries were woven to depict trees and shrubs of many types. Couches and chairs around the room were covered in wool fabric with silver trim. An elegant, silver chandelier of tall, burning candles hung from the recessed center of the ceiling.

"Welcome to my humble abode," the king said, spreading his arms.

"O king, I am speechless and undeserving to be in your presence."

"I heard voices and knew we had a guest." The soft, mellow voice came from just off Daniel's shoulder.

"Ah, Belteshazzar," the king exclaimed. "Meet my beautiful bride, Amytis."

So many things that Daniel had learned during his three years of indoctrination seemed to be surfacing. He recalled the alliance formed between Babylon and the Medes over a decade earlier in order to wage war against the Assyrians. Cyaxares, king of the Medes, signed a pact with Nabopolassar, king of Babylon and father of Nebuchadnezzar. Cyaxares gave his daughter, Amytis, to Nabopolassar's son, Nebuchadnezzar, to wed as a seal of the new alliance between the two empires. They had been married for only three years. Nebuchadnezzar had married his first wife, Nitokris, just before the campaign that dealt the final blow to Assyria. They had two daughters, Nitocris and Kashshaia. Because Nitokris had not borne the king a son in two births, he had banished her from the palace. It would be incumbent on Amytis to give him a son as heir to the throne.

"Indeed, a pleasure to meet you, Your Highness," Daniel said, bowing.

She was gorgeous. He judged her to be about thirty. The dark olive skin of her perfect face shone in the candlelight, taking the twenty-year-old's breath away. Being around very few females since his captivity had not affected his natural impulses, even after the traumatic events of the past few hours. His eyes couldn't avoid her coal black hair swept behind her ears, exposing her long, golden earrings that almost brushed her bare shoulders. Across her forehead was a chain of small golden disks that matched her bold necklace and bracelet. The blue, silk gown flowed gracefully from her shoulders to her feet.

And this is her casual dress for around the home.

"The king told me of your interpretation of his dream," she said. "He was very upset for days about the recurring dream and the failure of his sorcerers to tell him its meaning."

"Excuse us, my dear," Nebuchadnezzar interrupted. "I need to have an important conversation with Belteshazzar."

For the rest of the morning, the king related in detail the expectations he had for Daniel. He explained that he would relieve his current province ruler and give Daniel full authority over all provincial affairs. With all civil matters managed by Daniel, the king would focus mostly on his army and relationships with other kings. Bulludhu would step down from chief of the magicians, giving Daniel total oversight of all the advisors. Daniel would be the king's principal advisor on all aspects of governing.

"I am also appointing you chief of the court officials," the king said. "Ashpenaz will become my personal assistant. This way, you will answer to no one but me in the full breadth of your responsibilities. I will have a room furnished just off my outer chamber as your residence."

Daniel realized that would place both the king and Daniel just a few steps from the outer chamber, where they would meet frequently. Although still in a daze, he was able to organize his thoughts better by the end of the meeting. Realizing the risk, he decided to make one request before the meeting closed.

"Your Majesty, please consider one request from your grateful and humble servant."

The king nodded.

"I am so flattered by your confidence in me, and I want to be everything you expect of me. But I must remind you of my youth and inexperience. My three friends, the ones you recognized with me for being at the top of our studies, are also men of great wisdom and close to Yahweh, Who revealed your dream. I need their assistance in order to best serve the king."

"In what capacity do you need them? It will be done."

"Please consider appointing them my administrators for the province of Babylon and remove them from their advisor cohorts. Give them another place of residence and let them report to me. We will make an exceptional team for you."

"Done. I will have Ashpenaz make the adjustments to the court staff as his last official act."

Later that afternoon, Daniel headed to his room, anxious to see his three friends. A personal servant inherited from the predecessor of his new position had already been assigned to him. The man, Raviv, twice Daniel's age, accompanied him to carry his belongings from his previous room to his new quarters.

As they discussed their new relationship during the short walk, Daniel had to look up slightly to make eye contact with one of few people in the palace who was taller than he. His thin build, long legs, and darker skin gave away his Egyptian nationality. He explained that his grandfather was taken with many others from Egypt to Nineveh to serve the court of the Assyrian King Esarhaddon when he conquered Egypt seventy years earlier. His father was born in Nineveh and served in the palace there until his death by the sword of the Babylonians during the seizure of the city seven years ago.

Raviv would now serve Daniel as a eunuch, having been castrated in Nineveh. When he was fifteen, King Sinshariskun decreed that all palace servants become eunuchs. Daniel had learned from his indoctrination that his servant's condition was also shared by the other servants in Nebuchadnezzar's court.

Raviv had continued the family line of palace servants in Nineveh until being a victim of the Babylonian razing of the city. He told of being taken from Nineveh to Babylon by Nebuchadnezzar's father, Nabopolassar, to serve in the Babylon palace.

"You and I have a lot in common," Daniel said. "We are both exiles from the land of our birth and are living a lonely life without our families, even though surrounded by throngs of people."

"But, Your Greatness, we are worlds apart in many ways," Raviv replied. "You have risen to royalty, while I will always be a servant. And . . . you have your masculinity."

As Daniel entered his room, all three friends rushed to form a group hug.

"This is so very awkward," Daniel said. "I am not worthy of the honor bestowed on me today, and I am not deserving of your celebration."

"We are truly happy for you, Daniel, and you are indeed deserving," Mishael countered. "And I say that not because we, too, have been elevated to places of such high honor serving under you."

"You have already heard?" Daniel asked. "I have been rehearsing all the way here how I was going to announce the good news. Word travels quickly in the palace."

"Ashpenaz himself came to visit us and describe our new duties," Azariah explained. "He also will have servants come this evening to

move our belongings to a much larger room in the palace near where
you will live."

That reminded Daniel. "Oh, forgive me, this is my . . . ah . . . servant,
Raviv." Raviv bowed slightly from the doorway.

"You know, the events of this morning are not setting well with
Bulludhu, Arua, and all the advisors," Hananiah said. "Ashpenaz cautioned us to be on guard because of the chaos and hostility that has
arisen among the cohorts. He said Bulludhu is in a rage."

"Yes, our fortune is quite a mixed blessing," Daniel added. "My predecessor will be very upset about his dismissal and will no doubt blame
me for it. And the province administrators you will replace will not
become your friends. I did not expect gratitude for saving their lives."

Daniel peered out the window at the courtyard and surrounding
sections of the palace. "By the miracle of Yahweh, we have been placed
at the highest levels in the palace of the world's greatest kingdom. Yet
we are just young Hebrews in exile. The only explanation of this is
the miraculous work of Yahweh. But the upheaval in the king's court
places us at tremendous risk. We must pray constantly that the hand
of the One Who placed us here will give us protection and wisdom
for this seemingly impossible task."

Daniel turned to face his friends, dropped to his knees, and motioned for them to join him in crying out to Yahweh.

16

"The king is ready for your meeting," Ashpenaz announced.

Daniel gathered his parchments containing a couple of decrees for the provincial satraps and a palace proclamation that he had written for the king's approval. He strolled down the corridor to the king's quarters in his dark blue robe and white turban, the standard attire for these scheduled meetings. Although visiting with the king almost every day casually, this once-a-week meeting was set aside for specific agenda desired by both men. He took his seat as always next to the king's chair. He stood as the king entered and sat next to him.

"Well, how was Belteshazzar's week?" the king asked.

"Nothing too out of the ordinary, Excellency."

"So, then, you have been threatened, verbally abused, disobeyed, lied to, and plotted against," Nebuchadnezzar said with a wry smile.

"A typical week," Daniel returned the quip.

"I am really sorry and quite agitated that most of the court has not yet adjusted to your position over them after nearly three years. But as I have told you before, I am impressed with your patience and tolerance of their animosity. I am amazed that you have been so tremendously effective in your duties, despite rebellious subordinates. Even in their jealousy, they recognize your superiority and subject themselves to it.

Your attention to the details of managing this vast kingdom has released me to concentrate on the higher-level issues we face. Leaving you in charge twice as I waged the campaigns against the neighbors of your homeland was very difficult for you, but you have prevailed with honor."

"Thank you, as always, Your Highness. Your confidence in me is recognized by my adversaries within the kingdom who honor my directions as being ultimately yours."

"I'm glad you feel that way because I need to inform you of some plans that you will not want to hear. You know that after you left Jerusalem, King Jehoiakim led your people in full compliance with my orders as my vassal for three years but then began to dissent. He withheld taxes, reached out to other nations for help, and urged other kings to oppose me. I forced surrounding nations to launch harassing attacks on Jerusalem to convince him to remain loyal to the only king who could save him."

Daniel had heard all of this from the king over the last three years and wondered how long it could continue without retribution. His body tensed at what he assumed he was about to hear.

Nebuchadnezzar continued, "Your former King Jehoiakim was killed last month in a skirmish with my soldiers there to oversee Judah's vassal government. His son, Jehoiachin, assumed his throne. That childish eighteen-year-old is now demanding that my soldiers depart the country. Of course, that is totally treasonous. I plan to take my army back to Jerusalem and finish the job I should have done when I foolishly negotiated a bloodless take-over and brought you and your colleagues to Babylon."

Immediately, Daniel's thoughts exploded. *What will happen to my family? Will the king order Jerusalem to be completely destroyed? Do I have enough influence on him to rail against this plan? What is the will of Yahweh in this? Yahweh, this has caught me unprepared. I need Your guidance. Give me Your words.*

After a moment of silence, but not enough time to rehearse his words in his mind, Daniel responded. "Your Highness, your plan troubles me deeply. The word that my people will die in the streets of battle—perhaps my father and mother, sisters and brother—causes great agony."

Daniel fought back the tears. "I am torn between agonizing over my people's demise and knowing the justice of Yahweh is being poured out on the same people for their rebellion. As painful as it is, I must understand and accept that you, O king, are the one Yahweh is using to carry out His righteous wrath."

"Belteshazzar, you are not acting like the second most powerful man in all of Babylon! You no longer have a family in Jerusalem. You are no longer a disgusting Hebrew. You are a Babylonian! I am your brother. The palace court is your family."

Nebuchadnezzar's voice grew louder as Daniel became more agitated with each statement. He wanted to counter with a hail of curses toward the king but knew that Yahweh's will was for him to be restrained.

The king stood and took a step toward Daniel. "Pharaoh Necho has been threatening from the west ever since our armies clashed three years ago, and King Cyaxares, my father-in-law, has the Medes planning to conquer me from the east. I'm not going to tolerate disloyalty from a puppet Judahite king of a nothing nation. He will feel the sword, along with his ignorant people who follow him. Jerusalem's agony will be on his hands."

The king turned and strode in quick steps toward his quarters but turned to face Daniel just before entering.

"And you, Belteshazzar, had better support this invasion to the fullest. Do not forget that had I not rescued you from your paltry life in Judah and lavished you with fame and fortune, you would be lying in your own blood on a dusty street in Jerusalem a few weeks from now. But you are a privileged Babylonian ruler, and you must be ruthless."

Daniel struggled for words. "My commitment is to you, my lord. But you must know that my ultimate allegiance is to Yahweh. And although I will serve Babylon according to direction from Yahweh, I will always be a Hebrew."

Nebuchadnezzar scoffed. "What god you follow is of no concern to me as long as you serve me with complete loyalty. You just said that your God was using me to execute His vengeance. Then, you should be ensuring I can do that with great success. General Maoz is implementing my plans. We will take fifteen thousand men. I am depending on you to generate the support necessary for the army to launch their journey to Jerusalem a week from now. Act swiftly, Belteshazzar. You are already behind schedule."

Daniel immediately summoned Hananiah, Mishael, and Azariah. Soon, the four were seated at the table in Daniel's chamber as he shared the king's plans.

"This is tearing at my heart, but I remain convinced that Yahweh has miraculously placed us in our prominent positions for His purpose. Yet I feel like a traitor to our own homeland. How can I lead the support of an invasion of Jerusalem that will be deadly to my own people—probably to my own family? How can I ask you to prepare Babylon to dispatch thousands of soldiers to destroy the walls of the

Holy City and kill many men, women, and children of Zion, including your families?"

The three stunned young men, heads bowed low, breathed heavily.

Hananiah, who had been massaging his temples while trying to process what he had heard, spoke. "Your first statement was the truth we must anchor ourselves to. We will never understand why we are in this position, but we would not be serving at this level if it were not the will of Yahweh. To defy the king would be sure death for us, and we would be taking ourselves out of His plan. Perhaps Yahweh will show us ways to influence this attack to make it less destructive and deadly."

"Maybe they will not kill everyone," Mishael added. "They might be convinced to bring back many into exile here as they did with us. What if they brought our families here to be reunited with us? I know it is unlikely, but it is possible."

"Anything is possible with Yahweh," Azariah said. "Who is to say that Judah's warriors would not defeat the larger Babylonian army as it happened with Gideon?"

"All that is true; but Gideon was a godly man, and Yahweh honored his plea. Sadly, we can't say that for our current king Jehoachin or his father. I'm afraid we're seeing what our prophets have been proclaiming right up to our own Jeremiah," said Daniel. "The just punishment of Yahweh is being inflicted on Judah. Our people will not prevail. Many will die. I hope some are brought back with the conquerors. Let's pray we see all our families again. I would give my life to see my father and mother, brother, and sisters walk through the gates of this city, knowing they had survived."

Daniel opened a scroll that had been lying on their table. "Although my nature says resist, my spirit says to conduct the duties of our

positions. I'm not sure why Yahweh chose to involve us in the destruction of our own people, but I am confident He has rightful purpose
in the invasion and our roles in it."

Twisting the handles of the papyrus scroll to the intended section,
Daniel continued. "Here is the deployment plan for the army. It pre-
scribes the logistical support for the fifteen thousand soldiers on the
three-month journey to Judah and back. You three will be responsible
for gathering the supplies and equipment. You will call up the reserve
warriors of Babylon as requisitioned by General Maoz's staff. The men
will receive refresher battle training and physical training from the
standing army. The plan details how you will redistribute the labor
forces of the city and surrounding country to maximize commercial productivity during the absence of most men. Many of the tasks,
especially the food preparation, will require working day and night
for the rest of the week. Of course, we will need to add women and
children to the labor force."

Daniel sensed the three administrators of the Babylon province
had just realized the full weight of their responsibilities in surge mode.
They appeared astounded at his demeanor as he assumed his role as
provincial ruler, but he knew they respected his leadership.

"This job is not new to you. We supported the Egyptian invasion
shortly after we were appointed to these positions. We managed all of
Babylon during the king's absence as total novices for several weeks.
We did the same when the army cleared out the opposition tribes of
northwestern Arabia. However, this is much larger and complex, as
well as shorter notice. We can do it."

Daniel visited the hubs of activity for the readying of the army
daily for the next seven days. He ordered corrections needed and

directed changes in processes that weren't meeting his standards of efficiency and speed. After meeting each evening with his three administrators, he ended his day with a late-night final progress report to King Nebuchadnezzar.

The next day, the sun had just broken the Saturday darkness when the entire convoy of the deploying army was formed and ready to depart. Thousands of weeping parents, wives, and children of the soldiers were gathered along the road all the way to the bridge to bid farewell to their beloved warriors. The families remaining behind realized fully that many of the soldiers, perhaps their own, would not return. Daniel stood next to the king's carriage at the front of the convoy, preceded only by the chariots of the guards. He had received thorough instructions from his king regarding his duties and authority, having, yet again, full charge over the palace court and all the kingdom.

At the king's command, the trumpeters sounded the call to arms, and the wheeled conveyances began to roll. The king gave Daniel one last eye-to-eye look. Daniel nodded and raised his right hand high in salute. By mid-morning, with only Raviv and a few well-wishers remaining along the street with him, Daniel could see only the dust cloud on the northern horizon.

He stood stately, gazing past the northern wall. The contemplation of his responsibilities while the king was away was consuming him. *I am but a twenty-three-year-old Hebrew. I should be newly married and starting a family in Jerusalem. Perhaps I would be a fledgling administrator serving in the Jerusalem palace. I would be kissing my mother and father every day. My siblings would be swarming around me. But I must remember with every breath I take that I am here because Yahweh is orchestrating everything. Why else would the most powerful king among kings go to conquer a nation and leave an inexperienced young native of that nation in charge of his kingdom? Yahweh has everyone in that cloud of dust under his control, including the king. Oh, Yahweh of my people and of this humble servant, I depend on You completely for ability far beyond my capacity. Without You, I will crumble. Order my every step.*

"Your Excellency, pardon me for interrupting your thoughts, but we must be going," Raviv said. "You have many meetings and other obligations today."

"No, Raviv. Reschedule everything for tomorrow. Today is the Sabbath. The court will rest for what is left of today. Tell all the officials I said to send their subordinates home to their families. Everyone has worked exhaustively for the last six days. We shall all rest on the seventh, *the Sabbath.*"

*

Five weeks had passed since the army contingent had left. Daniel had noticed his own tenseness for the last few days. His unsettled feelings were partially due to the openly reluctant response to his leadership from most of the court, especially the seers and magicians. Their lack of requests from him was in great contrast to their almost daily tasks from King Nebuchadnezzar, who had become confident in them again. The musicians and harem dancers who frequently entertained the elite guests of the king and his wife were now relegated to practice sessions with no call to perform. Daniel had canceled all theatrical performances at the amphitheater, which he considered inappropriate while the army was at war.

Almost every evening, shortly after dinner, Daniel bathed in a room uniquely designed for that purpose. The bathing room, next

to the king's chambers, was used only by the king, his wife, and
Daniel. Normally, they bathed in that order. The room, about thirty
feet square, had mud brick walls with a floor of hard bitumen tar.
The floor sloped to the center, where a sophisticated system of narrow clay troughs drained the water into the brick sewer lines and
ultimately to the river.

Raviv always supervised the servants for Daniel's bath, which was
more like a shower. Ashpenaz directed the servants for the bathing of
the king and Amytis. The male servants, being eunuchs, were unfazed
by assisting Amytis in her daily bathing ritual. They poured water
into large clay jars at ground level and raised the jars to the second
floor bathing room by a mechanical device. The device's endless chain
around two wheels was cranked into lifting motion by the servants.
Servants in the bathroom collected the jars and poured cool, refreshing
water over the bathers.

Daniel walked the short corridor to the bathroom at his appointed
time to meet Raviv. He opened the door and stopped immediately with
a gasp. In the center of the room, Amytis stood wringing her long
black hair, her body covered only with glimmering water reflecting
the light of the lanterns held by her servants. Raviv was standing at
her side, holding a towel over his forearm.

Daniel froze. Amytis' eyes met his. She smiled and made no attempt
to reach for her towel. Time and motion seemed to suspend. Daniel
regained his composure.

"I am so sorry, Your Highness. I—I beg your forgiveness. I didn't . . .
um." Daniel exited quickly, closing the door behind him.

Soon, Raviv knocked at Daniel's door and let himself in.

"What was that all about?" Daniel snapped.

"Your Greatness, I beg your forgiveness. It was a very awkward situation."

"Awkward is an extreme understatement. I have never been so embarrassed. This has placed me in a very precarious position. I have to interact with Amytis every day. I am responsible to the king for her. What am I supposed to say the next time we meet? 'Good morning, Your Highness, you are as beautiful naked as you are clothed?' She will doubtless tell the king of my intrusion into her bath. At the least, he will be suspicious of my intentions, and at most, I could lose my position, if not my life. Why didn't you alert me that my bath time would be delayed? And what were you doing overseeing her bathing? That is the job of Ashpenaz's servants."

"Please, let me explain, Your Greatness. With short notice, Ashpenaz asked me to supervise the bathing of Her Highness as he was doing another personal task for her. There was plenty of time before your appointed bath time, so I agreed. However, she tarried longer than normal. I could not leave her. I feared that you would arrive before she finished, but I was unable to get word to you. She must have known she was taking extra time. It was like she wanted you to interrupt her."

Daniel delayed his response, mulling over why the queen would want him to enter her bathroom. "I understand why you were conflicted as to how to handle the situation. Why do you think she extended her bath in anticipation of my arrival?"

"That is a mystery, Your Greatness. If I may be so bold, she may have arranged for me to replace Ashpenaz, knowing I would be less likely to insist she not encroach on your time. I sensed that she wanted you to walk in on her."

"I need time alone to think about this. We will talk in the morning."

"So, you won't be having your bath tonight?"

"Certainly not. I'm not opening that bathroom door again for a while."

Daniel avoided contact with Amytis for the next few days, while immersing himself in administrative obligations. The rebellious nature of the palace court had subsided somewhat by the sixth week of the king's absence. There were still several principal men who were clear in their disdain for Daniel and his three friends. The only thing that was preventing a rebellion was their knowing the king would execute all participants on his return. Even the army reserve left in Babylon could have likely been convinced by Ashpenaz, Bulludhu, and other displaced court staff to take down Daniel's position. He understood plainly that he had been appointed to lead a very disgruntled opposing force that was hoping for eventual retribution.

Just before sunset, Daniel was surprised by a knock at his chamber door. He opened the door to a very disheveled and obviously exhausted soldier he recognized as being from the deployed army.

"Greetings from King Nebuchadnezzar, Your Greatness," the soldier said, smelling of many days without a bath.

"Please come in. Have a seat. Let me get you some wine," Daniel replied.

Filling a goblet from a leather flask, Daniel conversed briefly about the young man's week-long trip on horseback but was anxious to receive his field report. Pulling up a chair facing the messenger, he inquired, "So, tell me the important news."

"After several days' encampment around the walls of Jerusalem wearing down the spirits and bodies of the Hebrews and building a ramp to the top of the lowest wall, our army broke through to the inner city. The enemy put up a bold fight for two days with even the women and children joining in the final hours. There was much death and destruction. Hebrew casualties outnumbered ours five to one. Finally, King Jehoiachin sent word to King Nebuchadnezzar requesting a meeting. The palace had been virtually destroyed, and our king demanded the meeting be outside the walls of the city. There, King Jehoiachin surrendered his vassal country to the kingdom of Babylonia."

It was news Daniel fully expected but dreaded with anguish from the time the army had marched out the bronze west gate. *My homeland has been destroyed; my people, probably my family, have been killed; and I am living in luxury on the wrong side of the battle line.*

"Did the king give you anything to tell me about my family?" Daniel asked.

"No, Your Greatness. I understand your concern, but I have given you the king's complete message, except about the exiles."

"Exiles?"

"After the surrender, the king ordered our army to seek out and marshal ten thousand of the fittest, brightest, and most affluent of the remaining population of Jerusalem, including most of the enemy soldiers who survived. When I departed, those were forming up outside the city. They will be brought here to serve the king as he sees fit."

Daniel remembered his earlier speculation with his friends that possibly Jerusalem captives might be brought back to Babylon. He had studied about how the Assyrians did the same with the survivors of the northern nation of Israel 125 years ago. His mind jumped to the possibility of reuniting with his family as well as many of his friends after eight long years. *Surely, my father met the criteria for captivity and exile, and my mother and siblings would accompany him.*

"What about young King Jehoiachin?" Daniel inquired. "He is five years my junior."

"He will be walking through the gate in chains behind King Nebuchadnezzar and with the throng of his subjects."

"I'm thankful he wasn't executed."

"The early surrender probably saved his life."

The messenger provided a few more details of the army operation and relayed the king's orders to construct a temporary prison area for the captives. Daniel would gather his thoughts in the bed before sleeping—his best time for analyzing situations—and meet with his three friends the next morning. *We will need to begin quickly on the plans for the captives and the arrival of the army. Building a prison encampment for ten thousand people in five or six weeks will be a huge challenge.*

Daniel woke early, dreading to face Amytis for the first time since the bathing incident but knowing he had to inform her quickly of the king's anticipated return. He sent word to Ashpenaz to arrange for a meeting with her. Moments later, Daniel stood as she entered the outer chamber dressed exquisitely as always.

He bowed slightly. "Your Highness, I have important news from the king. But first, I want to humbly apologize for the intrusion into your bath. It was totally unintentional and a misunderstanding of schedule."

Amytis smiled, tilted her head, and ran her fingers through her hair. She stepped lightly toward Daniel. "No apology needed," she spoke softly. "Actually, I found the situation quite exhilarating."

Daniel inhaled deeply as she drew closer. She cupped his right hand in her left.

"I am so lonely. The king has been away more than at home for the past year."

Daniel stepped back, at a loss for words. Conflicted feelings overwhelmed him. He assessed the encounter for what it truly was but was surprised by how it tugged at him to surrender to it.

Yahweh, rescue me. I am weak.

He slipped his hand from hers and walked toward a window. "You must not look to me for relief from your loneliness. You are alluring, and your proposition is tempting." He faced her. "But, Your Highness, I could not bear to betray my king and, more importantly, my Yahweh."

"What am I supposed to do, Belteshazzar? I am alone most of the time in this cavernous palace with no one to relate to but my lowly servants. I long for Media with its beautiful mountains, luscious flowers, and trees. I crave my family. When the king is here, I can tolerate it; but alone, I am miserable." She sat and cried.

Daniel knelt in front of her. "I have found that happiness cannot be found in circumstances. Your contentment will only come from something greater than your own pleasures. My peace is in my Yahweh. You have observed the reality of Him in the miracle of my ascent in this position of authority."

"I am making efforts to be more spiritually aware. I summoned Bulludhu last week for advice."

Bulludhu! This should be interesting. "And what was his counsel?"

"He cautioned that his conversations with me must be strictly confidential. He inquired of the gods and recommended I pursue happiness where it could be found. He suggested I slowly, but seductively, draw you to myself, predicting you would be hesitant to acquiesce. He said the gods want me to be happy and that you could ultimately be my satisfaction when the king is away."

*Bulludhu's conspiracy to take me down! If I succumbed to the seduction,
he would alert the king, and I would be executed. My enemies are committed
to my demise, even by deceit if necessary.*

"So, the plan began in the bathing room?"

Amytis lowered her head. "I sent Ashpenaz on an errand and asked that
he have Raviv oversee my bath. I delayed, hoping you would walk in on me."

An awkward silence ensued as both mentally processed the revelation. Amytis wiped her remaining tears and forced a smile. "So, you
have a word from the king?"

Daniel stood. "Your Highness, the victory is won in Jerusalem. The
king is safe. He and the army have begun their journey home with
ten thousand exiles."

"Exiles! Ten thousand exiles?"

"Yes, it looks like many of my people who survived the invasion
will be residing here as slaves of Babylon."

"I . . . I'm so sorry. Here I have been burdening you with my longing
for my people and land. I tend to forget that you are as much a stranger
to Babylon as I am. I should be grateful that my people have not been
invaded and brought into bondage." She rose and stepped toward
Daniel, then stopped abruptly.

"I am deeply conflicted," Daniel said. "I want to defend and protect
my people, but my provincial ruler duties require that I exploit them
for Babylon."

"In many ways, we are both caught in the same trap, Belteshazzar.
My people may be next."

Daniel bowed, more formally this time, and began walking toward
his chamber. "I have some brutal weeks ahead preparing for the king's
arrival and provision for the exiles."

"Belteshazzar!" Amytis called out. "Be angry with my indiscretions, but please don't reject me."

He turned and gazed upon her momentarily and smiled. "Who could reject you?"

Later that morning, Daniel paid a visit to Bulludhu.

"What a surprise. The ruler finally visits his underlings," Bulludhu said. "Sad that we haven't seen you since the army deployed."

"I have had no need for advice sourced from pagan gods, signs in the sky, or animal entrails. My guidance comes from Yahweh. I will soon be meeting with you and the other seers to discuss how to begin considering the counsel of Yahweh."

"Do you really expect us to just disregard centuries of the sorcery traditions of the Sumerians and Chaldeans in favor of an unknown Hebrew God from Judah?"

"Yahweh is not unknown to you now. You have seen much evidence of His power in the interpretation of dreams and the miraculous rise of us Hebrew exiles over the past few years. You will need to begin advising the king and the Court from the guidance of Yahweh."

Bulludhu walked in a circle, his hands clasped behind his back. "The king chose the exact day to attack Jerusalem based on our counsel. When he returns, we will share the direction we have been given from the stars for him to erect a large golden image of himself for all of Babylon to worship. Our gods are elevating him to deity. Also, the gods desire the swift completion of the Babel tower."

"How soon you have forgotten the king's acknowledgement of Yahweh following my interpretation of his dream."

"I'm confident the king will be much more interested in our revelation of his ascent to deity than in humbling himself under a Hebrew God from the land he has just conquered."

Daniel worked to suppress his anger. "We will discuss this later. In the meantime, you will not approach the king with this nonsense of deity, golden images, and tower building."

Daniel walked away but stopped at a short distance to eye Bulludhu again. "Oh, your counsel to Amytis failed. Do not interfere further in her life. The king is a jealous man. But even if you don't incur the wrath of the king, I have the power to make your life miserable—and the will to do it. I hope you give me the opportunity."

watched disappear almost five months earlier was now reappearing on the late morning's northern horizon. An advance messenger from the army had notified him earlier that morning of the king's arrival at about noon with his almost fifteen thousand soldiers and ten thousand exiles.

Daniel had hoped to be physically fresh and mentally alert for the arrival ceremonies. But having had less than six weeks' notice to prepare for the exiles, he was exhausted. The planning, organizing, and directing of such a monumental undertaking had taken its toll on him and his assistants. The stress of selecting the location for settling the captives and designing its construction had caused many sleepless nights. He was conflicted, wanting to use his influence to provide a comfortable existence for his own people but knowing the king would not be pleased with more resources expended on them than the most basic subsistence.

Daniel and his three friends had chosen to construct a communal living settlement along the west bank of the Chebar canal just outside the east perimeters of the city. This irrigation channel, a tributary of the Euphrates River, was used to supply water to the gardens and farm plots in and around Babylon. It was relatively pure water and plentiful. Simple and austere shelters, each accommodating multiple families, had been built quickly by an augmented labor force.

Despite many complications, the project was completed just in time for occupancy. Daniel positioned himself near the west bridge entry about a hundred steps from the gate. He made a final visual sweep around him to confirm that the principal staff was all in place wearing their official robe and turban attire. Hundreds of the soldiers' family members and friends had lined the bridge after spreading palm branches on the surface. As the guards in chariots entered through the decorative stone archway, Daniel's memories of his arrival eight years ago overwhelmed him. He wondered whether the first impressions of the opulent walls, the imposing Babylon tower, and the terror of not knowing their fate were having the same impact now that he experienced then.

Soon, the king's entourage emerged from the gate, and Daniel could see the royal carriage. As it approached, Daniel saluted with his raised right hand. The carriage kept moving, and Daniel walked alongside.

"Welcome back, Your Excellency!" Daniel said loudly over the commotion. "All is well in Babylon and the kingdom. Ashpenaz will receive you at the palace. I will take charge of the exiles."

"Where are you establishing the exiles?"

"On the west bank of the Chebar, Excellency."

King Nebuchadnezzar smiled, nodded, and gave a slight wave of dismissal.

Apparently, we passed the first test. He seemed pleased. Now, to my people.

As he turned back toward the gate to await the first appearance of the Hebrew exiles, it struck him that he had been so caught up in the bustle that he had, for a moment, lost the thought of potentially welcoming his family. Tears formed. *Will I embrace them today?*

Seemingly, hours passed while the echelons of the army continued coming through the gate. Finally, Daniel recognized the break in the convoy as a very different-looking group appeared. The exiles were in ragged clothes, disheveled, and all on foot. Each was laden with a large bag containing what was obviously his or her total possessions. Guards walking alongside were bellowing instructions intended for many who didn't understand their language. Two of the guards a few steps in front of the exiles were holding up a man who was unstable in his walk. Daniel clearly identified the physical features of the first echelons as his beloved Hebrews. He couldn't suppress a broad smile, despite his heavy heart and tear-filled eyes.

My people of Judah. My people! O, Yahweh, they are captives under my authority. Yet they are my people. I belong to them. What do I do with this? Do not withhold Your wisdom from me. Please allow me to find my family among them. I am overcome. Yahweh, help me.

Daniel scanned each row. He was sure he recognized some faces but couldn't connect them with names. Suddenly, he focused on a young man, inconspicuous, but something was familiar. He walked toward him. *Is it really him? Yes!* He lifted his robe above his ankles and ran.

"Ezekiel! Ezekiel!

The young man snapped his attention to the direction of the voice and squinted to seek its source in the sun's midday brightness. Before he could focus, the man calling his name grabbed both of his arms tightly.

"Ezekiel! It is me, Daniel!"

"Daniel? Daniel, son of Karmiel?" Ezekiel stared at Daniel's face, his eyes bulging, as Daniel led him forcefully away from the others.

Ezekiel gaped. "What are you . . . why are you . . . you look official. Why are you not a slave of the Babylonians?"

"It's a long and complicated story. But first, I must know . . ."

Ezekiel looked back toward where he had been. A woman waved with a curious look. He waved back and motioned for her to continue walking.

"My wife, Peninah. I will catch up with her."

Daniel's eyes focused back at the exiles for another search. "My family. Tell me my family is with you."

Ezekiel looked deeply into Daniel's reddened eyes momentarily, then lowered his head.

Daniel gripped Ezekiel's forearms tightly.

"No! Please, no!" He dropped to his knees, still hanging on to his old friend. The sobs became wails. "My father, my mother, my brother, my sisters. Did they all die violently?"

"Your father was a very courageous man, Daniel." Ezekiel knelt in front of Daniel and placed a hand on his shoulder. "During our journey here, I learned more about what happened from some who witnessed your father's actions. When the invaders forced their way into the national treasury, Karmiel ordered his guards to defend it. After an initial clash leaving several dead, the guards fled. Your father stood in the entranceway alone, sword drawn. Someone said he yelled, 'This is Yahweh's provision for His people, and its protection is my duty.'"

Ezekiel's voice was breaking, "After looting the treasury, the Babylonian officer in charge ordered the rest of your family killed and your house burned in retaliation for your father's stand."

For a few minutes, the two embraced and wept uncontrollably, oblivious to the swirl of activity around them.

"This is of no consolation, but my family, except for my wife, didn't survive the attack either," Ezekiel said.

"I'm sorry." Daniel looked into Ezekiel's eyes. "I admired your father, Buzi, greatly. Our loss seems too great to bear, but Yahweh will comfort and strengthen."

Daniel stood and continued surveying the movement through the gate, imagining his family's appearance. He visualized each one of them eight years older than his remembrance.

"Would you walk with me to the Chebar canal?" Daniel asked Ezekiel. "Your wife will be there."

"Of course."

Raviv approached Daniel's side. "I will get your carriage and driver, Your Greatness."

"No, Raviv, I just need to walk."

"Very well, sir. I will get your guards."

"Your guards?" Ezekiel said in a hushed voice as two swordsmen came alongside the two men.

"As I said, it's complicated. I'll give you the short version of the story as we walk. But before that, what do you know about King Jehoiachin?"

"He is here with us, assuming he survived the journey. I have not seen him since Jerusalem, but our guards were ridiculing him along the way and said he was at the front of the line leading us into exile. The king's mother, Queen Nehushta, and five of his young sons from other wives and concubines are also among us, including Sheshbazzar, whom he has designated as his heir to the throne. Two other sons were killed in the attack."

Daniel remembered the man at the head of the exiles being stabilized by two guards. "That must have been King Jehoiachin I saw. The guards had symbolically placed him at the head of his people, taunting him as king of the Jews. Since Jehoiachin's children are with him, do the people remaining in Judah have a king?"

"Nebuchadnezzar installed Jehoiachin's uncle as king and changed his name to Zedekiah. He will reign over a disjointed nation of uneducated and low-skilled people now that the elite are enslaved to Babylon."

Ezekiel hardly said a word for the next half-hour as Daniel summarized his life since being taken away from his people.

"You were studying for the priesthood," Daniel said. "Did you continue that pursuit?"

"I was . . . I am a priest. I was serving in the temple under a mentor priest. You know they took all of the treasures from the temple, including the gold vessels Solomon had made three centuries ago."

The two men approached the ridge overlooking the Chebar. This spot had been Daniel's vantage point many times over the past weeks as he assessed the progress of the project and sent tasking messages to various foremen. But this time, he was watching his kinsmen file into the pathways between the many rows of shelters extending as far as could be seen in either direction along the banks of the canal. He could see hundreds of his supervisors assigning individuals and families to their austere accommodations. Soldiers were shoving and cursing. Many Hebrews were crying. He moaned, then turned to Ezekiel, seeking a comment or reaction. Ezekiel shook his head slowly as he viewed the clamor.

"Yahweh has purpose in all of this," Ezekiel said. "He still loves His people."

"That assurance is what has kept me sane for the last eight years. Praise be to Yahweh."

Daniel embraced his reconnected friend. "I must leave you now. One of my men will escort you to the compound and help you find your wife." He began the trek back to the palace. His heart felt like a millstone as he fought feelings of depression and anger.

For three days after his arrival, the king had not ventured from his chamber and had canceled all meetings and reports. Daniel had expected this, since it was his usual conduct after an arduous military campaign. On the fourth day, Ashpenaz set up a normal itinerary, beginning with an early morning meeting with Daniel. The king appeared rested and content.

"Ah, Belteshazzar, you have far exceeded my expectations in your preparation and settlement of the exiles. My dawn inspection of the compound from the ridge overlook gave me great confidence in the assimilation of our captives into our labor force."

"Thank you, Your Highness. The Hebrew people are known for their outstanding skills and craftsmanship as builders and artisans. Their agrarian culture also provides knowledge of crops and herds that will benefit the kingdom tremendously. With your permission, I will appropriate their unique talents toward accomplishments that were not possible prior their arrival."

"I do realize the Hebrews bring us special capabilities, but don't let your bias toward them affect your management of these people. They are servants of Babylon, Belteshazzar, and not to be given advantage over the lowest of Chaldeans. Besides, I have my own plans for their immediate efforts. I am directing two labor-intensive projects which will be accomplished by the Hebrews. They will apply the fine craftsmanship you tout to the erecting of a golden image of myself fifteen times my height. It will stand on the plain of Dura about a two-hour walk from our gates for all to see and pay homage to. At the same time, we must expedite our building of the Babel tower. It will be identical to the ancient original Tower of Babel, the highest structure in the world and a tribute to all the gods."

Direct from Balludim, I have underestimated him. He has gotten to the king inside of three days, perhaps with the help of Amytis. This cannot happen. The people of Yahweh must not use their precious skills to construct an idol or a tower to the pagan gods. Wisdom, Lord. Words, Yahweh.

"I understand, Your Excellency. Please allow me to think a few days on how best to accomplish your wishes."

"Granted, but I will not tolerate anything short of a full-scale effort on both projects."

Their meeting continued past midday as Daniel covered a multitude of reviews and updates and received guidance. The king reached for his meeting materials, signaling the end of the meeting.

"Excellency, if I may, I feel compelled to discuss something of a more personal nature with you. Please forgive me and send me away if this is inappropriate."

The king sighed. "Speak."

"I know you love Queen Amytis dearly with all of your heart, as she does you. When you leave for long periods, as the king must, I observe from a distance how her countenance falls. When I update her on your progress abroad, she often brings up how she misses her homeland with the beautiful trees and lush flowers on the mountainsides. When you are here, her mind is not occupied in this way. Only when she is lonely does her mind wander to the pleasures of her homeland, Median."

"You are talking nonsense, Belteshazzar."

"If it please the king, as your principal advisor, I humbly suggest you talk with the queen about her childhood memories and her longings for her former surroundings. I believe she will share her heart with you."

"You stretch me, Belteshazzar. I promise nothing. But if the time presents itself, I will consider your advice."

As the king's shifting in his chair signaled his readiness to end the meeting, Daniel lost hope that the loss of his family would even be mentioned.

"May I extend your patience just a moment longer, Your Excellency?" The king pursed his lips and nodded, not hiding his annoyance. "You probably know my entire family was killed in the invasion."

"No, I had not heard that," the king said unemotionally.

He sees no connection between my family and me, not even between the Hebrews and me.

"I understand my father was pierced by a Babylonian sword as he stood alone protecting the national treasury. In retaliation, my mother and siblings were killed and their house burned."

"Standing alone against the Babylonian army was not wise. Your father and his family could have been among the exiles."

"They were my family. I had hoped you would show some mercy to me by ensuring their survival."

The king stood abruptly. "Belteshazzar, conquering a city is complete chaos. It is rage and uncontrolled bloodshed. Do you really think the king can bestow favors on particular individuals in the heat of battle? And you, you have not had a family since leaving Jerusalem. You are a Babylonian. Your heritage is Chaldean. I thought you were beyond seeing yourself coming from Judah. You can't be my provincial ruler and keep thinking of yourself as a Jew, particularly now that they are our servants. The meeting is over."

Daniel returned to his room and went to bed immediately, although he didn't expect to be comforted by sleep. The king's words had been like a dagger thrust into his heart. *How am I going to fulfill the task Yahweh has given me?* Sleep deprivation overcame his depression, and he was asleep before sundown.

For the next three days, Daniel worked painstakingly with his three administrators to organize the settling of the exiles into the compound. He was determined to make the transition as easy as possible for his people while honoring his obligation to serve the best interests of the kingdom. This was proving to be a difficult balance.

A surprise visit from the king to the compound area during Daniel's on-site meeting with key staff was an unwelcomed distraction.

"Welcome, Your Excellency," Daniel said, raising his right hand.

"I thought it was a good afternoon to take a tour of the compound. You know I have never seen the project up close."

"Certainly. It will be my pleasure to show you around and inform you of our progress."

The king invited Daniel to ride next to him on his carriage, pulled by four horses and surrounded by palace guards. As the king was gazing at the compound, Daniel turned to his staff, shrugged, and stepped up on the carriage.

For the next two hours, Daniel and the king rode the full length of the compound. The king had many questions about the cost of the project, the mood of the exiles, logistics, and how best to use the capabilities of the captives for the benefit of the kingdom. Daniel had answers to every question that seemed to satisfy the king, although he admitted there were many unknowns to be resolved. When asked about capabilities, he was quick to reinforce the point that the Hebrews had special skills in building and agriculture management. He still hoped to dissuade the king from involving them in crafting an image of himself and from the completion of the Babel tower.

The king commanded the carriage driver to stop under a large shade tree, then asked his entourage to move some distance away to provide him some privacy.

"Belteshazzar, I am a strong-willed and cold-hearted man most of the time out of necessity as king. However, I am not ignorant, and I do know when to listen. I have given much thought to what you said at our last meeting about how Amytis longed for her homeland. We had a long talk last night about her displeasures. I know my absences don't help that emptiness inside her. Of course, I can't let her return to Media. But I do love her and desire the best for her. Do you have any advice for what a frustrated king can do to make his distraught queen happy?"

Daniel was caught off guard by this unprecedented display of humility and transparency. But he quickly recognized it as a God-given opportunity. He now understood why God had planted a strange idea in his mind over the past few days. "If it please the king, I would present something complex, but within the capabilities of the kingdom of Babylon. Since the queen can't return to Media, you can create a bit of Media here in Babylon. You have already cast a challenging vision for constructing many more large buildings within the city, along with redesigning walls and gates. You have the kingdom's finest engineers planning amazing waterworks and street pavings. You are a king with a penchant for elaborate building projects. Why not make Babylon the city of the most beautiful gardens and trees in the world, greater than anything in Media? I believe Amytis would be elated with such a project and might even become involved in it. It would be a gift from you to her."

Daniel was relieved to see the king smile and nod as he talked.

"That is an idea well worth considering," the king said. "Work up more preliminary details, and let's talk again soon."

"Absolutely. If I may suggest one more thing, sir, the exiles have the abilities and numbers to take the lead in such a venture. The other projects you plan can be accomplished successfully by Babylonian craftsmen and laborers. If it please the king, I request permission to factor the Hebrew work force into my initial planning for the gardens."

"We shall see," the king said after a pause. Daniel took that as a yes.

The next morning, Daniel and his three administrators met over breakfast and discussed the garden concept. Each of them was enthusiastic about the idea and prayed together for wisdom in how to proceed. Then all four paid an unannounced visit to a special resident of the city jail.

Daniel instructed the guard to unlock the iron door. He spoke in Hebrew. "Your Excellency, King Jehoiachin?"

The startled king looked up from a dimly lit corner of his room. "Who is it?"

"I am Daniel, son of Judah's treasurer, Karmiel. I was among those taken captive by King Nebuchadnezzar when your father was king."

King Jehoiachin stood quickly. "Ah, yes. I knew you were here. Ezekiel told me about your good fortune. Destiny has reversed our roles so that I am subject to you. It is humorous that you greet me as 'Your Excellency.'"

Daniel was struck by the king's appearing even more youthful than his age of eighteen. "Allow me to introduce my friends, who were taken from Jerusalem with me and many others. Meet Mishael, Azariah, and Hananiah." The three lowered their heads briefly to the king. "They are the administrators of the province of Babylon."

"Why do you visit me, and why the phony respect? I am lesser than the other Hebrew slave in this dreadful place. Few of them are imprisoned."

"Our respect is genuine, Your Excellency. You are still the king of Judah, and your people must recognize that while in exile."

"Of course, I am a king. Just look at my palace of thrown-together wood, my fine dirt floor, and my split-log throne. All my servants must be out sick. I'm not even allowed to see my wives."

"I cannot replicate your palace here, Excellency. But I will see what I can do to improve your conditions. It is essential that your people have a leader and some semblance of stability to avoid complete chaos. They need structure much like they are accustomed to." Daniel turned to his assistants. "See to it that all people in the compound, as well as our overseers and guards, understand that the exiles still have a king, King Jehoiachin, who will serve at the mercy of King Nebuchadnezzar."

"I'm not sure that will work in this environment," Jehoiachin said.

"I assume most of your staff members are somewhere in the compound," Daniel said. "Reorganize them and govern these ten thousand confused people from your prison room. You're the king. Make it work. One more thing. We have been given Babylonian names that must be used in public." He ensured Jehoiachin memorized the names and promised that all four of them would meet with him regularly.

Two weeks later, Daniel assumed temporary custody of King Jehoiachin and called the first meeting with him and his key staff members. He shared his vision for the monumental garden project. He explained that he wanted the exiles heavily engaged in the gardens to avoid their involvement in the building of the king's image and the Babel tower. He charged the king to organize and direct the most accomplished craftsmen and most expert agriculturalists among his people. They would design and plan the effort that could take several years to complete. Laborers for the construction would have to be selectively chosen according to age and skills. The king was enthusiastic and ready.

＊

Much activity and change of scenery had taken place since the arrival of the exiles four years prior. The Hebrew architects and landscaping experts had crafted a magnificent plan for the gardens. In cooperation with Babylonian engineers, huge wheeled equipment had been fabricated to haul rocks and dirt from outside the city to the steep, manmade mountain on the bank of the Euphrates. Gigantic columns shaped from baked brick were anchored into the sides of the mountain. These columns supported artistically carved troughs filled with rich Euphrates valley soil, where hundreds of shrubs, vines, flowers, and trees were being planted. These columns and plant-filled troughs cascaded from ground level to the top of the mountain, giving the appearance of lush greenery suspended in mid-air and rising to the sky.

Irrigation specialists among the exiles had designed a unique system that pumped water from the river to all levels of the gardens through a series of aqueducts. The pumps were powered by horses hitched to a large, horizontal wheel connected to a system of underground gears.

The entire project would take another three years. Finishing the intricate facades and adding the remaining plants, many of which were imported from Media, would be slow and tedious. Some of the trees and larger shrubs would not mature for another ten years.

Meanwhile, thousands of Babylonian laborers had been adding height and breadth to the Babylon tower for the past four years. It was a short distance from the gardens and was an affront to the Hebrews, who had to view it every day. It had been quite an architectural and engineering feat, as nothing else in the world had ever come close to its size and complexity. Completion of the specifications demanded by King Nebuchadnezzar would take at least another decade.

Daniel had purposely avoided giving much attention to the tower project. He had assigned the best leaders in Babylon to manage it and only took occasional reports from the project heads as necessary to brief the king on its progress. Daniel considered it a futile effort that accomplished nothing and was an insult to Yahweh.

Amytis usually accompanied her husband as they both inspected the garden project once or twice a week. She made many suggestions for designs more in keeping with the remembrances of her homeland.

King Nebuchadnezzar had only brought up the golden image a couple of times over the four years since he first mentioned it. Daniel assumed his silence on the subject was because he had cautioned the king against doing something that would upset the Hebrews, who were content with their focus on the gardens. The tower was offensive enough to the exiles, but a towering idol implying the deity of the king might take them over the edge. Besides, the labor intensity of the two ongoing projects left few workers for anything else in Babylon. Daniel hoped the whole idea of a golden image would ultimately be discarded.

The resourceful exiles, prodded by King Jehoiachin, had made major improvements in their shelters, adding rooms, improving furnishings, and landscaping with flowering plants and trees. Mishael, who was the administrator directly responsible for the compound, provided liberally the materials necessary for the enhancements.

Daniel had developed a close friendship with Ezekiel and visited him and Peninah often in the compound. They read together sections of the Torah and David's Psalms that Ezekiel had brought from Jerusalem. This had been the first access Daniel had to the Scriptures since leaving Judah. They prayed together in Ezekiel's shelter and occasionally knelt on the hill overlooking the compound. Ezekiel had been meeting regularly with skilled Hebrew scribes to develop a long-term effort to copy the scrolls of the Torah, as well as copies of writings by Joshua, Isaiah, David, Solomon, and others collected from among the exiles. His goal was that every Hebrew family would one day possess their own copies. Daniel ensured that the scribes had sufficient papyrus, reed quills, and ink to support the effort. He also made sure Ezekiel and the scribes were spared much of the duties of the other exiles, so they could devote ample time to studying and copying the scrolls.

During a visit from Daniel, Ezekiel unrolled a writing from Jeremiah that he had copied in the temple several years earlier while he and Daniel were being taught by the priest.

"Remember when I read this in your class in Jerusalem?" Ezekiel said.

"Yes!" Daniel said excitedly. "The priest invited you to our class to read what you had copied. I remember it like it was yesterday!"

Ezekiel read again the earlier warnings of God through his prophet, Jeremiah. Daniel placed his hand over the words as tears formed. "You last read this to me while we were young, free men in the land of Yahweh. Now, we read it again while living out the fulfillment of the prophecy. You and I occupy very different roles in this pagan nation that took us both captive. But we share the same status as strangers in a land that is not ours because our people have forsaken almighty Yahweh."

Ezekiel's hand covered Daniel's. "My brother, I need to share something with you. Yahweh is giving me a heavy burden for our people. Since leaving Jerusalem, they have had no prophet. They didn't heed the words of Jeremiah, Zephaniah, or Habakkuk, but at least they were hearing from Yahweh through them. Who do they have now? The last few weeks, my mind has been filled with thoughts and dreams of what Yahweh desires to say to His people of Abraham. I had recurring dreams of His trying to speak to them, but there is no voice to speak for Him. I strongly believed He is calling me to be a prophet to His people in captivity, but I felt so unworthy and incapable. Then, two days ago . . ."

Ezekiel paused and began to breath heavily, seeming to have difficulty with what he was about to say. "I . . . I was . . . sitting on the bank of the Chebar reading from the Torah. The breeze suddenly became a strong wind. It blew in a storm with dark, looming clouds and lightning brighter than anything I have ever seen. Out of this cloud came a glowing object with what looked like four human figures. As they came closer, they were very different from any human or animal on earth."

He paused again. "I can't find words to describe it. The scene seemed like a dream in a sense, yet so real I had to shield my eyes from the brightness and could feel the heat on my skin. I fell face-down. I can remember each word of a deep voice that called out to me. 'Son of man, stand on your feet that I may speak with you!' I felt a force that lifted my limp body to my feet. 'Son of man, I am sending you to the sons of Israel, to a rebellious people who have rebelled against Me; they and their fathers have transgressed against Me to this very day. I am sending you to them who are stubborn and obstinate children, and you shall say to them, *Thus says the Lord, GOD.* As for them, whether they listen or not—for they are a rebellious house—they will know that a prophet has been among them. And you, son of man, neither fear them nor fear their words, though thistles and thorns are with you and you sit on scorpions; neither fear their words nor be dismayed at their presence, for they are a rebellious house. But you shall speak My words to them whether they listen or not, for they are rebellious. Now you, son of man, listen to what I am speaking to you; do not be rebellious like that rebellious house.'⁴

"I'm sorry, Daniel. Again, I cannot find words that adequately express all that happened next. I plan to write it all down when I have time to concentrate on the words. I hope you believe what I am saying because it had to be a vision from Yahweh appointing me to be His prophet to His people in this strange land."

Daniel placed his hand on Ezekiel's shoulder. "My friend, the vision is shocking, but the calling is no surprise. Yahweh has been preparing you for this since we were students together. Surely, our people must have a prophet. They have other priests like yourself among them, but the priests understand little about what is really happening. They minister to the people and carry out the rituals, but they are not hearing from the heart of Yahweh and the messages He must be yearning to convey to them. In many ways, they still commit the same idolatrous

---

4 Ezekiel 2:1-6

acts as they did in Judah. Many have assumed the pagan behavior of their captors."

"When I speak the truth, it will often not be well-received by our people or by Babylonian officials. I will need you to stand in the gap for me when my words offend our captors."

"You know I will. Yahweh has just revealed yet another reason He has me in this position. Praise Him for revelations to both you and me!"

18

Daniel stood nearby as Ezekiel proclaimed the word of Yahweh amid a cluster of houses in the compound. Almost every day for five years, he had prophesied to all who would listen. He had been condemning his people's continuing rejection of God, both in Judah and Babylon. He had warned that God's judgment on His people would continue and that Jerusalem would someday be completely destroyed, including the temple. He had also prophesied that Nebuchadnezzar would attack Egypt.

Today, however, Daniel was hearing something new from his prophet friend. Ezekiel was proclaiming Jerusalem's destruction was eminent. "For the king of Babylon stands at the parting of the way, at the head of the two ways to use divination; he shakes the arrows, he consults the household idols, he looks at the liver. Into his right hand came the divination, 'Jerusalem,' to set battering rams, to open the mouth of slaughter, to lift up the voice with a battle cry, to set battering rams against the gates, to cast up ramps, to build a siege wall. And it will be to them like a false divination in their eyes; they have *sworn* solemn oaths. But he brings iniquity to remembrance, that they may be seized. Therefore, thus says the Lord GOD, 'Because you have made your iniquity to be remembered, in that your transgressions are uncovered, so that in all your deeds your sins appear—because you have come to remembrance, you will be seized with the hand."[5]

Daniel knew King Nebuchadnezzar had a large army contingent camped around Jerusalem. They were sent there soon after King Zedekiah sent messages of complaint to Babylon about tax increases and tighter restrictions on Judah's trade with neighboring nations. King Nebuchadnezzar had mentioned that he had been consulting with the sorcerers again regarding whether to invade Jerusalem a third time. Daniel took offense at such circumventing of his advice and counsel but could not control who the king trusted most. Bulludhu's advice often prevailed because he told the king what the king wanted to hear.

Ezekiel's prophesy was confirmed sooner than Daniel had anticipated. Late that afternoon, King Nebuchadnezzar summoned him to his chambers.

"Belteshazzar, I am leaving in a few days for Jerusalem with a small army contingent commanded by Nabonidus to reinforce the troops already there. Zedekiah has fortified the city more than we had anticipated with stronger walls and gates. Nabonidus will begin a siege of the city cutting off all food and supplies. You have seen the reports from my overseers there that Zedekiah has been communicating with Pharaoh Hophra, attempting to forge an alliance. I have no desire to go to war with Egypt again. Apparently, Zedekiah thinks I am a fool. Nine years ago, I showed mercy to him and over twenty-five thousand people remaining in Jerusalem, plus three times that many in all of Judah. I made him king with a level of independence. Now, he has betrayed me and will pay for it dearly."

---

5 Ezekiel 21:21-24

Daniel understood his limitations in influencing decisions regarding the king's many vassalages. "I understand, Your Excellency. I know my advice carries little weight in these matters, but I urge you to be as merciful as possible. Those twenty-five thousand people you speak of inside the walls are not your enemies. They are innocent. And the reports from there have noted that their prophet Jeremiah is passionately denouncing the move toward the pharaoh."

"You are a hopeless pacifist, Belteshazzar. If they want mercy, they will have to surrender the moment I arrive."

"How long will you hold siege before you attack?"

"Until they starve, if necessary."

Three days later, Daniel was directing the activities surrounding the early morning departure of the king, his army commander, Nabonidus, and about a thousand soldiers. Dejected mothers, wives, and children bade farewell to their loved ones while the musicians performed rousing instrumentals. As the royal party led the entourage through the gate, Amytis moved next to Daniel.

"I feel less lonely at times like this, now that the gardens are becoming so beautiful and occupy my time."

"I'm glad, Your Highness. The king has certainly provided you a wonderful gift to help ease the burden of his long absences necessary for preservation of the kingdom."

"I am not as naïve as you may think. My yearnings for Media that I shared with you had long fallen on the deaf ears of my husband. But you were sensitive enough to my needs to risk confronting him about it. Your influence on my behalf will not be forgotten, Belteshazzar. I will return the favor. But you will have to wait. I am finally pregnant. The king was convinced that being unable to conceive for fourteen years, I would bear him no heir to the throne. I believe this will be his heir."

Daniel forced a smile. "What wonderful news. I am happy for you and the king. Speaking of the gardens, I haven't been there in a while. I must see how it's going. Good day, Your Highness."

Six months later, Daniel dispatched a message to the king. *Your Excellency, you have an heir to the throne. He and his mother are doing well. As you commanded, he was named Amel-Marduk—Man of Marduk.*

*

The past two years had been a turbulent time for Daniel. King Nebuchadnezzar had remained with his army for six months, holding Jerusalem under siege. He had returned upset and frustrated at King Zedekiah's resistance. His vassal in Jerusalem had refused to even speak with him and had barred the city's gates. Zedekiah had sealed his city's ultimate demise with no food or supplies coming in. A famine had already depleted much of the grain stores, but they had an ample source of water through the underground tunnels built by King Hezekiah over a century prior for defense against a potential Assyrian siege.

What King Nebuchadnezzar viewed as suicidal intransigence by the Hebrews had caused his army to have to build a long siege ramp, fabricate battering rams, and confiscate food from nearby cities for an indefinite period. Upon arrival at Babylon, the king took his aggravation out on the exiles by clamping down on their food supply and other needs. It took Daniel over a month to calm the king and convince him that what he was doing was slowing progress on the gardens.

The king's return was primarily to see his blood succession to the throne. To Daniel's surprise, he was spending a lot of time with little Amel-Marduk, even carrying him proudly as he visited construction sites around the city. After eight months in Babylon, the king departed again to join his army in final readiness for invasion. They had completed the siege ramp and weakened the gate doors and walls to make a forced entry possible.

During this absence of the king, Bulludhu had organized a work slow-down among many in the palace court and on the Babylon tower project. And Amytis became bolder in her efforts to seduce Daniel by showing up frequently at places where she knew he would be alone.

A knock at the door woke Daniel just before dawn. Raviv had received a message from Ezekiel requesting a visit right away.

Ezekiel was waiting in his doorway. He was shaking. "Peninah has been ill for a couple of days. Last night, I had a dream. Yahweh told me that she was going to die soon."

Daniel interrupted. "No, my friend. It was probably just a bad dream."

"Only if that were true. This is another real-life drama to show His people their transgressions and His judgment. He commanded me not to mourn or weep but that He would give me words to say to my people."

Ezekiel continued. "You have been so busy; I have not been able to share with you a vision I had last week. I saw two angels escort the Spirit of Yahweh out of the temple of Jerusalem. I believe Yahweh no longer dwells with our people in the Holy of Holies but has given them over to Babylonia because of their rebellion."

"That would mean His dwelling with the Ark of the Covenant in the tabernacle of Moses and the temple of Solomon is now over after seven centuries," Daniel said.

Daniel remained with Ezekiel throughout the day, praying over Peninah and consoling Ezekiel. Ezekiel shed no tears. Peninah died just past midnight.

Shortly after sunrise, Ezekiel was on the streets telling of his wife's death but showing no sadness. He spoke the words the Lord put in his mouth. "Thus, says the Lord GOD, 'Behold, I am about to profane My sanctuary, the pride of your power, the desire of your eyes and the delight of your soul; and your sons and your daughters whom you have left behind will fall by the sword. You will do as I have done . . . You will not mourn and you will not weep, but you will rot away in your iniquities and you will groan to one another. Thus Ezekiel will be a sign to you; according to all that he has done you will do; when it comes, then you will know that I am the Lord GOD.'"

Although the message confused many of the people, Daniel and Ezekiel understood that not only would Jerusalem be attacked, but the temple would also be completely destroyed. And most likely, it had just happened that day, the day Peninah died.

As the people of the compound were leaving, mostly grumbling about what they had just heard, Daniel put his arm around Ezekiel. "Your obedience to Yahweh in showing no emotion over the death of your beloved Peninah strengthens me for my personal battles. Let's go now and prepare her for a proper burial."

Four weeks had passed since Ezekiel prophesied the destruction of the temple. Daniel was inspecting the gardens when an army officer

---

6 Ezekiel 24:21-22, 23-24

ran up to him and announced what had been anticipated. A young
soldier had just arrived from Jerusalem with a report for him. The
walls of Jerusalem had been broken down to the foundation in many
places. What remained of the palace had been finished off, and the
temple had been razed to the ground. Valuables from all public and
private places were being hauled back to Babylon as plunder. There was
not a lot of bloodshed because King Zedekiah, along with his entire
army and officials, had attempted to escape.

"So, the king and his army retreated without much of a fight?"
Daniel asked.

"Yes, sir. But the Chaldean army caught up with them in the plains
of Jericho. Some of Judah's army scattered, but most were captured."

"And King Zedekiah?"

"The general slaughtered his sons before his eyes, then put out his
eyes with the tip of a sword."

Grimacing, Daniel inquired further. "Is he still alive and among
the captives?"

"Yes, sir, and he is to be imprisoned as was Jehoiachin."

"Is the king bringing many exiles back with him?"

"Sir, that is the reason I was told to get here as swiftly as possible.
The king wants you to prepare for twenty thousand more exiles."

"Twenty thousand?" Daniel blurted out.

He dismissed the messenger and went straight to King Jehoiachin,
sending word for Mishael to join him there in the prison.

"Gentlemen, we have a major crisis," Daniel said to the king and
Mishael. "Twenty thousand more exiles from Jerusalem will be here
in less than six weeks. I want the three of us, along with Azariah and
Hananiah, to pray individually into the night. If it takes all night to get

an answer, so be it. The task seems impossible. We must have Yahweh's wisdom. All five of us will meet in my chamber for breakfast in the morning. If Yahweh has spoken by then, we will all be unanimous in the solution. Your Excellency, I will have the guards escort you to the palace for this meeting."

Raviv had set the table with five place settings of mixed fruit, cheese, wheat cakes, and pomegranate juice. The five men sat around the table and talked about King Zedekiah and what was now only a small remnant of poor, lame, and unskilled Jews left in Jerusalem. They also discussed the over seventy-five thousand Jews living elsewhere in Judah, mostly farmers and shepherds, who were apparently affected little by the routing of the city. After the meal was finished, Daniel got to the point of the meeting.

"Has everyone received an impression from Yahweh that you feel is His answer to our crisis?"

There were three nods and a lowered head.

"Your Excellency?" Daniel said.

"Yahweh knows I am not worthy to pray to Him. I tried, but I felt nothing," King Jehoiachin said.

"He will draw you to Himself in a personal encounter if you call on Him. As you observe His love and power in this meeting, He will reach out to you, but you must accept His hand."

Daniel eyed the other three. "I will reserve what he revealed to me until I hear from you, so there will be no influence on my part."

Mishael began. "I did not receive the details I would have preferred, but the general strategy came to me clearly. I believe Yahweh would have us move those occupying the compound into the city. They would intermingle with the citizens of Babylon, build themselves houses, and become part of the established communities. Then we could place the new exiles in the compound, since most of the shelters have been improved and enlarged. Still, many new shelters will have to be built quickly."

Hananiah stared at Mishael with raised eyebrows and smiled. "I had basically the same revelation, except that I saw many of the original exiles moving in with Babylonian families having extra room in exchange for domestic services."

"Same here," Azariah said. "I also visualized those moving into the city practicing their unique skills and knowledge for pay from the Babylonians. Some would set up shops and trade in the marketplace."

Daniel laughed. "That matches what was revealed to me exactly. Yahweh is so faithful and so good! Your Excellency, as you can see, Yahweh is still powerfully present among us here in this pagan land. He has not abandoned us."

"That is obvious," Jehoiachin said. "I want to be a worthier servant of His."

Daniel continued. "The enormous contributions to Babylon our people have made for the last eleven years and their peaceful coexistence have surely made a lasting impression on the city. Everyone is in awe of the gardens and credits the exclusive skills of our people with its beauty. I am convinced the city's residents will welcome them as a benefit, rather than a burden. This reminds me of the letter from Jeremiah urging us exiles to build houses, plant gardens, and eat with our captors. Your Excellency, you will need to prepare your people for an abrupt life change. Make sure they understand how crucial it will be for them to be good neighbors, honorable, helpful, and courteous."

Daniel turned to his administrators. "It is eleven years ago over again but doubled in accommodations, all in the next five weeks. We will temporarily terminate the work on the gardens and divert that workforce to this requirement. Assess the capacity of the existing compound and build new shelters as needed. Organize the moving out effort. I will distribute a letter to all residents and businesses in the city explaining the plan and exhorting them to be patient and accommodating. I will highlight how this will enhance their lives. When the first exiles arrived, we could have never envisioned this happening. But Yahweh has orchestrated what our minds could not conceive. Praise Him!"

Daniel dismissed his assistants but asked King Jehoiachin to remain. "Your Excellency, you must turn your attention to the new exiles after their arrival. Your staff will need to remain in their original shelters and receive your orders from your confinement. The new arrivals will need you far more than those moving into the city. You remember what it was like when you arrived. Prepare for double the chaos. Your palace will be your prison room."

Daniel was being realistic. He knew that King Nebuchadnezzar would never allow his conquered ruler to be released from confinement. King Jehoiachin understood.

*

The past six weeks had been the most challenging time Daniel, his staff, and his assistants had ever experienced. But with the obvious miracles of God undergirding the effort, twenty thousand additional captives from Jerusalem now occupied the compound. King Zedekiah was unable to walk by the end of their journey and was laid in a prison room not far from his nephew, Jehoiachin. Daniel had an all-day meeting with King Jehoiachin and King Zedekiah, where all three agreed that Jehoiachin would continue to act as the king of the exiles. Zedekiah, blind and in poor health, was pleased to abrogate any claim to kingship back to Jehoiachin.

The ten thousand original exiles had assimilated into the city, some boarding with host Babylonian families and some having built their own houses with materials provided by the kingdom. King Nebuchadnezzar's return had settled much of the effort of Daniel's antagonists to undermine his leadership. Amytis had ceased showing up at the most awkward times. Daniel turned the attention of the province back to the kingdom's former objectives. The new exiles, now with twice the manpower, began the accelerated finish work on the gardens.

At the end of the king's scheduled meeting with Daniel, he added an unexpected agenda item. "I've been greatly impressed with the relative ease with which you have settled the new exiles into the compound. Equally impressive is the integrating of the first exiles into the mainstream of our people and culture. Now, we must look at how we can best use the expanded labor force to accomplish my vision for this amazing city. I want Babylon and my kingdom to be known by all future generations, forever and ever, as the envy of all cities and kingdoms of the world. The gardens and the Babylon tower will contribute to that. I also want to build the most grandiose buildings ever constructed. I want gold cladding and colors on many of the facades. The lion, the fiercest of all animals, will be our kingdom's symbol known throughout the world. This animal will line our walls, overlook our gates, and dominate our sculptures. With the labor and craftsmanship of the Hebrews, the engineering skills of the Chaldeans, and the plundered treasures from our conquered lands, we have the resources."

Daniel was astonished by the arrogance of this man who could instantly shift from rational thinking to ego-driven mania. *My people will be expected to work brutally to satisfy his whims.* The king continued, "As a tribute to my power and reign over this magnificent society, I want to now begin the delayed project of erecting my golden image. The abundance of gold brought from Judah, added to our plunder of Egypt, should now be sufficient to build the image. Have our engineers and draftsmen draw up three or four optional plans from my general specifications, which I will give you."

"Excellency, your vision for such extravagant buildings and artisan works will make Babylon truly the envy of the rest of the world. Trade routes will be redirected to our door. Other kings will visit to observe and study the highest standards you set for a city. Such a monumental undertaking will occupy the full capacity of the workforce for many years. We will need to expedite the completion of the gardens and the tower, then turn attention to the long-term development of the city. As the majesty and beauty of Babylon becomes a testimony to your greatness, it will serve as a more impressive tribute to you than a golden image could ever be. Every man-hour dedicated to an image is a man-hour taken from your vision for the city."

"Do not try to sway me, Belteshazzar. I have dreamed of this golden image of myself since my coronation. The statue with the golden head described in your interpretation of my dream confirmed the gods want me to do this. You will begin now to coordinate with our designers, craftsmen, and labor managers. I want it completed within a year."

Daniel met with his three administrators the next day to begin the long-range planning for the king's objectives. They worked daily from morning to evening laying out the sequence of events and division of labor for completing the garden and the tower over the next few years while accomplishing the first stages of the complete rebuilding of the city. All exiled men and many of the women would be allocated to the gardens and city projects. Chaldean workers would continue on the tower. Daniel waited for several days to tell the three about the golden image. Silenced in astonishment, they listened until the end of his announcement.

"How can we be a part of this?" Hananiah said. "The basic laws of Yahweh say to not make a graven image."

"The law refers to an image to be worshipped like an idol," Daniel said. "If this is just a sculpture to remind future generations of the founder of this magnificent city, I don't support it; it's a waste of time and resources; and it's a huge overstatement. But I think I'll save my next battle for something more critical to the honor of Yahweh."

Daniel's acquiescence drew mixed comments, but the other three decided to not make it an issue.

"We will need to protect our people from working on such an offensive task. It will have to be a Chaldean project," Mishael said. All agreed.

"I expect the designers will use hardwood as the core material and clad it all with gold overlay," Daniel said.

"I'm sure much of the gold will be that which was plundered from Jerusalem," Hananiah said. "It sickens me that the gold from the temple will be used to honor a pagan king."

"Me, too," Daniel said. "But keep remembering, Yahweh has placed us in the middle of all this for His purpose. For many years now, we have lived a delicate balance fulfilling our duties without compromising our faith. There will be times when we must rebel, but I don't sense this is the time."

The four worked late into the night developing the framework for the enormous tasks ahead.

"One of the first requirements for the massive construction effort will be to enlarge the lime kiln furnace for substantially more mortar production capacity than we have now," Daniel said. "Thousands of loads of wood from nearby forests will be needed to fuel the fire to an extremely high temperature."

*

The golden image of King Nebuchadnezzar, fifteen times his height, loomed ominously in its remote location in the plain of Dura. It looked like a speck on the horizon from atop the city walls. But as visitors approached it, they felt goosebumps. The glistening gold figure rising ever skyward out of the flat, barren desert was mystifying. The conical base made up half of its height. The top half was a recognizable, full-body representation of King Nebuchadnezzar in his royal robe and cylindrical crown. His right hand grasped his long sword. The entire monument was covered with gold overlay, giving it a brilliant glow that burned the eyes on a typical sunny day.

Daniel had managed to distance himself from the statue project and to keep his Hebrew people occupied with other tasks ordered by the king.

Late afternoon, as Daniel entered the palace, Ashpenaz met him in the hallway and handed him a folded parchment with a wax seal. He recognized the document as an official order from the king. Ashpenaz smiled and walked away. Daniel broke the seal and read the order by the diminishing light from the window.

Seventy days from today, at mid-morning, you will assemble all the Babylonian satraps, prefects, governors, counselors, treasurers, judges, magistrates, and provincial rulers at the foot of the golden image on the east side for the official dedication. No one will be excused. I, King Nebuchadnezzar, so declare.

Daniel lay on his bed staring at the ornate ceiling, the order still in his hand.

O Yahweh, my greatest fear is not the king You have placed me under or my enemies inside the palace court or other threatening nations. I am not afraid of anyone or any force that can cause me physical harm. I do, though, constantly fear that I will fail You. I worry that I may not carry out the expectations You have of me in this complex role. Every day, I am torn between obeying You and obeying the pagan king You have led me to serve. Now, I appeal to You to grant me wisdom, yet again, regarding this order.

Daniel continued to pray when he awoke several times through the night. By morning, he felt a peace about carrying out the order. He had Raviv summon Mishael, Azariah, and Hananiah. After reading the king's command to them, he explained his confidence that they were to continue submitting to Nebuchadnezzar's demands, unless the demands violated the specific laws of Yahweh.

"Have our scribes copy the king's declaration and dispatch messengers to the listed Babylonian officials throughout the kingdom," Daniel said. "Make it clear that attendance is mandatory."

*

TEN WEEKS LATER

During the past week, scores of provincial officials had poured into the city. The journey for many had taken over a month. On the eve of the dedication, King Nebuchadnezzar had put on a lavish party for his kingdom's elite. Shortly after sun-up, all were dressed in their exquisite, colorful attire for the two-hour ride to the statue. Fighting hangover headaches and nausea from the previous night, they formed a long line beginning at the river bridge. Hundreds of trips by construction workers had formed a well-packed, sandy road to the site.

Once there, everyone was guided to their places by palace hosts according to rank and position. When Daniel arrived, accompanied by his three administrators, he was seated at the front on one of only three chairs available. The seats to his immediate right were reserved for the king and queen. Musicians with harps, lyres, drums, and trumpets performed a welcoming serenade for the guests. The crowd sang celebratory tunes until the music quieted. A trumpet trio sounded the king's arrival strain, followed by the herald's announcement. "His Majesty, King Nebuchadnezzar. Long live the king!"

The crowd responded, "Long live the king!"

King Nebuchadnezzar stood on a garish platform custom-made for the occasion. A host led Amytis to the chair beside Daniel. She gently touched his thigh momentarily while the king was looking away surveying the crowd. The king thanked everyone for attending, made a few remarks about the statue, and called his herald to the platform. The herald unrolled a parchment, accompanied by a three-note blast from the trumpet trio. He began to read.

"To you the command is given, O peoples, nations, and *men of every language*, that at the moment you hear the sound of the horn, flute, lyre, trigon, psaltery, bagpipe and all kinds of music, you are to fall down and worship the golden image that Nebuchadnezzar the king has set up. But whoever does not fall down and worship shall immediately be cast into the midst of a furnace of blazing fire."[7]

Daniel's sigh was loud enough to turn the heads of the king and queen. He didn't look in their direction but could feel their sharp stare.

How could I have been so naïve as to think this monstrosity was just a monument to a powerful king to ensure his reign would be recognized by future generations? No. It was an idol—a graven image as initially described by Bulludhu. And it must not be worshipped by any Hebrew.

The ride back to the city in Daniel's carriage seemed quick as his mind was totally occupied with the fate of his people under the decree. He determined he would have to convince the king to make an exception for the thirty thousand Hebrews.

---

7 Daniel 3:4-6

19

"Good morning, Kyle," Dr. McCarty answered.

Kyle was a little nervous calling the professor for the first time, but he was intrigued about what he had just read and couldn't wait until their next meeting to sort it out.

"Good morning, sir. I got your text about the time for our next meeting. Thanks. I'll be there. I'm sorry to bother you, but I'm perplexed about something I just read from Ezekiel's writing. I would like to discuss it when we meet again but wanted to give you time to think about it."

"Wow, you're reading beyond Daniel. I'm really impressed with how you're getting into this. You're not bothering me at all. Any time. What do you have for me?"

"Well, Ezekiel's writing is difficult for me to understand, but it appears that at some point, God departed from the temple in Jerusalem. Does God get so frustrated with His people that He actually abandons them?"

"This is complex and takes some study, but it is very important in understanding the nature of God. Before Christ came, God's Spirit did not dwell with individuals as He does today. He visited certain individuals, typically prophets and leaders, for limited periods of time.

However, beginning in Moses' day, He dwelled in the tabernacle with the Ark of the Covenant. This permanent presence—later termed 'shekinah glory,' meaning 'God's dwelling' in Hebrew—was evidenced by a cloud above the Ark and tabernacle visible to the people.

"Centuries later, after the temple was built, He dwelled with the Ark in a room visited only by the high priests. As prophesied by Moses and other prophets, this shekinah glory departed from the Hebrews just prior to Babylon's destruction of Jerusalem and the temple. For over five centuries, God's Spirit did not dwell among His people. Then the shekinah glory returned in the person of Jesus Christ. Shortly after Christ's death, resurrection, and ascension into Heaven, God's Spirit came to live in the souls of everyone in the world who became His followers. That presence of the Spirit in each Christ follower continues today. The shekinah glory of God no longer lives in a particular place but in the soul of each individual believer."

"That's hard for an engineering student to wrap his mind around. The Spirit of God Who dwelled with His people at a specific location for centuries now lives in each person's soul."

"Yes, but only in the souls of those who believe in Him and have committed their lives to Him. So, in essence, He still lives with His people, just in a more personal way. Our minds can't fully comprehend that, but we can see and feel the evidence of it."

"But where was God in Daniel's day in Babylon?"

"He continued to be with His prophets and certain others as He chose and for times of His choosing. Obviously, He was with Daniel and some others in Babylon as they called on Him, and He responded. It's exhilarating to know now that despite the disobedience of His people, God sacrificed His Son so that we no longer have restricted access to Him. He gives everyone who belongs to Him unlimited access to Himself."

"Okay, I think I've got the gist of that. I'll probably want to read more about it and talk further on it when we meet."

"Absolutely. I look forward to next time."

"Me, too. Thanks."

20

Daniel didn't speak a word on the ride from the golden image dedication ceremony.

"We have arrived, sir," Raviv said, realizing his master's mind was somewhere else.

"Of course," Daniel said, accepting his servant's assistance in disembarking the carriage. "Prepare my semi-formal attire. I will be meeting with the king this afternoon."

"But, Your Greatness, you are not on the king's schedule."

"I will be meeting with the king this afternoon!"

Later that afternoon, Daniel waited in the outer chamber after arranging an off-schedule meeting with the king through Ashpenaz. The king entered and took his seat.

"This has to be quick. I have dinner plans with my vassals from throughout the kingdom. So, what is the emergency?"

"Your Excellency, I was quite astonished by your decree to worship the image. When I interpreted your dream, you acknowledged Yahweh as the God of all gods and kings. This Yahweh is the one and only God worthy of anyone's worship. He, and He only, should be worshiped by all people and nations of the Earth. The Hebrew exiles, including I, cannot worship any other image."

The king's face reddened as Daniel spoke. He folded his arms across his chest.

"I acknowledge your God; I acknowledge Marduk; I acknowledge all gods of my advisors. You and your people are welcome to worship your Hebrew God, but they will also worship me and my image. Belteshazzar, we have discussed this before. You are a Babylonian. All exiles are now Babylonian. They will worship whomever the Babylonia king declares they will worship. When the palace musicians are dispatched to play their instruments in the streets of Babylon, all people of the city, native and foreign-born, will face in the direction of my image, fall to their knees, and bow to the grounds with hands raised. Anyone who doesn't will be thrown into the lime kiln. Do not come to me with this subject again."

King Nebuchadnezzar rose abruptly and walked swiftly to his chambers.

Raviv was preparing Daniel's bed as he entered the room. "Thank you, Raviv. Now, please go at once and summon Shadrach, Meshach, and Abednego."

"We knew it wouldn't take long for this meeting to be called," Mishael said as they were seated. "We were together praying for guidance when Raviv arrived."

"We were praying for you, too," Azariah said. "Have you talked with King Nebuchadnezzar?"

"The discussion was short," Daniel said. "He made it clear that the Hebrews would not be exempted from the decree. We four discussed earlier the line between submitting to the authority of those over us and doing nothing that would dishonor Yahweh. The act of worshiping an idol, even if not of the heart, would be disgusting to Him. Any

Hebrew that does such a thing would be adding to the disobedience that resulted in our present, deserved servitude."

"Of course, we agree, but ignoring the decree would sentence us all to being burned alive in the lime kiln," Mishael said.

"Would he actually execute thirty thousand of his hard-working labor force?" Hananiah asked.

"If I have learned anything about the king over these twenty years, it is that he is unpredictable," Daniel said. "So, yes. We can assume he would annihilate all exiles, including the four in this room. But we have no choice as servants of Yahweh. This is the line we cannot cross. We must conscientiously disobey this decree."

"How do we get the word to the exiles?" Mishael asked.

"This will be King Jehoiachin's first test of his faith and his displaced leadership. I will ask him to circulate a decree opposing King Nebuchadnezzar's decree. We should be honest with the people, explaining that disobeying King Nebuchadnezzar could be punishable by death, but we should trust Yahweh."

"We will monitor the communications and reactions," Mishael said.

The next two days were uneventful. Daniel assumed the king was allowing time for the entire city to be informed of the decree. Although his nerves were on edge the day after his meeting with the king, he felt an unexplainable peace as he awoke on the third day, which he attributed to the spirit of Yahweh.

However, shortly after the marketplaces began stirring on that day, Daniel heard a disturbing sound through his open window and ran quickly to the street in front of the palace. The palace musicians began to march in the streets, sounding their instruments loudly. Everyone he could see was on his or her knees. He ran to the gardens. He smiled as he observed all Hebrew workers going about their normal duties. Turning to some storefronts, he viewed the Babylonians bowing, while the Hebrews continued their activities. The music faded as he returned to the palace, and people around him were rising to continue their normal day.

Daniel reentered the palace and was proceeding to his chamber when Ashpenaz met him in the hallway.

"The king has requested a meeting in one hour to assess the response to the decree."

Daniel changed into his meeting attire, all the while praying for a seemingly impossible good outcome for his people. He also wondered who had ordered the musicians to play, since he would normally have been tasked with that. Entering the outer chamber, Daniel was surprised at seeing only two men present—Ashpenaz, as expected, and unexpected Bulludhu. He moved his chair between them and the king's seat as an intentional demonstration of his position. He did not speak. The king entered and sat.

"We have had our first call to worship, and, of course, I am very interested in your reports."

Daniel would normally have been the first asked to speak, but the king asked for reports from the other two. Ashpenaz stood and spoke first.

"O king, live forever! You have decreed that everyone who hears the sound of the horn, flute, lyre, trigon, psaltery, bagpipe, and all kinds of music will fall down and worship the golden image. Anyone who doesn't will be cast into a blazing furnace. Three of your Jewish administrators—Shadrach, Meshach, and Abednego—have disregarded you and have refused to serve your gods or worship the golden image."

The king stood and shouted, "This shall not be. Go immediately and bring these three to stand before me."

"As you command, O king," Ashpenaz said as he hurried out the rear door.

Daniel felt the long, penetrating leer from the king. Waiting for the anticipated question, he looked away. Suddenly, the king left the room. Daniel knew the king wanted to ask what he did when the music sounded, but he was evidently hesitant to ask, avoiding a response he couldn't stand to hear. Daniel turned to Bulludhu and spoke sternly.

"Why the administrators and not all Hebrews?"

Bulludhu grinned widely. "As you can appreciate, sir, why risk the annihilation of such a huge part of our labor force when the execution of three prominent administrators will send a powerful message to all exiles and Babylonians alike? The next worship event will be obeyed by all."

"And why not me?"

"You?" Bulludhu chortled. "The king would not execute you. You are indispensable to the kingdom. But if he knew you defied the decree and he failed to execute you, he would suffer much loss of credibility. The people must fear the king at all cost."

"So, you set up my friends."

"Your best friends. The king may have given you authority over us, but we still have his ear."

"Us and we being you and Ashpenaz?"

"The king's misguided elevation of you at our expense deposed many of the palace court, but when you eclipsed Ashpenaz and me, you toppled the wrong men."

"We would not be in this situation if the king's ego had not driven him to build the image."

"It was I who recommended he erect an image to be worshiped. His overwhelming victories that formed the great Babylonian empire qualifies him for deity. He has earned a place with the gods. The gods made that clear to my sorcerers, and our conjuring affirmed their revelations."

"And no doubt, you have advised the king throughout the image project and devised the punishment for disobedience."

"You are very astute, Your Greatness. With such psychic ability, there is little wonder the king made you his top advisor."

The rear doors opened abruptly. Soldiers escorted Daniel's friends, hands bound, to the front of the chamber. They were dressed in their robe and turban regalia. The king reentered with Ashpenaz at his side. He gazed into the eyes of each one, then paced back and forth a few times before stopping in front of them.

"Shadrach, Meshach, and Abednego, I am told that you have not obeyed my command to worship my golden image. In deference to your service to the kingdom, I will give you another chance to worship the image at the sound of the music. If you defy me again, you will be cast into the furnace. What god could save you from my punishment?"

Mishael replied, "O King Nebuchadnezzar, such an offer does not deserve an answer. Yahweh is able to save us from the fire, and He will rescue us from your hand. But even if He does not, let the king be assured we will not serve your gods or worship your golden image."

The king shook his head rapidly and made an eerie, growling sound, then looked at Ashpenaz and shouted, "Go now! Heat the furnace to seven times the temperature normally used for the mortar. Take these traitors out of my sight!"

He stepped toward Bulludhu. "You're in charge of casting the criminals into the fiery furnace. You conceived the punishment; you carry it out. Do it after dark, so the glow of the fire will be seen by everyone in the city."

Daniel returned to his chamber and prayed, crying out to God in intercession for his three friends. His piercing voice reflected his deep distress. He needed to hear his own words above the roar of the lime kiln fire a considerable distance away. Lying on the stone floor worried by his tears, he pleaded for the three innocent lives. Later, peering out his window at the bright yellow glow high in the night sky, he saw the streets filled with residents scurrying toward the execution site.

"Your carriage is ready, sir," Raviv announced from outside Daniel's door.

Looking down the street, Daniel could see the flames shooting out of both sides of the kiln and reaching high into the air. He knew that the fire was normally contained within the lime production kiln. However, the multiple box bellows being used constantly, along with the wood fuel being added unceasingly, had made the fire much hotter than had ever been attempted before.

Daniel exited his carriage at a safe distance from the kiln but could still feel the intense heat. He sighed at the large, curious crowd encircling the kiln, including many of the kingdom's high officials. Bulludhu was barking orders at the kiln operators. One of the operators was very animated in his conversation with Bulludhu, likely warning him about overheating the kiln.

A carriage enclosed with curtains pulled up next to Bulludhu. A soldier stepped out, followed by a man with his hands bound behind his back.

Mishael! Daniel fought to keep his composure.

Then another soldier disembarked with a firm grip on the arm of Hananiah, also with hands tied with a rope. Finally, a third soldier appeared with Azariah.

Daniel's lips quivered. *O Yahweh, have mercy!*

"Azariah! Hananiah! Mishael!" Daniel screamed, but his voice was not heard by anyone over the rumbling fire and chanting of the crowd.

Bulludhu stood the three men and their accompanying soldiers side by side with their backs to the kiln. Other soldiers parted the crowd, and out of a cleared lane appeared King Nebuchadnezzar on his chariot dressed in full regalia. The king nodded to Bulludhu, who lifted his right arm in salute, faced the convicted men, and ordered them to turn and walk toward the fire.

Daniel shook uncontrollably. *I should be there, too. Instead, I am spared by the deceit of Bulludhu and Ashpenaz. I would normally stand next to the king for an execution, although I would have refused to do so for this one. Relegated to the shadows tonight probably means my position has been* rescinded. *If not, and if Yahweh does not choose to save my friends, I will declare myself finished. I can no longer serve the king, and I cannot meet the demands of Yahweh. I am undone!*

The condemned men, with the soldiers pushing from behind, strode ceremoniously toward the fiery kiln, followed closely by Bulludhu. The three held their heads high in defiance and sang together a praise song from the Psalms. Daniel fell to the ground as his knees gave way.

The trio squarely approached the furnace opening, while the guards and Bulludhu crouched behind them to shield themselves from the unbearable heat. The flames were now lapping well outside of the furnace.

"They're afire!" someone shouted from the crowd. Onlookers began to cry out.

The three guards and Bulludhu were instantly engulfed in flames. They fell to the ground writhing in pain, screaming.

Daniel sprang to his feet gaping at the sight. The king's arms raised in reflex. Daniel sprinted to the king's side spontaneously. Within seconds, Bulludhu and the guards lay still near the mouth of the furnace, their clothing consumed and their smoldering bodies emitting the stench of burning flesh.

The three sentenced to die stood tall and continued to march forward under their own will. "Immanuel!" all three shouted. "Immanuel!" Daniel echoed. They leaped into the furnace. The crowd clamored with unintelligible outcries and profanities. Chaos ensued among the soldiers and officials.

King Nebuchadnezzar stepped from his chariot and took three slow paces toward the furnace, straining to look into the fire. He suddenly turned to his officials. "Didn't we cast three men into the fire?"

"Of course, O king."

"Look!" the king shouted. "There are four men walking freely in the roaring fire. One looks like a son of the gods."

Daniel saw it. "O Yahweh!" he cried.

The fire withdrew to the confines of the furnace, and the heat subsided to a temperature bearable to those nearby. The king moved closer to the door as the crowd followed. He paused as he came to the blackened and smoking bodies, shook his head, then stepped over them.

"Shadrach, Meshach, and Abednego, men of the Most High God, come out!"

Daniel watched in amazement as his three friends stepped out of the furnace. Their clothes were not scorched; their hair was unsinged; and their faces were not discolored. They peered around the king and smiled at Daniel. He bounded toward them like a playful child and hugged them tightly, wailing with joy.

Nebuchadnezzar turned to the crowd. "Praise the God of Shadrach, Meshach, and Abednego, Who has sent His angel to save His faithful servants. They were willing to lose their lives rather than obey my command to worship any other gods. Therefore, I decree that anyone who says anything against the God of Shadrach, Meshach, and Abednego shall be torn apart and their houses demolished. Obviously, no other god could have done what we have witnessed today."

The king returned to his chariot and departed the scene. The crowd, now quieted, pressed around the three survivors many reaching to touch them in disbelief.

"They are not even hot!" one exclaimed.

"They don't smell of fire!" another proclaimed.

The ranking soldier ordered the people to disperse. Then he turned to the three and loosed their bindings. "I suppose you're free to go."

"Did you see there was another person in the fire with you?" Daniel asked.

"Oh, yes." "Absolutely." "Certainly." All three responded at once.

"He appeared just as we were walking into the furnace, motioning us to enter with Him," Mishael said. "He looked like any other man. I thought someone else was being executed with us, but then there was something like an invisible shield encircling all of us that kept the fire away. When we stepped out, He was gone. It had to be an angel from Heaven."

"I prayed that Yahweh would extinguish the fire, but He chose to walk with you through it and protect you from it instead," Daniel said.

"We heard your response in kind to our code word, 'Immanuel.'" Hananiah said.

"We must thank Yahweh here and now," Daniel said as they all knelt in front of the kiln.

"O, Yahweh, we praise You and thank You for sending Your angel to rescue the friends I love more than anyone else on earth. You heard our cry and acted powerfully to preserve them for Your service. We should have expected no less. Forgive our lack of faith. Thank You for sparing all Your people—the exiles, including myself. We would have all eventually faced the same destiny for refusing to worship the golden image. May we never underestimate Your protective care. Also, I recognize Your mighty hand in turning my nemesis into the charred remains lying beside me. Amen."

"Do you have anything to eat at your chambers?" Azariah asked Daniel. "I'm starving."

The four boarded Daniel's carriage laughing.

Daniel opened the door to his chamber and was startled by the lamplight. Then he stiffened as his eyes adjusted to King Nebuchadnezzar seated at his table with a wine flask and cup in front of him.

slightly.

Mishael, Hananiah, and Azariah followed Daniel into his room, and the four joined the king at the table at his invitation. It was the first time he had ever been in Daniel's chamber.

"Please excuse my intrusion," the king said. "I am so overwhelmed by what I . . . what we . . . what Babylon just experienced. I will not be able to sleep until I resolve what happened. It is obvious your God miraculously saved you three from execution by my command. Your God is superior to all gods of Babylon. I have never seen such a miracle from my gods."

"O king," Daniel said. "Our Yahweh is not superior to other gods. He is the only God. He is the Creator of all things—the heavens, the earth, and all that is on the earth. All other gods are from the minds of men, and their images are merely formed by the hands of men. They are powerless and of no use to Babylon or any other nation."

Daniel was amazed by his own bold words directed to the king. They came with no forethought.

Nebuchadnezzar leaned back and looked to the ceiling. "I can accept that your God is more powerful than my gods, at least at present. But Marduk, the greatest god of Babylon, has empowered our nation to conquer the world and has made me the mightiest of all kings."

"If your humble servant may be so daring, Your Excellence, your rise to world power has been only by the allowance of Yahweh. He has ultimate purpose in your defeat of many nations, including our beloved Judah. Your reign is at His mercy and control. He gives power and takes power away. He is not to be found in impotent idols but commands that there will be no idols. Therefore, I respectfully advise that you destroy all idols in all of Babylon, beginning with the huge image of Marduk in the outer chamber of this palace."

The king was silent. Daniel could see the tenseness on the faces of the other three, but he felt at peace.

"I must do much thinking about this, Belteshazzar," the king finally spoke. "But I assure you I will consider your God mightier than Marduk or any other god in Babylon." He walked toward the door.

"Oh, and, Shadrach, Meshach, and Abednego, I will compensate you liberally for what I have put you through," the king said.

"Your Highness," Daniel said. "What about your golden image? Will you rescind your declaration that all people worship it?"

As he exited the room without looking back, he replied, "The people shouldn't worship an inferior image, should they? Circulate a retraction to my declaration throughout the kingdom."

Several days passed with no royal musicians calling the people to worship the golden image according to the king's declaration. Daniel presented the cancelation and replacement of the declaration to the king for his approval:

Nebuchadnezzar the king to all the peoples, nations, and men of *every language that live in all the earth: "May your peace abound!*

It has seemed good to me to declare the signs and wonders which
the Most High God has done for me.

"How great are His signs

And how mighty are His wonders!

His kingdom is an everlasting kingdom

And His dominion is from generation to generation."

I hereby declare the Most High God as the true God of
Babylon and all other gods and their images as false and
unworthy of worship.

"Well-crafted, Belteshazzar," King Nebuchadnezzar said. "I am anticipating great things for Babylon from your Most High God!"

Daniel nodded and smiled. *That was not exactly the response I wanted.*
His acceptance of Yahweh is from selfish motives, but it is a starting point.

"Just have the scribes remove the last sentence and place my seal
on copies to all rulers," the king continued.

"But, Your Highness, that statement is key to the declaration."

"Everyone must be free to worship their gods of choice. I welcome
your God, but I will not take the risk of denying other gods. I assumed
you would be pleased that the Hebrew exiles will be free to worship
their Most High God."

Daniel seethed, wanting to burst out with arguments that were
welling up inside, but he bit his lip to keep the words contained. Today,
he would live with his conflicted emotions, take the limited victory,
and wait for a better time to engage.

---

8 Daniel 4:1-3

*

A Few Months Later

Just after midnight, Daniel awoke abruptly and sat up in his bed. His dream vividly replayed in his mind. Nitocris, the twenty-four-year-old daughter of Nebuchadnezzar by his first wife, Nitokris, was standing on the steps of the Ishtar temple motioning with both hands for him to come to her. She was dressed as a bride prepared for a wedding. She turned to enter the temple, looking over her shoulder at him. Once more, she beckoned him to follow her, then disappeared into the temple.

Daniel could not get back to sleep. At the break of dawn, he began a long walk to Ishtar temple, overwhelmingly driven to respond to the invitation in the dream. It was not the day of worship of the temple's namesake goddess, but there was much activity in the courtyard and around the entrance. He soon realized he was witnessing the common ritual of temple prostitutes offering themselves as an act of worship. He knew all too well the dreadful practice of heathen men, especially traveling tradesmen. They professed to worship the fertility goddess, Ishtar, through sexual pleasures with the prostitutes.

Yahweh, my Lord, why did You lead me to this abhorrent scene? It invokes the memories of the sacrifice of the baby to Molech. I know about this, but You have protected me from ever having to see it. I cannot dishonor You by going into the temple, even though the dream implied I should. You must show me my next move quickly, or it will be to run away from this.

Daniel opened his eyes to catch a glimpse of a beautiful young woman in quite provocative attire passing to his right, heading toward the temple. A second glance took his breath away.

"Nitocris!"

"Belteshazzar! What is a pious Hebrew doing here?"

"Er—I would ask the same of the princess."

"Come walk with me, and I'll explain."

Yahweh, is this Your answer? I am not confident, but this is not coincidence. Protect me.

"Although I am following Chaldean tradition and the will of Ishtar, I am embarrassed to discuss it with you. But perhaps you are the one the goddess has sought out for me."

"Sought out?"

"I am a virgin, Belteshazzar. Before a virgin marries, she is required to gain Ishtar's blessing by lying with a stranger in the temple as her representative."

Daniel stopped and grasped her arm. "But that is for the temple prostitutes. This is beneath you, my lady. You can't be serious."

"It is tradition. And it is the wish of my father before I marry Nabonidus."

"Nabonidus? The army officer, Nabonidus?"

"We will marry next week."

Nitocris started up the temple steps as Daniel followed, dazed by the words.

"Why would you marry Nabonidus?"

"My father admires him and believes he should become commander of the army of Babylon. He is a courageous officer. Our marriage will enhance his connection with the palace and ensure he will never aspire to lead a coup against my father's throne."

Daniel vividly recalled Nabonidus leading his troops on the final brutal raid on Jerusalem just a few years ago. "As a Hebrew, my impression of Nabonidus is quite the opposite of the king's."

"This is my day to sacrifice my virginity for Ishtar, not to talk politics."

They both walked through the huge, arched entrance. "Nitocris, you can't go through with this."

"Please, Belteshazzar, come with me and be the one."

Daniel froze. The music was enticing, her perfume captivating, her beauty even more striking in the subdued light. She pulled him to her breasts, and her lips met his. He breathed deeply and rapidly. *Good could come from this. My surrender would save her from some obnoxious, perhaps violent, stranger. Maybe Yahweh meant this for both of us. Yahweh!*

"No, Nitocris! I must go. I'm . . . sorry."

He ran to the gate. His mind flashed back to his run from the baby sacrifice. *I'm almost old enough to be her father. What was I doing? Thank you, Yahweh, and forgive me. Your purpose was not my pleasure, but a test of my obedience to You.*

The next morning, Daniel got up early and walked to the army officers' quarters. "Belteshazzar, what a surprise. I haven't seen you in months," Nabonidus said. "Cup of tea?"

"No, thank you. This isn't a social call. I saw Nitocris yesterday. I learned a lot in a short time, which has me extremely agitated."

"Now, my friend, you needn't be worried about our marriage. Yes, I am away from Babylon for long periods at times, but Nitocris is an independent woman and can thrive in those circumstances. She is popular with the people and still considered by all to be their princess. She will be a great complement to an ambitious army officer."

"It takes little discernment to see what you are up to. Nitocris would be the only heir of Nebuchadnezzar if Amel-Marduk died. The status of Queen Amytis might complicate things, but I'm sure you have a solution for her. With no male successor to the throne, the princess would become queen, and her husband would be king by default."

"You are the great mystic, Belteshazzar—the seer, the interpreter of dreams, the wiseman. Think what you want, but the people of Babylon will be thrilled with the royal wedding of the princess and the general."

"What are your post-wedding plans? Will you convince the army to overthrow the king and expel the queen, making it convenient for the princess and her valiant soldier to assume the monarchy?"

With no reply as expected, Daniel departed.

Two weeks later, the city was buzzing with the news of the wedding of Nabonidus and Nitocris that had taken place that morning. It was the event of the year for Babylon. Nabonidus gained celebrity status from the popularity of Nitocris. Daniel had not attended the wedding but looked on as the bride and groom paraded through the main streets in their decorated carriage. Shouts of "Princess, Princess!" echoed from the tall buildings. She had captured the minds and hearts of the people. They were a royal couple without a kingdom.

*

582 B.C.

Late in the afternoon, Ashpenaz called Daniel to an urgent meeting with the king.

"I have been with a messenger from Judah most of the afternoon," the king began. "Gedaliah, my governor there, has been assassinated."

"No!" Daniel blurted spontaneously. He knew about the able leadership of the vassal governor, a Hebrew appointed by Nebuchadnezzar after the destruction of the city and temple. Gedaliah had been producing stability and prosperity for the remnant of poor Hebrew laborers. Many Judahites who had fled to neighboring countries after the devastation of Jerusalem had returned, and the still sparsely populated city had enjoyed a calmness for the last four years.

"A traitor named Ishmael claims to be king of Judah as a descendant of the royal line and is leading a revolt against my kingdom. He is backed by the king of Ammon, who no doubt looks to annex Judah. This Ishmael and his followers have routed my small army contingent there, and the few remaining skilled and intelligent Hebrews have fled to Egypt. I was told your friend, Jeremiah, discouraged the mass exodus."

"Did Jeremiah stay in Judah? Did he survive?"

"The refugees forced him to go with them to Egypt, according to the messenger."

"What do you plan to do?"

"Two hundred soldiers are preparing for deployment with me tomorrow. I will return with Ishmael's head."

"Will you appoint another governor?"

"Never again. Your homeland has been impossible to rule ever since I first conquered it. I trust no Hebrew to serve me there. They have all failed me. I will leave the soldiers to rule by the sword. Those few Hebrews who did not follow the others to Egypt, I will bring back to do the worst jobs in all of Babylon."

The next day, the king departed with his entourage of soldiers and guards.

After three months, the king returned with his guards and yet another group of Hebrew exiles, this time only about five hundred, to be assigned to hard labor. Daniel learned that by the time Nebuchadnezzar arrived in Judah, Johanan, one of Gedaliah's army commanders, had pursued Ishmael, but he had escaped to Ammon. Daniel remembered Jeremiah had prophesied that Jerusalem would eventually be uninhabited. The city was now virtually empty, except for a few Babylonian soldiers. Its future would now depend on the fulfilling of another of Jeremiah's prophecies—the eventual return of the exiles.

＊

Except for the year surrounding the assassination of Gedaliah, King Nebuchadnezzar had been increasingly kind to the exiles in Babylon. The experience at the furnace still had a profound influence on him. Now the father of four sons who occupied much of his time, he seemed to be mellowing somewhat. Well, short of giving the exiles total freedom, he expanded their access to many benefits previously restricted to those of Chaldean descent. Daniel and Ezekiel had mixed feelings about this and discussed it often as they visited in each other's homes. They had observed their people becoming more at ease with the traditions of the Babylonians, even experimenting with their pagan gods. On a particular visit, Ezekiel placed on a table before Daniel a long piece of papyrus on which he had written.

"God will return His people to their homeland," Daniel.

"I have all confidence in the prophesies that one day all of us will have the opportunity to return to Judah," said Daniel. "But I worry that our people are getting so comfortable here, some of them will not be inclined to return. And there are thousands of children here who have not known any other place but Babylon."

"I haven't shared this with you, but Yahweh gave me a vision a few days ago that showed me His plan to raise up His people and lead them back to their land. It is yet another confirmation of His eternal and unconditional love for us. I wanted to wait to tell you until I had written it down for you to read and, perhaps, copy." He pointed to his words.

The hand of the LORD was upon me, and He brought me out by the Spirit of the LORD and set me down in the middle of the valley, and it was full of bones. He caused me to pass among them round about, and behold, there were very many on the surface of the valley; and lo, they were very dry. He said to me, "Son of man, can these bones live?" And I answered, "O Lord GOD, You know." Again He said to me, "Prophesy over these bones and say to them, 'O dry bones, hear the word of the Lord.' Thus says the Lord GOD to these bones, 'Behold, I will cause breath to enter you that you may come to life. I will put sinews on you, make flesh grow back on you, cover you with skin and put breath in you that you may come alive; and you will know that I am the LORD.'" So I prophesied as I was commanded; and as I prophesied, there was a noise, and behold, a rattling; and the bones came together, bone to its bone. And I looked, and behold, sinews were on them, and flesh grew, and skin covered them; but there was no breath in them. Then He said to me, "Prophesy to the breath, prophesy, son of man, and say to the breath, 'Thus says the Lord GOD, Come from the four winds, O breath, and breathe on these slain, that they come to life.'" So I prophesied as He commanded me, and the breath came into them, and they came to life and stood on their feet, an exceedingly great army.[9]

---

9 Ezekiel 37:1-10

Daniel looked up and smiled. Ezekiel continued, "I haven't written the rest yet. But Yahweh explained in my vision that the bones were the whole house of Israel. He said He would renew their lives and bring them back into the land of Israel. He is also giving me visions of the rebuilding of the temple and the division of the land among the tribes. I have a lot of writing to do."

"You certainly do, and you must finish writing the many prophesies you have publicly proclaimed over the last several years. These must be preserved by our scribes. Your vision is also affirmed by Jeremiah's prophecy that the period of exile would end after seventy years.

"Yes, I refer to those words often. The seventy-year period also relates to the land sabbath God directed in the Torah. His people were to raise crops for six years and rest the land for the seventh year. We stopped doing that as we transitioned from His judges to our kings for leadership. Since then, we have failed to observe seventy land sabbath years. God is requiring us to repay those seventy years by resting the land of Judah while we are in exile. We are at about the halfway point of our seventy years now. I feel an urgency to study, write, and prophesy like never before, my friend. But my health is beginning to fail me. I am becoming weaker by the day."

That comment caught Daniel by surprise. He had noticed Ezekiel's face seemed to be paler but had attributed that to the long hours he was spending inside documenting his prophecies. "I will get you some help from the scribes and will send the palace physician to you."

Over the next few weeks, Daniel gave much attention to Ezekiel and ensured all the prophet had heard from Yahweh was recorded on the finest parchment available. The palace doctor reported Ezekiel's heart was very weak, and he needed much more rest than he was getting.

On a Sabbath morning with a rare, light rain, a lone scribe found Ezekiel still lying on his bed with no sign of life. The scribe ran to the palace to inform Daniel. As Daniel sat on the floor of his room after hearing the news, his head in his hands, the scribe offered some positive news.

"I hope it will bring some ease to your pain that Ezekiel finished writing the last of his visions from Yahweh just yesterday. It was as if he was allowed to die the moment he finished his calling."

"At fifty-one years of age, he still had a lot to offer Yahweh, but we should not question His sovereignty," Daniel said. "All His ways have purpose. We must praise Him in all things, even in those things that give us much pain."

As the scribe departed, Daniel wiped the fog from his window and saw a vivid rainbow spanning the eastern sky. With tears still flowing, he gave thanks for the life of his friend and servant of Yahweh.

22

The sun had yielded its light to the first stars as Daniel, Hananiah, Azariah, and Mishael sat on the ground in front of the lime kiln to pray and celebrate. The only evidence of the brick baking fire that had raged all day in the kiln was a few glowing embers made brighter by the ensuing darkness.

"What a solemn and joyful time as we look back fifteen years ago today," Daniel said. "Yahweh not only saved the lives of my closest friends but also freed our people to openly worship Him."

"That miracle also turned many Babylonians from idols to Him and ultimately allowed them to live out that new belief without risk of death," Hananiah said.

"Looking at that kiln takes my breath away, even after all these years, as I relive walking into the fire," Mishael said. "Believing in miracles cannot match being a part of one."

"We have so much to be thankful to Yahweh for," Daniel said. "We have been allowed to live to see a long period of peace in Babylon, to lead the building of the most beautiful city in the world, and to see our Hebrew people prosper even while in captivity. Freed from the influence of Bulludhu, most of the magi advisors are now following my leadership and depending on Yahweh for their counsel. Many of them are studying the Torah and the Prophets. Oh, yes, and all three of you ugly men have beautiful wives and teenage children, who have somehow managed to put up with you."

At that last statement, Daniel found himself wrestled to the ground by the other three, who playfully mussed his hair. They all laughed long and hard, then joined hands and prayed until well into the evening.

For the past few years, Daniel's contact with King Nebuchadnezzar had been progressively less frequent. The king had been away for many months on a sweeping army campaign through Ammon and Moab. Now, two years after his conquests, several days would often pass with the king never leaving his chamber. Daniel was assuming more responsibility for governing the kingdom by default.

Daniel had just gotten in bed one night when he heard his door open. Grabbing his sword lying next to the bed, he sat up instantly.

"It's me, Belteshazzar," Amytis' quiet voice announced.

Daniel rose, wrapped himself in his blanket, and lighted the lamp. Amytis, dressed in her sleepwear, ran to Daniel quickly and embraced him.

"It's all right," she said. "The children are asleep, and he has been asleep for an hour. He would not miss me if he awoke as we haven't slept in the same bed for almost a year. He moves and groans in his sleep so much that I can't sleep with him."

"Why are you telling me this, and why are you here?"

"He is not well. He often says things that make no sense and can't remember important things. He sleeps most of the day."

"Then we need to get him medical attention."

"I've tried. He won't hear of it. I wanted to tell you much sooner, but he threatened my life if I told anyone. He thinks it would make people question his ability to rule."

"You needed to tell me. I must think about how to approach him and urge him to see the palace physician."

"All in good time, Belteshazzar. But tonight, I just need to be held. I have been so lonely. I am sixty years old with an ill husband who has lost his desire for me."

"Amytis, we can't. We have been through this before. I will never betray my king. More importantly, I will not disobey the law of Yahweh. You are still a beautiful woman, and everything within me wants you; but you must go back to your husband now."

"Don't deny me, Belteshazzar. I am the queen of Babylon. I can make you regret rejecting me."

"You must go." Daniel clinched her arms, turned her around, and gently pushed her to the door, closing it behind her, then bracing the door with his shoulder. He could hear her sobbing. He broke out in a cold sweat.

The next morning, Ashpenaz interrupted Daniel's breakfast with a message to meet the king in his chamber.

"Not the outer chamber?" Daniel inquired.

"No, the king's chamber."

Amytis answered Daniel's knock. With stoic expression, she motioned for him to enter. The king sat in the corner of the room still in his undergarment. His face was ashen.

"Ah, Belteshazzar, excuse my informality. I have not been well and not very motivated to assume my normal activities for the last few days."

"The last few weeks," Amytis whispered.

The king was not making eye contact but was focused on the wall. "I have not slept well but have had a vision, maybe a dream, that keeps repeating every night. I have called on your magicians to determine its meaning, but none of their explanations were believable. Since your interpretation of the strange statue as a young man, you have never failed to enlighten me concerning my dreams, Belteshazzar. Your God always gives you the meaning."

"I am honored, my lord. If it pleases the king, describe your dream."

The king closed his eyes and began. "There was a tree that grew large and strong, reaching to the sky. All the earth could see it. It had beautiful leaves, and its fruit was plentiful enough to feed everyone. Even all the animals were fed from it as they enjoyed its shade and nested in its branches.

The king paused momentarily and seemed troubled. "Then a heavenly being descended and shouted, 'Chop down the tree, remove its branches and leaves, and scatter its fruit! Drive the animals away from it! Leave the stump and roots with a brass and iron fence around them. Let him be soaked with dew and eat grass like the animals. Let him have the mind of an animal and remain in this condition for seven periods of time.' This was decreed by the heavenly being speaking for the Holy One, so that everyone will know that the Most High rules over mankind through whomever He wishes, even the lowest of men."

Opening his eyes, the king said, "This is my dream, Belteshazzar, which none of my wise men could interpret. But I know you are able because the spirit of the holy gods is in you."

"Your Highness, even while you were speaking, the one true God began revealing to me the meaning of your dream, and it alarms me greatly."

"Belteshazzar, do not let my dream or its interpretation alarm you."

"But, my lord, I only wish the dream and its interpretation applied to your enemies!"

Daniel swallowed hard and continued. "The tree in your dream represents you, O king. You have become great and strong, and your authority has reached to the sky. Your kingdom has spread to the ends of the earth.

"The Most High has decreed that you will be driven from your palace to a wilderness, where you will eat grass with the animals and be soaked with dew. You will remain in this condition for seven periods of time until you recognize the Most High rules over all mankind through whomever He wishes, even the lowest of men. Therefore, O king, be pleased with my advice. Repent of your sins and do good by showing mercy to the poor, and perhaps the Most High might extend your reign and your good fortune."

Daniel had watched the king's countenance fall as his interpretation progressed. His expression turned to anger.

"Your one true God is no more capable than the gods of your magicians, Belteshazzar. My mind has weakened with my illness, but I am not insane. Depart from me! I will hear no more of your rubbish!"

Daniel hesitated, then bowed and walked out of the room, followed by Amytis. She closed the door behind her and hugged him tightly.

"I'm afraid."

"Be sorry for what Yahweh will take him through, but do not be afraid for your safety. Remember, the dream assured that he will regain his kingdom in the end."

"Amel-Marduk is not prepared to rule Babylon," she said.

"Your husband will be king as long as he lives. If he is not capable for a time, I can govern in his stead, but I will be loyal to him as my king—and you will be his wife, the queen."

*

One year later

King Nebuchadnezzar had shown no change in character or genuine acceptance of the one true God since the foreboding interpretation of his dream. To the contrary, his degenerating health seemed to bring on more frequent fits of rage against anyone who disagreed with him. His punishment meted out to wrongdoers had become progressively crueler.

Daniel was midway through a morning meeting when the door swung open.

"Where is the king?" Amytis yelled.

Everyone stood, and Daniel quickly stepped around the table to her side. "I haven't seen him this morning."

Her voice quivered. "He wasn't in his bed this morning. I've looked everywhere in the palace."

"I'm sure he is close by. He may be out for a walk or taking a carriage tour of the gardens."

"Belteshazzar!" she scolded. "His guards and his carriage driver have not seen him either. None of his clothes are missing."

"Gentlemen, we're adjourned," Daniel said as he took Amytis' arm and walked her out the door.

"He acted very strange last night," Amytis said. "I was awakened by his shouting from his room. He was rambling about his building of Babylon for his glory and by his own power. I followed him into the outer chamber and watched him climb up the stairway to the rooftop. I waited a few moments, then went back to bed. I'm afraid he wandered away from the palace during the night."

"It doesn't seem that he could have gotten past the guards and the watchmen, but in the dark and as he was dressed, they may have thought he was a commoner."

"I should have been more sensitive to his condition and moved back into his room."

"I'll organize some of our soldiers and search the city and out into the country if necessary."

About an hour later, as Daniel watched part of the military search team depart through the gate, he was approached by Mishael.

"Daniel, the king's mind has left him, and he is out there in the wilderness somewhere, just as Yahweh revealed through your interpretation last year."

"I believe you are right. If so, no amount of search efforts will succeed until Yahweh is ready for him to be found."

Before Daniel's breakfast was delivered the next morning, Amytis entered his chamber.

"Did the soldiers find anything, any clue as to the king's whereabouts?"

"Nothing. Every search team leader checked in with my administrators. They are certain he is not in the city. Most of the countryside within a day's walk has been covered, but there is no evidence of where he might have gone."

"We must get them out again early. Have them look farther out. Maybe he has been taken prisoner. Check the outlying villages."

Daniel clasped her hands gently. "In any other situation, I would agree, but further searches would be futile in this case. Plus, it is a security risk to have so much of our army scattered outside the city."

"Other situation? This case? What are you saying?"

"The dream that Yahweh placed in the head of the king a year ago was His plan for him. I believe my interpretation revealed the will of Yahweh, and nothing will interrupt that plan. I am relieved that the dream included the king's return to the throne and his rule after a period of time."

"I'm sure you're not surprised that I don't believe that. It is very convenient for you to give meaning to a dream that eliminates the king and leaves you in a position to rule the kingdom unrestrained. Maybe you arranged for his disappearance."

Daniel's grasp of her hands tightened.

"Don't be ridiculous! Your son would become ruler if something happened to the king, not I."

"Amel-Marduk is only seventeen. He would become king, but you would make decisions for him. He would be just a figurehead—someone to seal your proclamations. Don't forget who would still be queen."

"Amytis, do you really think I would be so disloyal to your family?"

"I don't know what to think!" Amytis ran out the door crying and disappeared down the hallway.

The next afternoon, Daniel was meeting in the outer chamber with his administrators and the chief architects.

"I am pleased with the progress of the many new construction projects throughout the city. The lion images on the gates and public buildings have set a high standard for the world's craftsmen. The chief of commerce reports that trade with other nations has doubled in the last ten years. They credit not only our agriculture and fabrication markets, but people are also drawn to Babylon for the gardens, the buildings, and the fine artisan works. In the king's absence, let us not relax our pursuit of the world's finest of everything. May he see great progress on his return."

Everyone's attention to Daniel's comments was suddenly interrupted by the entrance of Amytis and Amel-Marduk. He was in full regalia, including his father's turban. Daniel and his leaders stood.

"Your Highness, what does this mean?"

"We do not know the whereabouts of my husband or even whether he is alive. If, by a miracle, he returns, he will not be fit to be king. We need to have a coronation for my son."

"Gentlemen, please excuse us," Daniel said, and the meeting attendees left the room, looking back over their shoulders.

"Amytis, what are you doing? I have every confidence the king will return in due time and will be completely restored, as his dream predicted. In the meantime, the kingdom will run as normal—"

"In the meantime," Amytis interrupted, "you see yourself as king. Never! Not while I am queen and my son is heir to the throne. You have no bloodline authority to rule Babylon. You are not even a Babylonian. You are a Hebrew slave. I don't know what the king even saw in you."

"How quickly you have changed—from admiring me to despising me."

"Perhaps it was not a wise choice for you to have rejected me at several inviting opportunities. Maybe you could have been king. And I could have been your queen."

Daniel's jaw tightened as he looked away.

"You poor, Hebrew fool," she continued. "You came to Babylon as a boy with nothing, and the king gave you riches and power. Now, you are fifty; you govern the kingdom; you are known worldwide; but you still lack one thing. You are still not the king. I can give you that one thing you lack, Belteshazzar. Marry me, and we will rule Babylon."

"Mother!" Amel-Marduk snapped.

"Think about it," Amytis said. "Be my king, or be my young son's administrator."

The queen and her son returned to their chamber, and Daniel sat on the floor looking at the high, ornate ceiling. "Yahweh, what now?"

Daniel had not been able to fall asleep until the early hours of the morning. He was praying repeatedly that the dream's seven periods of time away meant seven months and not seven years. He was awakened by a knock. He opened the door to Ashpenaz. Amel-Marduk stood behind him.

"The queen wants her son to begin spending each day with you. She wants him to learn how the palace is organized and who is responsible for what in the kingdom," Ashpenaz said.

Daniel strained to keep from saying what he really wanted to say. "Certainly, I can show and explain the many things he will need to know someday when he succeeds his father on the throne. It will take months of confidence-building and testing to qualify him for ruling the kingdom. Of course, when his father returns, he will resume that responsibility."

"Mother will be talking with you soon about arranging my coronation," Amel-Marduk said.

For the next several weeks, Amel-Marduk met Daniel each morning and stayed by his side all day through meetings, inspections, hearing complaints from the city's overseers, visiting army units, studying various reports, and appearing at major social events. They made numerous overnight trips to outlying cities. Daniel was training the young man to be king but, in his mind, not any time soon.

At least once a month, Daniel visited the Shamash Gate, where the Hebrew elders and community leaders met daily at noon to discuss their religion and social issues. This time, Amel-Marduk accompanied him. Daniel's presence and contribution to the conversations were always welcome, but his guest was not well-received. Daniel had always arranged for King Jehoiachin to join the group under the watch of two Babylonian guards. He introduced Amel-Marduk to the king.

"I am indeed honored to meet you," Amel-Marduk said. "I have grown up admiring the contributions you and your people make to the economy and aesthetics of our fine city. The Hebrews have assimilated well into our culture while maintaining their heritage. I have been concerned that your people are not being properly rewarded for their role in Babylon's ascendance to greatness. As soon as I am crowned king, I will see that you are given your freedom and the other Hebrews are more properly cared for."

Daniel was quite surprised by this statement. Some of the men within hearing distance motioned for others to come and witness what was being said.

"I, uh, really appreciate your kind recognition of our efforts and—and—willingness to treat us fairly," Jehoiachin responded.

Amel-Marduk turned to face Daniel. "We need to visit the king's prison room soon to see whether we might need to make his accommodations more suitable for the king of the Hebrews."

Daniel nodded, hardly able to believe what he was hearing.

Later that afternoon, as Daniel expected, word had gotten around the palace court that Amel-Marduk had shown respect for the exiles and honor for their captive king and that he intended to improve their treatment. Neriglissar, an army officer with aspirations to become emperor of the kingdom's army, approached Daniel on the palace portico. His father had been a highly decorated general and had paved the way for his son's ascension through the ranks. Nitocris' husband, Nabonidus, was currently emperor of the imperial army.

"Sir, I'm sure you know that the people of Babylon are rather troubled about the prospects of Amel-Marduk becoming king," Neriglissar said.

"Yes, I am aware anxiety is building, and I, too, am concerned. There are laws in place that initiate royal succession when a king dies or is incapable of ruling the kingdom. But a missing king is unprecedented, and there is no plan in place for that."

"My opposition to his coronation will forever prevent me from attaining the position of emperor of the army if he becomes king and may cost me my life. But, sir, he will devastate our empire with his youthful, idealist whims. He is at a dangerous age to be king. He is too old to be subject to the tutelage of advisors and too young to think wisely on his own. His showing of favor to the Hebrews by significantly increasing their compensation for their labor would obliterate the treasury. And he is a borderline pacifist, more interested in the comforts of the people than the conquest of nations."

"Neriglissar, Yahweh revealed to me, based on King Nebuchadnezzar's dream, that the king would disappear for a time, then reappear to rule again. I want you to begin sending small search teams out each day in anticipation of his reappearance. I believe the king will return soon. I will do everything I can to avoid the coronation of Amel-Marduk."

"The survival of Babylonia hinges on that, Your Excellence."

23

For the next three months, Amel-Marduk continued to shadow Daniel. At the young heir's persistence, he wrote a few innocuous proclamations that Daniel authenticated by his seal. Finding it difficult to meet privately with principals of the palace court because of the constant presence of his companion, Daniel often sent notes to his leaders, assuring them that he, rather than the king's son, was in charge of the affairs of the kingdom. The notes seemed to be having the intended effect of minimizing the apprehension about a potential coronation.

Returning late in the afternoon from inspecting the crops that were soon to be harvested, Daniel and Amel-Marduk had just entered the gate in their carriage when three of the guards ran to them each waving a sheet of papyrus. All three spoke loudly at once until one finally prevailed.

"Your Excellence, you have assured us this would not happen!"

Daniel took the sheet and read:

> I hereby proclaim that my father, Nebuchadnezzar, the former king of Babylon, has been missing for almost seven months. I declare him dead. My mother, Queen Amytis, and

286

I will arrange my coronation to take place in two weeks. Considering the critical need to expedite this ceremony due to the risks of being without a king, participation of the governors, satraps, and administrators from beyond two weeks' journey will not be required. Preparation for the coronation will begin immediately.

The new seal of Amel-Marduk was applied to the proclamation.

Daniel turned to Amel-Marduk. "Is this you or your mother?"

"You knew, Belteshazzar, that Babylon could not continue forever without a king."

Daniel shouted to his driver to rush to the palace. Once there, he leaped from the carriage leaving his passenger behind.

"What have you done?" Daniel said sharply as he burst into Amytis' chamber unannounced.

"How dare you charge into my room uninvited!"

He waved the proclamation in front of her face. "How could you do this without my knowledge or approval?"

"Your approval? *Your* approval? A Hebrew exile has to approve who is king of mighty Babylon? No! You swine. My son will be king, and you will arrange the coronation."

"Nebuchadnezzar is still king—and still your husband. We may be approaching the time of his return. No, I cannot participate in a coronation."

"Then you no longer have any authority over Babylon. Leave the palace now. Go peacefully, and perhaps my son will spare your life when he is king."

"Surely, you can't be serious. Babylon will be in chaos within a few weeks after the coronation."

"Guards!" she yelled. The two door guards immediately appeared inside the doorway. "Escort Belteshazzar out of the palace after he gathers his belongings from what was his chamber. Take his robe, sash, and turban."

The stunned guards stood motionless, exchanging glances between Daniel and Amytis.

"Bind him if necessary," the queen said.

"I won't give you the pleasure of seeing that." Daniel departed the room with the guards following closely.

Raviv was in Daniel's chamber, having been alerted to his expulsion. He helped bundle the personal belongings and wept as Daniel embraced him on the way out the door.

With a large bag over his shoulder, Daniel walked the long street to the residence halls of Babylon officials. He passed a lamplighter in the corridor tending the oil lamps for the evening as he knocked on the door of Mishael's quarters.

"Daniel! I thought I would see you soon after receiving the proclamation, but why are you not in your official attire?"

Mishael's wife and toddler son appeared from the adjacent room.

"Galya, would you please bring Azariah and Hananiah to us?" Daniel asked Mishael's wife. "We have a lot to discuss."

Moments later, Daniel was explaining to his three friends what had happened and gave them instructions pertaining to the upcoming coronation. They discussed the preparations and how to hold the kingdom together as much as possible in Daniel's absence.

"You are welcome to stay with Galya and me," Mishael said.

"I appreciate the kind offer. I will do that tonight. But I may be a prisoner soon, if allowed to live. Amel-Marduk may find it in his best interest to have me executed."

Daniel rose early the next morning and sat alone on the stone land-ing behind Mishael's quarters. He eyes were fixed on the palace. The rising sun shimmered on the majestic dome. Uncontrollable emotions welled up inside his soul from conflicted feelings.

Am I agonizing for Babylon, for my Hebrew people, or for me? O, Yahweh, awaken. Correct this wrong. Do not let Babylon fall under a mindless king and a ruthless queen. I feel like your prophet Isaiah, who said, "Woe is me, for I am ruined."[10] *You must have no further use for me.*

For the next two weeks, no one attempted to look for or contact Daniel. He stayed inside Mishael's quarters around the clock, careful to not remind anyone that he was still around. He observed a lot of activity near the palace as the entire city focused on preparing for the coronation. Mishael kept him updated on the progress of the corona-tion preparation and always had questions about how to plan it properly. Finally, on a warm and breezy Thursday morning, palace trumpeters were sounding the call for the city to assemble in and around the palace courtyard. The planners had avoided a Friday or Saturday, the Jewish Sabbath, in order to accommodate Amel-Marduk's insistence that all the Hebrews attend the event.

Daniel had decided to attend as just another Hebrew, wearing com-mon attire and blending into the crowd. Many near him bowed as he passed, but he waved them off. Working his way forward as much as possible in the press of the crowd, he stopped a short distance from the courtyard entrance. He stood with thousands of others, barely able to see the proceedings and well outside of hearing distance. Few of those present were pleased about the coronation, but everyone knew they had to appear supportive and excited about it.

---

10 Isaiah 6:5

All regional officials within two weeks' journey of Babylon had gathered in the city and were seated among the palace elite directly in front of an elevated platform. On the platform was the throne that had been moved from the outer chamber room. Strategically placed behind the throne, but clearly visible, was a replica of the larger Marduk image in the outer chamber. Immediately below the platform was the one hundred-musician royal orchestra. Daniel recognized the flowers and green plants prominent throughout the courtyard as coming from the hanging gardens.

The orchestra music stopped when the throngs had filled the courtyard and as far as Daniel could see in every direction. Commotion ceased, and voices silenced. Trumpeters blared a short fanfare. Formally dressed soldiers with spears and shields filed out of the main palace door and lined the rear and sides of the platform perimeter. Another trumpet fanfare sounded. A low-level murmur from the crowd ensued as the heir-apparent to the throne appeared from the rear of the platform, accompanied by two guards walking closely behind. Trailing her son, escorted by two more guards, strode the queen.

Loud applause by all in attendance began mixed with shouts of "Hail the king!" The orchestra played a rousing royal anthem arranged specifically for the honoree. The chief priest of Babylon stepped forward to read the public proclamation of coronation. Next to him stood his assistant with the royal crown the priest would place on the king. Another assistant held the regal robe over his outstretched forearms. Even from the distance, Daniel recognized the robe as Nebuchadnezzar's.

Daniel was straining to hear the proclamation but was finding it difficult because of the rising of distant voices behind him. He turned around to see some sort of disturbance developing across the street.

Several guards were pushing their way through the crowd toward the commotion. His instinct drove him to move in that direction until he reminded himself he had no authority now. The voices grew louder. More guards ran in the direction of the noise. Hundreds of heads turned from the platform to the disruption. The clamor increased and progressed forward through the crowd.

"Make way! Royal guards! Make way!" the guards ordered.

Daniel could see the guards' helmets close by as they marched through the press of people shoving many out of their path. On his tiptoes, he saw what appeared to be someone being escorted by the guards. He got a quick look through a momentary parting of people beside him. The guards were having to carry their man, whose arms were around their shoulders.

"It's the king!" yelled a bystander.

"Hail the king!" yelled another.

"The king is back!" shouts came from every direction.

Daniel's heart raced as he pushed others aside, forcing his way forward. *Praise You, Yahweh! Praise You!* The mass of people pressed toward the courtyard, making it impossible for Daniel to move farther, but he was within hearing range of the platform. The priest had stopped reading. All eyes on the platform were glued to the guards as they started up the steps with their mystery guest. Gasps could be heard from officials on the stage.

The man between the guards was in tattered and soiled clothing. His limbs and back were exposed, and he was barefoot. Even with his long and matted hair and beard, he was recognized by everyone on the platform, including the occupant of the throne and his mother.

"Ahh!" Amel-Marduk blurted, his eyes bugged with shock.

All the palace guards and the priests dropped to their knees. Amel-Marduk, in a daze, hesitated, then bowed from the throne. Amytis, agape, knelt beside the throne.

King Nebuchadnezzar dismissed his two guards, looked around the platform, and turned to the crowd. "Where is Belteshazzar?" he asked in a hoarse voice.

Daniel moved through the crowd, pushing and shoving as necessary, making his way through the courtyard to the bottom of the steps. Bowing, he responded, "Your Highness."

"Come up here, Belteshazzar."

Daniel charged up the steps and bowed again before the king. Nebuchadnezzar turned to face his wife and son. "It is obvious what is happening here. Guards, remove this unworthy animal from my throne, along with his mother. Imprison them for swift execution."

"Have mercy on us, my king," Amytis said, as the doomed mother and son were led away.

The priest placed the crown on Nebuchadnezzar as his assistant wrapped his robe around his shoulders. The king took his place on the throne as the silenced crowd erupted in roaring shouts of praise and applause.

Running up to Daniel, Raviv bowed before him. His broad smile turned to joyful laughter. Daniel broke protocol and hugged him tightly.

"I believe you have a job to do. Get my things from Mishael's quarters and carry them back to my palace chamber. But first, find Ashpenaz and ask him to prepare the king's bath and ready his wardrobe."

Daniel was organizing his chamber when the anticipated visit by Ashpenaz brought the expected invitation to meet with the king as soon as possible.

"Belteshazzar!" The king met Daniel at the door and embraced him tightly. The thought flashed through Daniel's mind of his own impulsive embracing of Raviv the day before. *Sometimes, protocols of authority need to be disregarded.* He was wearing the royal clothing and had a fresh haircut and shave. His fingernails and toenails were nicely trimmed. "Please sit down." Nebuchadnezzar motioned to a chair next to his. "Words cannot express how sorry I am for what you have had to endure in my absence. I am also so sorry and regretful for my dismissal of your interpretation of my dream many months ago. I realize fully your message to me from your God was true, and I have been the receiver of the wrath of the one true God."

"Your Excellence, my greatest desire is that you would accept Yahweh as not only the one true God, but also as your one true Yahweh."

"Oh, I have, Belteshazzar. For just as your interpretation said, I survived many weeks in the wilderness, crawling on my hands and knees, eating what plants I could find. My hair and beard grew long, and my fingernails were like those of bird claws. I did not know who I was or where I belonged."

The king paused and lowered his head, then continued.

"Then a few days ago, I woke up, lying on the ground drenched with dew as always, and my mind seemed to be clear. I remembered the palace, my wife and son. I remembered the dream, and I sensed the direction to Babylon. On the way, some soldiers found me. I voiced a prayer to the Most High God that I still remember precisely: 'God is the Most High, and His kingdom is everlasting. All the inhabitants of earth and heaven are subject to His will. No one can deny or question His will."

"I am pleased and thankful to Yahweh that He has restored you as He promised in the dream. I also celebrate your statement of commitment to Him. However, Your Excellence, you know how you turned to Him after the first dream interpretation and after the miracle at the furnace. But your acceptance of Him as the one true God was short-lived."

"I know, Belteshazzar, those were profound movements by the one true God, but they didn't affect me personally. This time, He spared my life. He rescued me—not my advisors or your friends, but me. He has my attention. He has my faithfulness."

"O king, live forever, Yahweh has again shown His superiority to the other gods of Babylon; I will pray that His favor shines on your kingdom and on your throne. May your health be renewed for many more years of rule in Babylon followed by your son and your son's sons."

Daniel referenced the succession to the throne to bring up an essential point. He watched the king's countenance change.

"My son's betrayal has ensured he will never succeed me. His head will be severed before sundown along with his mother's."

"If I may intercede, Your Excellence. Your commitment to Yahweh has just been tested. He has shown undeserved mercy by forgiving you of repeated rejection and restoring you to health and to your throne. I believe if you give Him full attention, He will guide you to show the same mercy to your wife and son."

After a long silence with no eye contact, the king looked at Daniel. "You challenge me beyond my capacity, Belteshazzar. I will promise nothing but to think on it."

"Think and pray, Your Excellency. You can now pray to Yahweh."

The next morning, Daniel paid an early visit to the jail where Amel-Marduk and Amytis had been cast. They were together in an austere room with no windows normally reserved for miscreants of the most egregious crimes. The morning sun shone directly through the door as a guard opened it for Daniel. They shielded their eyes, unable to see their visitor at first. The room was cold and damp. Still dressed in formal attire, their contrast with the abysmal surroundings was bizarre.

"It is Belteshazzar," Daniel said. "I am relieved that you remain alive."

Amytis walked to a corner and faced the wall.

"We were told by the chief guard last evening that our lives would be spared, but we would be forever confined here," Amel-Marduk said.

Daniel smiled. "You should thank Yahweh for sparing your lives."

He exited back into the warm, fresh air. *Thank You, Yahweh.*

24

The empire of Babylon had been relatively quiet and peaceful over the six years following King Nebuchadnezzar's wandering in the wilderness and his subsequent campaign into Egypt. He and his army marched on Egypt and overran population concentrations along the Nile collecting great riches from the land. The invasion was a show of strength for any who might doubt his power after his seven-month absence. The king was prevented from extending his empire to all of Egypt, but the Babylonian treasuries benefitted exceedingly from the battles.

The dark, damp prison room took its toll on Amytis. She died four years after her imprisonment and was buried next to the commoners with no special ceremony. The king and his daughters, Nitocris and Kashshaia, grieved in private, but it was short-lived with no public mourning. Daniel mourned her death privately, despite the extremes of their relationship. He had conflicted feelings about her that he never really understood. Amel-Marduk blamed her for his situation and felt no loss from her death. His animosity was further fueled by their close proximity incarceration for four years.

To Daniel's knowledge, neither Amel-Marduk's father nor his half-sisters had visited him. Neither had Daniel. Only a few steps from his prison room were those occupied by the two kings of Judah, Jehoiachin and Zedekiah. Zedekiah had become almost totally incapacitated, unable to even sit up and feed himself.

King Nebuchadnezzar's health had continued to deteriorate, requiring Daniel to again assume even more of the governing responsibilities. The great city of Babylon was inundated with more major building projects the king was initiating from his bed. Lavish structures built within the last two decades were receiving more elaborate facades and second or third stories. Nitocris was starting to exercise her creativity in her stepmother's absence by overseeing much of the further embellishment of the gardens. The king insisted that she be allowed to showcase her talents in developing the city's opulent landscape.

One hot summer evening, Daniel was walking with Raviv from his bath to his chamber when Nitocris ran to him in the hallway.

"Belteshazzar, my father is having difficulty breathing. I'm very worried."

Daniel instructed Raviv to get the palace doctor and meet them in the king's chamber. Nebuchadnezzar's face was very pale, and he was breathing erratically. His forehead felt cold and clammy.

"Belteshazzar," the king struggled to form words. "Believe my time has come. Wanted to give you more instruction . . . and time to prepare. But Most High God is choosing this hour. You know what to do. My son . . . must become king . . . only because there is no other heir. Not fit to rule, so that falls on you. Must trust you . . . keep him controlled."

"Father!" Nitocris began to weep.

"It is all right, Princess. I am in . . . hands of one true God." His quivering hand raised slowly to touch her cheek.

"I am speechless, O king, and my heart is heavy," Daniel said, tears forming as quick, random glimpses of the past forty-plus years flashed through his mind.

The king's other hand reached for Daniel's. "I leave this life indebted to you beyond measure. You guided my stubborn soul to see . . . truth of the Creator . . . and futility of other gods."

The palace doctor entered and knelt at the king's side. He touched the side of his neck, then cupped his hand under his nostrils. He turned to Daniel, then looked at Nitocris. "I'm sorry."

Nitocris placed her head on her father's chest and sobbed.

Few officials in the palace slept that night. Almost all were scurrying about and huddling in meetings within their departments to take initial actions in response to the death of their king. While the embalmers were preparing the body for burial, Daniel wrote the announcement that would be circulated around the city, the province, and, ultimately, throughout the empire. His mind constantly went back to the issue of succession. As the king said on his death bed, Amel-Marduk, the prisoner, would rightly become king. The very next day, he would have to begin the difficult transition process.

During a breakfast planning meeting with the five high court judges, everyone agreed on the next steps. They all went to the prison to conduct the most historical release in the history of the kingdom.

"Your Excellence, we're here to inform you that King Nebuchadnezzar departed this life last night," Daniel said. "You are the king of Babylon. We will begin immediately to prepare for your coronation."

Amel-Marduk sat on his bed stunned, still squinting from the sun invading the dark room.

"The judges will accompany you to the palace. The prison guards will serve temporarily as your bodyguards. You can bathe and acquire appropriate clothing in your father's—in your chamber. I will meet with you in the outer chamber in two hours to begin our coordination."

"Then, as of this moment, I have authority over the kingdom," Amel-Marduk said looking to the judges. They all nodded.

"Belteshazzar, release Jehoiachin immediately."

"As you say, Your Highness. May I humbly suggest that you also offer the same freedom for Zedekiah?"

"Certainly. We have all been unjustly imprisoned."

Daniel walked to Jehoiachin's jail room.

"Greetings, Your Highness."

The king was sitting at his dimly lit small table reading from what Daniel recognized as Jeremiah's writings he had borrowed from Ezekiel. "Ah, Daniel. To what do I owe this honor?"

Daniel told him about King Nebuchadnezzar's death and what that meant for Amel-Marduk and him. "I am sick with sorrow that you have had to endure over thirty-six years of this pig sty. But praise Yahweh, you are now free. Gather your things and go with the guards to your family."

Finally, Daniel went to King Zedekiah's bedside. He had just awakened and was being attended to by a prison medical official. "Hail, King Zedekiah. It is Belteshazzar."

The king's voice was very weak. He reached slowly for Daniel's hand. "You have come to see me one last time before I die?"

"On the contrary, I have come to set you free. King Nebuchadnezzar died last night, and no one in authority desires your further imprisonment."

"Oh, Belteshazzar, that is wonderful news. But there has been no freedom for me since Jerusalem, and now I am a slave to this body that cannot see and will not move."

"I know, O king. And I so deeply regret that the king of Yahweh's people has had to endure such pain and misery."

"I have settled with my Creator, Who told me long ago through Jeremiah that I would die in peace. Now that my enemy, Nebuchadnezzar, is gone, I can do just that."

Daniel directed the medical official to take the king to the infirmary nearby and to give him the best treatment available.

Later, as Daniel entered the palace, there was much commotion among the servants, and he heard yelling from across the outer chamber. Nitocris ran to him.

"My brother has banished Nabonidus and me from the palace, which didn't shock me. But now he has commanded the guards to remove my father's body and drag it through the streets."

Daniel rushed to Amel-Marduk, who was barking out orders to the guards. "What is going on, sir?"

"I am going to remove any supposition by the people of Babylon that my father might have disappeared into the wilderness again. My coronation will not be questioned or delayed. They will see his body for themselves this very morning as it is displayed before their eyes. They and those throughout the kingdom will enjoy a bit of justice for the forty-three years of his tyranny."

"Don't be a fool, sir. Such an evil act will begin your reign with a reputation worse than your father's. I will assist you in an orderly transition of power, and I—"

"Your influence in this palace is over, Belteshazzar," Amel-Marduk interrupted as he walked to the bier where Nebuchadnezzar's body lay half-dressed and partially embalmed. Those preparing the body for a lavish ceremony had been abruptly dismissed. "I have been dreaming of this moment for years. And my dream needs no interpretation from you."

"I must object!"

"Guards, do as you were told."

The six guards whispered among themselves, then looked alternatively between Amel-Marduk and Daniel with expressions of confusion. Finally, the lead guard instructed the others to take the body into the street.

An hour later, Daniel lay on his bed, gazing at the ceiling. Through his open window, he heard the moaning and wailing of the people. He could not look but visualized the scene of the king being dragged behind horses through the main streets. He stretched his arms upward.

O Yahweh, I am afraid and needy of Your presence. I mourn the loss of my king, whom I have served my whole adult life. I thank You and joy in his turning to You in genuine faith. Although I have often been conflicted about my role in the kingdom, You have always convinced me that You have purpose in placing me here. You have shown me when to oppose and when to support. Now, apparently my work here has ended. Perhaps my life will soon end. If so, I die in obedience to You. Do not abandon me. Show me what to do in the midst of this madness.

The next morning, after a most restless night, Daniel was awakened by a knock. At the door was King Jehoiachin. Astonishment immediately replaced Daniel's grogginess. The king was dressed as a palace official. The two sat at a table after Daniel poured each of them a cup of papaya juice.

"I don't know where to start," Jehoiachin said. "I have a message from Amel-Marduk. I was summoned to the palace late last night. Amel-Marduk told me I was to be his provincial ruler and chief advisor—exactly what you were for King Nebuchadnezzar, Daniel. He said I would reside in your chamber, and he would see that I was compensated well and had all the amenities of the palace. He said the Hebrews his father had enslaved deserved their freedom and would be represented in the palace by their Hebrew king, meaning me. I am still in shock, Daniel. A lowly prisoner one day, and a high palace official the next. I don't know how to handle this."

"Yahweh is in control, Your Excellence. I see this as His perfect will in keeping His servant in the palace to effect His will in the kingdom. I was blessed beyond measure to serve Yahweh in that capacity under King Nebuchadnezzar. Now, the mantle shifts to you. This could be a blessing for us Hebrews."

"But I am not worthy or prepared to replace you. I will need your counsel immediately as I have already been placed in charge of the coronation. But Amel-Marduk has ordered that you be banned from the palace and that I not consult you after this meeting."

"I pledge my support to you and will do whatever you are comfortable with. You may want to meet with me at a secret location at times. I will accept that risk if you will. Also, I encourage you to keep Mishael, Hananiah, and Azariah in their positions, if possible. They have the experience, knowledge, and wisdom that will serve you well. They can help you immediately with the coronation."

Jehoiachin hugged Daniel and turned toward the door. "Oh, forgive me for not mentioning this at the first. King Zedekiah died last night at the infirmary. The community will give him the proper honor and burial."

"I'm sad to hear that. He suffered terribly in prison, but he died in peace as a free man, just as Jeremiah prophesied."

Daniel moved out of the palace and into a modest house in the Hebrew community the next day. He made no contact with Amel-Marduk. Within a week, he learned from talk in the marketplace that Nabonidus had been relieved of his command of the army and replaced by Neriglissar. It became quickly evident most people were very displeased with the king-to-be and were offended by the treatment of his late father's body. Nebuchadnezzar was buried on the palace grounds next to his father but with no ceremony. Daniel assumed he would not be welcome at the coronation and chose to not attend.

*

560 B.C.

For two years, Daniel observed Amel-Marduk's reign from a distance. Although a more benevolent king than his father, he made many unwise decisions. He reduced the size of the army; he had no desire to expand the territory of Babylon; and his reluctance to grow the trade economy was bankrupting the kingdom.

He had ordered all the gold cladding removed from Nebuchadnezzar's golden image, leaving only the wooden core to depict his father's legacy as worthless and decaying. The gold was reused by craftsmen to make many images of Chaldean gods that were placed in various temples.

Occasionally, Jehoiachin had requested secret meetings with Daniel to receive counsel on these and other complex and often frustrating issues. Daniel's three friends had retained their positions within the new government and were paying him a subsistence for much needed advice. Their advisory source was not revealed to the king. Daniel's contacts with Jehoiachin and the three provincial administrators provided him with an indirect, but valuable, connection to the governance of Babylon.

He was becoming troubled that he had received very little guidance from God since assuming the role of a common Hebrew exile. Nevertheless, he continued to reserve three meditation times each day in solitude, facing Jerusalem as he prayed. His prayers had become almost totally inquiries regarding his purpose and future.

One evening, Daniel and his friends were meeting at Mishael's house discussing some economic issues over dinner. The women were clearing the table when Mishael's principal assistant banged on the door. He was pale and breathing heavily. "You must come quickly, all of you! Babylon troops have stormed the palace, and the word is they have assassinated King Amel-Marduk."

The four men grabbed their cloaks and ran up the street to the palace. Throngs of people had already gathered in the street. Some were crying. Most were shouting. Torches and lanterns cast an ominous glow on the palace wall. The steps were filled with soldiers standing shoulder to shoulder. Daniel recognized one of the royal guards in uniform standing in the shadows.

"What happened?" Daniel asked.

"I was on duty at the front gate with three other guards when our own soldiers marched up the street. They must have been ten abreast as far as I could see in the dark. Their commander, Neriglissar, was on horseback leading them. He ordered them to charge the gate, swords drawn. We were powerless. We dropped our swords and ran."

"Then?"

"I don't know. Someone came out later screaming the king is dead."

Moments later, Daniel noticed some people coming out a side door, barely visible in the dark. A closer look revealed several palace officials and servants. One was a Hebrew domestic servant that used to clean his chamber.

"Uzi! Are you all right?"

Daniel hugged him and felt blood on his arm.

"No one tried to kill me, but as I was fleeing, I got in the way of a wielded sword."

"What did you see?"

"I was sweeping the outer chamber when the soldiers burst in. They ran their swords through the guards and broke open the doors to the king's chamber. I heard the king cry out for mercy; then there was silence."

"What about Jehoiachin?"

Uzi hesitated, then answered, "Our king also died by the sword."

Daniel walked away, his face buried in his hands.

The constant roar of voices from the front of the palace abruptly ceased. Daniel ran back into the street. Neriglissar stood at the top of the steps surrounded by soldiers, each with lanterns held high. The lights encircled the coup leader with an eerie halo.

"Citizens of Babylon, you have been rescued. You have been spared further oppression from the incompetent king that has occupied your palace for too long. I, Neriglissar, am now king of the great empire of Babylon."

The soldiers raised their voices in chants of "All hail, King Neriglissar" and "King Neriglissar, live forever."

"And, behold your queen, Kashshaia." The king motioned for his wife to stand next to him.

Kashshaia! Daniel maneuvered through the crowd and strained to see the new queen. *It is Kashshaia, daughter of Nebuchadnezzar. How could Nitocris' little sister, whom I watched grow up in the palace, now have the blood of her own half-brother on her hands?*

A few chants continued sporadically from the street, but most were just murmuring and milling in confusion. Daniel and his three friends returned to Mishael's house, where they spent the rest of the night praying and talking about what had just transpired.

A week later, a quickly organized coronation ceremony had a rather small attendance, since time had not allowed governors and officials from far-reaching regions of the kingdom to attend. Daniel had stayed isolated in his house since the coup to avoid calling attention to himself. He took advantage of everyone's preoccupation with the coronation to slip out and visit one of the many synagogues built by Hebrews over the years. Without a temple, these places of worship and study had been constructed throughout the Jewish communities.

"Welcome," the man said as he looked up from the parchment on a high table. "I am Yadid. What a surprise, sir. I didn't know whether we would see you again."

Daniel vaguely remembered seeing the man somewhere. He was obviously one of the scribes copying sacred Hebrew writings.

"I know it was tragic for you to witness such a bloody upheaval in the palace where you served so long and faithfully. I'm aware you had issues with Amel-Marduk, but he had certainly made the life of the

Hebrews less burdensome. Neriglissar will show us no favors. Then to lose our king, Jehoiachin, was painful. His son, Sheshbazzar, is still in deep mourning. What did they do with the body of the king?"

"Amel-Marduk was buried next to his father and grandfather unceremoniously."

"How sad. And what of you, Daniel? What is Yahweh showing you in all this?"

"I've been perplexed for the last two years. I'm not getting an answer from Yahweh, but He has protected me. Honestly, the main reason I wanted to visit was to seek the wisdom of someone very close to Yahweh. I seem to be having a dry spell with Him of late."

"Truly, you have been Yahweh's emissary in this pagan land for many years. Perhaps He is teaching you patience while preparing you for a new role."

"Perhaps. Would you be open to my coming here every day to assist you and pray with you?"

"Of course. We can pray and read from the Scriptures until Yahweh reveals his new direction to you. There is also much to be done in the Lord's work among the Hebrews. We can partner in leading the Sabbath services. Your administrative strengths will make up for my weaknesses in that area."

Yadid pointed out a stack of parchment sheets with an assortment of scrolls lying around it. "Several scribes have been organizing and copying the Torah and other sacred writings, such as the prophecies of Jeremiah, Isaiah, and Habakkuk. I am presently copying Ezekiel's prophecies. We must record as much as possible for future generations. What about records of your life and service, Daniel? Your extraordinary story must be preserved."

"The palace scribes have kept a detailed history of the kingdom, which includes my role in it. The exile of the Hebrews is well-documented from our childhood to present in those annals. We need to combine those with the history of Israel for a full account of Yahweh's people."

"That is already in process, but it needs capable management. Will you help with that?"

"Certainly. Maybe I'm beginning to get a glimpse of my new assignment from Yahweh."

556 B.C.

Four years into King Neriglissar's reign, Daniel had become just another common Hebrew to the monarchy and hardly recognized by the Babylonian community. Belshazzar, the son of Nabonidus and Nitocris, had been appointed as King Neriglissar's administrator in a move to lessen the animosity among the two sisters and their husbands. Daniel remained very popular among the Hebrews. He had organized the scribes into a highly productive team to compile copies of the Torah and many other historical and prophetic writings. He had requisitioned historical records of his years in the palace and had closely monitored the scribes as they summarized his story in the Aramaic language. The language would permit it to be read by both Babylonians and Hebrews.

King Neriglissar and Queen Kashshaia had a son, Labashi-Marduk, during the first year of their reign. In their third year, a daughter, Gulah, was born. Neriglissar's rule was characterized by numerous advances in expanding the kingdom's boundaries and adding to the elegance of the city of Babylon. Kashshaia was instrumental in embellishing the gardens and directing the aesthetic improvement in structures and landscapes. Although the general welfare of the citizens had improved with the economy, it was often offset by their harsh treatment by palace officials, guards, and the army.

Early one morning in the fifth year of King Neriglissar's reign, Daniel was setting up his table in the synagogue for writing more of his memoirs when Hananiah burst into the room.

"The king is dead! His servants couldn't awaken him, and the physician pronounced him dead just moments ago."

Daniel, acting on instinct, grabbed his tunic and ran with his friend to the palace courtyard. *This palace intrigue is becoming too common.*

"Permission to enter the palace," Daniel said to the guard he recognized. "I know I'm needed to advise and help with the crisis."

"Belteshazzar, what you know is you are not welcome here."

"Please, I respectfully ask that you send word to Queen Kashshaia that Belteshazzar requests her invitation to enter."

The guard paused, shook his head, then whispered something to a subordinate. The subordinate disappeared into the crowd around the entrance. Fifteen minutes later, he exited the palace and whispered to his boss. The guard motioned for Daniel to follow the subordinate. Hananiah waited in the courtyard.

Despite the thousands of times he had entered through the door, this time felt strange, as if he had never been there. Once inside, he could hardly recognize anything from his day. Into the outer chamber, his eyes met Kashshaia's.

"Belteshazzar!" She ran to him and embraced him tightly. "Your being here brings me peace. Neriglissar was always jealous of you and kept you at a distance. I honored his wishes, but I know how wise and strong you are." Daniel felt her tears on his neck. He thought she might welcome his presence but never imagined such an emotional greeting. It was awkward.

"I'm so sorry, Your Highness. Does anyone know what happened?" Daniel asked.

"No." She wiped her eyes. "He seemed perfectly all right when he went to bed. He just . . . didn't wake up."

"Where is his administrator? Who is in charge?"

"He is meeting with the other palace officials. They are arranging the transition."

"Transition to whom? The king has no heir, except your four-year-old son."

"Labashi-Marduk will be king, and I will be queen."

"Kashshaia! Babylonia cannot be ruled by a child!"

"The child will grow up. In the meantime, he will be the assurance of my right to rule as his proxy."

I can't believe we're having this conversation before Neriglissar's body is cold. The tears ceased awfully fast.

Kashshaia continued, "Your wisdom wasn't lost on me as I was growing up. I watched admiringly as you managed the kingdom for my father, often solely during his long absences. Nitocris and I grew up watching you handle the affairs of government with great wisdom. I want to bring you back to the palace, Belteshazzar. I have a right to the throne through my son, and the people love me. But I am wise enough to realize I don't have the ability to rule this vast empire on my own. I will pay you three times what my father paid. You will be cared for lavishly. You and I will make a powerful team."

"I am stunned, but deeply flattered, Your Highness. Allow me a few days to pray and process all of this. For now, can we discuss the immediate actions that must take place?"

For the next two hours, Daniel and Kashshaia sat in her chamber, while he offered advice and caution regarding the proper honor for the deceased king and the orderly transition of power.

Afterward, Daniel told Hananiah of his experience with Kashshaia. "She asked me to return to the palace in my former role as the kingdom transitioned to Labashi-Marduk."

"That would be a mistake," Hananiah responded.

Daniel was surprised by his bluntness. "Why do you say that? Babylon cannot be ruled by a child and an inexperienced mother without an experienced surrogate. I would continue to represent Yahweh in the kingdom and ensure the welfare of the Hebrews from my position."

"Remember, I have been closer to palace officials than you have in recent years. I predict the boy's time on the throne, indeed his life, will be very short. You will be considered his right arm and mouthpiece. The likelihood of you surviving his assassination is not great."

Daniel slumped in his chair, dumbfounded by his friend's words. Hananiah continued, "Your influence on the kingdom is not over, Daniel, but this is not the time."

"I know you hear from Yahweh as I do, and I take your counsel seriously. I will pray for Yahweh to reveal His guidance further to me."

That night, Daniel prayed until early morning for the Lord to give him wisdom in what his response to Kashshaia should be. He yearned for the power, the excitement of being back in the palace again. This time, it would be with full authority, not having to second-guess a king. Except for the title, he would be king! He rationalized that he could be the conduit for Almighty God to rule the greatest kingdom in the world. *Surely, Yahweh is presenting me this opportunity for His glory.*

Strangely, though, he received nothing recognizable as the voice of God. The words of Hananiah kept coming to his mind. Shortly after sunrise, he answered a knock at his door to find Belshazzar, Nitocris' son and former administrator for King Neriglissar.

"The queen requests your presence at the palace, sir."

After a pause to collect his thoughts, Daniel replied, "Please give the queen my deepest regrets. Tell her I am honored by her request for my assistance, and I will be petitioning Yahweh on her behalf and that of the . . . new king. Tell her my place is with my people now."

Belshazzar's raised eyebrows reflected his disbelief as he nodded and departed.

Daniel collapsed on his bed, hardly believing he had just refused what would have been the most powerful position in Babylonia. He thought about the repercussions that could come from this decision. But it wasn't a decision as much as a surrender to the counsel of Hananiah in the silence of Yahweh.

Oh, Yahweh, I hope I have understood You rightly. I accepted Your silence as my status quo. Please give me a sign soon that I have heard You rightly.

For the next few months, Daniel did not give much attention to the affairs of the kingdom. The writings of Moses, the prophets, and King David and King Solomon were being meticulously transcribed under his supervision. The standard was absolute perfection. If even a minor mistake was made, the scrolls were discarded. Many historical accounts carried from the palace and temple of Jerusalem by the exiles were sorted and copied.

Although immersed in these projects, Daniel was frequently visited by officials from the palace, expressing their disillusionment with the dearth of leadership and their disgust of paying homage to a child.

The growing sentiment in the palace court was that the young queen was incapable of ruling the kingdom. And she was not inclined to receive advice well

Furthermore, the worship of Marduk rigidly enforced by King Neriglissar was abruptly halted at his death. In a few weeks after the coronation of Labashi-Marduk, Nitocris' husband, Nabonidus, who was an Assyrian zealot of the sun god, Sin, began proclaiming Sin's dominance over the god, Marduk. Nabonidus was the son of a priestess of Sin. He became very successful in convincing the people their god, Marduk, had left the Babylonians as evidenced by the governmental chaos of the past six years. Many people were converting to the Sin god in desperation for a better future.

Daniel arrived at Mishael's house just in time for dinner. Mishael had also invited Hananiah and Azariah. While Galya was still preparing the meal, the four began a troubling conversation.

"The three of us have, by the will of Yahweh, maintained our positions of responsibility, but we are without direction," Mishael said. "Nine months after the death of King Neriglissar, the palace is in disarray. Even the queen's administrator has no influence on her."

"We are hearing rumors that the followers of this sun god fanatic, Nabonidus, are planning to overthrow the boy-king and establish the worship of Sin as Babylon's forced religion. He still has strong connections with the upper ranks of the army he commanded. We have religious upheaval on top of a governmental crisis," Azariah added.

"The present emperor of the army seems determined to sit this one out," Hananiah said. "He doesn't believe the people would passively accept another army take-over of the kingdom like Neriglissar's.

However, he makes no secret of his frustration with receiving orders from a child king and his mother."

"How I long for the days of King Nebuchadnezzar, especially his last years as a follower of Yahweh," Daniel said. "The turmoil since then may well be Yahweh's means of judging the kingdom for its captivity of His people as Jeremiah prophesied."

"But we have concluded long ago that Babylon was the instrument of Yahweh to pass judgment on the nations of Israel and Judah for our sins," Hananiah said.

"Yes, but if the Hebrew people humble themselves before Yahweh and seek forgiveness, He will show mercy and eventually return us to our homeland," Daniel said. "But it can only happen if Babylon falls. We may be seeing the beginnings of Babylon's end."

After the meal, the four men knelt and cried out to God for peace in Babylon and freedom for the Hebrews.

Four days later, Daniel was awakened in the middle of the night by the faint sound of trumpet blasts in the distance. He opened his door to the sight of people running toward the palace, some in their night clothes. He dressed hurriedly, put on his cloak, and joined the others in running.

This emergency run to the palace is all too familiar.

This time, the steps and the courtyard were not full of uniformed army troops but with normally dressed men carrying swords. Several of them spoke at the same time.

"People of Babylon, you are liberated. The child king is dead. Hail the god of Sin! Hail Nabonidus!"

Nabonidus? Nabonidus has done it! He has taken the palace!

Daniel could not get through the press of the insurrectionists on the steps. Realizing he might be placing himself in grave danger, he worked his way slowly to one who acted with some authority. "Sir, I am Belteshazzar, advisor to the queen. I need to be with her to assist her in a peaceful transition of power."

In swift motion, the man pressed the edge of his sword on Daniel's neck. "I doubt the queen will be needing advice. Perhaps her need is for someone to prepare her body for burial." He pushed Daniel back down the steps.

Daniel stood in the street, stunned by the assault on the palace with no military resistance. He contemplated other options for getting into the palace but rejected each one as futile. Apparently, Kashshaia had been assassinated, along with her son, so there was nothing he could do.

Moments later, he opened the door to the unlighted interior of his house. Feeling his way to his bed, his eyes slowly adjusted to the darkness. Someone was crouched in the corner of the room!

"Who is it?" Daniel blurted.

"Kashshaia," returned a soft, broken voice.

"Kashshaia! I thought you were dead!" Daniel fumbled in the darkness to light a lamp, but his hands were not steady enough. He knelt to embrace her, barely able to see her face. "What happened? How did you get here?"

Hardly able to control her sobbing, she managed to speak a few words between each rapid breath. "They burst in. Took my son. A man in my room held me down. Labashi-Marduk was screaming. Suddenly, my administrator ran into my room. He ran his sword through my captor. He took my arm, and we escaped out a side door in the midst of the confusion. The last thing I heard was my son's screaming abruptly turn silent." She collapsed into Daniel's chest sobbing uncontrollably.

Daniel carried her to his bed, covered her with a blanket, and whispered, "We will talk more in the morning. Try to be as quiet as possible. If you are discovered here, we will both be killed." He lay on the floor beside her through the three hours left before sunrise. Neither of them slept.

As the morning lighted the room, Daniel served her a cup of pomegranate juice and a piece of stale bread. She removed the blanket and sat up on the bed, arranging a thin nightgown over her legs and bare feet.

"This isn't breakfast fit for a queen, but it is all an old, single man has at present," Daniel said softly, so as not to be heard outside his walls. "How did you get here last night?"

"Belshazzar led me down some dark alleyways and eventually to your house, which he remembered from my sending him here a few months ago with my invitation. I didn't have time to dress."

"I will get you some clothes and sandals from a friend this morning. This evening, I will take you to my friend, whose wife will look after you."

Wham! The door flew open, and two men bolted in with swords in hands. Daniel sprang to the front of Kashshaia. One of the men shoved him aside.

"Ah, Kashshaia. How long did you think you could avoid the inevitable?" the man asked boisterously. Belshazzar stood in the doorway.

"I'm so sorry, Your Highness," Belshazzar said. "They were going to kill me if I didn't lead them to you." He began to weep.

The two men grabbed each of her arms and dragged her out the door and into the street as she pleaded for her life. Daniel stood shaking in the middle of the room, shocked but thankful he was still alive.

Belshazzar stared at him momentarily, then lowered his head. "I have sentenced my own aunt to death," he said, then ran out of sight.

Daniel fell to his knees and called out, "Yahweh, dear Yahweh, thank You for sparing me! I implore You to spare Kashshaia. Bring some order to the kingdom. Give me wisdom as to what to do."

Daniel walked to the synagogue by a circuitous route through alleyways so as not to be seen by any palace officials. He thought it best to stay there out of sight for a few days.

Five days later, he was startled by a frantic voice outside the synagogue door. "Belteshazzar! Belteshazzar! Are you in there?" He recognized the voice of Belshazzar.

"Belshazzar," Daniel called as he opened the door. "Are you hiding from your father? Come inside quickly."

"Actually, I am back in the palace, but as a servant to my father—the king. He is punishing me for attempting to rescue Kashshaia."

"How did you know I was here?"

"I inquired at some other synagogues, and one scribe suggested I check this one.

"Come inside."

They sat on a stone bench along the wall as Belshazzar spoke. "Kashshaia is in prison. My father plans to execute her tomorrow."

"What?" Daniel exclaimed.

"He has reinstituted beheading as the death sentence. I humbly ask that you be present and to pray to your Hebrew God to spare her life."

Daniel bent forward, his head in his hands. "Of course, I will."

"It could be very dangerous for you. Father will not likely do anything to you if you are peaceful but will imprison or execute you if he feels you are the slightest threat. I'm only allowed to live because I am his only heir to the throne."

Daniel thanked Belshazzar for his loyalty to his aunt and assured him he would pray for her.

The next day just before noon, Daniel sat on the grass at a distance from the execution platform behind the palace and prayed as many people gathered. The executioner, resting a heavy, iron ceremonial axe on his shoulder, stood next to a large, wooden block set to be coated with its first blood stain. Soon, Kashshaia appeared wearing a plain, gray gown and escorted by two palace guards. Next, King Nabonidus and Queen Nitocris stepped up onto an elevated stand and sat on red, fabric-covered chairs.

The guards instructed Kashshaia to kneel in front of the block with her head face-down on the block's surface. The mother of Nabonidus recited a ritual prayer to the sun god while standing next to the executioner. Daniel, with eyes open, prayed a specific prayer for God to intervene to save Kashshaia's life. *Yahweh, instill compassion in the heart of Nitocris for her sister.*

The king nodded; the executioner raised the axe over his head. Daniel stood as Kashshaia screamed and shook.

"Stop!" Nitocris shrieked as she ran toward the executioner.

The king caught up with her, grasping both of her arms from behind. "What are you doing?"

The executioner held the axe above his head.

"She is my enemy, but she is my sister! I beg you, Your Excellence, spare her."

The king and his queen spoke in low, inaudible voices for several minutes. Then the king called for his guards. After receiving a short instruction, the guards escorted Kashshaia away. Without any further word of explanation, the king and queen walked back into the palace. Daniel learned later that Kashshaia was returned to prison. He returned to the synagogue. *O Yahweh, all praise to You from a thankful heart. Your mercies never cease.*

*

The reign of Nabonidus was fraught with dissension from his subjects. His Assyrian heritage was a constant irritation. But even more aggravating was his aggressive move to establish the sun god, Sin, as the god of Babylon. The Babylonians had worshiped the god Marduk as their god of gods for generations. Just days after his coronation, the king ordered the large statue of Marduk removed from the palace and destroyed publicly at the Ishtar Gate. Almost all images of Marduk throughout the empire were ordered destroyed and replaced by images of Sin. The priests of the two gods led fanatical followers in frequent bloody clashes that left many mutilated bodies in the streets.

*

553 B.C.

After almost four years of constant strife with his antagonists, King Nabonidus began plans to rule in absentia choosing friendlier environs. He declared Belshazzar co-regent of the empire with eventual sole authority over the province of Babylon. His advisors began to plan for his relocation to the oasis of Tayma in western Arabia. Tayma was along the main trade route from Medo-Persia through Babylon to Egypt and the Mediterranean Sea. The Tayma oasis had a well that supplied the only water source along the Arabian desert route. King

Nabonidus ordered the building of a remote palace and other facilities necessary for his continued reign over the kingdom while absent from Babylon. He also dispatched excavation teams throughout the kingdom to explore and, if possible, rebuild ancient Sin temples.

The priests of Marduk eventually gained the confidence of most of the Babylonians in the religious civil war that had been raging. They were bringing heavy pressure on the king and the palace court. The army was sending signals that brought its allegiance to the king into question. The time had come for Nabonidus to relocate permanently to avoid being overthrown. He dispatched letters throughout the empire that he would be moving his palace court and an army contingent to Tayma. The letter announced that his son would be his regent for the province of Babylon. The queen would remain with their son.

After the death of King Jehoiachin, the Hebrews were without a recognized leader for almost a year before Sheshbazzar, Jehoiachin's son, became their obvious choice. He represented them before the king of Babylon, although he was never allowed to be called king. Nebuchadnezzar had referred to him as the prince of the Hebrews. Sheshbazzar received a parchment copy of the king's announcement. He took the announcement to Daniel for an assessment of how the new king and regent arrangement would affect the Hebrews.

"So, Babylon now has a yet another king or, as Nabonidus calls him, a regent," Daniel said. "I had no relationship with Nabonidus, but I can speak freely with Nitocris. She will be making most of the decisions for her son. That should be to our advantage. But I will only intervene when prompted by Yahweh. Otherwise, I have lost my desire for things of the palace. Babylon's years of glory are gone. My soul senses a greater purpose."

Daniel often heard complaints from both Babylonians and Hebrews about poor governing from the throne by a substitute king. He was careful to avoid comment on anything regarding the king. Supervising the scribes and occasionally leading gatherings at the synagogue occupied all his time. He found comfort in the assumption that he would no longer be called on for counsel or even recognized by the monarchy. The absence of responsibility and stress had become very satisfying. He considered the calm in the elderly stage of his life to be a reward from God.

Studying the writings of Isaiah late one night, the scroll dropped from Daniel's hands as he drifted into a deep sleep. He awoke in the morning in a heavy sweat. His dream had seemed so real, he thought he had actually been transported miraculously to another location. Changing from his bed clothes quickly, he hurried to the synagogue, scrambled to arrange his parchment and ink on the writing table, and began to write while the dream was fresh on his mind. He wrote in Hebrew, since the vision was meant primarily for his people.

I was looking in my vision by night, and behold, the four winds
of heaven were stirring up the great sea. And four great beasts

were coming up from the sea, different from one another. The first was like a lion and had the wings of an eagle. I kept looking until its wings were plucked, and it was lifted up from the ground and made to stand on two feet like a man; a human mind was also given to it. And behold, another beast, a second one, resembling a bear. And it was raised up on one side, and three ribs were in its mouth between its teeth; and thus they said to it, "Arise, devour much meat!"

After this I kept looking, and behold, another one, like a leopard, which had on its back four wings of a bird; the beast also had four heads, and dominion was given to it. After this I kept looking in the night visions, and behold, a fourth beast, dreadful and terrifying and extremely strong; and it had large iron teeth. It devoured and crushed and trampled down the remainder with its feet; and it was different from all the beasts that were before it, and it had ten horns. While I was contemplating the horns, behold, another horn, a little one, came up among them and three of the first horns were pulled out by the roots before it; and behold, the horn possessed eyes like the eyes of a man and a mouth uttering great boasts.

I kept looking until thrones were set up, And the Ancient of Days took His seat; His vesture was like white snow And the hair of His head like pure wool. His throne was ablaze with flames, Its wheels were a burning fire. A river of fire was flowing And coming out from before Him; Thousands upon thousands were attending Him, And myriads upon myriads were standing before Him; The court sat, And the books were opened. Then I kept looking because of the sound of the boastful words which the horn was speaking; I *kept looking until the beast was slain, and its body was destroyed and given to the burning fire.*

As for the rest of the beasts, their dominion was taken away, but an extension of life was granted to them for an appointed period of time. I kept looking in the night visions, And behold, with the clouds of heaven One like a Son of Man was coming, And He came up to the Ancient of Days And was presented before Him. And to Him was given dominion, Glory and a kingdom, That all the peoples, nations and men of every language Might serve Him. His dominion is an everlasting dominion Which will not pass away; And His kingdom is one Which will not be destroyed.

As for me, Daniel, my spirit was distressed within me, and the visions in my mind kept alarming me. I approached one of those who were standing by and began asking him the exact meaning of all this. So he told me and made known to me the interpretation of these things:

"These great beasts, which are four in number, are four kings who will arise from the earth. But the saints of the Highest One will receive the kingdom and possess the kingdom forever, for all ages to come."

Then I desired to know the exact meaning of the fourth beast, which was different from all the others, exceedingly dreadful, with its teeth of iron and its claws of bronze, and which devoured, crushed and trampled down the remainder with its feet, and the meaning of the ten horns that were on its head and the other horn which came up, and before which three of them fell, namely, that horn which had eyes and a mouth uttering great boasts and which was larger in appearance than its associates. I kept looking, and that horn was waging war with the saints and overpowering them until the Ancient of Days came and judgment was passed in favor of the saints of the Highest One, and the time arrived when the saints took possession of the kingdom.

Thus, he said, "The fourth beast will be a fourth kingdom of the earth, which will be different from all the other kingdoms and will devour the whole earth and tread it down and crush it. As for the ten horns, out of this kingdom ten kings will arise; and another will arise after them and will be different from the previous ones and will subdue three kings. He will speak out against the Most High and wear down the saints of the Highest One, and he will intend to make alterations in times and in law; and they will be given into his hand for a time, times, and half a time. But the court will sit for judgment and his dominion will be taken away, annihilated and destroyed forever. Then the sovereignty, the dominion and the greatness of all the kingdoms under the whole heaven will be given to the people of the saints of the Highest One; His kingdom will be an everlasting kingdom, and all the dominions will serve and obey Him."

At this point, the revelation ended. As for me, Daniel, my thoughts were greatly alarming me and my face grew pale, but I kept the matter to myself.[11]

At the end of the day, Daniel secured his writing and returned to his house weak and exhausted. Deeply burdened by the revelation,

---

11 Daniel 7:2-28

and with no guidance as to what to do with it, he lay on the floor and called out to God. "O Yahweh, I am laid low and am void of direction. Truly, You have revealed something of extreme importance to your servant. But I am just a man, not a prophet. I do not understand Your mysteries as Jeremiah and Ezekiel did. You have gifted me with miraculous abilities to interpret dreams, counsel kings, and discern motives. But You have not placed prophetic visions in my mind since the statue of many years past. There are no prophets in Babylon to whom I can go. Oh, that You would have allowed Ezekiel to remain longer. He could have helped me with this burden. I feel so alone. I want to be all You desire of me, but woe am I. I am just a man. Speak, Yahweh. I need You."

After almost an hour of silence, no impressions, and no word from God, Daniel suddenly alerted to a seemingly audible Voice. It felt as if the words were filling his entire soul.

Rise up, Daniel. I am answering you. I am honoring your life of obedience in the face of great adversity. I am not finished with you. You will be my prophet, following a long line of prophets. I will show you the rise and fall of kingdoms for generation after generation. Your message will be about My sovereignty over the destiny of nations and My dominion of everything in Heaven and on earth. You will impress My plan upon My people for the ages to come.

Daniel could not move. He remained face-down on the floor through the night, half-conscious until daybreak. He felt his strength renew and slowly sat up. He wanted to respond in some way to God's answer, but the words would not form on his lips. In quiet reverence, he meditated all day on both the vision he had documented and the answer to his prayer.

Two days later, composed but still mystified, he was standing with a bucket at his side in a long line for water from the well not far from his house. Someone grasped his arm from behind. "Come with me." It was a palace guard. Pulling him along for about twenty steps, the guard stopped next to a plain-covered carriage drawn by two horses. Daniel assumed he was being arrested as he had anticipated for some time. The guard, glancing back at the well to make sure he hadn't drawn attention, lifted the leather side panel of the carriage and motioned for Daniel to board. As he stepped up, his eyes focused on the passenger.

"Nitocris!"

"Forgive me. We had to meet in secret. I have been having the guard observe your habit of gathering water around this time every day, so I planned this covert meeting."

The carriage began to move as Nitocris continued. "I'll be brief. The people of Babylon were not happy with Nabonidus. But they are no more supportive of being ruled by our son. Many are offended that the king has chosen to rule from another land. Although they know I am ensuring my son does nothing foolish, hardly anyone is comfortable with that arrangement. The people won't serve a figurehead king, regardless of the respect they have for his mother. My brother was assassinated after two years for his incompetence—with my sister as an accessory. I must gain the people's confidence in my son."

"I am afraid your assessment is true. I anticipate another coup soon. But what does that have to do with me?"

"It has everything to do with you, Belteshazzar." She raised her voice, and her jaws tightened. "You are the only one in the province who knows how to run it and how to lead the people. You refused to help Kashshaia when Labashi-Marduk was king, and they killed him."

Daniel wanted to remind her that it was the present king, her husband, who killed her nephew. Hananiah's warning against returning to the palace at that time came to his mind.

"King Nabonidus would not tolerate me in the palace. He would consider me a threat and would return to remove me and probably my head," Daniel said.

"I have a plan for that. I want you to advise me through Belshazzar's administrator, Arah Nisanu. You and he will make a wise consultant team. He also realizes my son will not survive without drastic changes. He can meet with you at your house briefly at the end of each day to discuss the events of that day and plans for the next. My husband and our son will never know. I will be inclined to follow your guidance, knowing it will be in the best interest of the people and the kingdom. The people will not be aware of your involvement. They will gain confidence in my son and accept the king in absentia."

Daniel stared at the carriage panel in front of him, astounded by the proposal. The same feelings he had when asked to serve Kashshaia and her child king welled up in his chest. His suppressed craving for the duties and rewards of nobility pierced his soul. But those feelings clashed with the word he had just received from his God.

"Your Highness, you flatter me and appeal to my nature. This will be an agonizing decision because Yahweh has placed me on an entirely different course. I must humbly request that you give me a day to consult with Him."

"I have no time to lose, Belteshazzar. I am pressed from every side. One day. But don't disappoint me." She leaned toward him, looking straight into his eyes. "I need you. I really need you. Your answer will mean success or a death sentence for the king, my son, and me."

The carriage stopped near the well. Daniel filled his bucket and walked home. For the rest of the afternoon, he conversed earnestly with his Lord.

"All-powerful, all-knowing Yahweh, I would never fail to abide by Your direction. But you know the desires of my heart. The empire You allowed to rule the world for many years is slowly crumbling. The nation conquered Your people and held them captive, yet You saw fit to elevate this common Hebrew to the king's right hand to represent You and protect Your people. Now, I may be the only hope for Babylon's survival. I believe You are judging this nation like You judged Israel and Judah. Nebuchadnezzar's dream long ago and the dream You gave me just days ago revealed the looming collapse of this kingdom. The time may be at hand to destroy Babylon and rescue Your people. But if Your people will suffer as the empire falls, I appeal to You to delay until Your people are set free. And allow me to renew my role in Babylon's survival during that delay."

By late evening, exhausted from the stressful exchange with his Lord, he finally felt a peace about where he was being led. He awakened rested the next morning. As anticipated, Arah Nisanu arrived mid-afternoon.

"Do we have a partnership?" Arah Nisanu asked with no introductory formalities.

"I look forward to our meetings each evening," Daniel replied. "I will be honest and straight-forward with you. We may not always agree, but I must insist that my full counsel reaches the ears of the queen whether you agree or disagree."

"I would want it no other way, and I will also clearly state my opinion to both you and Her Majesty."

From that day forward, Arah Nisanu and Daniel met each evening in Daniel's house. Most of the discussions were about Babylon's security. From Tayma, Nabonidus had negotiated lucrative trade routes going through Babylon from Medo-Persia to Egypt. This was bolstering the empire's economy tremendously. However, the army had been seriously diminished over the past few years. Finances were being diverted from pay and supplies for the soldiers to infrastructure and beautification projects for the city, as well as building up the national treasury. Collection of taxes from vassal nations was being neglected, and several strategically deployed army units had been recalled in order to reduce the total number of soldiers needed. Knowing an enemy attack was on the not-too-distant horizon, Daniel was also concerned about the decreased training and physical conditioning of the men. The attempts of Nitocris to heed Daniel's advice and reverse some of this decline in the army's readiness were being resisted by Belshazzar and many in his court.

*

547 B.C.

After three years, void of another revealing dream or vision, Daniel had become depressed. He agonized over whether he had heard God correctly in what he understood to be a promise of further prophetic insights. He wondered whether he had mistaken God's direction in advising Nitocris. He reminded himself of learning long ago that when God was silent, it usually meant He was satisfied. Nevertheless, being assigned by the Creator to prophesy followed by no prophetic revelations was unsettling.

Then, after several days of calling out to God for a word, the heavens opened while he was praying in a secluded setting outside the walls of the city. It was like God had put him into a trance and carried him to another city to speak to him. Afterward, he was physically ill from the burden of the episode. Recuperating after a few days, he again wrote a precise record of the entire vision in the Hebrew language.

I looked in the vision, and while I was looking, I was in the citadel of Susa, which is in the province of Elam; and I looked in the vision and I myself was beside the Ulai Canal. Then I lifted my eyes and looked, and behold, a ram which had two horns was standing in the front of the canal. Now the two horns were long, but one was longer than the other, with the longer one coming up last. I saw the ram butting westward, northward, and southward, and no other beasts could stand before him nor was there anyone to rescue from his power, but he did as he pleased and magnified himself.

While I was observing, behold, a male goat was coming from the west over the surface of the whole earth without touching the ground; and the goat had a conspicuous horn between his eyes. He came up to the ram that had the two horns, which I had seen standing in front of the canal and rushed at him in his mighty wrath. I saw him come beside the ram, and he was enraged at him; and he struck the ram and shattered his two horns, and the ram had no strength to withstand him. So, he hurled him to the ground and trampled on him, and there was none to rescue the ram from his power.

Then the male goat magnified himself exceedingly. But as soon as he was mighty, the large horn was broken; and in its place there came up four conspicuous horns toward the four winds of heaven. Out of one of them came forth a rather small horn which grew exceedingly great toward the south, toward the east, and toward the Beautiful Land. *It grew up to the host of heaven and caused some of the host and some of the stars to fall to the earth, and it trampled them down. It even magnified itself to be equal with the Commander of the host; and it removed the regular sacrifice from Him, and the place of His sanctuary was thrown down. And on account of transgression the host will be given over to the horn along with the regular sacrifice; and it will fling truth to the ground and perform its will and prosper. Then I heard a holy one speaking, and another holy one said to that particular one who was speaking, "How long will the vision about the regular sacrifice apply, while the transgression causes horror, so as to allow both the holy place and the host to be trampled?" He said to me, "For 2,300 evenings and mornings; then the holy place will be properly restored."*

When, I, Daniel, had seen the vision, I sought to understand it; and behold, standing before me was one who looked like a man. And I heard the voice of a man between the banks of the Ulai, and he *called out and said, "Gabriel, give this* man *an understanding of the vision." So he came near to where I was standing, and when he came, I was frightened and fell on my face; but he said to me, "Son of man, understand that the vision pertains to the time of the end."*

Now while he was talking with me, I sank into a deep sleep with my face to the ground, but he touched me and made me stand upright. He said, "Behold, I am going to let you know what will occur at the final period of the indignation, for it pertains to the appointed time of the end. The ram which you saw with the two horns represents the kings of Media and Persia. The shaggy goat represents the kingdom of Greece, and the large horn that is between his eyes is the first king. The broken horn *and the four* horns that *arose in its place* represent *four kingdoms* which *will arise from* his *nation, although not with his power. In the latter period of their rule, When the transgressors have run their course, A king will arise, Insolent and skilled in intrigue. His power will be mighty, but not by his* own *power, And he will destroy to an extraordinary degree And prosper and perform* his will; *He will destroy mighty men and the holy people. And through his shrewdness He will cause deceit to succeed by his influence; And he will magnify* himself *in his heart, And he will destroy many while* they are at ease. *He will even oppose the Prince of princes, But he will be broken without human agency. The vision of the evenings and mornings Which has been told is true; But keep the vision secret, For* it *pertains to many days in the future." Then I, Daniel, was exhausted and sick for days. Then I got up again and carried on the king's business; but I was astounded at the vision, and there was none to explain* it.[12]

While Daniel was not feeling well, he sent word to Arah Nisanu to postpone their meetings for a while. Meanwhile, he meditated each day on the vision. Although, he did not understand fully the future kingdoms represented, it was obvious that God would soon bring an end to Babylon and that Media and Persia would dominate the world. He hoped that he would be allowed to die before this happened.

The professor and Kyle, having over-indulged on Mrs. McCarty's special chicken cacciatore dinner, nestled comfortably into the brown leather sectional arranged around the mahogany coffee table. The crystal goblets resting on the Princeton insignia coasters had just been refilled with freshly brewed raspberry iced tea. Kyle was anxiously awaiting his second private session on biblical prophecy. Since their last meeting, he had read the entire book of Daniel from his new Bible app.

"A few decades and many challenging circumstances transpired in the life of Daniel since the times we last covered," Dr. McCarty said. "I have copied some of my notes on the people and events of those years. You may keep them for your own study. However, this evening, I want to concentrate on Daniel's first two prophetic visions, which are essential to understanding God's total sovereignty and the revelation of His plans for our future."

The professor opened his large study Bible and unfolded a map on the surface of the coffee table and began to teach.

"Well, God raised up Daniel to preside over Babylon's glory years. It was like God installed a strong buffer between King Nebuchadnezzar and the exiled Hebrews. Only through the power of God could Daniel have fulfilled his illogical and seemingly impossible role. As the king's righthand man, he masterfully advanced the world's most powerful dominion while protecting and guiding his own people the king brought to Babylon as slaves. But after Nebuchadnezzar's death, God directed Daniel off center stage as He initiated the beginning of Babylon's destruction. Five kings crowned in nine years, if you include Belshazzar, led to no less than abject chaos in the land virtually void of Daniel's influence. Daniel's calling for over fifty years had seemed to take a completely different direction. He was receiving prophetic visions during King Belshazzar's reign. Perhaps this was a reward from His loving heavenly Father for his life of unwavering faithfulness. Maybe he had to prove himself worthy of being the mouthpiece for the Lord's message to future generations. In any case, he was the one man God was trusting with the message of His plan. Let's review Daniel's account of the first vision."

The professor placed his Bible in his lap.

"The first six chapters of the Book of Daniel are chronological history. The last six describe his prophetic visions. His visions, recorded in chapters seven and eight, actually fit between chapters four and five in the timeline. The history section may have been from a compilation of his official records drafted by his administrative assistants, since they are written in third person and Aramaic. His visions were personally written in first-person and Hebrew."

The professor read the vision aloud from Daniel chapter seven, then laid the Bible on the table.

"God chose Daniel to receive the most comprehensive foretelling of the future world power structures found anywhere in history. Through this prophet, the people of his day and generations to come, including us today, could anticipate and prepare for what was to come.

God wanted His people, then and now, to have this information. Much of Daniel's visions reinforced the dream of King Nebuchadnezzar interpreted by Daniel almost a half-century earlier.

"In our twenty-first century, we can look back on how most of this prophetic vision was fulfilled completely, but there is a part of the vision that we are still waiting to see materialize. Just as surely as the sixth century B.C. predictions for the rise and fall of specific nations are now ensconced in our history books, the prediction of the world empire yet to come will materialize in the relatively near future. Let's look closely at these predictions."

Dr. McCarty focused on the map.

"It was probably the angel Gabriel, the heavenly chief messenger, who gave the interpretation of the first vision during Daniel's dream. The angel explained that the four beasts coming out of the water are four kings who rise in succession to world dominance. King Nebuchadnezzar's dream consisted of a man's body made of four different metals representing nations. Daniel's dream consisted of four animals representing kings of the same nations.

"Representation advanced from the inanimate to the living. The first beast was a lion, the most ferocious of beasts. A lion with wings had long been the symbol of Babylon depicted in its statues and facades. This beast ruled the golden head of Nebuchadnezzar's dream, which was the powerful empire of Babylon as Daniel's dream interpreted.

"The second beast, the bear, we now know was Cyrus, king of Persia. This correlated to the silver upper body of the man in Nebuchadnezzar's dream representing Medo-Persia. Silver is inferior to gold. Just as a bear is weaker than a lion, the king of Medo-Persia ruled a kingdom of lesser power than Babylon but defeated the intimidating kingdom with hardly any bloodshed. The bear's prone position chewing on bones was probably a foretelling of how easily Medo-Persia would conquer Babylon in 539 B.C. Keep in mind, this defeat happened fourteen years after Daniel's dream predicted it. He knew the Medes and the Persians were becoming a credible threat to Babylon, but he couldn't have imagined they would conquer the empire so soon with relatively little effort. Medo-Persia ruled the known world for over two centuries.

"Next, the leopard with four wings and four heads would represent the king of a swiftly rising and expanding empire from the west that would dominate all other kingdoms in a sweeping conquest. The leopard would defeat the bear by its speed and agility. We look back and clearly see this kingdom as Greece, the bronze midsection of the man in Nebuchadnezzar's dream. Bronze is stronger than silver. The four heads of the leopard described the four regional rulers of the Greek empire after Alexander the Great died. That empire lasted from 331 to 63 B.C. We'll talk more about the four regional kings when we get to Daniel's second dream. Are you hanging in there with me?"

"My mind is racing, sir, but I think I'm getting it. It's so amazing that God showed Daniel the world rulers for the next five hundred years, and today we can look backward and see it all happened as He planned. I just wonder how many people realize this. I personally know of no one who is aware of fulfilled prophecies over twenty-five hundred years ago. It seems this last kingdom, the fourth beast, was the most significant."

The professor chuckled. "Not many people are into ancient prophecy, Kyle, which is unfortunate because it has so much connection to our modern world, what we can expect, and what we need to prepare for. You are right that this fourth beast is the one which grabs our attention. The other three represent kings long past, but the fourth, although beginning many centuries ago, also involves our future."

Dr. McCarty circled the perimeter of the Roman Empire on the map with his finger as he began to explain the fourth beast.

"This beast symbolized the Roman Empire. The species of this beast is not described as if it were too mighty and terrifying to be classified as a particular animal. It was a monster. Its large, iron teeth—like the iron lower body of the image in Nebuchadnezzar's dream—would crush the territories of all the previous kings. Iron was stronger than any metal describing the previous beasts. The focus of the dream was on this beast's horns. There were ten of them, representing ten kings. Then an eleventh horn grew larger than the others and subdued three of the others. The Roman caesars ruled the known world from 63 B.C. to A.D. 476. Of course, there were other people groups in Asia, Africa, even in what is now the Americas in these times. But these ten kings ruled what we consider the ancient civilized world.

"After establishing the fourth beast as the kings of the Roman Empire, Daniel's dream takes an interesting twist. The time periods obviously change from ancient times to the future beyond our present day. It jumps to the time surrounding the second coming of Jesus Christ, making the latter period like a second Roman Empire. The angel didn't reveal this time-skip to Daniel, so he would have seen the horns as simultaneous or immediately successive kingdoms. But the description of the Ancient of Days, or God, giving the Son of Man, or Jesus, rule over the everlasting kingdom places the event in our future, rather than in the old Roman kingdom. Only because we now see the prophecy in retrospect do we realize the horns are many centuries into the future of the fourth beast."

Kyle interrupted. "Excuse me, but this is getting complicated. So, the fourth beast represents the kings of the Roman Empire we know from the history books. But the ten horns of the beast also foretell of rulers of ten nations in our future years?"

"Exactly. Ten nations in our future will be like a new Roman Empire. They will dominate the world, acting as a cartel. Some scholars believe they will be powerful nations of the Western world, perhaps including the United States. Others maintain they will be nations corresponding to the geographic area of the ancient Roman Empire, including the Middle East.

"The small horn that grows to defeat three of the other nations is the principal focus of the end times. His appearance in Daniel's later visions reinforces his importance. This king will become a world leader to which all nations will ultimately acquiesce. This king, or dictator, will be more cunning and ruthless than any ruler before him. He will be particularly cruel to Christians because they will be the most antagonistic toward him, understanding much of who he is based on these prophecies. According to the angel, he will denounce God and commit unthinkable atrocities in order to establish his global authority. He will change the culture and the government laws to his favor. God will allow this horrific oppression for 'a time, times, and a half-time,' which means three-and-a-half-years. Ultimately, God will destroy this world ruler, and His people will assume oversight of all nations under an everlasting kingdom on Earth ruled by Jesus Christ.

"Daniel's second dream indicates the world dictator will rule for longer than the three-and-a-half-years, which means God's people will be rescued before his oppression becomes unbearable. The apostle John, in his writings, refers to this ruthless dictator as the antichrist.

Other Scriptures indicate that at some point in the despotic and ruthless rule of the world dictator, God will take His people off the Earth and into Heaven in an instant. We have since come to call this cosmic event 'the rapture.'"

"I've not read the rapture books or seen the movies, but I know they're all about that event. I guess I need to give it more attention," Kyle said.

"What we term 'the rapture' is an important event in the Bible, and we should learn all we can about it. However, don't get too caught up in when it will happen and what it will be like. The most important thing to understand and anticipate is that someday, there will be a world dictatorship, a new Roman Empire, that will persecute God's people—Christians—for a number of years. Before that persecution becomes unbearable, Jesus will rescue His saints by taking them off the Earth to be with Him in Heaven. Later, God will remove the dictator and ultimately establish his eternal kingdom on Earth. Ready to look at Daniel's second dream?"

"Ready!"

The professor read chapter eight of Daniel. "In this vision, there were two beasts, a ram and a goat, representing the two kingdoms immediately following Babylon.

"This time, the angel Gabriel was identified by name in a voice from Heaven. Gabriel revealed the ram's two horns represented the kings of Media and Persia. The goat's horn represented the king of Greece. Remember, Daniel would have been aware of Medo-Persia's potential overthrow of Babylon, but Greece was hardly recognized in his day as a factor in world affairs. That Greece, coming from the west, would eventually conquer Medo-Persia was no doubt a shock to him. The

Mede kingdom was dominant well before the combined Mede and Persia take-over of the Babylonian empire, but its king became less powerful than the king of Persia in the years leading up to Babylonia's fall. Thus, we see the symbolism of the initially shorter ram's horn becoming longer than the other.

"The vision was primarily about the goat, Greece. Its conspicuous single horn obviously symbolized Alexander the Great, who we now know viciously destroyed the Medo-Persian armies in 331 B.C., over two centuries after Daniel's dream. The goat's large horn being broken and replaced by four horns facing in different directions precisely describes the death of Alexander and the rise of four kings of the Greek Empire, as we discussed a moment ago. After Alexander died in 323 B.C. at the age of thirty-three, several civil wars across the empire ultimately divided it into what is modern-day Greece and Macedonia; Turkey; Egypt; and the combined regions of North Africa, Syria, and Israel."

Kyle's confused look caused the professor to pause.

"Am I losing you?"

"No, sir. I vaguely remember the four regional kingdoms of Greece from my freshman Western Civ. course. That boring study is just now coming to life. But I don't remember an additional king, the small horn of Daniel's vision."

"Although he is well-documented in secular history, scholastic history books don't usually highlight this king. But he is vitally important to God's revelation of the end times ahead of us. His inhumane actions during the Greek rule foreshadow the end times actions of the antichrist.

"Daniel wrote that this fifth horn became mighty toward the south, east, and the Beautiful Land. The Beautiful Land was a moniker for

Judah, or more specifically, Jerusalem. We now recognize the fifth horn as King Antiochus IV. The history of the Greek Empire includes lots of intrigue, corruption, and assassinations in the Syria and Israel region. As a result, Antiochus IV, through deception and murder, became ruler of Judah and the surrounding region. He was a tyrannical king, forcing Hellenistic culture on the Jews and disallowing their religious practices. He proclaimed himself a god and assumed the title of Epiphanes, or 'god-like.' He occupied the temple of Jerusalem and transformed it into a shrine for worship of himself.

"Notice that one of the angels in the vision asked how long this desolation of the temple would last. The other angel proclaimed the temple would be restored in twenty-three hundred evenings and mornings, which would be 1,150 days. Today's historians agree that the temple was reclaimed by the Jews and cleansed in 164 B.C. on the twenty-fifth of the Hebrew month relating to our December. This restoration was after a group of Jewish rebels, called the Maccabees, routed Antiochus' army from the temple. The removal of Antiochus is now celebrated by the Jews as Hanukkah.

"Counting back 1150 days from the Maccabees' raid takes us to the day in 167 B.C. when history records Antiochus desecrated the temple with pagan sacrifices. So, the 1150 days duration declared by the angel happened exactly as confirmed by secular history. The goal of Antiochus was to annihilate the Jews and become a deity. So, the little horn sprouting from one of the four horns of the goat was the ultimate focus of Daniel's dream."

"It's fascinating how accurately recorded history follows Daniel's prophetic vision centuries earlier," Kyle said. "But I'm not clear what the angel meant by the vision pertaining to the time of the end. The

Greek Empire period was not the end times, or we wouldn't be waiting for the end times twenty-three centuries later."

"You're getting ahead of me," Dr. McCarty said. "But I like it. You're thinking. Often, biblical prophecies have double meaning. In seminary, the study of biblical interpretation is called hermeneutics. And hermeneutics dealing with double-meaning prophecies is called dual fulfillment. The dual fulfillment revelations are about the near future as well as the distant future.

"For instance, some of King David's Psalms describe his own destiny, while the same words specifically describe the life of Jesus a thousand years later. In Daniel's vision, the goat's fifth horn predicts the rise of Antiochus Epiphanes, whose ruthless actions against the Jews are almost identical to the actions of the antichrist, or eleventh horn, of Daniel's earlier vision. History is repeating itself over two thousand years later.

"In the New Testament, Jesus' words, along with those of Paul and John in their writings, tell of a despotic and deceptive dictator to which all nations of the world will give autocratic authority. He will establish himself as the world deity to be worshiped in the temple of Jerusalem. As I alluded to previously, he will order the persecution and killing of Jews and Christians. This will happen in the end times. Daniel predicted this same scenario at the hand of the fifth horn, Antiochus Epiphanes, as part of the Greek Empire. It actually happened in 167 B.C., almost four hundred years after Daniel's vision.

"The same specific actions and timelines will happen in our future end times. Although the temple of Jerusalem has not been rebuilt since its destruction in 70 A.D., it may be by the time this despicable man rules. Or it could be a temporary temple—a tabernacle-like facility built quickly."

The professor picked up his Bible. "In the New Testament book of Matthew, Jesus said, 'Therefore, when you see the ABOMINATION OF DESOLATION which was spoken of through Daniel the prophet, standing in the holy place (let the reader understand), then those who are in Judea must flee to the mountains.' The antichrist, as John called him, like Antiochus Epiphanes, will occupy the temple and declare himself God at some point in the future. From the vision, we know this ruler will be destroyed, but not by human action. Antiochus died of an illness, and the antichrist will be destroyed by Jesus Himself on His return to set up His kingdom on earth."

"When I read this, it just makes me want to know more. I wonder why the vision didn't include more on the end times," Kyle said.

"No prophecies pertaining to our future give us everything our inquisitive minds want, but they give us an amazing amount of information. When you study them all and correlate them with each other, you can get a much better picture. The Bible is full of prophecies, many about our future times, and they all complement each other, coming together in a tapestry of truth. They unfold in time as we get glimpses of stepping stones to the future being revealed through world events year by year. Jesus told us to watch for the signs of the end times, meaning to watch in expectation for the progressive events of the prophecies to happen."

Dr. McCarty closed his Bible and began to fold the map. "What questions do you have?"

"I have to soak this in. I'll probably have a bunch for you later." Kyle hesitated. "There is one thing I'm wrestling with, but . . . I don't want to seem skeptical."

---

13 Matthew 24:15-16

"What about?'

"Well, how can anyone really be certain that these prophecies were actually written in real time and not by someone else after the events happened?"

"Ah, a very good question. I assumed we would go there sometime during our discussions. Let me assume my high-brow theologian position," the professor said, stiffening his posture and cocking his head back. "We have a Latin word for that skepticism. *Vaticinium-ex-eventu* means 'foretelling after the event.' Some critics of all prophecies advocate they were written after the events prophesied, so they are historical records made to look as if they were written earlier.

"First and most importantly, I believe the entire Bible is inerrant. That is, although it may have some seemingly contradictory content, when considering the whole of the Scriptures, it is accurate in every sense. God influenced Paul to write, 'All scripture is inspired by God.'[14] Why would God inspire anyone to write anything that is not true and accurate? But for the persistent skeptic, here are some more facts to consider relating to Daniel's writing."

Dr. McCarty took his last sip of tea and leaned forward in his chair.

"Considerable research has gone into the linguistics of the Book of Daniel. The earliest anyone could have looked back on most of Daniel's prophecies as having happened would have been in the second century B.C. I mentioned earlier that chapters two through seven were originally written in Aramaic, while subsequent chapters were in Hebrew. The prophetic non-biblical writings of the second century B.C. were all in Greek. The Aramaic of Daniel's day was considerably different from that of the second century B.C. The words, phrases,

---

spellings, and grammar were not anything like those of the second century B.C.

"Think of how much the English language in the 1600s differs from our modern English four hundred years later. Ancient languages changed even more rapidly. Also, the Hebrew language style of Daniel is nearly identical to that of the historical books of Ezra, Nehemiah, Chronicles, and Esther. Yet no scholars question the fifth century B.C. origin of those books.

"The relatively recent discovery of the Dead Sea Scrolls of Qumran have allowed great advances in dating ancient writings. All Qumran evidence points to the sixth century B.C. dates for Daniel's writing. The oldest Qumran copies of the Book of Daniel were copied in the second century B.C. The authentications processes of those ancient scribes would have disqualified Daniel's writings if they were of a later date than the sixth century.

"Daniel's writing contains twenty-five different words from Old Aramaic and Hebrew languages that were unlikely to have been known four centuries later. The Book of Ezekiel, Daniel's colleague, references Daniel by name twice. Yet hardly any biblical scholar doubts the date of Ezekiel's book. Josephus, the renowned historian of the first century, wrote about Alexander the Great coming to conquer Jerusalem and being met by a priest who showed him the prophecies of Daniel written two hundred years earlier predicting the conquest of Alexander. That placed Daniel well previous to Alexander."

The professor leafed through his Bible to find the verse he wanted. "Finally, and most importantly, as I mentioned earlier, Jesus is quoted in both Matthew and Mark as saying, 'Therefore, when you see the ABOMINATION OF DESOLATION which was spoken of through Daniel the prophet . . . '[15] Would Jesus have used Daniel's writing as a source for teaching if it were untrustworthy?"

Kyle nodded and smiled. "That's good enough for me. I've really enjoyed this special time, but I don't want to overstay my welcome. I believe Mrs. McCarty went upstairs. Please tell her how much I appreciated her hospitality and the delicious meal."

"Next time, let's meet in the student center after classes. I'll bring some burgers. How does next Friday look?"

Kyle checked his phone calendar. "Great!"

---

15 Matthew 24:15-16; Mark 13:14

For the past ten years, the consulting sessions with Arah Nisanu became increasingly sporadic. Nitocris felt less need for advice. She was becoming more comfortable with the governing of Belshazzar and more confident in her own counsel. She was also directing several projects throughout the province. To resolve the frequent flooding of the river that flowed through the city, she had a series of reservoirs constructed with a network of canals that drained excess water into the reservoirs.

The economy was at peak performance and filling the treasury to record levels, even though tax receipts had dwindled due to Belshazzar's neglect to collect them. King Nabonidus was profiting nicely from levying trade route taxes from his palace in Tayma. He was a consummate negotiator of lucrative deals with commercial caravans from distant lands. He required all traders from the East and the West to travel through Babylon for supplies. Babylon was enjoying peace and prosperity, but little attention was being paid to a looming threat.

Daniel was deeply concerned that he had not received any dreams or visions in over a decade. His concern was relieved somewhat by his receiving what seemed like supernatural insight into what was happening beyond the Babylon Empire. Since his childhood classes

with the priest, he had always had a passion for studying history.
During his years with King Nebuchadnezzar, he closely scrutinized
potential enemy nations. He had recently made a few journeys to
the eastern perimeters of the kingdom, where outlying cities were
keenly aware of the build-up of the Median and Persian armies.
Their movements and strikes against cities on their western front
were increasing. Daniel had immersed himself in the study of the
strategies of this formidable combined empire. Running his cache
of knowledge through the filter of his prophetic visions, he realized
God's next clash of empires was imminent.

Although Daniel treasured the roles and responsibilities God had
entrusted him with, he was also recognizing his mortality. At eighty
years of age, he was growing physically weaker and feeling less capable.
Azariah's recent death had brought on a deep depression for weeks as he
mourned the loss of his precious friend. Mishael and Hananiah were
both in poor health. The void of close friends that he could interact
with frequently had led him to become closer to his people's leader,
Sheshbazzar. He knew Sheshbazzar would be ending his meetings
with supervisors of a building project just before dark, so he set out
on the half-hour walk after the evening meal.

"Greetings, my friend," Sheshbazzar said, smiling as he folded
some parchment sheets into his wooden case. "I was just finishing
up for today."

"The storage facility is progressing well. Your oversight of the project has been outstanding," Daniel said.

"The king is always in a rush to build new structures for keeping
the increasing amount of trade items exchanged with other nations.
He wants the buildings strong and elaborate but won't give us the time

it takes to build them that way. Queen Mother Nitocris makes the rounds of the city every day, insisting we all work harder and faster."

"As we have discussed before, I'm afraid it is futile to keep building and hoarding treasures because this will all be overtaken and possessed by another people soon."

The two sat on a perfectly hewn stone readied for its place in the building's wall. "How long do you think we have, Daniel?"

"Ever since Persia's Cyrus the Great dethroned Media's King Astyages ten years ago, he has been developing both the Persian and Median armies to be superior to our army. Combined, they outnumber us significantly. Persia has now conquered our vassal state, Elam, and destroyed its capital, Susa. Cyrus is just waiting for the opportune time to attack Babylon."

"And our lion army is a sleeping lion."

"King Belshazzar is in denial as he wallows in the luxury of his privilege and amenities. I have overhead some say that King Nabonidus understands the situation and is furious with his son. Some even say he will be returning to the Babylon palace soon to take back control of the province."

"I fear it is too late."

"There is a dangerous storm on the eastern horizon, my friend."

*

539 B.C.

A blast from a shofar interrupted Daniel's nap. He walked to the palace, arriving just in time to see the entourage of charioteers in regal uniform parading past the palace steps. Following the chariots, the royal carriage, bearing the insignia of King Nabonidus, stopped adjacent to the palace entryway. As the king, with his bodyguards, approached the gate guards, they awkwardly bowed before him. Some other guards scrambled to lay out a carpet as still others ran inside the palace. The king and his escorts disappeared through the front entrance.

Within a few hours, the city was crawling with soldiers in full battle gear. Watchmen were positioned on the wall. Daniel sensed what had happened. The empire's king had returned from fourteen years of ruling from Tayma and was shaking up the province of Babylon, putting them on full alert.

Daniel, still hopelessly inquisitive long after his term in Nebuchadnezzar's palace, maintained a few sources on the inside. He arranged to rendezvous with one of Belshazzar's domestic servants, Noam, that evening.

"It was not a good scene," Noam said. "King Nabonidus took his seat on the outer chamber throne and called for the full palace court and army generals. His arrival was a shock to both Belshazzar and Nitocris. They remained in the shadows as Nabonidus shouted orders to the court."

"Did he banish King Belshazzar?"

"No, his son Belshazzar will apparently remain in charge of the palace, at least for now. Nabonidus is leaving in a few days to meet with Cyrus the Great somewhere on the Tigris River. The armies of the Persians and the Medes are encamped at Gutium, about a three-day march to the east. Nabonidus is going to try to negotiate a peace treaty with Cyrus."

A week later, Daniel was in the synagogue, where he frequently spent his afternoons praying. He suddenly sensed he wasn't alone and looked up to see Noam in the doorway.

"I'm sorry to interrupt, sir, but I thought you would want to know what I just learned."

Daniel rose from his knees, his face showing pain as his joints cracked. "Yes, proceed."

"King Nabonidus and a few generals left the day after we last spoke to meet with Cyrus. The generals returned this morning without the king."

"What happened to the king?"

"I don't know. Those discussions are well above my level. I do know the generals just ended a meeting with Belshazzar, and he has dispatched a command for all governors and satraps throughout the empire to meet with him about a month from now."

Over the next month, Daniel observed a mystifying relaxation of the readiness posture King Nabonidus had ordered for the army. Watchmen were no longer consistent in their positions in the wall towers. Few soldiers were seen on the streets, and those that were had no shields with them. There was much chatter on the streets reflecting the fear and confusion of the workers and shoppers. Trade caravans from far-away regions were conducting business as usual without any challenge to their credentials. Strolling by the palace, Daniel looked for any unusual activity, but observed none.

In Nebuchadnezzar's day, if an enemy had been within striking distance, he would have been in full scale preparation for battle and rallying the people. I would have been meeting with the court officials day and night. Actually, in Nebuchadnezzar's day, the enemy would not have gotten within striking distance.

During the next three days, Daniel did observe activity around the city that was very much out of the ordinary. However, it had no connection to military operations. Public workers were erecting poles along the main streets on which they were hanging extra oil lanterns. Bright-colored flowers from the hanging gardens were lining walkways and common areas. A finely woven Asian carpet had been laid from the palace entrance to the street's edge. The flurry of activities signaled the anticipation of a celebratory festival of some sort. Also obvious were increasing numbers of ornately decorated carriages parked on the sides of the streets. Daniel approached one of the workers, who was polishing the palace gate.

"What is the special occasion?"

"The big festival and feast later this week. The administrator must intend to work us to our grave."

"Who or what are we honoring?"

"The mighty Marduk and all the lower gods who have made Babylon the greatest of all kingdoms of the world. King Belshazzar has mandated the attendance of all the empire's regional rulers, their wives and families, and many from their courts. All the gods of every region will be worshiped and honored. Hundreds have already arrived, and about a thousand will finally be here for the feast."

"What is the purpose?"

"They don't tell me these things. But my guess is the king wants to get everyone's mind off the reality of pending war. Or maybe he thinks this is the last opportunity he will have to make merry with his friends."

Daniel asked a few more questions, thanked the worker, and began to walk to the synagogue to pray. *Oh, Yahweh, how much more will You tolerate before you crush this dynasty? My deepest concern is for Your people, the Hebrews. Cyrus' army will attack as soon as You pour out Your wrath on the kingdom that has become a stench in Your nostrils. But what of Your people? I feel so helpless. I am no longer an influence but only a common, aged Hebrew in a pagan land. My Lord, save Your people. I don't see any way out, but You are Yahweh. I trust in You.*

After four days of praying in agony and with inability to sleep, Daniel sat on the ground in front of his house, his chin on his chest. The tunes of the palace musicians could be heard from the palace. Lamps lighted the entire city. Some were dancing in the streets. The feast was under way. He visualized God at a great distance away with His back to the city and His hands over His ears. He rose to his feet with difficulty and went to his bed. "Yahweh, forgive them."

"Belteshazzar! Belteshazzar!" Arah Nisanu shouted as he approached Daniel's house.

"The king sent me. You must come with me to the palace quickly. I'll explain on the way."

Daniel dressed immediately, and they both embarked in the waiting carriage. "Keep a slow pace," Arah Nisanu instructed his driver. "I need some time."

"Are we going to the palace," Daniel asked.

"Yes. We have . . . a situation. Toward the end of the festive meal, as everyone was laughing, drinking, and being entertained, something exactly like a man's hand with no arm or body appeared out of nowhere and began writing on the wall. It was like ink was flowing from His finger. Some people near the wall screamed; everyone looked; and suddenly, the room was completely silent. The hand disappeared, and the letters remained. My first thought was that the magicians were giving us a show. But it was too real to be a trick. I have never seen anything so mysterious. I am still frightened."

"Did the hand write something readable?"

"The letters are in Aramaic, but there is no sense to them. The king called for his Chaldean magi, including the conjurers and diviners. I brought them into the room. They came up with some nonsensical interpretations, and the king sent them away angrily."

"So, what am I supposed to add to this occasion?"

"The queen approached her son and reminded him there was a man in his kingdom in whom is the spirit of the gods. She, of course, was describing you. She said that in the days of the king's grandfather, King Nebuchadnezzar, the wisdom of the gods was found in you. She told how her father, Nebuchadnezzar, appointed you chief of all the Chaldean magi conjurers and diviners after you had interpreted his dreams. She then asked him to summon you for the interpretation of the writing on the wall."

"Ah, Nitocris. I should have guessed."

Daniel and Arah Nisanu entered the outer chamber, where at least a hundred tables were placed about the room. The stuffy room reeked of a combination of wine, meat, and body odor. Almost all were in some state of drunkenness, their elitist attire rumpled. Everyone appeared frightened by the mysterious phenomenon just witnessed. Numerous women were on men's laps, but what had obviously been an orgy-like atmosphere was now very solemn. Daniel gasped as he recognized the relic gold and silver plates and goblets from the temple of Jerusalem. *Despicable people.*

"Ah, yes. Daniel, I believe," the king greeted Daniel as he stepped onto the raised podium for the king's table. Daniel was surprised at being addressed by his Hebrew name. Apparently, Belshazzar felt no need to use his Chaldean moniker. "Are you Daniel, one of the exiles my grandfather, King Nebuchadnezzar, brought from Judah? I have heard a spirit of the gods is in you and that you have the wisdom of the gods."

Daniel started to speak but was cut off by the king's further slurred words. "Earlier, the wise men and the conjurers were unable to interpret the message on the wall. But I understand that you will be able to interpret and discern the meanings of this mysterious writing. If you are successful, I will clothe you with purple and place a necklace of gold around your neck, giving you authority as the third ruler of Babylon."

"Keep your gifts and rewards for someone else, Your Highness; however, I will interpret the inscription for the king and make known its meaning."

Daniel eyed the black script of Aramaic letters. MNMNTKLPRSN. *Yahweh, this is meaningless to my finite mind. I humbly ask You to form its interpretation in the mind of Your servant.*

Slowly, the letters added vowels in Daniel's head for pronunciation. *Mene Mene Tekel, Upharsin. Mene is numbered. Double Mene is numbered and finished. Tekel is weighed as money is weighed. Upharsin is to divide into two pieces. The singular of Upharsin is Peres, which is also Aramaic for Persian.*

Daniel closed his eyes and concentrated heavily. It all began to form in his mind.

He instinctively turned to the crowd while he remained standing beside the king's table. "O king, the Most High Yahweh granted a vast kingdom to Nebuchadnezzar, your grandfather. Because of his great power, all people of the earth feared him. He killed or let live according to his wishes. He advanced or crushed whomever he wanted. But when he became too arrogant and prideful, Yahweh banished him to the wilderness to live like a wild animal. He was missing from his kingdom for months until he recognized that the Most High Yahweh rules over mankind through whomever He wishes.

"Yet you, his grandson, Belshazzar, have followed the same manner of rule, even though you knew all this. You have exalted yourself against Yahweh. They have brought the vessels of His holy temple to your tables, from which you, your nobles, your wives, and your concubines have been drinking wine. You have worshiped idols you cannot see, hear, or understand, while not glorifying the One True Yahweh Who holds your life in His hand. So the hand from this Yahweh has written you a message which I am about to reveal.

Daniel glanced at the king whose eyes were fixed on him. Looking back at the crowd, he continued. "This is what was written on the wall: 'MENE, MENE, TEKEL, UPHARSIN.' This is the interpretation: 'MENE'—God has limited your kingdom, and it is ending. 'TEKEL'—you have been evaluated and found deficient. 'PERES'—Babylon has been divided and turned over to the Medes and Persians.'

The silence of a thousand revelers was broken as murmuring began to fill the chamber. Derisive shouts began to echo at random. Daniel was looking for exits he might take if he were rushed by a drunken, riotous group. The king stood and motioned for constraint.

"My friends, we will not kill the messenger tonight. This man is only conveying what has been revealed to him by the one he refers to as Most High Yahweh. That is what I asked him to do. If his interpretation offends you, take it up with your own gods. As for me, I will keep my promise. Arah Nisanu, bring the awards I described."

Arah Nisanu exited the chamber, and the king directed some other servants to make quick arrangements for a formal presentation.

"But, Your Highness . . . ," Daniel uttered as Nitocris appeared instantly next to him with her finger on her lips, signaling silence. "The king is speaking from his inebriation," Nitocris whispered. "Don't challenge him. He can just as easily become belligerent. Let him do as he promised. The people will abide. He is the king, second in authority after his father, who is not present. It appears you are now third in line for the throne."

When Arah Nisanu returned with the regalia, King Belshazzar ordered him to place the purple satin robe around Daniel's shoulders and the gold necklace around his neck.

The king placed his hands on Daniel's shoulders. "Before these governors and satraps, palace officials and families, I decree you, Daniel, to have authority as the third ruler in the kingdom."

Daniel bowed to the king and took his seat next to him. *O Yahweh, I am conflicted beyond measure. Until an hour ago, I was content in Your purpose for me as Your humble prophet. Now, I am thrust into the highest position of authority I have ever held, at least until the king sobers. Babylon's* **pending doom makes any position in the kingdom short in duration. The only desire I have is for Your will to be done. If this is Your will, so be it.**

Daniel stared at the gold chalice in front of him that had just been filled with a fine wine. He was repulsed. The king had not said a word after they were seated but just kept a permanent drunken smile. *He either didn't understand any of my interpretation, or he is resigned to it and doesn't care.*

A few of the celebrants were huddled around tables in deep conversation, but most went back to their party mode, bordering on an orgy. The musicians played a soft, sultry rendition. Daniel was shaking. The ominous atmosphere was heavy with the weight of impending calamity.

Ka-bam! The chamber's main door burst open. Soldiers in full battle gear stormed into the crowd. Hundreds at the tables shrieked. The invaders waved their swords wildly and toppled the tables while heading directly to the raised podium. Most of the celebrants stood frozen. Others ran.

The king sat paralyzed by shock and inebriation. Daniel felt strangely at peace wondering why he, himself, was not in a panic. Several soldiers mounted the podium, turned over the head table, and placed all at the table in an armlock with swords at their throats. Three of the table occupants tried to run but were grabbed before they could leave the podium. Daniel was lifted out of his seat with a strong arm around his chest. He felt the sharp edge of the sword press into the flesh of his neck. A closer look at the soldiers revealed their Median army uniforms. The room filled with a few hundred soldiers in full battle dress. Babylonian men were moaning, and the women were wailing. A few lay injured, but apparently, no one had been killed.

Through the main door strode a man whose uniform displayed high rank. The other soldiers parted to open a path to the podium. The decorated man approached King Belshazzar. The king's knees buckled, but the captor held him up.

"I am General Gubaru, commander of the army of the Medes," the man said in Aramaic with a Mede accent. "I come in the name of King Cyrus of Persia. Tonight, Babylon is given into the hands of Persia. Long live the king!"

Daniel recognized the general's name as the governor of Gutium, a Babylonian province formerly of Media located east of Babylon. He knew him as the son of the Mede king, Astyages, whom King Cyrus had conquered eleven years prior. That made him the nephew of Amytis.

Gubaru nodded to the soldier holding Belshazzar. The soldier slammed the king's head, face-down, on the table. Gubaru drew his sword and raised it high.

Daniel slumped against the arm around his chest and closed his eyes. *O, Yahweh, have mercy!* He heard the thud, the cracking of bones. He felt the splattering of blood on his hand. Men and women throughout the chamber were sobbing uncontrollably. Many women fainted.

Gubaru punched Daniel in the stomach. "Who are you?"

"I am Daniel, a Hebrew prophet."

Gubaru laughed. "A Hebrew prophet in royal regalia at the king's table? Is that the best you can come up with? Before I sever your head, I need to know how to identify you to my superiors."

"Bring in the Babylonian general to identify this man," Gubaru shouted to his aide near the door.

The Babylonian army general stepped forward, saluted Gubaru, and identified Daniel.

"He is a Hebrew exile whom King Nebuchadnezzar appointed to be his provincial ruler. He is also a religious leader among the Hebrews. Nebuchadnezzar gave him the Chaldean name of Belteshazzar. I was just told he was tonight made a ruler of Babylon under Belshazzar."

Gubaru gazed at Daniel for a moment, then instructed the soldier holding him. "Let him go. We are not here to kill Hebrews or take prisoners. We are here to take Belshazzar's head to King Cyrus and to set up the new kingdom of Persia." He turned to the crowd.

"You rulers will return to your provinces. Go now before I change my mind. Put your houses in order. You will be replaced soon by Persian rulers."

As the room cleared frantically, Daniel stopped the general.

"What happened? Where was the Babylonian army?"

"Our army's leaders defected to King Cyrus. The other generals and I who accompanied King Nabonidus to the meeting with Cyrus became convinced that Cyrus would conquer Babylon. At Cyrus' urging, we conspired to grant a bloodless takeover of the kingdom in exchange for some concessions allowing us to maintain our military rank and positions under Persian rule. We handed Nabonidus over to Cyrus."

"Is King Nabonidus dead?"

"No, he was exiled to Carmania, east of Persia."

"So, the entire Babylonian army deserted their king?"

"As the generals go, so goes the army, although some of the lower ranks resisted and paid for it with their lives. Some civilians were killed trying to be heroes. We planned the take-over with Cyrus' Mede and Persian generals. Even though Cyrus defeated the Mede king Astyages eleven years ago, the Mede army still operates somewhat autonomously under Cyrus. We showed them how to open the canal gates to drain the Euphrates River for crossing. Then, we opened the city gates for the Medes to enter without opposition. Babylon will probably be a better kingdom under Persian rule, and we're all still alive, so I would call that a Babylonian army victory."

Daniel thanked the general for his explanation. He dropped his royal, blood-stained robe on the floor. Holding the necklace—also splattered with blood—in his hand, he started to drop it, too. *Maybe I should keep it as a souvenir. I suppose I need something to show for my hour as third king.* He was surprised he could force a grin after witnessing the instant fall of the greatest empire in history and almost breathing his last breath. He put the necklace back around his neck and hid it under his garment.

Making his way to the exit door, Daniel heard a commotion behind him. He was astonished to see Nitocris in the custody of two Persian officers. *Yahweh, please, don't let them kill her!* He braced to confront them.

"It's all right, Belteshazzar. They say they are taking me to Nabonidus in Carmania. I will be spared. It was part of the generals' negotiation."

She looked at the two officers. "Please give me a moment." They obliged. She embraced Daniel tightly.

"I have always loved you, Belteshazzar."

"And I, you, my sweet one. Your mother as well."

"You will always have a special place in my heart." Her voice cracked. "Try to arrange a proper burial for . . . my son."

The officers took her arms and continued down the corridor. She shouted out, "Don't let the people forget our great Babylonia!"

Daniel clutched his beard, still wet from her tears and savored her sweet perfume.

Not surprisingly, the following week was tumultuous for Babylon. The Mede army had soldiers on every street. Some Babylonian soldiers who had been permitted to assimilate into the prevailing army had already been issued Mede uniforms. About a dozen Babylonian zealots had attempted ambush attacks on a few soldiers, both Babylonian and Mede, all of which had resulted in their brutal death. The trade caravans had been avoiding Babylon, and the local merchants feared for their livelihood.

Daniel and Sheshbazzar were meeting daily with the Hebrew district leaders to allay their fears about the destiny of the exiles. Every evening, Daniel prayed past midnight for wisdom and understanding in this confusing time. Gubaru had not made a public appearance since the interrupted feast.

Daniel entered his house at mid-morning carrying his pail of water from the well and saw a parchment sheet on the floor. Breaking the palace seal, he read, *General Gubaru requests your presence at a noon meal in the palace.* It was stamped by Gubaru's new administrator, Amata.

Gubaru doesn't know me. What possible reason would he have to invite me to meet with him? Maybe this will bring the clarity I've been praying for. Or it could be a ruse for my convenient arrest. Yahweh, guide me.

Daniel felt very uneasy presenting himself to the Mede palace guards. Although confident this was God's will, he couldn't shake feeling treasonous accepting the invitation of the enemy's leader.

"Welcome, Daniel," Gubaru said after Daniel was announced in the doorway of the king's dining room. Daniel's mind flashed to when he and King Nebuchadnezzar had discussed many crucial issues over meals in this room. "I want you to meet two of my newly appointed commissioners, Fravarti and Gaumata."

Daniel nodded politely, still wondering why he was invited.

"Please be seated at the table. The meal will be served soon."

Daniel sat at the place setting left unoccupied between the two commissioners. Gubaru unrolled a parchment containing a diagram of his governing organization for the former Babylonian kingdom. He handed it to Daniel.

"One-hundred-twenty of my finest army officers have already been dispatched to provinces throughout the kingdom. These governors, or satraps, will replace all the Babylonian governors as judges, law enforcers, and tax collectors, as well as recruiters and trainers for the Persian army."

Daniel was impressed with how rapidly the general had implemented his structure of governance.

"In the few days since my arrival, I have learned much about you, Daniel. You not only practically ran the kingdom for Nebuchadnezzar, but you are also the Hebrew connection between the thousands of exiles and the Chaldeans. You are the miraculous interpreter of dreams and supernatural happenings—the leader of the magi. You even foretold my overthrow of Babylon, but it was too late. I am a merciless commander, who would normally have imprisoned you to stifle your influence. However, I am also a wise man, who can see the benefit of having you act as a buffer between me and your people, both Chaldean and Hebrew. Therefore, I am appointing you as a third commissioner over forty satraps, including those governing the province of Babylon and the western region of Judah and its neighbors."

Daniel felt numb as he glanced at his Mede colleagues and looked back at Gubaru.

"I am honored beyond measure, Your Excellency. But I am old, and my influence among the Babylonians is not what it was. I am sure someone else would be of greater value to you."

"With your age has come much wisdom. My observation is that you continue to enjoy great respect among the people. I need your leadership and your wise counsel. I'll want you within close reach at all times."

After about two hours of instruction to the commissioners, Amata showed them to their palace offices.

"All of you will move your belongings to the three houses directly across the street from the palace. You may employ five assistants each, including your house servants. Everything and everyone in the palace are at your disposal."

Daniel was leaving as Gubaru intercepted him at the main door. "King Cyrus is traveling from Pasargadae. He will arrive at the palace next week. I will need your experience in helping to give him the proper ceremonial courtesies. We will meet the day after tomorrow to discuss plans."

Daniel needed a long walk to process this overwhelming responsibility. He walked the full length of the Chebar canal, where he had arranged for the first exiles to reside. Almost all Hebrews had since integrated with the Babylonians. Remnants of the small houses could still be seen along the banks. His heart was filled with memories of the first years of the captivity. He prayed all afternoon as the struggles of his people over more than six decades consumed his thoughts. He spoke intimately with God about the incredible life journey He had led him through and confirmed undoubtedly where He was leading him now.

He asked God to give him a youthful body and mind, despite his age.

Returning to the synagogue, he reviewed the writings of Jeremiah and retrieved the scroll containing Isaiah's writings. Reading Isaiah, he came to a section that astonished him.

"How have I not noticed this before?" he said to himself. He reread it.

"It is I who says of Cyrus, "He is My shepherd! And he will perform all My desire.' And he declares of Jerusalem, 'She will be built,' And of the temple, 'Your foundation will be laid.'"[16]

"Cyrus!" Daniel's voice echoed off the walls. "Over 150 years ago, Isaiah named Cyrus as the one Yahweh would direct to rebuild Jerusalem and the temple." Yahweh gave Isaiah the specific name of the king who would free His people to return to Jerusalem—a king who wouldn't exist for a century-and-a-half!

The next week, the city was fully prepared to receive King Cyrus. Crowds of unwilling Babylonians had been forced by threat of death to show respect and line the streets for his arrival. The sting of submission to Persia was pervasive in every native of the land. The exiles, at the urging of Daniel and Sheshbazzar, remained neutral, choosing to accept the invasion and show respect to the new king.

King Cyrus's carriage arrived mid-afternoon, preceded by a long column of soldiers with gold-plated shields and trailed by an entourage of officials. He was greeted by Gubaru and escorted onto the palace courtyard. He stood on a decorative dais with Gubaru at his side. Palace

---

16 Isaiah 44:28

guards, three layers deep, encircled the dais. Daniel and his three colleagues stood facing the king just inside the guard's formation. Gubaru signaled silence, and King Cyrus began to speak.

"Men and women of Babylon, seventeen days ago, Persia conquered the empire of Babylon by the powerful arm of the Mede army. Little blood was shed in the invasion, which is fitting for the peaceful transition that I desire. This magnificent kingdom founded by the great King Nebuchadnezzar is now part of the Persian Empire to which you are now subject. You will be ruled by Persia, pay tribute to Persia, and fight for Persia. Your Chaldean culture will change very little as long as you honor your king. Oppose my rule, and you will become slaves to Persia with heavy burdens."

The crowd responded with muffled grumblings but quieted as King Cyrus continued.

"A coward was put in charge as king of this empire—not a lion, but a kitten who ran from his own people. With evil intents, he did away with the regular offerings to the gods and desecrated the worship of the greatest of his gods, Marduk. Today, I have ordered all statues and shrines of the sun god, Sin, to be destroyed and all Sin priests imprisoned. In the coming weeks, your Marduk images will be returned to their deserved places inside the city walls."

Suddenly, the people roared with praise for this unexpected favor.

"You will find that my further concessions will be in proportion to your further concessions. I will continue to rule from Pasargadae in Persia and my most excellent commander and governor, Gubaru, will be the king of the former Babylonia under my authority."

King Cyrus took a gold crown held by his assistant and placed in on the head of the kneeling Gubaru.

"You will no longer be called Gubaru. I crown you King Darius, holder of the scepter of Babylonia. All former subjects of the Babylonian Empire will bow to you and serve you as their king. Now rise and take your place among the great and mighty rulers within the Persian Empire."

The soldiers chanted, "Hail, King Darius," and "Long live King Darius." Soon, the chants rippled down the streets of onlookers. Musicians stationed in the background began a Persian anthem that resounded throughout the city. There was spontaneous dancing in the streets.

King Cyrus planned to remain in Babylon for two weeks before returning to Pasargadae. The day after Darius was crowned king, he summoned Daniel and the other two commissioners to meet with King Cyrus. King Darius presented to King Cyrus the territorial boundaries of the commissioners' responsibilities. As if the meeting had been rehearsed many times, Cyrus presented the governing strategies, and Darius gave the three their tasks to accomplish the strategies. Cyrus ended the meeting by asking whether anyone needed any clarifications.

Daniel responded, "Your Excellency, I am sure the three of us will lead well and please both you and King Darius. However, there is one important issue in the realm of my responsibility that I need to call to your attention."

Daniel's two colleagues eyed each other with expressions of concern as he continued.

"My Hebrew people have been held as exiled slaves in Babylon for many years, some for almost seventy years. Yahweh, the Creator of the heavens and the earth, told my people through Jeremiah the prophet that our captivity would be only seventy years, after which He would restore us to our homeland. Just last night, I read again from the writings of Jeremiah, where he prophesied, 'When seventy years have been completed for Babylon, I will visit you and fulfill My good word to you, to bring you back to this place.'[17]

"Moreover, the Hebrew prophet Isaiah wrote over 150 years ago that a man named Cyrus would allow the Hebrews to return to Jerusalem to rebuild their temple and the entire city. Your Excellency, the years of captivity of the Hebrews and the time of your conquering of Babylon are aligning with these prophecies."

King Cyrus mulled Daniel's statement for a moment. "Your prophet identified me by name 150 years ago?"

"Yes, Your Highness."

"Do you possess the documents relating these prophecies?

"Yes, Your Highness."

"Bring them to my chamber tonight. I must see them."

Daniel obtained the scrolls of Jeremiah and Isaiah from the protective shelves in the synagogue and returned to the king's chamber just after sundown. Just the two of them, Daniel and King Cyrus, sat at a table with the two scrolls containing the writings of Isaiah and Jeremiah respectively. Daniel carefully translated the Hebrew writing into Aramaic as his host listened with great interest. The king broke his silence only after Daniel had read the pertinent passages.

"So, this prophet—Isaiah—wrote many years ago that I—I specifically—would release the Hebrews to return to Jerusalem."

"That is correct, Your Excellency."

"And this Jeremiah wrote before Nebuchadnezzar brought the Hebrews to Babylon that they would be conquered and exiled but only for seventy years, which is upon us."

---

17 Jeremiah 29:10

"Right, again, Your Excellency."

The king's eyes scanning the walls of his chamber for a time made Daniel uneasy. The king finally spoke. "This God of the Hebrews has proven Himself superior to other gods on many occasions, as I understand. What His prophets say must be true. This places me in a rather precarious position. After I return to Pasargadae, I will decide on the action to take. In the meantime, I know you will serve me well in Babylon, regardless of the destiny of your people."

"Of course, Your Excellency."

extremely demanding on the people of Babylon. King Darius produced new decrees almost every day that the commissioners had to implement. Daniel found it easier to communicate new laws and governing processes to his governors and satraps because of their closer proximity to the capital city. In addition, Daniel's many years of experience with the people gave him an advantage over Fravarti and Gaumata, who were new to the Babylonian culture. Although the two commissioners were much younger than Daniel, they became frustrated by their inability to progress in their duties as rapidly as their counterpart. Language barriers and unfamiliarity with customs stifled their progress. At a weekly update meeting with the three commissioners, King Darius expressed his disappointment in the performance of Fravarti and Gaumata.

"I have just finished studying the reports from the three of you. As you know, I also receive feedback directly from the satraps of the regions concerning how my directives and policies are being implemented. Some are complaining of being directed heavy-handedly and even under the threat of death. Although I realize the people's difficulties in adjusting to control by a foreign power, we must make this transition work without rebellion. Almost all of the discontent and lagging progress is within the regions overseen by the two of you."

The king was eyeing Fravarti and Gaumata.

"Daniel's people seem to be accepting of his implementation of my decrees. I am already seeing excellent cooperation and productivity from the Babylonians under his authority. I want you other two to give attention to his methods and demeanor. You will meet with Daniel weekly to discuss your plans and problems. Heed his advice and counsel regarding the manner in which you conduct oversight of your regions. I expect improvements. If you do not learn from Daniel, I will make him ruler of the whole kingdom with authority over both of you."

Daniel's appreciation of the king's commendation was more than offset by his concern for his relationship with his fellow commissioners. Immediately after the meeting, he initiated a conversation with them to head off inevitable ill feelings.

"My friends, I deserve no credit for my success in leading my region. These people have known me for years and have grown to trust me. I speak their dialect, and I know their culture. Unfortunately, you have no such advantages. I want us all to succeed and have no desire to rule over you. I pledge that I will help you in every way possible in our weekly meetings. My advice will be for the sole purpose of helping you to understand and communicate with your subjects."

"We will meet with you only because the king has forced us to," Fravarti said. "Our subjects are servants of our empire and bound to the laws of the Medes and Persians. Why would we take guidance from a gray-haired Hebrew?"

After several weekly meetings with the other two commissioners, Daniel was very frustrated with their lack of response and cold demeanor. His advice was always challenged and often rejected outright.

It was late afternoon when one of his satraps from a rural area of Babylon came to his palace chamber escorted by a palace guard.

The satrap bowed at the doorway. "Your Excellence, I apologize for coming unannounced, but I have an urgent message for you."

"Enter and be seated."

"Sir, I have close relationships with some of the other satraps of our province. We are all Medes or Persians, and some are my kinsmen. As you would expect, we visit frequently and share successes and failures in our rule of the people. Your fellow commissioners have been urging us to find corruption or negligence on your part for which they could accuse you before the king. You know your satraps are loyal to you and have no reason to accuse you. So, their efforts with us have failed. However, satraps under the other two commissioners have been told that soon they may be ruled by a ruthless Hebrew who hates Medes. They were told to appeal to the king to keep their commissioners or else risk losing their positions."

The satrap's words struck deeply into Daniel's soul. He knew the animosity the other commissioners had toward him but never suspected they would generate a kingdom-wide conspiracy against him.

"You are a courageous leader. I am eternally grateful for your message. I know I can trust you. Please continue to inform me of further attempts to sabotage my service to the king."

"You are the courageous one, Your Excellence. I will continue to watch and report to you."

Daniel chose to keep the satrap's information to himself and depend on God for protection. Over the following month, the abuse from his fellow commissioners seemed to subside somewhat. He assumed that they had not been able to find anyone who would corroborate their accusations. They had become more civil in the weekly advisory meetings.

In a regularly scheduled meeting with the commissioners, King Darius closed with an announcement as he handed official documents to each of them.

"After four months of my reign over Babylon, the prefects, satraps, high officials, and governors appear to be gaining the respect of the inhabitants of the empire. I have received word that these men believe a show of solidarity from people throughout the kingdom is in order. Therefore, the decree in your hands orders that no one will make a petition to any god besides me for thirty days. Anyone violating the decree will be cast into a den of lions nearest to their city."

Daniel turned immediately to the other two commissioners. They were looking for his reaction. He wanted to object but decided he didn't have the influence to fight the action.

"Your Highness," Gaumata said. "Be reminded that you, even as king, will not have the option of revoking this decree according to the law of the Medes and Persians."

"I do not need to be reminded that once a king signs a decree, it cannot be changed."

"Of course, Your Highness."

After the meeting, Daniel went straight to his house and up to the top floor. The source of the king's decree was obvious to him. His leadership skills and integrity had made it impossible for the other two commissioners to find incompetency or corruption in his duties. But they knew if they could cause his devotion to his God to be a crime, he would commit such a crime. He opened the west window facing Jerusalem, knelt, and prayed just as he had done three times a day throughout his sixty-six years of exile. Twice more that day, he humbled himself in front of the window, calling out to God; the last prayer came in late afternoon.

"O long-suffering Yahweh, how tolerant will You continue to be of these pagans who despise you? How long will you contend with those who seek to harm me? How much more will I, your faithful servant, have to bear from those who seek my destruction? If it is time for this old man to be gathered with my family, I am grateful that my execution will be from my love for You and my obedience to Your commands. I cry out to You now to rescue all Your people, the people of Abraham, Isaac, and Jacob. As the end of seventy years of captivity spoken of by Jeremiah approaches, be merciful to them and let them return to the land You promised them. Although I am unworthy, I ask that You—"

"Daniel! What are you doing?" the boisterous voice of Fravarti interrupted. "We have observed you in the window three times now praying to your Hebrew God."

Fravarti and Gaumata stood just inside the doorway. Two soldiers were behind them.

"You certainly know that no one in the kingdom is allowed to petition any god except King Darius for thirty days. We came to meet with you, never suspecting that you would be violating the decree on the first day of its declaration."

"This unscheduled meeting is conveniently timed and with soldiers accompanying you," Daniel said. "What a coincidence."

Fravarti nodded toward the soldiers. They clutched Daniel by the arms and escorted him to the palace. Moments later, he was standing before King Darius, who was notified in advance of his arrival.

"Your Highness, did you not sign an injunction that any man who makes a petition to any god or man besides you, O king, for thirty days is to be cast into the lion's den?" Fravarti asked.

"The statement is true," the king said. "It is according to the law of the Medes and Persians, which may not be revoked."

"Daniel, who is one of the exiles from Judah, pays no attention to you, O king, or to the injunction which you signed, and he keeps making his petition three times a day," Gaumata said.

"But the decree was meant for the masses to ensure their submissiveness, not to test the loyalty of my commissioners."

"Your order has no exemptions, Your Excellence," Fravarti said.

"Daniel, you are dear to my heart. I did not foresee this consequence. Tell me that you were petitioning me instead of your God. I will accept that."

"Your Highness, I cannot deny almighty Yahweh for any reason, not even to save my life. From the time He breathed life into me, He has protected me and has set me on high ground with authority over Nebuchadnezzar's dynasty. He honored me through your elevating me again to a position of high esteem, and I have sought to serve you well. I have nothing more to say concerning this matter. I am ready to face your sentence. Yahweh, Whom I serve, is able to deliver me from the mouths of the lions. But even if He does not, let it be known to you, O king, that I am not going to serve you as a deity or petition you as a god. Yahweh is the one true God! I will love Yahweh with all my heart, with all my soul, and with all my might."

King Darius eyed the other two commissioners. "I must seek other counsel in this matter."

"Recognize, O king, that it is a law of the Medes and Persians that no injunction or statute which the king establishes may be changed. Daniel is guilty of disloyalty to the king," Fravarti said emphatically.

The king walked to his throne, fell into it, and slumped forward with an audible sigh. "Do it without delay before I act in a manner that will cost me my kingdom. Daniel, I have no recourse. I cannot deliver you."

"According to His will, Your Highness," Daniel replied.

The soldiers led him out of the palace and placed him in a waiting carriage. They sat on either side, still grasping his arms. Fravarti and Gaumata accompanied the king in his royal carriage.

The brisk twilight brought a chill to Daniel's arms and legs. He wasn't given time to get his cloak. The only sounds were of the horses' hooves on the stone street and the constant whining of the carriage wheels. He savored the aroma of mutton being seared on an outdoor grill, realizing it would probably be the last food he would smell.

Daniel was familiar with executions by lions. He had learned as a teenaged exile that the lion was the symbol of the Chaldeans and Nebuchadnezzar's empire. As a young man, he had supervised the building of the Ishtar gate with lion images accenting the deep blue façade. Wild lions captured by royal hunters were caged in stone structures outside most large cities of Babylonia specifically for executing the kingdom's miscreants. Symbolically, the lions of Babylon would devour the domestic enemies of Babylon. It was particularly the death sentence of choice for traitors. As Nebuchadnezzar's provincial ruler, he had overseen some of these executions. The lions were sparsely fed, so they would be constantly hungry.

Daniel's mind was filled with remembrances of his childhood, his family, the exile journey, the miracle of his ascension to power, and governing with his three friends. He had never felt so lonely as now. He had always hoped to die in his homeland. Now, he was going to die in a foreign land at the hand of yet another foreign kingdom. All his friends had preceded him in death. He longed for Ezekiel's encouragement and the presence of Mishael, Hananiah, and Azariah. Approaching the destination, he began to feel a strange peace. The tense muscles relaxed. Filled with the Spirit of God, he prayed silently.

O Yahweh, my Comforter, how I have depended on You and You alone through the highest mountains and deepest valleys. You protected me in the positions of authority and power, so I could protect Your people, the sons of Judah. You have given me undeserved abilities to interpret dreams and signs for Your glory. In trouble and temptation, You have rescued me. Who has had a fuller life than I, Your servant? Now, my Lord, I am old and tired. This is likely my call to Paradise, my rest, my reward. I accept it willingly. Yes, I welcome it. For what more need could You have of me? Only one more thing I ask of You. Have mercy on Your people. Let them return to the land You promised them. Let them be free to worship You unshackled. Lift Your hand of wrath from them. They are Your people. Love each of them as You have loved me. Now, I am ready to receive what You have for me. If it is Your will, I ask for it to be quick and as painless as possible, yet not my will but Yours be done.

The carriage halted in front of the gray, stone structure. Several men stood by with blazing torches that expelled the darkness of the moonless night. Daniel sat with his escorts as the men moved the heavy stone entry cover enough to throw a torch into the den. A deep roar echoed from inside. Daniel visualized the lions fleeing from the torch and away from the opening. The soldiers exited the carriage with Daniel and stood facing the den. To the side hardly visible in the darkness, Daniel caught sight of the king, flanked by the other two commissioners. The stone was moved further until the entry was just wide enough for its guest. The soldiers commanded Daniel to remove his robe and sandals, leaving him covered only by his under garment.

"Your God, Whom you constantly serve, will Himself deliver you," King Darius shouted.

In a violent motion, he was lifted off his feet and shoved through the narrow opening. Landing face-down on the cold, dirt floor, he heard the stone slam closed. He rose quickly to his knees. The embers from the burned-out torch provided just enough light to make out the eye reflections and faint silhouettes of four lions pacing back and forth in the background. The largest one roared loudly enough for Daniel's body to feel it.

"Yahweh, have mercy on me!" Daniel screamed.

The animal loped toward him. Stopping short by an arm's length, the male of the pride opened his mouth to show his long, sharp teeth as he let out a bloodcurdling roar that blew Daniel's hair back. In the dim light, the ferocious beast's shadowy head and mane looked monstrous. The other three surrounded their prey, walking slowly in a circle while emitting muffled growls. Daniel could smell their breath. He closed his eyes tightly, awaiting the first excruciating pain of teeth sinking into his flesh. *Where will the first strike be? My leg, my arm, my neck?*

Suddenly, the commotion ceased. Silence. Daniel opened his eyes slowly. The glow of four sets of eyes were circled around him near the ground. As he focused on the animals, now barely visible, he could see they were all lying down with their heads on their front paws. An eerie silence had replaced the roars. All mouths were closed.

He was startled by a faint silhouette behind the lions. Thinking at first it was another lion, he strained to see the figure more clearly. It was like a man. He blinked his eyes to focus better and could see the man's right hand extended palm-down toward him. The man walked backward slowly into the darkness. Daniel instantly remembered the mysterious man who had appeared in the furnace with his three friends to save their lives.

Yahweh, what have You done? Are You going to rescue me yet again? Have You sent Your angel to protect me as You did for Your servants in the furnace? The miracles You have performed on my behalf, I cannot comprehend. How can I be worthy of this? He began to weep. *This morning, by Your grace, I was advising the king at his table; tonight, I am in a den of wild lions that are tamed by Your mercy. Who am I, Yahweh, and what do You desire of me?*

Daniel sat without moving for most of the night, staring at the docile lions and marveling at the faithfulness of God. Finally, exhausted, he stretched out quietly, wincing as his bare skin made contact with the cold, damp floor. He continued prayers of praise from the songs of David until he drifted off to sleep.

"Daniel!" The loud voice woke him with a start.

"Daniel!" Although muffled by the thick wall, Daniel recognized the voice of the king.

"Daniel, has the God you serve been able to save you from the lions?"

The grinding noise of the stone being slid back echoed through the den. The lions were on their feet but standing in place. Daniel shaded his eyes from the morning sun as he turned sideways to squeeze through the opening.

"Don't worry about the lions escaping. They're content where they are," Daniel said, smiling.

The soldiers were muttering about not seeing even a scratch on Daniel's body. King Darius came swiftly to Daniel, picked up his outer garment from the ground, and draped it around him. Daniel noticed Fravarti and Gaumata standing next to the king's carriage. Both looked very troubled.

"O king, live forever! Yahweh sent His angel to shut the lions' mouths, and they have not touched me because I was innocent before Him and you. O king, I have committed no crime."

"Daniel will ride back with me." The king instructed the soldiers to walk Daniel to the king's carriage.

"Your Excellence," Fravarti called out. "There will be only one seat left on the carriage with the addition of Daniel. Whom do you want to return with you, Gaumata or me?"

"Neither."

King Darius spoke to the soldiers in a voice inaudible to Daniel. The soldiers took Fravarti and Gaumata forcefully and began walking toward the den entrance. Both stopped walking and had to be dragged while screaming.

"No, no, O king, have mercy, mercy, mercy!"

They were stripped bare and pushed through the opening. Before the cover stone was completely over the entry, Daniel heard the lions roaring while the two men shrieked. Then there was silence. Daniel was instantly nauseated, breathing deeply to avoid vomiting. The king sat in the rear seat of the carriage next to Daniel. One of the soldiers approached.

"Highness, what shall I record as the crimes of the executed?"

"The same as was Daniel's. Disloyalty to the king. Record this man as innocent and the two serving as food for the beasts as guilty. And see that their wives and children meet the same fate."

The carriage driver snapped the reins and turned the horses back toward the city with the new passenger on board.

"Daniel, I am sorry you had to go through this. I knew you shouldn't be punished for praying to your God, but I was legally bound, under the circumstances, to sentence you to death."

Daniel's overwhelming emotion left him speechless. He just looked the king in the eye, nodded, and smiled. During the trip back to the palace, the king told Daniel he would be appointing three new commissioners. Daniel was relieved that he would be out from under the brutal leadership pressures. But that relief soon evaporated.

"I want you to be over all three commissioners. Train them, equip them, and oversee their performance. You will be third ruler of the kingdom after King Cyrus and me. My administrator, Amata, will assist you as well as me."

Daniel's breathing stopped as he pondered what he had just heard. From commissioner to criminal, to the lions' den to third ruler of Babylonia, all in less than a day. This was the second time he had been named third ruler of Babylon. Deep inside, he hoped this title would be as short-lived as the one received from King Belshazzar. *O Yahweh, how I need guidance and wisdom now. You know the desire of my heart is to rest in my old age. But if this is from You, I accept it willingly.*

The next morning, a palace messenger came to Daniel's door with a copy of a decree from the king.

To all the peoples, nations, and men *of every language who [are] living in all the land: May your peace abound! I make a decree that*

in all the dominion of my kingdom men are to fear and tremble
before the God of Daniel;

For He is the living God and enduring forever,

And His kingdom is one which will not be destroyed,

And His dominion will be forever.

He delivers and rescues and performs signs and wonders

In heaven and on earth,

Who has also delivered Daniel from the power of the lions.[18]

The decree gladdened Daniel's heart, but he received it with some skepticism. He recalled that King Nebuchadnezzar issued a similar decree after the miracle at the furnace, but it had little lasting effect on the hearts and minds of the Babylonians.

Throughout the day, he had difficulty concentrating on the extensive amount of work that he needed to accomplish in order to govern the kingdom effectively. He was honored and grateful for the confidence the king had in him, but his mind and heart didn't seem up to the huge tasks at hand. He kept thinking about the return of his people to Jerusalem. He left his chamber sooner than planned, deciding to go home and pray. This time he wouldn't have to be concerned about being arrested for praying.

---

18 Daniel 6:25-27

31

MESSIANIC PROPHECY

ON THE WAY TO HIS house, Daniel passed several homes of Hebrews. Stopping momentarily at each one, he extended his hand toward the house and prayed for their return to Jerusalem. By the time he reached his house, he was weeping uncontrollably but wasn't sure why. *Is it the recent traumas that are catching up with me? Is Yahweh speaking to me through my emotions, or is it just my emotions?* He hurried up to his upper room, opened the west window, and dropped to his knees. God's Spirit gave him words.

"Alas, O Lord, the great and awesome God, who keeps His covenant and lovingkindness for those who love Him and keep His commandments, we have sinned, committed iniquity, acted wickedly and rebelled, even turning aside from Your commandments and ordinances. Moreover, we have not listened to Your servants the prophets, who spoke in Your name to our kings, our princes, our fathers, and all the people of the land."[19]

He continued to confess the sins of God's people that had led to their exile. He appealed for God to hear their remorse and pleaded for Him to forgive them. With tears flowing, he petitioned the Lord to reestablish His people in their Promised Land.

---

19 Daniel 9:4-6

Suddenly, he felt a hand on his shoulder. *The soldiers again!* flashed in his mind. The room flooded with light brighter than a thousand lamps. He looked up, shading his eyes, then fell on his face. Standing beside him was the brightly shining form he recognized from before as the angel Gabriel.

"Have mercy on me; I am unworthy."

"O Daniel, I have now come forth to give you insight with understanding. At the beginning of your supplications the command was issued, and I have come to tell *you*, for you are highly esteemed; so, give heed to the message and gain understanding of the vision."

Daniel repositioned to his knees facing the angel, his hands stretched upward in surrender. Gabriel began his proclamation.

"Seventy weeks have been decreed for your people and your holy city, to finish the transgression, to make an end of sin, to make atonement for iniquity, to bring in everlasting righteousness, to seal up vision and prophecy and to anoint the most holy *place*. So you are to know and discern that from the issuing of a decree to restore and rebuild Jerusalem until Messiah the Prince, there will be seven weeks and sixty-two weeks; it will be built again, with plaza and moat, even in times of distress. Then after the sixty-two weeks, the Messiah will be cut off and have nothing, and the people of the prince who is to come will destroy the city and the sanctuary. And its end *will come* with a flood; even to the end there will be war; desolations are determined. And he will make a firm covenant with the many for one week, but in the middle of the week he will put a stop to sacrifice and grain offering; and on the wing of abominations will come one who makes desolate, even

---

20 Daniel 9:22-23

until a complete destruction, one that is decreed, is poured out on the one who makes desolate."[21]

As his last word was uttered, Gabriel faded away, and the brightly illuminated room became dark again. Acting with more reflex than thought, Daniel took his lamp and bounded through his doorway. Seeing no sign of his visitor, he headed to the synagogue. No longer able to run, he was nevertheless surprised at his liveliness of step. *Yahweh, help me remember. Freeze Your messenger's words in my mind.*

Once inside, he clumsily grabbed sheets of parchment and opened the container of ink. He was amazed at how clearly he could remember each word he had just heard. Finishing the last word, he bowed his head and thanked the Lord for his mental capacity, despite his age.

He read the words over and over for most of the night. *Yahweh, You have made me an interpreter of dreams. Allow me the gift of interpreting Your message.* He began to understand that days represented years. The seventy weeks were representative of 490 years. Seven weeks, or forty-nine years, would apparently be for rebuilding Jerusalem. But he was baffled about the Messiah, the sixty-two weeks (or 434 years), and the destruction of the temple. He assumed the temple would be rebuilt when the people returned to Jerusalem. Did this mean it would be destroyed again? He wasn't getting clear answers.

"Yahweh, You have chosen me to receive this message. Now, please give me its full meaning. If not now, will I receive further explanation later? Don't leave me the heavy burden of hearing Your words directly but not sensing what to do with them. Is Your sending of the Messiah to be our King being revealed in this message? I will trust You to reveal further meaning in due time. I feel there is more here than I am worthy

---

21 Daniel 9:24-27

or qualified to understand. If Your revelations are to be the work of my last years, I will gladly step down from my position with the king. Speak to me, Yahweh. I am listening."

By the time he got to bed, Daniel felt a relaxing sense of peace about resigning from his position as third ruler of the kingdom in order to devote himself constantly and fully to whatever God had for him. He knew being God's hearer and spokesman was infinitely more important than anything he would ever do for Babylonia.

Early the following morning, he sat in the outer chamber awaiting the king's appearance. The announcement of his decision didn't set well with the king at first, but after considerable discussion, respect overcame disappointment.

"I suppose the empire will survive without your knowledge and wisdom, but I will not rule as well without you, Daniel. I know I can still call on you in a crisis."

"Certainly, Your Excellency. I will never be far from you, and my loyalty has not diminished."

With that, Daniel felt a massive burden lift from his shoulders. He spent most of the following week reading and re-reading the message from the angel Gabriel. He prayed about it and meditated on it for hours at a time. Apparently, God was not going to satisfy him with a total understanding of it, but he had become sure that it had multiple meanings. He was reminded that prophecies of Isaiah, Jeremiah, and Ezekiel, as well as the songs of David, spoke of the immediate future, as well as the distant future in the same words. He would continue his disciplined study and wait for the Lord to give him further revelation.

32

Daniel was walking to the synagogue for the Sabbath worship and prayer when a carriage pulled up next to him. He recognized one of the soldiers who had cast him into the den of lions.

"I knew you would want to know. King Darius died last night."

"Oh-h-h." Daniel's voice cracked. His mind raced through the four previous messengers who had come to him announcing the demise of other kings. "What happened?"

"His aide found him dead when he came to wake him this morning."

After the soldier left, Daniel walked to the synagogue, knowing there would be a lot of questions about the news. He would have rushed to the palace under normal circumstances, but God had called him away from that responsibility. His head was pulling him to the palace, but his heart was drawing him away. *Yahweh, what am I to do?*

As he approached the synagogue, he could already hear the commotion inside. He suddenly felt a strong urging from the Lord. *I have permission to do both. I will settle my people's anxiety and curiosity, then go quickly to the palace.*

After a short period of discussion and prayer, he heard his name called from the synagogue entrance. It was the same soldier.

"Daniel, I have been sent from Amata, the administrator. He requests your presence at the palace."

Amata greeted Daniel with a sigh of relief and led him to a private room.

"Daniel, I know you declined the king's request yesterday, but we are in a crisis. We must have your wisdom and experience. We have to plan ceremonial last respects to our king. I dispatched a messenger to Pasargadae to inform King Cyrus. But it will take over thirty days for the king to be notified and travel to Babylon. The kingdom must maintain a credible sovereignty, give King Darius a ceremonial burial, and prepare for King Cyrus' visit. Just last night, King Darius gave me the names of new commissioners to appoint. I need you to oversee their indoctrination. It is obvious the palace is overwhelmed."

"I will do the best I can. King Cyrus is not here; King Darius had no queen; so, apparently you and I are left to fill the gap."

"I must depend on your many years of experience. I am but an administrator and ignorant of the ways of Babylonians. May your God give you wisdom and strength."

Daniel had sensed God's permission to yet again respond to the emergency needs of the kingdom. He pondered how many times he had been assured of God's direction just to have it change with equal assurance on a moment's notice. For five weeks, he worked long and stressful days in the palace and hosted meetings throughout the city to coordinate and direct the many actions and events necessary. He had to bridge the gap between the death of King Darius and whomever King Cyrus was going to install as the next ruler of the Babylonia region of the Persian empire. The ceremonial rites for King Darius were done with dignity and honor. His body was transported to Ecbatana, the Median capital, to be buried next to his father, Astyages.

Babylon remained peaceful and normal following the death of their king. The welcoming ceremony for King Cyrus was at ready with all the musicians, soldiers, guards, and necessary decorum in place for his arrival. As the king entered the Ishtar Gate, the city came alive with staged excitement. Musicians played; choruses sang; and soldiers lined the streets in full dress uniforms—all in line with Daniel's and Amata's plans.

The king seemed very pleased with his welcome and the appearance of the city. A few hours after his arrival, he called for Daniel and Amata.

"You have managed exceedingly well in the leadership crisis of King Darius's death. The acceptance of Babylonians to Persian rule has been better than I could have imagined. That is to the credit of both of you. Therefore, I will not replace Darius with another regional king. Instead, I will entrust Babylonia to the three regional commissioners. I will rule the entire empire from Pasargadae. I will depend on you two to implement this plan and prepare the leaders."

"Your Highness, I'm sure I speak for both of us in saying we are humbled by your trust, and you can be assured we will prove your faith in us well-placed," Amata said.

"I have every confidence in you. And you, Daniel, are an extraordinary man. Your God is powerfully evident in you. I have brought with me a decree that I wish you to make one of your highest priorities." The king unrolled a parchment sheet and handed it to Daniel. His eyes widened as he read it. He breathed heavily.

The next morning, just before noon, the palace trumpeters were dispatched throughout the city, beckoning the people to gather around the palace for a special message from King Cyrus. From the palace courtyard, the king stood on a dais high above the packed crowd that filled the streets as far as eye could see. Standing next to the king was Daniel, Amata, Sheshbazzar, and Sheshbazzar's nephew, Zerubbabel. Daniel had requested the presence of the Hebrew prince and his probable successor based on the subject of the decree. This would be the most significant event for the exiles since the beginning of their captivity. The king read from the decree.

Thus says Cyrus, king of Persia, "The LORD, the God of heaven, has given me all the kingdoms of the earth and He has appointed me to build Him a house in Jerusalem, which is in Judah. Whoever there is among you of all His people, may his God be with him! Let him go up to Jerusalem which is in Judah and rebuild the house of the LORD, the God of Israel; He is the God who is in Jerusalem. Every survivor, at whatever place he may live, let the men of that place support him with silver and gold, with goods and cattle, together with a freewill offering for the house of God which is in Jerusalem."[22]

Cheers of "hallelujah!" and "praise Yahweh!" erupted spontaneously from the Hebrew people scattered in pockets throughout the crowd. Daniel and his two fellow Hebrews on the dais raised their voices and hands in praise. This was the moment. A moment that

---

22 Ezra 1:2-4

culminated almost seventy years of exile. The tribe of Judah—God's
people—were free. They were going home. The decree also applied
to the small number from the tribe of Benjamin, who had also been
part of the exile.

That evening, there was dancing in the lighted streets and mer-
rymaking among the Hebrews well past midnight. Most of the
Babylonian residents were skeptical of the decree and chose not to
celebrate. The thought of tens of thousands of laborers and merchants
abruptly leaving their economy was worrisome and unwise in their
assessment. Daniel walked among the celebrants as they lavished praise
on him for his incredible leadership over the decades of their bondage.
Most didn't know of his exact role in their liberation, but they realized
he was largely responsible for it. Daniel's deference to God followed
every compliment and accolade. Nevertheless, it was the most joy he
had felt since his childhood.

The next day, King Cyrus met privately with Daniel to discuss the
details of the repatriation of the Hebrews.

"I want to fund sufficiently the return to Jerusalem and the rebuilding of the temple," the king said. "The request for friends and neighbors
to give parting gifts to your people will help sustain them, but much
more will be needed. Our treasury is well-stocked, but of course, we
can't draw it down to a dangerous level of reserves. What are your
thoughts on what will be needed and how it should be distributed?"

"Your Excellence, King Nebuchadnezzar, took thousands of articles
of gold and silver from the Jerusalem temple before he destroyed it.
He brought them here and distributed them throughout the houses of
his gods. He even carried back the gold plating from the temple walls.
Many of those articles were sacred and consecrated for the sacrifices

and worship of Yahweh. They need to return with us. Articles not necessary for the temple can be sold to supplement the cost of our return and resettlement. You are also aware of the abundance of idols in the temples. Much of the gold for those was taken from Jerusalem, used for Nebuchadnezzar's golden image, and later reused for making the idols. I beg you to consider returning all articles and precious metals taken from my people. Yahweh will reward you for such righteousness."

"This would be a very risky move. I'm sure my people now look on these articles and gold as possessions of their generation and as committed to their gods. I will have to seek wise counsel on this."

The next month was chaotic, but joyous. Daniel found his coordination efforts for his people's repatriation to be one of the easiest tasks he had ever done. Preparing for the move was tedious, but the mood among all the Hebrews was festive. Daily celebrations and farewell parties lasted well into the night as more Babylonians were coming to accept the departure of their neighbors. Families were filling wagons and carts with possessions from daylight to dark. They were selling and bartering their houses and businesses. Surprisingly, many Babylonians were freely giving their Hebrew neighbors food, clothing, gold and silver articles and coins, oils, and even livestock. However, there were still some dissenting local citizens who tried to discourage the mass exit to the point of sabotaging their wagons and carts. Some of their animals were killed.

The priests and scribes were packing up the large volume of copied Scriptures, both scrolls and flat sheets, with meticulous care. Leaders and servants of the synagogues cleared the buildings of all articles of worship and left the bare stone facilities for the Babylonian merchants.

Many Hebrew families had decided to stay in Babylon. Especially some of the younger population, who had never known their homeland, felt they had little practical reason to return. Daniel and others encouraged every Hebrew to return, noting it was a blessing of God for His people. Also, the oldest of the exiles, although remembering the homeland of their childhood, were choosing to remain in Babylon. Some felt they were too old to survive the trip, while others were simply hesitant to start a new life with only a few years left. Seven young priests felt called by God to stay to serve those remaining behind. They would keep a few of the synagogues operating. God had given Daniel a peace about staying when he first realized the exile was approaching seventy years. He was convinced the Lord was going to reveal more visions to him, and he wanted to remain constantly available for them without distraction.

One morning, he noticed numerous horse-drawn wagons going down the streets loaded with what appeared to be some of the temple articles from the houses of the gods. He hailed one of them, climbed on board, and spoke with the driver.

"What are you hauling, and where is it going?"

"Idols and valuable articles from the houses of our gods. I don't like it. It is wrong to test the gods. It will bring us calamity. But I have orders."

"Where are you going with them?"

"My orders are to leave the wagons loaded and parked in a field near the palace. The palace guards are watching over them day and night. I haul them there, unhook the horses, pick up an empty wagon, and go to another house of the gods. It will take ten of us three days to finish the job."

The driver complained that every horse and wagon within a day's journey of Babylon had been confiscated by the army to transport the Hebrews back to Jerusalem. Daniel smiled, encouraged the driver, and stepped off the wagon. He looked to the sky and raised his hands. *Yahweh, I praise You. You are doing a mighty work for Your people.*

Four days later, the exiles were in position before dawn. The serpentine caravan began at the Enlil Gate, crossed the bridge, wound through the city, and ended at the eastern wall. The count was just over fifty thousand people, distributed among about ten thousand wagons full of belongings. Each wagon was pulled by two horses and had two cows tied to it. Camel riders with goats tethered to their harnesses were scattered throughout the caravan. Sixty more wagons were loaded with the temple articles. Five hundred soldiers—Medo-Persian and Babylonian—commanded by a Persian general, would escort the caravan during the eight-week journey.

At the first light of dawn, Prince Sheshbazzar rode his decorated white stallion from the end of the caravan to the front, ensuring everything was in order and giving final instructions. His nephew and heir-apparent to rule Judah, Zerubbabel, rode with him. They would make most of the trip on horseback, riding with the general at the head of the caravan. Daniel stood at the gate to bid farewell to the entire line of his departing people. It would be about two hours from the first to the last through the gate.

King Cyrus and his chariot driver pulled up alongside Daniel. He was flanked by two guards on horseback with swords drawn.

"Come aboard, Daniel." He offered a hand to help him step up to the chariot. "I want your people to see you and me together on this momentous occasion."

"Your Excellence, my people are deeply grateful to you not only for their freedom, but also for the resources you have provided for their return. Your giving back of the temple articles and gold is so gracious and greatly appreciated."

"It is only right that as they rebuild the temple, the original articles that honored your God in the past will be there for the future."

"My Yahweh will bless you and your kingdom for this, Your Highness."

"Pray that He will, Daniel. Pray that He will."

Daniel stood proudly but emotionally overwhelmed as the wagons of people and possessions paraded before him. He returned their waves until he could raise his arms no longer. He breathed heavily as he saw children and grandchildren of the boys who had been torn from their families with him as the first of Nebuchadnezzar's servants. Tears streamed. None of Daniel's friends from that first exile were returning. Most had died; several were in very poor health; and a few, like himself, simply elected to stay. He wept uncontrollably as the children and families of Mishael, Azariah, and Hananiah waved to him with shouts of praise. Hananiah's recent death was the last of the three.

Daniel was impressed and appreciative that the king had stayed until the last wagon disappeared through the gate.

"I will soon be returning to Pasargadae, Daniel. Prince Sheshbazzar will be governor of Judah. As promised, I will instruct my treasurer to provide him the additional resources he needs to rebuild the temple of your God."

King Cyrus stepped down from his chariot and helped Daniel down. "I am aware of what you have done throughout your life to keep Babylon thriving through years of upheavals in the palace. You have my utmost respect and gratitude. You will be provided everything you need as long as you live. You will want for nothing. Relax and live easy, my friend."

"O king, I am undeserving of such honor. You are exceedingly gracious. How can I show my gratitude?"

"You are one with your God. Just pray to Him that I will be blessed with success and a long life. And long live the Persian Empire."

33

Cyrus' departure, Daniel was at the palace almost every day advising the new commissioners and assisting other officials in setting up their governing operations. He developed a liaison process for assimilating the remaining Hebrews into the new government, since they no longer had an official leader. He led many discussions with the heads of the Hebrew families, encouraging them to maintain strict adherence to their religious traditions while adapting to the Persian culture.

After the most critical transition processes were established, he began devoting most of his day to helping the few priests who had stayed with the remnant in their synagogue duties. He helped the remaining scribes, who continued to copy the Scriptures with the ample papyrus, ink, and quills that were left behind. He led one synagogue group every Saturday evening.

After a year away from the palace, Daniel became increasingly concerned about not receiving another vision from the Lord. He was confident in his understanding that God had reserved profound, prophetic revelations for him to receive in his final days. He prayed for hours every day that he would receive more messages about future times that would complement those received over the last twelve years. God was showing Himself through Scriptures, prayer, and His creation; but Daniel craved more. He begged God for an intimate connection that would reveal another message to God's people for generations to come.

*

Daniel had been fighting depression for the past year. His life of prominence and adventure had become a mundane existence. He wondered whether he might have misinterpreted God's purpose for his last days. He prayed that if he were not going to hear a message of eternal importance from God, he would be allowed to die. He was tired and without purpose.

On an unusually hot day, Daniel decided to pray on the roof top, where the breeze might provide some relief from the heat. As soon as he faced west and began reaching out to God, he felt a strange sensation to turn around. Fearing that he might see the angel again, he bowed low as he turned to the east. Nothing. No one was there. As he looked up at the afternoon eastern sky, he felt a strong urging to travel in that direction. He began to hear God speak, not audibly, but much like when he received the interpretation of dreams. No words in a particular language, yet an unmistakable message. God wanted him to travel east to a river. *What river?* The closest river to the east was the Tigris, a two-day journey. He had to go to the palace.

"Daniel, what a nice surprise," Amata greeted. "I haven't seen you in months. How have you been?"

"Yahweh has seen fit to keep me alive. He has an assignment for me, and I need your help."

"Your God has an assignment for you?"

"Yes, He wants me to travel to the Tigris River. At my age and condition, I cannot travel alone. I am requesting a wagon and three of your soldiers to accompany me. I will need their protection and their help with supplies."

"Your God told you to go to the Tigris. And what will you do there?"

"Wait for Him."

"You're going to meet your God at the Tigris. Then, what will the two of you do?" Amata smirked.

"I know you don't understand. Honestly, I don't either. But I'm sure that is what I am to do. Will you help me?"

Amata chuckled. "Of course, I will help you. It sounds mysterious, but you are a man of mystery, Daniel. Besides, King Cyrus told me to do whatever you asked. I will have three soldiers ready tomorrow morning with food and supplies. How long will they be away?"

"I'm not sure. As long as Yahweh wants."

Amata raised an eyebrow, then shook his head and wished Daniel well.

*

THREE DAYS LATER

Daniel and his three soldier escorts had set up a tent in an open grassy area on the west bank of the Tigris River. The soldiers had brought bread, cured meat, vegetables, and wine, sufficient for four people for several days. Daniel had told them that he would not be eating from their supply but would be fasting on wild berries, nuts, and water from the river.

As soon as he awoke each morning, he walked into a wooded area and prayed until nightfall, only pausing briefly to gather a few morsels from vines and trees. He cried out to God, begging for the long-anticipated message, constantly expecting an audible Voice from Heaven or the appearance of an angel. Day after day, he found the energy to keep praying. Night after night, he fell asleep disappointed but confident in the next day. The soldiers became frustrated after three weeks of boredom and grumbled about their duty. Daniel reminded them that they were getting paid to do nothing and should be happy.

*

"Gentlemen, I go again this morning to appeal to Yahweh. I am weak and hungry. I wish I could tell you how much longer we will be here. But who am I to be impatient with Yahweh? We will be here until I receive His message."

Just then, the faint light of dawn became blindingly bright. All four men shaded their eyes and lowered to their knees. Daniel turned around quickly. The light was emanating from a figure on the edge of the riverbank about twenty steps away. It appeared as a man dressed in white linen that glowed like the late afternoon sun's reflection on water. He had a belt of pure gold. His arms and legs shined like highly polished bronze. His face was like lightning, and his eyes like fire.

Daniel turned to look at the soldiers, hoping they could see what he knew to be a heavenly being. They were gone!

"Hail, Daniel," the angel spoke with a voice like thunder. Daniel fell on his face and lost consciousness.

Then he felt a hand under his chest lifting him to his hands and knees. He was trembling. The angel's deep echoing voice spoke again in the Hebrew language that Daniel loved but seldom heard anymore.

"O Daniel, man of high esteem, understand the words that I am about to tell you and stand upright, for I have now been sent to you."[23]

Daniel stood with difficulty, weak and trembling. Even after many days of anticipating this visit, the presence of God's messenger was more than he could bear.

"Do not be afraid, Daniel, for from the first day that you set your heart on understanding *this* and on humbling yourself before your God, your words were heard, and I have come in response to your words. But the prince of the kingdom of Persia was withstanding me for twenty-one days; then behold, Michael, one of the chief princes, came to help me, for I had been left there with the kings of Persia."[24]

Twenty-one days. He was to meet me here on my arrival but was stopped by the spiritual warfare demons of Persia. Did my prayers and fasting sustain him in that battle?

"Now, I have come to give you an understanding of what will happen to your people in the latter days, for the vision pertains to the days yet *future*."[25]

A finger touched his lips. "You can speak, Daniel."

"O my lord, I am completely overwhelmed by your presence. How can I speak? My strength fails me, and I feel faint and short of breath."

The angel gently placed his hand on Daniel's shoulder, and he could feel an infusion of energy. His breathing normalized.

"O man of high esteem, do not be afraid. Peace be with you; take courage and be courageous!"

"Please continue to speak as I am beginning to regain my strength."

---

23 Daniel 10:11
24 Daniel 10:12-13
25 Daniel 10:14

"Do you understand why I came to you? But I shall now return to fight against the prince of Persia; so, I am going forth, and behold, the prince of Greece is about to come. However, I will tell you what is inscribed in the writing of truth. Yet, there is no one who stands firmly with me against these forces except Michael your prince."

Daniel recognized the angel as Gabriel, God's messenger, from his previous visions. Now, he understood that the angel, Michael, was God's warrior who fought against the angels of Satan. *No doubt Michael has fought many battles on my behalf unseen by human eyes.*

Gabriel continued. "In the first year of Darius the Mede, I arose to be an encouragement and a protection for him. And now, I will tell you the truth. Behold, three more kings are going to arise in Persia. Then a fourth will gain far more riches than all of them; as soon as he becomes strong through his riches, he will arouse the whole empire against the realm of Greece. And a mighty king will arise, and he will rule with great authority and do as he pleases. But as soon as he has arisen, his kingdom will be broken up and parceled out toward the four points of the compass, though not to his own descendants, nor according to his authority which he wielded, for his sovereignty will be uprooted and given to others besides them."

Gabriel continued revealing in detail how four kings would rule the four respective regions of Greece. The kings of the northern and southern regions would continually war against each other. A ruthless king of the north would ultimately enter Jerusalem, which Gabriel called the "Beautiful Land," and desecrate the temple, stopping the sacrifices. He would exalt himself above every god and profane the God of gods.

"But rumors from the East and from the North will disturb him, and he will go forth with great wrath to destroy and annihilate many. He will pitch the tents of his royal pavilion between the seas and the beautiful Holy Mountain; yet he will come to his end and no one will help him."[27]

This was more than Daniel could comprehend, but he prayed God would plant the words firmly in his mind to be recalled later. He continued to listen intently.

"Now at that time Michael, the great prince who stands *guard* over the sons of your people, will arise. And there will be a time of distress such as never occurred since there was a nation until that time; and at that time, your people, everyone who is found written in the book, will be rescued. Many of those who sleep in the dust of the ground will awake, these to everlasting life, but the others to disgrace *and* everlasting contempt. Those who have insight will shine brightly like the brightness of the expanse of heaven, and those who lead the many to righteousness, like the stars forever and ever. But as for you, Daniel, conceal these words and seal up the book until the end of time; many will go back and forth, and knowledge will increase."[28]

A flash of light brightened the area even more, causing Daniel to look around. Standing on the riverbank just a few steps from him was another man with a glow that caused the outline of his body to blur. On the other side of the river stood yet another man with the same appearance. Gabriel was no longer standing in front of him but was now hovering mid-air over the river between the two men.

The man close to Daniel looked to Gabriel and asked, "How long will it be until the end of these wonders?"[29]

---

27 Daniel 11:44-45
28 Daniel 12:1-4
29 Daniel 12:6

Gabriel raised both hands, looked upward, and exclaimed, "As surely as He 'who lives forever' . . . it [will] be for a time, times, and half *a time*; and as soon as they finish shattering the power of the holy people, all these *events* will be completed."

"My lord, what *will* be the outcome of these events?" Daniel asked.

"Go *your way*, Daniel, for *these* words are concealed and sealed up until the end time. Many will be purged, purified and refined, but the wicked will act wickedly; and none of the wicked will understand, but those who have insight will understand. From the time that the regular sacrifice is abolished and the abomination of desolation is set up, there will be 1,290 days. How blessed is he who keeps waiting and attains to the 1,335 days! But as for you, go *your way* to the end; then you will enter into rest and rise again for your allotted portion at the end of the age."

Daniel had kept his head bowed in deference to the majesty of the heavenly visitors. He also needed to shield his eyes from the intense and pervasive brightness of the area. An eerie silence ensued in stark contrast to the reverberating voice of Gabriel. Slowly raising his head, Daniel could see normally again. The visitors were gone. The only sound left was the flow of the river. He ran to the tent, scrambled for his supply of parchment, ink, and a writing reed. Spreading the parchment on a flat river rock, he wrote rapidly as the words of Gabriel flowed unconstrained from his mind. He was again amazed that he could remember every word as if it were being repeated by the angel. *Thank you, Yahweh, for allowing me this revelation and this recall.*

As he finished the last words and placed a wax seal on the rolled-up parchment sheets, he heard a rustling behind him. The three wide-eyed soldiers were coming out of the woods.

"Are you all right, Daniel?" the ranking soldier asked. "We were afraid we would find you dead!"

Daniel snickered. "No, you were just afraid. And I thought you were here to protect me. It was an angel sent from Yahweh with the message I was sent here to receive."

"We heard no message, but the light was blinding. We knew the gods were among us, and we fled for our lives."

"The gods were not among you. Your gods are never among you. You have to be among them. They stay where you place them. Yahweh of the Hebrews is everywhere. He sent His messenger angel, Gabriel, to speak His special announcement to His humble servant. You have witnessed something amazing here that you will never see from your gods. Go back to Babylon and worship the Yahweh of the Hebrews Whom King Darius proclaimed following my rescue from the lions."

Daniel handed the roll of parchment sheets to the soldier. "These are the words spoken by the angel. Take them to the chief priest at the synagogue. He will know what to do with them. If you break the seal, may Yahweh punish you severely. You have experienced His presence."

"Why are you placing the writing in my care? Why will you not carry it to the priest?"

"I may not be returning with you, at least not in the condition to accomplish a task."

The men showed their confusion but didn't press for clarification.

That night, Daniel enjoyed a delicious meal and bedded down in the tent just after the stars came out. He was emotionally exhausted. But his spirit was very much rested and content. There was extra room for sleeping on this night because all three soldiers, rather than the normal single soldier, stood watch. They would be scanning the night skies.

Daniel lay still, reviewing his incredible life in his mind. He whispered praise and thanksgiving to His beloved Yahweh for eighty-four years of experiences beyond the normal capacity of any mortal man. He thanked Him for the privilege of receiving the prophecies that would provide hope for many generations after him. He closed his eyes, smiled, and immediately awakened in a place of eternal joy, peace, comfort, and contentment. He entered into rest to rise again for his allotted portion with the promised Messiah.

34

Kyle entered Dr. McCarty's office with a bag of cheeseburgers and fries. He had texted earlier to insist on providing the grub for the evening session. The professor was clearing a table for the meal.

"Thank you for your kindness of bringing dinner. You know I would have been glad to buy. College students are on a tight budget."

"A couple of burger meals from the student union didn't set me back too much. Besides, I should be paying you for this graduate course in biblical prophecy."

"Nonsense. I'm thrilled to be feeding a genuinely inquisitive mind. Have you read chapters nine through twelve of Daniel?"

"Yes, sir, and it's pretty awesome."

During their first half-hour, the professor summarized the momentous and rather bizarre fall of Babylon to the Persian Empire and King Cyrus' installing of the Median King Darius as the ruler of Babylonia. He reviewed the circumstances of King Cyrus' release of the Hebrew exiles to return to Judah.

"The fall of Babylon to Persia was the first fulfillment of Daniel's prophecies about the rise and fall of kingdoms. It was revealed over sixty years beforehand in his interpretation of Nebuchadnezzar's dream and later in the visions of the four beasts. I'm sure this first fulfillment in his lifetime was a welcomed affirmation to Daniel, although he would not see the subsequent fulfillments relating to Greece and Rome."

"But we can look back today and see them all fulfilled, except those pertaining to the end times," Kyle said.

"Yes, that is why I find this field of study so engaging. God revealed it, and then it happened as He said in every detail. So, let's delve right into Daniel's visions during the reign of Darius. You may have noticed how meticulous God was in revealing these visions and dreams progressively. Each successive message adds more specifics than the previous one. First was Nebuchadnezzar's dream of the four kingdoms. Then came the four beasts and the introduction of the antichrist. Next was the vision of the ram and goat with empires named and the prediction of Antiochus Epiphanes. A few years later, Gabriel brought the message of the seventy weeks, which we are about to discuss. It gave further clarity as to what to anticipate from the antichrist. Then, we will look at the final vision, which gets into some amazing detail of the future tribulation."

The professor unfolded a timeline chart and handed it to Kyle as an aid to following the vision he was about to discuss.

"First, let's analyze the reference to seventy weeks. That might appear to mean 490 days. However, Gabriel said such a period was the time decreed for five things to happen: finish the transgression, or the payment for the sin of the exiles; atone for sin, or Jesus' death; achieve everlasting righteousness, or the condition of those who placed their trust in Jesus; fulfill all prophecy, or the second coming of the Messiah; and anoint the Most Holy, or the reign of Jesus in Jerusalem.

"It would have been obvious to Daniel, and certainly clear to us today, that such events weren't going to happen within seventy weeks.

But other prophecies use days to represent years. For instance, God used a similar days-to-years comparison in His revelations to Ezekiel. Assuming 490 years, the message is understandable. The first period mentioned was seven sevens, or forty-nine years, plus sixty-two sevens, or 434 years. The forty-nine years was the time from a decree to rebuild Jerusalem until the work was complete. The 434 years was the additional time to the death of the Messiah. When Gabriel referred to the decree to rebuild Jerusalem, Daniel only knew about Cyrus' decree in 538 B.C. to rebuild the temple. But a later decree by Persian King Artaxerxes to rebuild Jerusalem was issued to Nehemiah in 445 B.C. This was the decree Gabriel referred to."

"Excuse me. This chart is a great graphic, but the footnote says one year equals 360 days. Why not 365?"

"Here's where the math and the Hebrew calendar are very important. We now count years throughout history according to the 365-day Julian calendar. However, in Daniel's day, years were measured in 360 days. Therefore, the forty-nine sixth century B.C. years would have been about forty-eight years as we measure them today. Then, the remaining 434 years would be about 428 years in today's calculation. So, forty-eight years and 428 years would be 476 years from the decree of Artaxerxes to the time of the crucifixion, which would place the crucifixion at A.D. 31, within the time period most biblical scholars place the crucifixion."

Kyle was feverishly clicking the numbers on his phone's calculator app. "It all works out. That's crazy!" He felt his face flush. "I mean . . . it's not crazy. I shouldn't have said that. I have to plead the engineer's mentality. We get excited when numbers surprise us."

"Don't be sensitive. It is crazy in a good sort of way. But should we expect anything less from God's revelation to Daniel? He entrusted

Daniel with a heavenly message to all future generations that revealed his eternal plan for the world—and accurate to the year. He pinpointed the time of the Messiah's sacrifice for our sinful condition from five centuries prior."

"Wow. Amazing."

"Then Gabriel said, afterward, the people of the prince would destroy the city and the sanctuary. That happened in A.D. 70 when Satan—often referred to in the Bible as the prince of this world—influenced Rome's army to level Jerusalem and destroy the second temple. The Jews were uprooted yet again from their homeland and dispersed throughout the world."

"Don't be shocked, but I was so confused when I read about all this in my Bible, I googled some articles on it. I was particularly interested in the remaining week of the seventy weeks. It is apparently a separate time from the continuous sixty-nine weeks."

"Great! What do you understand about it?"

"Well, as we discussed about the vision of the four beasts, it sort of jumps to the end times when the antichrist takes control of the world and rules from the temple in Jerusalem. But it gets confusing with different articles explaining it differently."

"You are correct on both counts. There is a gap in time between the sixty-nine weeks representing 476 years and the remaining week representing seven years. And, yes, this is probably the most controversial of all of Daniel's prophecies. Many differing interpretations have been proposed concerning this period. Will the antichrist be an individual? If so, who will he be? Will there be a rescuing of God's people from the worst of God's wrath before Christ comes again—something we call the rapture? If so, when will this happen? The questions and theories are endless. God didn't choose to give us every detail in His revelations. The important thing to understand is that Christ will come again and set up His kingdom on the Earth at a time unknown to us. I will give you my understanding of these seven years based on my life-long study of the subject."

"Good enough for me."

"We know now that the timing of events revealed in the 476 years were precise. God wanted His people to be absolutely assured of the first coming of the Messiah. The entire Old Testament writings pointed to that event, but He punctuated the promise with exact timing in His message to Daniel through Gabriel. The Old Testament also alludes to the second coming of Christ to establish Heaven on Earth. However, the timing of this second coming is not revealed as specifically, although a description of it and the occurrences leading up to it are clearly divulged. The timing is in God's hands, and He plainly states in the Bible that no one knows but Him. God could have chosen for the events of the remaining seven years to occur immediately after the 476 years without a gap. In fact, the first generation of Christians seemed to be expecting that, according to some of the New Testament writings. But in His perfect wisdom and His merciful patience, He keeps choosing to delay the glorious event."

Kyle was eager to offer his thoughts. "Perhaps he wants more generations to have the opportunity to spend eternity with Him. I have thought a lot about myself in this revelation. If Christ had come again before my lifetime, I would not have had the chance to experience life and spend eternity with Him."

Dr. McCarthy paused to let that statement soak in. "Very insightful, Kyle. Gabriel went on to briefly describe the seven years that are called the years of tribulation and the wrath of God in other parts of the Bible. The prince of the world, Satan, through his human servant, the antichrist, will make a seven-year peace covenant, or treaty, with Israel. But the antichrist will break it after three-and-a-half years. His atrocities will repeat those of Antiochus Epiphanes. He will stop the temple sacrifices and ruthlessly persecute the people of God. Daniel's visit from Gabriel in the first year of King Darius ended there. Daniel longed for more understanding of the end times to pass along to future generations, but nothing further was revealed for three years."

"But those three years void of further revelation were filled with reason for joy as Cyrus released the exiles to return to their homeland."

"You surprise me, Kyle. You are picking up on this beyond my expectation."

"I can't get enough of it, Dr. McCarty. I even went to the seminary library and checked out a few books on Daniel and end times prophecy."

"Wow! Next, you'll be teaching me something. I love it! So, let's look at the final vision that Daniel recorded. Again, an angel paid him a last visit on the bank of the Tigris River. Although not identified by Daniel, I see no reason this angel would not have been Gabriel again. A precursor to this vision was a twenty-one-day stand-off that interrupted Gabriel's journey to meet Daniel. He said he was attacked by the prince of Persia. This referred to a demonic angel of Satan, who ruled through the demons of the Persian Empire. Since Daniel was in Persia, Gabriel had to penetrate this evil to get to him.

"This information gives us insight into the reality of spiritual warfare. Satan's angels apparently have an organizational hierarchy within geographical regions. Angels are not infinitely powerful. Gabriel couldn't fight his way through the evil realm of demons who enshrouded the Persian Empire. God had to send His warrior angel, Michael, perhaps with an army of angels, to beat back the spiritual enemy. Today, there are spiritual wars among nations on the macro-level and spiritual battles involving individuals on the micro-level. We cannot imagine what goes on in the spiritual realm. Occasionally, God allows His angels to transcend the spiritual dimension and enter our physical realm temporarily as Gabriel was doing in delivering the messages to Daniel."

"Do you think angels appear physically in today's world?"

"Perhaps. If so, they appear as normal humans and not as recognizable angels. With the full Bible and the Holy Spirit to guide us, we have had less need for direct intervention by angels than in the times before Jesus came. However, the New Testament makes mention of angels and that we may experience them without awareness.

"Okay, let's get back to Gabriel's meeting with Daniel on the bank of the Tigris River three years after the seventy weeks message was delivered."

"Sorry, I got us off-track."

"Not at all. That was a valid question. Gabriel added yet more specifics than was given in previous visits saying there would be four more kings of Persia, and the fourth would be the richest and strongest. This fourth king would lead the Persian Empire against Greece. There were more than four kings of Persia after Cyrus, but Gabriel was referring to the next four. We now know them as Camabyses II; Bardiya; Darius I, not to be confused with Darius the Mede of Daniel's day; and Xerxes, probably the king called Ahasuerus in the Book of Esther.

"As Gabriel predicted, we know Xerxes did attack Greece in 480 B.C., but was ultimately defeated. The mighty king who arose later was, of course, Greece's Alexander the Great, whose domain was broken up and ruled by four other kings who were not his descendants. This part of the last prophecy reinforced Gabriel's previous reference to the goat's large horn being broken and sprouting four horns. Looking back in secular history, we identify those four regional kings as Cassander of Greece and Macedonia; Lysimachus of Asia Minor; Seleucus of Syria, Israel, and lands to the east; and Ptolemy of Egypt and North Africa. These kingdoms rose over two centuries after Daniel's encounter with Gabriel. The four kingdoms fought wars against each other for another two centuries until Rome overthrew Greece in 146 B.C."

Kyle was writing rapidly in his notebook, connecting the historical names and dates with the prophecy. "I would never have thought biblical prophecy given years in advance could play out so perfectly with historical record."

"I wasn't going to cover this, but let me show you some fulfilled prophecy that will really light your fire. Gabriel stated that, after some years, the king of the South will form an alliance with the king of the North, and his daughter will come to the king of the North in a peaceful arrangement. But Gabriel said she will not retain her position of power but will be given up, along with the one who sired her. Gabriel spoke this almost three centuries prior to the reign of these kings. History books detail the alliance of Ptolemy II of Egypt in the South with Antiochus II of Israel and Syria in the North. Ptolemy II arranged for his daughter, Berenice, to marry Antiochus II as a gesture of peace. After Ptolemy II died, and Berenice was no longer a political benefit, Antiochus II disowned her and sent her back to Egypt. How is that for prophetic fulfillment in detail?"

Kyle shook his head. "Why was that level of detail necessary in the prophecy?"

"I like to think God wanted future generations, like yours and mine, to read the Bible and be in awe of how much assurance we can have in its accuracy. If every prophecy proves reliable beyond question down to such specific details, how can we doubt the prophecies about our future?"

"Can't believe all this has been there all the time, but I never gave it a thought until now."

"You are a blessed and wise young man. Most people die never giving it a thought. Now, let's dive into what Gabriel revealed about our future.

"Gabriel retold of the abomination of Jerusalem and the temple by Antiochus Epiphanes. Remember, he was the little horn that grew from the goat's big horns. This abomination is recorded in history as happening in 168 B.C. As I explained before, the historic desolation doubles as a revelation of what is to happen to Jerusalem and the temple under the future rule of the antichrist. God just kept repeating the comparison of Antiochus to the future antichrist so we would not underestimate the catastrophic nature of the end times tribulation.

"He cries out to us in these prophecies to warn us to be ready. Actually, it will be far worse than what people suffered under Antiochus. Jesus said in the book of Matthew the "great tribulation" would be "such as has not occurred since the beginning of the world until now, nor ever will."[31] In addition to what was previously revealed to Daniel about the antichrist, this last vision, along with John's vision in Revelation, describes horrifying battles against the

---

31 Matthew 24:21

antichrist that will ultimately end with God intervening and casting him, along with his allies, into hell. Then the final event on the Earth as we know it will be Christ establishing His physical kingdom ruled from Jerusalem."

"Toward the end of the vision, Gabriel told Daniel to conceal it or something until the end times."

"Yes, this is interesting. I believe God's final words to Daniel were for him to not try to understand everything about the visions because the message was for generations far into the future. When Daniel asked for further explanation, Gabriel essentially told him to not worry about it. He said the revelation was for those living in the end times who would become keenly interested in it and would pursue knowledge and understanding of the prophecies. That is evident today. That is why the end times prophecy is striking a chord in your heart now, Kyle."

"And why we are seeing books, articles, movies, and songs about the end times like never before."

"Exactly. Gabriel closed the vision with a reminder of the three-and-a-half-years of suffering among the Earth's inhabitants. Then, he mentioned a couple of mysterious numbers. He implied this period would last 1290 days. Well, three-and-a-half years of 360 days would be 1260 days. Perhaps the extra thirty days will be the duration of the final judgment after the antichrist has been destroyed by Christ. But then, he says blessed is the one who endures 1,335 days. Some biblical scholars believe that allows for the restoration of the Earth after the seven years of destruction. If so, he may be referring to some who were not saved at the rapture but became believers afterward. The exact understanding of both these periods may be reserved for those who are living during the tribulation and not for us to know."

"So, Daniel's visions are mostly meant for us who now live in the end times, but some parts may only become obvious to those who will actually experiencing their fulfillment. There are other end times events I have read about that were not part of Daniel's visions and dreams. Are they in other parts of the Bible?"

"Oh yes, you could spend hours upon hours reading the end times prophecies in the Old and New Testaments. In the last book of the Bible, Revelation, the apostle John records in rather cryptic style his vision from God of the end times that expands on Daniel's. He was transported to Heaven in a vision to witness the tribulation and wrath of God that Daniel wrote about from the perspective of God, Jesus, the angels, and all those who had died previously. He wrote of two resurrections of the dead and two judgments of all people.

"In beautiful language, he described how God's original intent of a perfect Earth will be restored to what He purposed for all eternity. The Gospel books of Matthew, Mark, and Luke include the teachings of Jesus about the end times and how to know when they are approaching. The apostle Paul's letters in the New Testament have much to say about the rapture, the resurrection of the dead, and the judgment when everyone will stand before Jesus. In addition to the Revelation, John writes in other books of the Bible details of the antichrist and how to prepare for the end times. Several other prophets of the Old Testament allude to the end times. Even though my life's work has been to research the Bible's references to end times from cover to cover, I'm not sure I have found every last one. But this I am absolutely sure of. God has given us everything we need to know to make sure we won't fail to recognize the approaching of the tribulation period, the antichrist, and the arrival of Jesus Christ on this Earth for the second time. It could happen in our lifetime."

Dr. McCarty faced Kyle and leaned back in his chair.

"Kyle, most people go through life with a perspective based on current times and immediate experiences with hardly any thought of what has shaped their world or where their world is headed. They live totally for the present. Their purpose is little more than to get the most of what the world has to offer in the short time they have to enjoy it. God desires us to be happy but based on a much different perspective. Happiness is found in our relationship with Him in worship and making much of who He is. That can only be realized through understanding His character and how He has related to His creation through the ages and for the age to come. When we understand that He has been in control of all things from the beginning and will continue to be through eternity, we are freed from ourselves and others to be free in Him. That total surrender of ourselves to Him is the ultimate purpose of life. And it is all in full display in the life of Daniel."

"Well, thanks to you, I am way more prepared for what life brings than I was before we met."

"It's essential, Kyle, that you understand being knowledgeable is not the same as being ready. Only those who have been drawn to Jesus and genuinely believe His death on the cross has paid for their sin and who have committed themselves fully to Him are ready. Only those who have placed their total trust in Him exclusively will be rescued from God's final wrath and from eternal separation from God. The Bible is very clear about that."

Kyle lowered his eyes and did not respond.

"Daniel's revelations pointed to the promised Messiah, and he trusted in that promise. Other prophets before and after Daniel received messages about the coming of the Lord to Earth in physical form.

In fact, as I have mentioned repeatedly, the central theme of the whole Old Testament is the coming of the Messiah, Jesus Christ. If you miss forging a personal, committed relationship with Him, you miss God's eternal plan for your life. I want you to read John, chapter three, to see what Jesus said He requires for you to enter His kingdom, become a child of His, and live eternally. Then read Romans ten, verses nine and ten, and pray as guided by those Scriptures. The decision to be a loyal follower of Christ can't come out of an infatuation with prophecy or from respect for a person such as I. It has to come from a personal encounter between an individual and Jesus Christ."

The redness in Kyle's eyes and his flush face was all the feedback the professor needed to know that his words had struck a chord in the young man's heart.

"Let's call it a night. We can continue these discussions as long as you find them helpful."

"I want to learn more, sir, if you are willing to teach me."

"Let's make it a regular Thursday evening session for now. Next Thursday, I will want to hear what you are hearing from God regarding those Scriptures I shared."

"Sure thing."

Kyle excused himself and walked to his fraternity house in the chilled February night air. He felt warm inside as his mind swirled with the words of the professor. The next morning, he was at his desk before sunrise poring over the Scriptures suggested by Dr. McCarty. He was reading by the dim illumination of his desk lamp so as not to wake his roommate.

"What are you doing?" his roommate asked, causing Kyle to flinch with surprise after an hour of silence.

"Just reading."

"Your head was on your open Bible. You were either asleep or . . . praying."

"I had been reading something Dr. McCarty had recommended, and, yes, I was praying."

"Whoa! You have come a long way since you started meeting with that seminary prof. You're not going to start preaching to me, are you?" His roommate chuckled.

"No, I'm not going to be a preacher. But I am thinking about not enrolling in the master's in engineering program."

His roommate stretched and yawned. "Gonna go right into the corporate world?"

"No, I'm thinking about enrolling in seminary."

QUESTIONS FOR GROUP DISCUSSION

life relates to serious issues we face today in our personal lives and in our society. As you dwell on these questions, apply them to yourself and the world around you. Each question is associated with its corresponding chapter.

1. Why do you think Dr. McCarty chose the Book of Daniel as the main source for teaching Kyle how God revealed future world events through prophets?

2. Considering all God had done for His chosen people and the messages from His prophets, why did so many of them abandon Him?

3. How could anyone rationalize sacrificing the life of his or her own child for personal wellbeing?

4. In what ways is Jesus prophesied in the sacrifices of Yom Kippur?

5. How could the Hebrews be so committed to the rituals of the Day of Atonement when most of them lived such ungodly lives the rest of the time?

6. Was King Jehoiakim's agreement with King Nebuchadnezzar a wise decision, or did he betray his people to save himself?

7. How did young Daniel find peace in his bondage and convey that peace to his friends?

8. In what ways did God use the treacherous journey to Babylon to prepare Daniel for his leadership responsibilities?

9. How did Daniel gain the acceptance of other exiles regarding his leadership assignment?

10. Why did Daniel make the Hebrew diet such an important issue?

11. Why was Daniel's firm response to the challenge of his leadership the best approach for that situation?

12. What was causing the priests to misrepresent God by ignoring the messages of the prophets Isaiah and Jeremiah?

13. Why did Nebuchadnezzar single out Daniel and his three friends from all the other Hebrew exiles?

14. How was Daniel's assurance to Nebuchadnezzar that he could interpret the king's dream an act of exceptional faith?

15. How did the Babylonian wisemen respond to Daniel's saving them from certain execution?

16. How did Daniel cope with his conflicted loyalties to both King Nebuchadnezzar and his own Hebrew people?

17. What allowed Daniel to avoid hating King Nebuchadnezzar for the tragic death of his family?

18. What was Daniel's plan for accommodating the huge influx of more exiles?

19. Can you comprehend that the shekinah glory of God once in the tabernacle and temple now actually abides in you upon salvation?

20. Would you have the faith and courage of Shadrach, Meshach, and Abednego to walk calmly into the fire?

21. Why did God allow Daniel to be tempted by Amytis and Nitocris, and how did Daniel react?

22. What was God's purpose in King Nebuchadnezzar's dream and mental breakdown?

23. Was Amytis' motive in her son's coronation pure?

24. What was the driving force behind all the take-overs of the throne?

25. How important was Hananiah's honest counsel to Daniel?

26. In what ways were Daniel's dreams about the future kingdoms meant for us today?

27. In what ways did Daniel's revelations provide evidence that we are drawing close to the end times?

28. What lessons can we learn from the period of Belshazzar's Babylonia?

29. What factors caused the fall of the Babylonian Empire?

30. In what manner was justice wrongly denied, then rightly applied, in Daniel's conviction, punishment, and release?

31. Why is it probable that the seventy weeks vision was contingent on Daniel's confession?

32. What evidence indicates that Cyrus was being influenced by God in his freedom decree and support for the exiles?

33. Is the same level of warfare in the spiritual realm going on today as in Daniel's day?

34. Why do so many people have such little interest today in the prophecies of Daniel, particularly his final revelation?

ADDITIONAL ENDORSEMENTS

"Daniel comes alive in this marvelous, well-crafted story that gives the reader unique insights into the Hebrew people of Judea during their period of captivity in Babylon. "You will feel as if you are walking among the Hebrew people of the 6th century B.C. sensing their culture, religion, and traditions. "I highly recommend this book and believe it will have a significant impact on Christians, traditional Jews, and Messianic Jews alike."

DR. IVAN MELHOSKY
Professor of Messianic Jewish Studies
Chesapeake Bible College and Seminary

"Terry Thompson weaves a tale that lifts a well-known individual from the pages of the Bible breathing life into text recorded thousands of years ago. *Daniel: Prophet at the King's Command* is a captivating story of a youthful man from 600 BCE whose growing courage and leadership shapes Israel's future. We see Daniel's prophesies unfolding daily in our modern era, and this book easily complements Old Testament Bible studies. Terry entwines the curiosity of a present-day college student with recorded accounts of Daniel and catapults the reader through a time portal. To understand Daniel on a personal level, this book fulfills that purpose."

DAVID HARDER
Award-winning Author, *Final Grains of Sand* and *Persuaded*

"Terry Thompson has accomplished multiple objectives in his excellent work, *Daniel: Prophet at the King's Command*. Through a compelling presentation of Daniel's captivating story, he has provided solid lessons on leadership, a panoramic description of biblical prophecy, and a detailed historical sweep of the days in which Daniel lived. His style makes his content especially accessible and enjoyable. As Terry's pastor and fellow elder at Crossgate Church, I wholeheartedly commend this work to others."

PHIL KRAMER, PHD
Lead Pastor, Crossgate Church, Hot Springs, AR

"Here is a modern retelling of the Daniel story that is based on careful research and fidelity to historical fact. The reader will find a tale that is plausible and gripping—one that stirs up renewed interest in these ancient accounts and brings them to life for a modern audience in fresh ways."

PAUL ALLEN, PHD
Yale University, Lecturer in Religious Studies and Biblical Hebrew

Thank you for reading this book. Please consider leaving us a review on your social media, favorite retailer's website, Goodreads or Bookbub, or our website.

Miriam, a widow in Judea, has only one hope for survival: she must go to Capernaum and live as a beggar. Meeting unlikely friends along the way, Miriam's path winds from Capernaum to the Sea of Galilee to Jerusalem. As she searches for friends and security, she eventually meets a man named Jesus of Nazareth.

Naomi is the central character in the book of Ruth, but few books focus on her and retell her story from start to finish. This book is different.

Her husband died, then her sons. She is in shock. What she endures after that is worse than anyone can imagine. Can she recover and experience restoration?

From the prison colony on Patmos, the Apostle John entrusts Nicodemus with manuscripts for the Christian fellowships increasing throughout the Roman Empire. While transcribing the manuscript, Nicodemus is prompted to recall his former life and his encounter with Yeshua—a man of mystery, a healer, a teacher, and a prophet. An encounter that changed everything.

Made in the USA
Coppell, TX
21 October 2022

85054190R00249